D1564083

STACKS

Strange BUT NOT A Stranger

*With an
Introduction by
Connie Willis*

GOLDEN GRYPHON PRESS • 2002

Introduction, copyright © 2002, by Connie Willis.
"10^{16} to 1," first published in *Asimov's Science Fiction*, June 1999.
"Lovestory," first published in *Asimov's Science Fiction*, June 1998.
"Feel the Zaz," first published in *Asimov's Science Fiction*, June 2000.
"Unique Visitors," first published in *Redshift*, edited by Al Sarantonio, November 2001.
"The Prisoner of Chillon," first published in *Asimov's Science Fiction*, June 1986.
"Candy Art," © 2002, by James Patrick Kelly.
"The Propagation of Light in a Vacuum," first published in *Universe 1* (Doubleday), edited by Robert Silverberg & Karen Haber, April 1990.
"Hubris," first published in *Realms of Fantasy*, April 2002.
"Glass Cloud," first published in *Asimov's Science Fiction*, June 1987.
"Proof of the Existence of God," first published in *Asimov's Science Fiction*, August 1998.
"The Cruelest Month," first published in *Fantasy & Science Fiction*, June 1983.
"Chemistry," first published in *Asimov's Science Fiction*, June 1993.
"The Pyramid of Amirah," first published in *Fantasy and Science Fiction*, March 2002.
"Fruitcake Theory" first published in *Asimov's Science Fiction*, December 1998.
"Undone," first published in *Asimov's Science Fiction*, June 2001.
Afterword © 2002, by James Patrick Kelly.

Copyright © 2001 by James Patrick Kelly

LIBRARY OF CONGRESS CATALOG CARD NUMBER:
Kelly, James P. (James Patrick)
    Strange but not a stranger / James Patrick Kelly ; with an
introduction by Connie Willis.
        p.   cm.
    ISBN 1-930846-12-6 (alk. paper)
        1. Science fiction, American.   I. Title.
PS3561.E3942   S77   2002
813'.54—dc21   2002002464

Printed in the United States of America

First Edition

Contents

CONTENTS

For Connie Willis

In Memory of
Jim Turner
(1945–1999)
Founder of Golden Gryphon Press

Introduction

WHY DO THEY CALL THESE THINGS INTRODUCTIONS? THEY aren't anything like a real introduction. In a real introduction, you'd say, "Reader, I'd like you to meet James Patrick Kelly. He's a writer and lives in New Hampshire."

And the reader would say, "Oh, really, where in New Hampshire?" and the two of them would take it from there.

But in "An Introduction," *you* have to be the one to say, "Where in New Hampshire?" and then answer your own question:

He lives on a cross between Walden Pond *and* Golden Pond *in downstate New Hampshire, where he writes Hugo Award-winning short stories, a regular column for* Asimov's *magazine, audio plays for Seeing Ear Theater, and even now and then a planetarium show. The internationally known author of* Wildlife *and* Think Like a Dinosaur, *James Patrick Kelly . . .*

Which sounds ridiculous. After all, you've known him for over twenty years and have never once called him James Patrick Kelly.

So you try again, on a more personal note:

I first met Jim in Denver in 1980, where he was an up-and-

coming young writer and the cutest thing I'd ever seen. He's still cute, with a sly wit that once nearly got us thrown out of the Tupperware Museum in Orlando, Florida. He's also charming, and relentlessly sunny, even when you've gotten him lost in the Hampton Court Maze.

Which makes him sound like something out of a Meg Ryan movie, so you go back and make it edgier:

It was on that trip to Hampton Court that I first saw the darker side of Jim's personality. We were playing Twenty Questions—the boat trip took hours and there was nothing else to do—and I discovered to my horror that he cheats. *The ham and eggs you had for breakfast is* not *a fictional character. And furthermore, that time in Denver, he was involved with an incident concerning a hot tub that . . .*

But this is an introduction, not a Kitty Kelly exposé, and besides, aren't you really supposed to be introducing people to his short stories, not to him?

So you talk about "Lovestory" and "The Cruelest Month" and "Feel the Zaz," and the other great stories in *Strange But Not A Stranger.* But you can't just say, "They're all terrific," because you've already told people you're old friends, and they'll assume you're just being nice—even though the stories are terrific. And when you try to get more specific, you either end up sounding like a book report:

"The Prisoner of Chillon" is a near-future story about artificial intelligence and even more artificial relationships . . .

or a doctoral thesis:

Although Kelly cites Cordwainer Smith and Alfred Bester as authors who influenced his work, such stories as "Unique Visitors" and "Hubris" also show the sharp-edged humor of William Tenn . . .

and if you aren't careful, you give away the plot:

In "Glass Cloud," Bambi's mother dies, and Scarlett tries to get Rhett back, but it's too late because Gatsby . . .

That isn't actually what happens in "Glass Cloud," of course, but if you tell what *does* happen, you'll ruin the ending. So you decide you'd better go back to James Patrick Kelly the person. But writers' lives are essentially boring:

Jim works on an HP Pentium III with a Canon S600 printer, using Microsoft Word . . .

And the few juicy stories there are, like that one about the hot tub, you can't tell, because he also knows scurrilous stories about you.

Which leaves you with exactly nothing to say.

Except this:

I love Jim's stories.

When I find a new one in Asimov's or a year's best anthology (where he nearly always has a story—or two—or three) I'm thrilled at the prospect of reading it, which is really saying something. Writers have to read hundreds of stories, and most of them are a chore, if not a downright ordeal.

Not Jim's. Jim's stories are always a treat, even when he's e-mailed one to you for a last-minute critique and has an already-passed deadline and an irate editor waiting so could you please read it right now?

No matter what the circumstances, I can't wait to read a James Patrick Kelly story. Because I know when I do, I'll be surprised. Or touched or amused or made to think about candy or the nature of reality or toy telephones or those long lists of begats in the Bible in a brand-new way. Or that I'll be all of the above.

Because every one of his stories is unique, so unique, in fact, that he can even make you reconsider the meaning of the word:

There are currently eight hundred and forty-two unique visitors monitoring this session. The average attention quotient is twenty-seven percent.

"Unique Visitors"

Your attention quotient, on the other hand, will be a hundred percent, because you're in the hands of a master.

There aren't a lot of them around. Most writers view the short story as A) something to write till you can get some publisher to look at your novel, or B) something to write between those novels "to relax." As if the short story were a decaff latté. Or a nap.

Jim, on the other hand, sees the short story as a separate and special art form requiring infinite care and craft. And he's a master of that craft. At writers' conferences and as a teacher at the Clarion Writers' Workshop, he is affectionately known as Dr. Jim for his ability to diagnose and take a scalpel to seemingly terminal stories, perform surgery, and suture the story back together without the patient feeling any pain at all.

Dr. Jim always knows exactly what needs to be done to fix a broken plot or a dislocated character (or an over-extended metaphor, such as that in the last two paragraphs), and he applies that surgical skill to his own stories, which are beautifully constructed.

They are also more complex than they seem, because even though he's written a number of stories that could be called cyberpunk (a genre famous for its prose fireworks) Kelly never resorts to pyrotechnic displays.

He prefers subtler techniques, such as a transparent style and weapons like the stiletto and the delayed action bomb, so that you think you've read a simple, straightforward little story about Christmas or architecture or chemistry, and days—or even years—later, you find yourself bleeding, and thinking about Amirah in her pyramid. Or the Mondale administration. Or what T. S. Eliot really meant.

Craft alone, of course, can't do that, no matter how skilled. It's the mind exercising the craft that makes Jim's stories so memorable, a mind that looks at everything from repressed memories to Byron to fruitcake from a unique angle:

There are currently fourteen million, two hundred and sixty-three thousand, one hundred and twelve unique . . .

and with a unique touch.

Who else would include a crash course in Greek literary terms in a story of a guy on the make? Or tell a story from the point of view of . . . Oops, I almost gave away the plot. Sorry.

Who else would start out with a scam and end with a revelation? Or something even more unexpected?

Not even tried-and-true formulas are safe. We've all read that story about the unlikely hero who suddenly finds the fate of the world resting on his ill-equipped shoulders, but only James Patrick Kelly would take a level-headed look at the realities of such a task. And the likelihood of success.

Or at the ever-shifting shapes of clouds and marriages. Or at what technology could do to our relationship to our parents. Romantic comedy, zombies, and time travel to the future all go into a James Patrick Kelly story and come out transformed.

And so do we.

He changes our attitudes and our perceptions and even our understanding of what the short story can be, and he does it in stories which are disturbing, clever, affecting, funny, and **unique** in every sense of the word.

So allow me to introduce you to them. *Reader, this is "Undone,"
and this is "10^{16} to 1," and this is "The Propagation of Light in a
Vacuum." I know you'll love them, and all the other stories in* Strange
But Not A Stranger.

*And I guarantee your attention quotient is going to go right
through the stratosphere.*

> Connie Willis
> Greeley, Colorado
> February 2002

Strange But Not A Stranger

10^{16} to 1

But the best evidence we have that time travel is not possible, and never will be, is that we have not been invaded by hordes of tourists from the future.

Stephen Hawking, "The Future of the Universe"

REMEMBER NOW HOW LONELY I WAS WHEN I MET Cross. I never let anyone know about it, because being alone back then didn't make me quite so unhappy. Besides, I was just a kid. I thought it was my own fault.

It looked like I had friends. In 1962, I was on the swim team and got elected Assistant Patrol Leader of the Wolf Patrol in Boy Scout Troop 7. When sides got chosen for kickball at recess, I was usually the fourth or fifth pick. I wasn't the best student in the sixth grade of John Jay Elementary School—that was Betty Garolli. But I was smart and the other kids made me feel bad about it. So I stopped raising my hand when I knew the answer and I watched my vocabulary. I remember I said *albeit* once in class and they teased me for weeks. Packs of girls would come up to me on the playground. "Oh Ray," they'd call and when I turned around they'd scream, "All beat it!" and run away, choking with laughter.

3

It wasn't that I wanted to be popular or anything. All I really wanted was a friend, one friend, a friend I didn't have to hide anything from. Then came Cross, and that was the end of that.

One of the problems was that we lived so far away from everything. Back then, Westchester County wasn't so suburban. Our house was deep in the woods in tiny Willoughby, New York, at the dead end of Cobb's Hill Road. In the winter, we could see Long Island Sound, a silver needle on the horizon pointing toward the city. But school was a half-hour drive away and the nearest kid lived in Ward's Hollow, three miles down the road, and he was a dumb fourth-grader.

So I didn't have any real friends. Instead, I had science fiction. Mom used to complain that I was obsessed. I watched *Superman* reruns every day after school. On Friday nights Dad used to let me stay up for *The Twilight Zone*, but that fall CBS had temporarily canceled it. It came back in January after everything happened, but was never quite the same. On Saturdays, I watched old sci-fi movies on *Adventure Theater*. My favorites were *Forbidden Planet* and *The Day The Earth Stood Still*. I think it was because of the robots. I decided that when I grew up and it was the future, I was going to buy one, so I wouldn't have to be alone anymore.

On Monday mornings I'd get my weekly allowance—a quarter. Usually I'd get off the bus that same afternoon down in Ward's Hollow so I could go to Village Variety. Twenty-five cents bought two comics and a pack of red licorice. I especially loved DC's *Green Lantern*, Marvel's *Fantastic Four* and *Incredible Hulk*, but I'd buy almost any superhero. I read all the science fiction books in the library twice, even though Mom kept nagging me to try different things. But what I loved best of all was *Galaxy* magazine. Dad had a subscription and when he was done reading them he would slip them to me. Mom didn't approve. I always used to read them up in the attic or out in the lean-to I'd lashed together in the woods. Afterwards I'd store them under my bunk in the bomb shelter. I knew that after the nuclear war, there would be no TV or radio or anything and I'd need something to keep me busy when I wasn't fighting mutants.

I was too young in 1962 to understand about Mom's drinking. I could see that she got bright and wobbly at night, but she was always up in the morning to make me a hot breakfast before school. And she would have graham crackers and peanut butter waiting when I came home—sometimes cinnamon toast. Dad said I shouldn't ask Mom for rides after five because she got so tired keeping house for us. He sold Andersen windows and was away a lot, so I was pretty much stranded most of the time. But he always made a point of being home on the first Tuesday of the month, so he could take me to the Scout meeting at 7:30.

No, looking back on it, I can't really say that I had an unhappy childhood—until I met Cross.

I remember it was a warm Saturday afternoon in October. The leaves covering the ground were still crisp and their scent spiced the air. I was in the lean-to I'd built that spring, mostly to practice the square and diagonal lashings I needed for Scouts. I was reading *Galaxy*. I even remember the story: "The Ballad of Lost C'Mell" by Cordwainer Smith. The squirrels must have been chittering for some time, but I was too engrossed by Lord Jestocost's problems to notice. Then I heard a faint *crunch*, not ten feet away. I froze, listening. *Crunch, crunch* . . . then silence. It could've been a dog, except that dogs didn't usually slink through the woods. I was hoping it might be a deer—I'd never seen deer in Willoughby before, although I'd heard hunters shooting. I scooted silently across the dirt floor and peered between the dead saplings.

At first I couldn't see anything, which was odd. The woods weren't all that thick and the leaves had long since dropped from the understory brush. I wondered if I had imagined the sounds; it wouldn't have been the first time. Then I heard a twig snap, maybe a foot away. The wall shivered as if something had brushed against it, but there was nothing there. *Nothing*. I might have screamed then, except my throat started to close. I heard whatever it was skulk to the front of the lean-to. I watched in horror as an unseen weight pressed an acorn into the soft earth and then I scrambled back into the farthest corner. That's when I noticed that, when I wasn't looking directly at it, the air where the invisible thing should have been shimmered like a mirage. The lashings that held the frame creaked, as if it were bending over to see what it had caught, getting ready to drag me, squealing, out into the sun and. . . .

"Oh, fuck," it said in a high, panicky voice and then it thrashed away into the woods.

In that moment I was transformed—and I suppose that history too was forever changed. I had somehow scared the thing off, twelve-year-old scrawny me! But more important was what it had said. Certainly I was well aware of the existence of the word *fuck* before then, but I had never dared use it myself, nor do I remember hearing it spoken by an adult. A spaz like the Murphy kid might say it under his breath, but he hardly counted. I'd always thought of it as language's atomic bomb; used properly the word should make brains shrivel, eardrums explode. But when the invisible thing said fuck and then *ran away*, it betrayed a vulnerability that made me reckless and more than a little stupid.

"Hey, stop!" I took off in pursuit.

I didn't have any trouble chasing it. The thing was no Davy Crockett; it was noisy and clumsy and slow. I could see a flickery outline as it lumbered along. I closed to within twenty feet and then had to hold back or I would've caught up to it. I had no idea what to do next. We blundered on in slower and slower motion until finally I just stopped.

"W-Wait," I called. "W-What do you want?" I put my hands on my waist and bent over like I was trying to catch my breath, although I didn't need to.

The thing stopped too but didn't reply. Instead it sucked air in wheezy, ragged *hooofs*. It was harder to see, now that it was standing still, but I think it must have turned toward me.

"Are you okay?" I said.

"You are a child." It spoke with an odd, chirping kind of accent. Child was *Ch-eye-eld*.

"I'm in the sixth grade." I straightened, spread my hands in front of me to show that I wasn't a threat. "What's your name?" It didn't answer. I took a step toward it and waited. Still nothing, but at least it didn't bolt. "I'm Ray Beaumont," I said finally. "I live over there." I pointed. "How come I can't see you?"

"What is the date?" It said *da-ate-eh*.

For a moment I thought it meant data. Data? I puzzled over an answer. I didn't want it thinking I was just a stupid little kid. "I don't know," I said cautiously. "October twentieth?"

The thing considered this, then asked a question that took my breath away. "And what is the year?"

"Oh jeez," I said. At that point I wouldn't have been surprised if Rod Serling himself had popped out from behind a tree and started addressing the unseen TV audience. Which might have included me, except this was really *happening*. "Do you know what you just . . . what it means when. . . ."

"What, what?" Its voice rose in alarm.

"You're invisible and you don't know what year it is? Everyone knows what year it is. Are you . . . you're not from here."

"Yes, yes, I am. 1962, of course. This is 1962." It paused. "And I am not invisible." It squeezed about eight syllables into invisible. I heard a sound like paper ripping. "This is only camel." Or at least, that's what I thought it said.

"Camel?"

"No, camo." The air in front of me crinkled and slid away from a dark face. "You have not heard of camouflage?"

"Oh sure, camo."

I suppose the thing meant to reassure me by showing itself, but the effect was just the opposite. Yes, it had two eyes, a nose, and a mouth. It stripped off the camouflage to reveal a neatly pressed gray three-piece business suit, a white shirt, and a red and blue striped tie. At night, on a crowded street in Manhattan, I might've passed it right by—Dad had taught me not to stare at the kooks in the city. But in the afternoon light, I could see all the things wrong with its disguise. The hair, for example. Not exactly a crewcut, it was more of a stubble, like Mr. Rudowski's chin when he was growing his beard. The thing was way too thin, its skin was shiny, its fingers too long and its face—it looked like one of those Barbie dolls.

"Are you a boy or a girl?" I said.

It started. "There is something wrong?"

I cocked my head to one side. "I think maybe it's your eyes. They're too big or something. Are you wearing makeup?"

"I am naturally male." It—he bristled as he stepped out of the camouflage suit. "Eyes do not have gender."

"If you say so." I could see he was going to need help getting around, only he didn't seem to know it. I was hoping he'd reveal himself, brief me on the mission. I even had an idea how we could contact President Kennedy or whoever he needed to meet with. Mr. Newell, the Scoutmaster, used to be a colonel in the Army—he would know some general who could call the Pentagon. "What's your name?" I said.

He draped the suit over his arm. "Cross."

I waited for the rest of it as he folded the suit in half. "Just Cross?" I said.

"My given name is Chitmansing." He warbled it like he was calling birds.

"That's okay," I said. "Let's just make it Mr. Cross."

"As you wish, Mr. Beaumont." He folded the suit again, again and *again*.

"Hey!"

He continued to fold it.

"How do you do that? Can I see?"

He handed it over. The camo suit was more impossible than it had been when it was invisible. He had reduced it to a six-inch square card, as thin and flexible as the queen of spades. I folded it in half myself. The two sides seemed to meld together; it would've fit into my wallet perfectly. I wondered if Cross knew how close I was to running off with his amazing gizmo. He'd never catch me. I could see flashes of my brilliant career as the invisible superhero. *Tales to Confound* presents: the origin of Camo Kid! I turned the card over and over, trying to figure out how to unfold it again. There was no seam, no latch. How could I use it if I couldn't open it? "Neat," I said. Reluctantly, I gave the card back to him.

Besides, real superheroes didn't steal their powers.

I watched Cross slip the card into his vest pocket. I wasn't scared of him. What scared me was that at any minute he might walk out of my life. I had to find a way to tell him I was on his side, whatever that was.

"So you live around here, Mr. Cross?"

"I am from the island of Mauritius."

"Where's that?"

"It is in the Indian Ocean, Mr. Beaumont, near Madagascar."

I knew where Madagascar was from playing *Risk*, so I told him that but then I couldn't think of what else to say. Finally, I had to blurt out something—anything—to fill the silence. "It's nice here. Real quiet, you know. Private."

"Yes, I had not expected to meet anyone." He, too, seemed at a loss. "I have business in New York City on the twenty-fifth of October."

"New York, that's a ways away."

"Is it? How far would you say?"

"Fifty miles. Sixty, maybe. You have a car?"

"No, I do not drive, Mr. Beaumont. I am to take the train."

The nearest train station was New Canaan, Connecticut. I could've hiked it in maybe half a day. It would be dark in a couple of hours. "If your business isn't until the twenty-sixth, you'll need a place to stay."

"The plan is to take rooms at a hotel in Manhattan."

"That costs money."

He opened a wallet and showed me a wad of crisp new bills. For a minute I thought they must be counterfeit; I hadn't realized that Ben Franklin's picture was on money. Cross was giving me the goofiest grin. I just knew they'd eat him alive in New York and spit out the bones.

"Are you sure you want to stay in a hotel?" I said.

He frowned. "Why would I not?"

"Look, you need a friend, Mr. Cross. Things are different here than . . . than on your island. Sometimes people do, you know, bad stuff. Especially in the city."

He nodded and put his wallet away. "I am aware of the dangers, Mr. Beaumont. I have trained not to draw attention to myself. I have the proper equipment." He tapped the pocket where the camo was.

I didn't point out to him that all his training and equipment hadn't kept him from being caught out by a twelve-year-old. "Sure, okay. It's just . . . Look, I have a place for you to stay, if you want. No one will know."

"Your parents, Mr. Beaumont. . . ."

"My dad's in Massachusetts until next Friday. He travels; he's in the window business. And my mom won't know."

"How can she not know that you have invited a stranger into your house?"

"Not the house," I said. "My dad built us a bomb shelter. You'll be safe there, Mr. Cross. It's the safest place I know."

I remember how Cross seemed to lose interest in me, his mission and the entire twentieth century the moment he entered the shelter. He sat around all of Sunday, dodging my attempts to draw him out. He seemed distracted, like he was listening to a conversation I couldn't hear. When he wouldn't talk, we played games. At first it was cards: Gin and Crazy Eights, mostly. In the afternoon, I went back to the house and brought over checkers and *Monopoly*. Despite the fact that he did not seem to be paying much attention, he beat me like a drum. Not one game was even close. But that wasn't what bothered me. I believed that this man had come from the future, and here I was building hotels on Baltic Avenue!

Monday was a school day. I thought Cross would object to my plan of locking him in and taking both my key and Mom's key with me, but he never said a word. I told him that it was the only way I could be sure that Mom didn't catch him by surprise. Actually, I doubted she'd come all the way out to the shelter. She'd stayed away after Dad gave her that first tour; she had about as much use for nuclear war as she had for science fiction. Still, I had no idea what she did during the day while I was gone. I couldn't take chances. Besides, it was a good way to make sure that Cross didn't skin out on me.

Dad had built the shelter instead of taking a vacation in 1960, the year Kennedy beat Nixon. It was buried about a hundred and fifty feet from the house. Nothing special—just a little cellar without anything built on top of it. The entrance was a steel bulkhead that led down five steps to another steel door. The inside was cramped; there were a couple of cots, a sink, and a toilet. Almost half of the space was filled with supplies and equipment. There were no windows and it always smelled a little musty, but I loved going down there to pretend the bombs were falling.

When I opened the shelter door after school on that Monday, Cross lay just as I had left him the night before, sprawled across the big cot, staring at nothing. I remember being a little worried; I thought he might be sick. I stood beside him and still he didn't acknowledge my presence.

"Are you all right, Mr. Cross?" I said. "I bought *Risk.*" I set it next to him on the bed and nudged him with the corner of the box to wake him up. "Did you eat?"

He sat up, took the cover off the game and started reading the rules. "President Kennedy will address the nation," he said, "this evening at seven o'clock."

For a moment, I thought he had made a slip. "How do you know that?"

"The announcement came last night." I realized that his pronunciation had improved a lot; *announcement* had only three syllables. "I have been studying the radio."

I walked over to the radio on the shelf next to the sink. Dad said we were supposed to leave it unplugged—something about the bombs making a power surge. It was a brand new solid-state, multi-band Heathkit that I'd helped him build. When I pressed the on button, women immediately started singing about shopping: *Where the values go up, up, up! And the prices go down, down, down!* I turned it off again.

"Do me a favor, okay?" I said. "Next time when you're done would you please unplug this? I could get in trouble if you don't." I stooped to yank the plug.

When I stood up, he was holding a sheet of paper. "I will need some things tomorrow, Mr. Beaumont. I would be grateful if you could assist me."

I glanced at the list without comprehension. He must have typed it, only there was no typewriter in the shelter.

To buy:

    –One General Electric transistor radio with earplug

    –One General Electric replacement earplug
    –Two Eveready Heavy Duty nine volt batteries
    –One New York Times, Tuesday, October 23
    –Rand McNally map of New York City and vicinity
To receive in change:
    –Five dollars in coins
    –twenty nickels
    –ten dimes
    –twelve quarters

When I looked up, I could feel the change in him. His gaze was electric; it seemed to crackle down my nerves. I could tell that what I did next would matter very much. "I don't get it," I said.

"There are inaccuracies?"

I tried to stall. "Look, you'll pay almost double if we buy a transistor radio at Ward's Hollow. I'll have to buy it at Village Variety. Wait a couple of days—we can get one much cheaper down in Stamford."

"My need is immediate." He extended his hand and tucked something into the pocket of my shirt. "I am assured this will cover the expense."

I was afraid to look, even though I knew what it was. He'd given me a hundred dollar bill. I tried to thrust it back at him but he stepped away and it spun to the floor between us. "I can't spend that."

"You must read your own money, Mr. Beaumont." He picked the bill up and brought it into the light of the bare bulb on the ceiling. "This note is legal tender for all debts public and private."

"No, no, you don't understand. A kid like me doesn't walk into Village Variety with a hundred bucks. Mr. Rudowski will call my mom!"

"If it is inconvenient for you, I will secure the items myself." He offered me the money again.

If I didn't agree, he'd leave and probably never come back. I was getting mad at him. Everything would be so much easier if only he'd admit what we both knew about who he was. Then I could do whatever he wanted with a clear conscience. Instead he was keeping all the wrong secrets and acting really weird. It made me feel dirty, like I was helping a pervert. "What's going on," I said.

"I do not know how to respond, Mr. Beaumont. You have the list. Read it now and tell me please with which item you have a problem."

I snatched the hundred dollars from him and jammed it into my pants pocket. "Why don't you trust me?"

He stiffened as if I had hit him.

"I let you stay here. I didn't tell anyone. You have to give me *something*, Mr. Cross."

"Well then . . ." He looked uncomfortable. "I would ask you to keep the change."

"Oh jeez, thanks." I snorted in disgust. "Okay, okay, I'll buy this stuff right after school tomorrow."

With that, he seemed to lose interest again. When we opened the *Risk* board, he showed me where his island was, except it wasn't there because it was too small. We played three games and he crushed me every time. I remember at the end of the last game, watching in disbelief as he finished building a wall of invading armies along the shores of North Africa. South America, my last continent, was doomed. "Looks like you win again," I said. I traded in the last of my cards for new armies and launched a final, useless counter-attack. When I was done, he studied the board for a moment.

"I think Risk is not a proper simulation, Mr. Beaumont. We should both lose for fighting such a war."

"That's crazy," I said. "Both sides can't lose."

"Yet they can," he said. "It sometimes happens that the victors envy the dead."

That night was the first time I can remember being bothered by Mom talking back to the TV. I used to talk to the TV too. When Buffalo Bob asked what time it was, I would screech *It's Howdy Doody Time* just like every other kid in America.

"My fellow citizens," said President Kennedy, "let no one doubt that this is a difficult and dangerous effort on which we have set out." I thought the president looked tired, like Mr. Newell on the third day of a camp-out. "No one can foresee precisely what course it will take or what costs or casualties will be incurred."

"Oh my God," Mom screamed at him. "You're going to kill us all!"

Despite the fact that it was close to her bedtime and she was shouting at the President of the United States, Mom looked great. She was wearing a shiny black dress and a string of pearls. She always got dressed up at night, whether Dad was home or not. I suppose most kids don't notice how their mothers look, but everyone always said how beautiful Mom was. And since Dad thought so too,

I went along with it—as long as she didn't open her mouth. The problem was that a lot of the time, Mom didn't make any sense. When she embarrassed me, it didn't matter how pretty she was. I just wanted to crawl behind the couch.

"Mom."

As she leaned toward the television, the martini in her glass came close to slopping over the edge.

President Kennedy stayed calm. "The path we have chosen for the present is full of hazards, as all paths are—but it is the one most consistent with our character and courage as a nation and our commitments around the world. The cost of freedom is always high—but Americans have always paid it. And one path we shall never choose, and that is the path of surrender or submission."

"Shut up! You foolish man, *stop this.*" She shot out of her chair and then some of her drink did spill. "Oh, damn!"

"Take it easy, Mom."

"Don't you understand?" She put the glass down and tore a Kleenex from the box on the end table. "He wants to start World War III!" She dabbed at the front of her dress and the phone rang.

I said, "Mom, nobody wants World War III."

She ignored me, brushed by and picked up the phone on the third ring.

"Oh thank God," she said. I could tell from the sound of her voice that it was Dad. "You heard him then?" She bit her lip as she listened to him. "Yes, but. . . ."

Watching her face made me sorry I was in the sixth grade. Better to be a stupid little kid again, who thought grownups knew everything. I wondered whether Cross had heard the speech.

"No, I can't, Dave. No." She covered the phone with her hand. "Raymie, turn off that TV!"

I hated it when she called me Raymie, so I only turned the sound down.

"You have to come home now, Dave. No, you listen to *me.* Can't you see, the man's obsessed? Just because he has a grudge against Castro doesn't mean he's allowed to . . ."

With the sound off, Chet Huntley looked as if he were speaking at his own funeral.

"I am *not* going in there without you."

I think Dad must have been shouting because Mom held the receiver away from her ear.

She waited for him to calm down and said, "And neither is Raymie. He'll stay with me."

"Let me talk to him," I said. I bounced off the couch. The look she gave me stopped me dead.

"What for?" she said to Dad. "No, we are going to finish this conversation, David, do you hear me?"

She listened for a moment. "Okay, all right, but don't you dare hang up." She waved me over and slapped the phone into my hand as if I had put the missiles in Cuba. She stalked to the kitchen.

I needed a grownup so bad that I almost cried when I heard Dad's voice. "Ray," he said, "your mother is pretty upset."

"Yes," I said.

"I want to come home—I *will* come home—but I can't just yet. If I just up and leave and this blows over, I'll get fired."

"But, Dad. . . ."

"You're in charge until I get there. Understand, son? If the time comes, everything is up to you."

"Yes, sir," I whispered. I'd heard what he didn't say—it wasn't up to *her.*

"I want you to go out to the shelter tonight. Wait until she goes to sleep. Top off the water drums. Get all the gas out of the garage and store it next to the generator. But here's the most important thing. You know the sacks of rice? Drag them off to one side, the pallet too. There's a hatch underneath, the key to the airlock door unlocks it. You've got two new guns and plenty of ammunition. The revolver is a .357 Magnum. You be careful with that, Ray, it can blow a hole in a car but it's hard to aim. The double-barreled shotgun is easy to aim but you have to be close to do any harm. And I want you to bring down the Gamemaster from my closet and the .38 from my dresser drawer." He had been talking as if there would be no tomorrow; he paused then to catch his breath. "Now, this is all just in case, okay? I just want you to know."

I had never been so scared in my life.

"Ray?"

I should have told him about Cross then, but Mom weaved into the room. "Got it, Dad," I said. "Here she is."

Mom smiled at me. It was a lopsided smile that was trying to be brave but wasn't doing a very good job of it. She had a new glass and it was full. She held out her hand for the phone and I gave it to her.

I remember waiting until almost ten o'clock that night, reading under the covers with a flashlight. The Fantastic Four invaded Latveria to defeat Doctor Doom; Superman tricked Mr. Mxyzptlk into saying his name backwards once again. When I opened the door to my parents' bedroom, I could hear Mom snoring. It spooked me; I hadn't realized that women did that. I thought about sneaking in to get the guns, but decided to take care of them tomorrow.

I stole out to the shelter, turned my key in the lock and pulled on the bulkhead door. It didn't move. That didn't make any sense, so I gave it a hard yank. The steel door rattled terribly but did not swing away. The air had turned frosty and the sound carried in the cold. I held my breath, listening to my blood pound. The house stayed dark, the shelter quiet as stones. After a few moments, I tried one last time before I admitted to myself what had happened.

Cross had bolted the door shut from the inside.

I went back to my room, but couldn't sleep. I kept going to the window to watch the sky over New York, waiting for a flash of killing light. I was all but convinced that the city would burn that very night in thermonuclear fire and that Mom and I would die horrible deaths soon after, pounding on the unyielding steel doors of our shelter. Dad had left me in charge and I had let him down.

I didn't understand why Cross had locked us out. If he knew that a nuclear war was about to start, he might want our shelter all to himself. But that made him a monster and I still didn't see him as a monster. I tried to tell myself that he'd been asleep and couldn't hear me at the door—but that couldn't be right. What if he'd come to prevent the war? He'd said he had business in the city on Thursday; he could be doing something really, really futuristic in there that he couldn't let me see. Or else he was having problems. Maybe our twentieth century germs had got to him, like they killed H. G. Wells's Martians.

I must have teased a hundred different ideas apart that night, in between uneasy trips to the window and glimpses at the clock. The last time I remember seeing was 4:16. I tried to stay up to face the end, but I couldn't.

I wasn't dead when I woke up the next morning, so I had to go to school. Mom had Cream of Wheat all ready when I dragged myself to the table. Although she was all bright and bubbly, I could feel her giving me the mother's eye when I wasn't looking. She always knew when something was wrong. I tried not to show her anything. There was no time to sneak out to the shelter; I barely had time to finish eating before she bundled me off to the bus.

Right after the morning bell, Miss Toohey told us to open *The Story of New York State* to Chapter Seven, "Resources and Products" and read to ourselves. Then she left the room. We looked at each other in amazement. I heard Bobby Coniff whisper something. It was probably dirty; a few kids snickered. Chapter Seven started with a map of product symbols. Two teeny little cows grazed near Binghamton. Rochester was a cog and a pair of glasses. Elmira was an adding machine, Oswego an apple. There was a lightning bolt over Niagara Falls. Dad had promised to take us there someday. I had the sick feeling that we'd never get the chance. Miss Toohey looked pale when she came back, but that didn't stop her from giving us a spelling test. I got a ninety-five. The word I spelled wrong was *enigma*. The hot lunch was American Chop Suey, a roll, a salad, and a bowl of butterscotch pudding. In the afternoon we did decimals.

Nobody said anything about the end of the world.

I decided to get off the bus in Ward's Hollow, buy the stuff Cross wanted and pretend I didn't know he had locked the shelter door last night. If he said something about it, I'd act surprised. If he didn't . . . I didn't know what I'd do then.

Village Variety was next to Warren's Esso and across the street from the Post Office. It had once been two different stores located in the same building, but then Mr. Rudowski had bought the building and knocked down the dividing wall. On the fun side were pens and pencils and paper and greeting cards and magazines and comics and paperbacks and candy. The other side was all boring hardware and small appliances.

Mr. Rudowski was on the phone when I came in, but then he was always on the phone when he worked. He could sell you a hammer or a pack of baseball cards, tell you a joke, ask about your family, complain about the weather and still keep the guy on the other end of the line happy. This time though, when he saw me come in, he turned away, wrapping the phone cord across his shoulder.

I went through the store quickly and found everything Cross had wanted. I had to blow dust off the transistor radio box but the batteries looked fresh. There was only one *New York Times* left; the headlines were so big they were scary.

US IMPOSES ARMS BLOCKADE ON CUBA
ON FINDING OF OFFENSIVE MISSILE SITES;
KENNEDY READY FOR SOVIET SHOWDOWN
Ships Must Stop   President Grave   Prepared To Risk War.

I set my purchases on the counter in front of Mr. Rudowski. He cocked his head to one side, trapping the telephone receiver against his shoulder, and rang me up. The paper was on the bottom of the pile.

"Since when do you read the *Times,* Ray?" Mr. Rudowski punched it into the cash register and hit total. "I just got the new *Fantastic Four.*" The cash drawer popped open.

"Maybe tomorrow," I said.

"All right then. It comes to twelve dollars and forty-seven cents."

I gave him the hundred dollar bill.

"What is this, Ray?" He stared at it and then at me.

I had my story all ready. "It was a birthday gift from my grandma in Detroit. She said I could spend it on whatever I wanted so I decided to treat myself but I'm going to put the rest in the bank."

"You're buying a radio? From me?"

"Well, you know. I thought maybe I should have one with me with all this stuff going on."

He didn't say anything for a moment. He just pulled a paper bag from under the counter and put my things into it. His shoulders were hunched; I thought maybe he felt guilty about overcharging for the radio. "You should be listening to music, Ray," he said quietly. "You like Elvis? All kids like Elvis. Or maybe that colored guy, the one who does the Twist?"

"They're all right, I guess."

"You're too young to be worrying about the news. You hear me? Those politicians. . . ." He shook his head. "It's going to be okay, Ray. You heard it from me."

"Sure, Mr. Rudowski. I was wondering, could I get five dollars in change?"

I could feel him watching me as I stuffed it all into my bookbag. I was certain he'd call my mom, but he never did. Home was three miles up Cobb's Hill. I did it in forty minutes, a record.

I remember I started running when I saw the flashing lights. The police car had left skid marks in the gravel on our driveway.

"Where were you?" Mom burst out of the house as I came across the lawn. "Oh, my God, Raymie, I was worried sick." She caught me up in her arms.

"I got off the bus in Ward's Hollow." She was about to smother me; I squirmed free. "What happened?"

"This the boy, ma'am?" The state trooper had taken his time

catching up to her. He had almost the same hat as Scoutmaster Newell.

"Yes, yes! Oh, thank God, officer!"

The trooper patted me on the head like I was a lost dog. "You had your mom worried, Ray."

"Raymie, you should've told me."

"Somebody tell me what happened!" I said.

A second trooper came from behind the house. We watched him approach. "No sign of any intruder." He looked bored: I wanted to scream.

"Intruder?" I said.

"He broke into the shelter," said Mom. "He knew my name."

"There was no sign of forcible entry," said the second trooper. I saw him exchange a glance with his partner. "Nothing disturbed that I could see."

"He didn't have time," Mom said. "When I found him in the shelter, I ran back to the house and got your father's gun from the bedroom."

The thought of Mom with the .38 scared me. I had my Shooting merit badge, but she didn't know a hammer from a trigger. "You didn't shoot him?"

"No." She shook her head. "He had plenty of time to leave but he was still there when I came back. That's when he said my name."

I had never been so mad at her before. "You never go out to the shelter."

She had that puzzled look she always gets at night. "I couldn't find my key. I had to use the one your father leaves over the breezeway door."

"What did he say again, ma'am? The intruder."

"He said, 'Mrs. Beaumont, I present no danger to you.' And I said, 'Who are you?' And then he came toward me and I thought he said 'Margaret,' and I started firing."

"You did shoot him!"

Both troopers must have heard the panic in my voice. The first one said, "You know something about this man, Ray?"

"No, I-I was at school all day and then I stopped at Rudowski's. . . ." I could feel my eyes burning. I was so embarrassed; I knew I was about to cry in front of them.

Mom acted annoyed that the troopers had stopped paying attention to her. "I shot *at* him. Three, four times, I don't know. I must have missed, because he just stood there staring at me. It seemed like forever. Then he walked past me and up the stairs like nothing had happened."

"And he didn't say anything?"

"Not a word."

"Well, it beats me," said the second trooper. "The gun's been fired four times but there are no bullet holes in the shelter and no bloodstains."

"You mind if I ask you a personal question, Mrs. Beaumont?" the first trooper said.

She colored. "I suppose not."

"Have you been drinking, ma'am?"

"Oh that!" She seemed relieved. "No. Well, I mean, after I called you, I did pour myself a little something. Just to steady my nerves. I was worried because my son was so late and . . . Raymie, what's the matter?"

I felt so small. The tears were pouring down my face.

After the troopers left, I remember Mom baking brownies while I watched *Superman*. I wanted to go out and hunt for Cross, but it was already sunset and there was no excuse I could come up with for wandering around in the dark. Besides, what was the point? He was gone, driven off by my mother. I'd had a chance to help a man from the future change history, maybe prevent World War III, and I had blown it. My life was ashes.

I wasn't hungry that night, for brownies or spaghetti or anything, but Mom made that clucking noise when I pushed supper around the plate, so I ate a few bites just to shut her up. I was surprised at how easy it was to hate her, how good it felt. Of course, she was oblivious, but in the morning she would notice if I wasn't careful. After dinner she watched the news and I went upstairs to read. I wrapped a pillow around my head when she yelled at David Brinkley. I turned out the lights at 8:30, but I couldn't get to sleep. She went to her room a little after that.

"Mr. Beaumont?"

I must have dozed off, but when I heard his voice I snapped awake immediately.

"Is that you, Mr. Cross?" I peered into the darkness. "I bought the stuff you wanted." The room filled with an awful stink, like when Mom drove with the parking brake on.

"Mr. Beaumont," he said, "I am damaged."

I slipped out of bed, picked my way across the dark room, locked the door and turned on the light.

"Oh jeez!"

He slumped against my desk like a nightmare. I remember thinking then that Cross wasn't human, that maybe he wasn't even alive. His proportions were wrong: an ear, a shoulder and both feet sagged like they had melted. Little wisps of steam or something curled off him; they were what smelled. His skin had gone all shiny and hard; so had his business suit. I'd wondered why he never took the suit coat off and now I knew. His clothes were part of him. The middle fingers of his right hand beat spasmodically against his palm.

"Mr. Beaumont," he said. "I calculate your chances at 10^{16} to 1."

"Chances of what?" I said. "What happened to you?"

"You must listen most attentively, Mr. Beaumont. My decline is very bad for history. It is for you now to alter the time line probabilities."

"I don't understand."

"Your government greatly overestimates the nuclear capability of the Soviet Union. If you originate a first strike, the United States will achieve overwhelming victory."

"Does the President know this? We have to tell him!"

"John Kennedy will not welcome such information. If he starts this war, he will be responsible for the deaths of tens of millions, both Russians and Americans. But he does not grasp the future of the arms race. The war must happen now, because those who come after will build and build until they control arsenals which can destroy the world many times over. People are not capable of thinking for very long of such fearsome weapons. They tire of the idea of extinction and then become numb to it. The buildup slows but does not stop and they congratulate themselves on having survived it. But there are still too many weapons and they never go away. The Third War comes as a surprise. The First War was called the one to end all wars. The Third War is the only such war possible, Mr. Beaumont, because it ends everything. History stops in 2009. Do you understand? A year later, there is no life. All dead, the world a hot, barren rock."

"But you. . . ?"

"I am nothing, a construct. Mr. Beaumont, please, the chances are 10^{16} to 1," he said. "Do you know how improbable that is?" His laugh sounded like a hiccup. "But for the sake of those few precious time lines, we must continue. There is a man, a politician in New York. If he dies on Thursday night, it will create the incident that forces Kennedy's hand."

"Dies?" For days, I had been desperate for him to talk. Now all I wanted was to run away. "You're going to kill somebody?"

"The world will survive a Third War that starts on Friday, October 26, 1962."

"What about me? My parents? Do we survive?"

"I cannot access that time line. I have no certain answer for you. Please, Mr. Beaumont, this politician will die of a heart attack in less than three years. He has made no great contribution to history, yet his assassination can save the world."

"What do you want from me?" But I had already guessed.

"He will speak most eloquently at the United Nations on Thursday evening. Afterward he will have dinner with his friend, Ruth Fields. Around ten o'clock he will return to his residence at the Waldorf Towers. Not the Waldorf Astoria Hotel, but the Towers. He will take the elevator to Suite 42A. He is the American ambassador to the United Nations. His name is Adlai Stevenson."

"Stop it! Don't say anything else."

When he sighed, his breath was a cloud of acrid steam. "I have based my calculation of the time line probabilities on two data points, Mr. Beaumont, which I discovered in your bomb shelter. The first is the .357 Magnum revolver, located under a pallet of rice bags. I trust you know of this weapon?"

"Yes." I whispered.

"The second is the collection of magazines, located under your cot. It would seem that you take an interest in what is to come, Mr. Beaumont, and that may lend you the terrible courage you will need to divert this time line from disaster. You should know that there is not just one future. There are an infinite number of futures in which all possibilities are expressed, an infinite number of Raymond Beaumonts."

"Mr. Cross, I can't. . . ."

"Perhaps not," he said, "but I believe that another one of you can."

"You don't understand. . . ." I watched in horror as a boil swelled on the side of his face and popped, expelling an evil jet of yellow steam. "What?"

"Oh *fuck*." That was the last thing he said.

He slid to the floor—or maybe he was just a body at that point. More boils formed and burst. I opened all the windows in my room and got the fan down out of the closet and still I can't believe that the stink didn't wake Mom up. Over the course of the next few hours, he sort of vaporized.

When it was over, there was a sticky, dark spot on the floor the size of my pillow. I moved the throw rug from one side of the room to the other to cover it up. I had nothing to prove that Cross existed but a transistor radio, a couple of batteries, an earplug and eighty-seven dollars and fifty-three cents in change.

I might have done things differently if I hadn't had a day to think. I can't remember going to school on Wednesday, who I talked to, what I ate. I was feverishly trying to figure out what to do and how to do it. I had no place to go for answers, not Miss Toohey, not my parents, not the Bible or the *Boy Scout Handbook*, certainly not *Galaxy* magazine. Whatever I did had to come out of me. I watched the news with Mom that night. President Kennedy had brought our military to the highest possible state of alert. There were reports that some Russian ships had turned away from Cuba; others continued on course. Dad called and said his trip was being cut short and that he would be home the next day.

But that was too late.

I hid behind the stone wall when the school bus came on Thursday morning. Mrs. Johnson honked a couple of times, and then drove on. I set out for New Canaan, carrying my bookbag. In it were the radio, the batteries, the coins, the map of New York, and the .357. I had the rest of Cross's money in my wallet.

It took more than five hours to hike to the train station. I expected to be scared, but the whole time I felt light as air. I kept thinking of what Cross had said about the future, that I was just one of millions and millions of Raymond Beaumonts. Most of them were in school, diagramming sentences and watching Miss Toohey bite her nails. I was the special one, walking into history. I was super. I caught the 2:38 train, changed in Stamford, and arrived at Grand Central just after four. I had six hours. I bought myself a hot pretzel and a coke and tried to decide where I should go. I couldn't just sit around the hotel lobby for all that time; I thought that would draw too much attention. I decided to go to the top of the Empire State Building. I took my time walking down Park Avenue and tried not to see all the ghosts I was about to make. In the lobby of the Empire State Building, I used Cross's change to call home.

"Hello?" I hadn't expected Dad to answer. I would've hung up except that I knew I might never speak to him again.

"Dad, this is Ray. I'm safe, don't worry."

"Ray, where are you?"

"I can't talk. I'm safe but I won't be home tonight. Don't worry."

"Ray!" He was frantic. "What's going on?"

"I'm sorry."

"Ray!"

I hung up; I had to. "I love you," I said to the dial tone.

I could imagine the expression on Dad's face, how he would tell Mom what I'd said. Eventually they would argue about it. He would shout; she would cry. As I rode the elevator up, I got mad at them. He shouldn't have picked up the phone. They should've protected me from Cross and the future he came from. I was in the sixth grade, I shouldn't have to have feelings like this. The observation platform was almost deserted. I walked completely around it, staring at the city stretching away from me in every direction. It was dusk; the buildings were shadows in the failing light. I didn't feel like Ray Beaumont anymore; he was my secret identity. Now I was the superhero Bomb Boy; I had the power of bringing nuclear war. Wherever I cast my terrible gaze, cars melted and people burst into flame.

And I loved it.

It was dark when I came down from the Empire State Building. I had a sausage pizza and a coke on 47th Street. While I ate, I stuck the plug into my ear and listened to the radio. I searched for the news. One announcer said the debate was still going on in the Security Council. Our ambassador was questioning Ambassador Zorin. I stayed with that station for a while, hoping to hear his voice. I knew what he looked like, of course. I knew Adlai Stevenson had run for President a couple of times when I was just a baby. But I couldn't remember what he sounded like. He might talk to me, ask me what I was doing in his hotel; I wanted to be ready for that.

I arrived at the Waldorf Towers around nine o'clock. I picked a plush velvet chair that had a direct view of the elevator bank and sat there for about ten minutes. Nobody seemed to care but it was hard to sit still. Finally I got up and went to the men's room. I took my bookbag into a stall, closed the door and got the .357 out. I aimed it at the toilet. The gun was heavy and I could tell it would have a big kick. I probably ought to hold it with both hands. I put it back into my bookbag and flushed.

When I came out of the bathroom, I had stopped believing that I was going to shoot anyone, that I could. But I had to find out for Cross's sake. If I was really meant to save the world, then I had to be in the right place at the right time. I went back to my chair, checked my watch. It was nine-twenty.

I started thinking of the one who would pull the trigger, the unlikely Ray. What would make the difference? Had he read some story in *Galaxy* that I had skipped? Was it a problem with Mom? Or Dad? Maybe he had spelled *enigma* right; maybe Cross had lived another thirty seconds in his time line. Or maybe he was just the best that I could possibly be.

I was so tired of it all. I must have walked thirty miles since morning and I hadn't slept well in days. The lobby was warm. People laughed and murmured. Elevator doors dinged softly. I tried to stay up to face history, but I couldn't. I was Raymond Beaumont, but I was just a twelve-year-old kid.

I remember the doorman waking me up at eleven o'clock. Dad drove all the way into the city that night to get me. When we got home, Mom was already in the shelter.

Only the Third War didn't start that night. Or the next.

I lost television privileges for a month.

For most people my age, the most traumatic memory of growing up came on November 22, 1963. But the date I remember is July 14, 1965, when Adlai Stevenson dropped dead of a heart attack in London.

I've tried to do what I can, to make up for what I didn't do that night. I've worked for the cause wherever I could find it. I belong to CND and SANE and the Friends of the Earth and was active in the nuclear freeze movement. I think the Green Party (www.greens.org) is the only political organization worth your vote. I don't know if any of it will change Cross's awful probabilities; maybe we'll survive in a few more time lines.

When I was a kid, I didn't mind being lonely. Now it's hard, knowing what I know. Oh, I have lots of friends, all of them wonderful people, but people who know me say that there's a part of myself that I always keep hidden. They're right. I don't think I'll ever be able to tell anyone about what happened with Cross, what I didn't do that night. It wouldn't be fair to them.

Besides, whatever happens, chances are very good that it's my fault.

Lovestory

ONE

MAM SHOULD HAVE GUESSED SOMETHING WAS WRONG as soon as the father entered the nursery. His ears were slanted back, his ruby fur fluffed. He smelled as sad as a cracked egg. But Mam ignored him, skimming her reading finger down the leaf of her lovestory. It was about a family just like theirs, except that they lived in a big house in the city with a pool in every room and lots of robot servants. That family loved one another, but bad people kept trying to drive them apart.

"How's the scrap tonight?" The father shut the door behind him as if it were made of glass.

It was then that Mam realized the mother wasn't with him. "What is it?" She bent the corner of the leaf back to mark her place. The father and mother always visited together. She loosened her grip on the lovestory and it rewound into its watertight case.

"Wa-wa, it's the lucky father!" The scrap tumbled out of the dark corner where she had been hiding and hugged the father's legs. "Luck always, Pa-pa-*pa!*" The father staggered, almost toppled onto the damp, spongy rug, but then caught himself. The scrap had been running wild all night, talking back to the jokestory she was only half-watching on the tell, choreographing battles with her mechanical ants, making up nonsense songs, trying to crawl in and out of Mam's pouch for no good reason. It was almost dawn and the scrap was still skittering around the nursery like a loose button.

"Oh, when the father swims near," sang the scrap, "and he comes up for air, all the families cheer."

He reached down, scooped her into his arms and smoothed her silky brown fur, which was wet where it had touched the floor. It had only been in the last month that the scrap had let anyone but Mam hold her. Now she happily licked the father's face.

"Who's been teaching you rhyme?" he said. "Your mam?" He laughed then, but his wide, yellow eyes were empty.

"Mam is fat and Mam is slow. If I'm a brat, well, she don't know."

"Hush, little scrap," said the father. "Your tongue is so long we might have to cut some off." He snipped two fingers at her.

"Eeep!" The scrap wriggled in his arms and he set her down. She scrambled across the room to Mam's settle and would've wormed into her pouch, but Mam was in no mood and cuffed her lightly away. The scrap was almost a tween, too old for such clowning. Soon it would be time for them to part; she was giving Mam stretch marks.

"Silmien, what *is* it?" Mam waved at the tell to turn the scrap's annoying jokestory off. "Something has happened."

The father stiffened when she named him. This was no longer idle family chatter; by saying his name, she had made a truth claim on her mate. For a moment, she thought he might not answer, as was his right. But whatever it was, he must have wanted to tell her or why else had he come to them?

"It's Valun," he said. "She's gone."

"Gone?" said Mam. "Where?"

"To Pelotto." There was an angry stink to the father now. "She went to Pelotto, to live with the aliens."

"Pelotto?" Mam was confused. "But the scrap is almost weaned."

"Obviously," said the father. "She knows that."

Mam was confused. If she knew, then how could she leave? "What about her patients?"

"Gone?" The scrap whimpered. "Mother gone, mother?"

"Who will give the scrap her name?" Mam reached an arm around the little one to comfort her. "And it's time to quicken the new baby. The mother, Valun and I have to. . . ." She paused, uneasy talking about birthing with the father. "What about the baby?" she said weakly.

"Don't you understand? She has left us." The father's anger was not only in his scent, but spilled over into his words. "You. Me. She's left the family. She's an out, now. Or maybe the aliens are her family."

Mam rose from her settle. She felt as if she were hefting a great weight; if she did not bear the load, the whole house might collapse around them. "This is my fault," she said. "She does not trust me to carry the baby, nurse it into a scrap."

"It's not you!" the father shouted. "It's *her*." The scrap shrank from the crack of his voice. "We're still here, aren't we? Where is she?"

Mam stooped to let the scrap wriggle into the pouch.

"She thinks I'm stupid," said Mam. She felt the moisture in the rug creep between her toes. "She has nothing to say to me anymore."

"That's not true."

"I heard her tell you. And that all I read are lovestories."

The father squished across the room to her then, and she let him stroke the short fur on her foreleg. She knew he meant to comfort, but this unaccustomed closeness felt like more weight that she must bear. "This has gone very badly," he said. He brought his face up to hers. "I'm sorry. It's probably *my* fault that she's gone." He smelled as sincere as newly split wood and Mam remembered when she had fallen in love with them, back at the gardens. Then it was only Valun and Silmien and her. "Something I did, or didn't do. Maybe we should've stayed in the city, I don't know. It has nothing to do with you, though. Or the scrap."

"But what will happen to the new baby?" Mam said. Her voice sounded very small, even to her.

"I love you, Mam." The father pricked his ears forward, giving her complete attention. "Maybe Valun loves you too, in her way. But I don't think you and I will ever see that baby."

Mam felt the scrap shiver inside her.

The father lingered for a few moments more, although everything important had been said. Mam coaxed the scrap out of hiding and she slipped her head from the pouch. She stared at the father as he rubbed the fluff around her nose, saying nothing. The scrap had just started her tween scents, another sign that it was time for them to part; she gave off the thin, bright smell of fear, sharp as a razor. The father made warbling sounds and her edge dulled a little. Then he licked the side of her face. He straightened and took Mam by surprise when he gave her an abrupt good-day lick, too. "I'm sorry, Mam," he said, and then he was gone.

Mam collapsed onto her settle. The heated cushion was blood hot, but did little to ease the chill that gripped her neck. For a moment she sat, brittle as ice, unsure what to do. The next ten minutes without Valun were harder to face than the next ten years. In ten years they'd probably be dead, Mam and the father and the mother, their story forgotten. But just now Valun's absence was a hole in Mam's life that was too wide to cross over. Then the scrap stirred restlessly against her.

"Time to sleep," Mam said, tugging at the scrap's left ear. "Almost dawn." No matter what happened, she was still this one's mam.

The scrap shook her head. "Not tired not."

"You want the sun to scratch your eyes out?" Mam rippled her stomach muscles, squeezing her from the pouch like a seed. The scrap mewled and then slopped across the wet rug as if she had no bones. "You pick up your things and get ready." Mam gave the scrap a nudge with her foot. She might have indulged the little one; after all, the scrap had just lost her mother. But then Mam had just lost her mate and there was nobody to indulge her. "Make sure you clear all your projects off the tell."

The scrap formed up her ants and marched the little robots back into the drawer of her settle. She ejected her ID from the tell, flipped it onto the tangle of ants and shut the drawer. She sorted the pillows she had formed into a nest. She turned off the pump that circulated water through her rug, dove into the nursery's shallow egg-shaped pool at the narrow end and immediately slid out at the wide end. "Does this mean I can't go to the gardens?" She shook the water from her fur.

"Of course not. This has nothing to do with growing up. You'll be a tween soon, too big for the pouch."

"But what about my name?"

"The father will give you one. I'll help him."

"Won't be the same."

"No." Mam hesitated. "But it will be enough."

The scrap smoothed the fur flat against her chest. She was almost two and her coat had begun to turn the color of her mother's: blood red, deepening like a sunset. "They're the parents," she said. "They were supposed to take care of us."

Mam tried not to resent her. The scrap *had* been taken care of. She was about to leave the family, go off to the gardens to live. She'd fall in love with a father and a mam and start a new family. It was Mam who had not been taken care of, Mam and the new baby. "They did their best."

"I wish she were dead," said the scrap. "Dead, red, spread on a bed." She was careful as she wriggled into Mam's pouch. "Do you think she'll come to visit me at the gardens?"

"I don't know." Mam realized then that she didn't know anything about Valun. The mother had always been restless, yes, and being a doctor in this little nowhere had only made things worse. But how could aliens be more important than the family? "But I'll come visit."

"You have to, you," said the scrap. "You're my old, fat mam."

"That's right." Mam tickled her behind the ears. "And I will never leave you." Although she knew that the scrap would leave her soon enough, just like she had left her mam.

Mam got up to darken the windows against the rising sun. It was a chore getting around; the scrap bobbed heavily against her belly as she crossed the room. In the last few days, the scrap had begun to doze off on her own settle; Mam was once again getting used to the luxury of an uninterrupted day's sleep. But it felt right to carry the little one just now, to keep her close.

Mam waddled back to her settle through the soothing gloom. She wasn't tired and with the scrap in the pouch, it was hard to find a comfortable position. The scrap was fidgety too. Mam wondered whether the father was sleeping and decided he was probably not. He'd be making a story about what had happened, trying to understand. And the mother? No, Valun wasn't a mother any more. She was an out. Mam focused on the gurgle of water in the pool and tried to let the sound quench her thoughts.

There were never aliens in the kinds of lovestories Mam liked to read. Fathers and mothers might run off to be an out for a while, but everyone would be so unhappy that they'd come back at the end. Of course, mams never ran. Or else one of the three mates might die and the others would go to the city and try to find a good out to take their place.

She started when the scrap's lips brushed the tender skin near her nipple. At first she thought it was an accident, but then she felt it again, tentative but clearly deliberate, a question posed as loving touch. Her first impulse was to push her away; the scrap had fed that afternoon. But as the nubbly little tongue probed the edges of her aureole, Mam knew that it wasn't hunger that the scrap sought to ease. It was grief. Mam shivered and the underfur on her neck bristled. Had the scrap tried to nurse out of turn on any other day, Mam would certainly have shaken her from the pouch. But this day they had each been wounded; this feeding would ease not only the scrap's pain but Mam's as well. It was something they could do for each other—maybe the only thing. With a twitch of excitement, she felt her milk letting down. It wasn't much, it wasn't time, but the scrap had a such warm, clever mouth.

"Oh," said Mam. "*Oh.*"

The father had told her once that, when she nursed, chemicals flooded her brain and seeped into her milk. He said this was how Mam was making the scrap into who she was. He told her the names of all the chemicals, but she had forgotten them. Mam had a simpler explanation. She was a mam, which meant that her emotions were much bigger than she was, so they spilled onto whoever was nearest. The mother always used to say that she was a different person when she was with Mam, because of her smell. Even the father relaxed when the family came together. But it was the scrap Mam was closest to, into whom she had most often poured the overflow of feelings. Now, as they bonded for one of the last times, perhaps *the* last time, Mam was filled with ecstasy and regret. Of all the pleasure the scrap had given her, this was the most carnal. When she sucked, she made a wet, little sound, between a squeak and a click, that made the top of Mam's head tingle. Mam enfolded her bulging pouch with both arms and shifted the scrap slightly so that she came at the nipple from a different angle. She could smell the bloom of her own excitement, heady as wine, thick as mud. She thought she might scream—but what would the father say if he heard her through the walls? He would not understand why she was taking pleasure with the scrap on this night of all nights. He would . . . not . . . understand. When the urgent sound finally welled up from the deepest part of her, she closed her throat and strangled it. "My . . . little," she gasped, and it was as if Valun had never gone, the aliens had never come to plague the families with their wicked wisdom. "My little . . . *scrap.*"

The weight lifted from her and for a brief, never-ending moment, she felt as light as air.

TWO

Silmien was proud of his scrap. "Tevul," he corrected himself, cupping the name he had given her on his tongue. He was so proud that losing her mother almost didn't matter anymore. He spotted her and some of her friends splashing in the pond across the bone garden. She was so quick, so carefree, so beautiful in the chill, blue light of the mothermoon.

"What?" Mam had stopped to smell the sweetbind that wound through the skeleton of someone's long dead ancestor; she hurried over to him. "What?"

He pointed. Mam was already nearsighted from spending so much time indoors, the curse of the nursery. Distance seemed to confuse her. "She hasn't seen us yet," he said.

"The scrap?"

"The tween," said Silmien. "Tevul."

Silmien was proud of Mam, too. She had been a good parent, considering everything that had happened. After all, Tevul was their firstborn. Silmien knew just how lonely the long rainy season had been for Mam, especially since she didn't exactly understand about Valun and the aliens.

But that wasn't right. Silmien was always surprised at how much Mam understood, even though she did not follow the news or query the tell. She engaged the world by means that were mysterious to him. If she did not always reach for the complex, her grasp of essentials was firm. Silmien drew strength from her trust in him— and her patience. Even though it was a burden on her not to be nursing a scrap, she had never once nagged him to start looking for a mother to take Valun's place.

"I'm glad you came tonight, Mam." He wanted to put an arm around her, but he knew that would make her uncomfortable. She was a mam, not a mother. Instead he stooped and picked a pink buttonbright and offered it to her. She accepted it solemnly and tucked it behind her ear.

There was something about visiting the gardens that revived Silmien, burned troubles away like morning mist. It was not only nostalgia for that simple time when Valun had chosen him and he had found Mam. It was the scent of the flowers and ponds, of mulch and moss, of the golden musk of old parents, the sharp, hormone-laden perfume of tweens and the round, honest stink of chickens. It was the fathermoon chasing the mothermoon across an enormous sky, the family obelisks pointing like fingers toward the stars. Valun always used to tease him about being such a romantic, but wasn't that a father's job, to dream, to give shape to the mud? The garden was the place where families began and ended, where futures were spun, lives honored.

"Over here!" Tevul had finally caught sight of them. "Come meet my friends!"

Silmien waved back. "More introductions," he whispered to Mam. "I don't recognize a single face in this batch." It was only his second visit of the dry season, but he was already having trouble keeping them all straight. Although he was glad Tevul was popular, he supposed he resented these fortunate tweens for stealing his little scrap away from him. Tevul, he reminded himself again, Tevul. At home, he and Mam still called her *the scrap*. "Come along, Mam. Just a long smile and short bow and we'll have her to ourselves."

"Not me," said Mam. "You."

Silmien blinked in surprise. There was that odd smell again, a dusty staleness, like the corner of an empty closet. If Valun had been here, she would have known immediately what to do, but then if she were here, Mam wouldn't be. "Nonsense," said Silmien. "We're her family."

Mam crouched abruptly, making herself as small as possible. "Doesn't matter." She smoothed her sagging pouch to her belly self-consciously.

"Why did you come then," said Silmien, "if not to see Tevul?"

"You wanted me."

"Mam, the scrap wants you too."

"I'm not here." Mam was staring at her feet.

They had to stop arguing then, because a clutch of old parents entered the garden, giggling and stroking the bones. One, a father with thin, cement-colored fur, noticed the buttonbright behind Mam's ear and bent to pick one for himself. His companions teased him good-naturedly about acting his age. Then a shriveled mam popped one of the flowers into her mouth, chewed a few times and spat it at the father. Everyone laughed except Silmien and Mam. Ordinarily, he enjoyed the loopy antics of the old, but now he chafed at the interruption.

"I'll bring Tevul to you," he whispered to Mam. "Is that what you want?"

She made no reply. She curled her long toes into the damp soil as if she were growing roots.

Silmien grunted and left her. Mam was not getting any easier to live with. She was moody and stubborn and often reeked of self-loathing. Yet he had stuck by her, given her every consideration. Not once, since he had first told her about Valun, had he let his true feelings show. It struck him that he ought to be proud of himself, too. It was small comfort, but without a mate to share his life, all he had were glimmers and wisps.

"Pa-pa-*pa*." Tevul hauled herself partly out of the pond and perched on the grassy bank. "My father, Silmien." Her glistening coat clung to her body, making her as streamlined as a rocket. She must have grown four or five centimeters since the solstice. "Here is Mika. Tilantree. Kujalla. Karmi. Jotan. And Putket." Tevul indicated each of her friends by splashing with her foot in their direction. Karmi and Jotan and Putket were standing in the shallows and acknowledged him with polite but not particularly warm bows. Kujalla—or was it Tilantree?—was treading water in the deep; she just stared at him. Only Mika clambered up the bank of the pond to greet him properly.

"Silmien," said Mika as they crossed hands. "It is truly an honor to meet you."

"It is you who honor me," Silmien murmured. The tween's effusiveness embarrassed him.

"Tevul tells us that you write stories."

Silmien shot Tevul a glance; she returned his gaze innocently. "I write many things," he said. "Mostly histories."

"Lovestories?" said Mika.

Tilantree's head disappeared beneath the surface of the pond.

"I wouldn't call them lovestories, exactly," Silmien said. "I don't like sentiment. But I do write about families sometimes, yes."

Tilantree surfaced abruptly, splashing about and making rude, blustery sounds. The three standing tweens smirked at her.

"Silmien has been on the tell," said Tevul. "Write, bright, show me the light."

"My mam was on the tell last year," said one of the standing tweens, "and she's a stupid old log."

"Even aliens get on the tell now," said another.

"Have you written any lovestories about aliens?" Mika was smirking too.

With a sick lurch, Silmien realized what was going on. The tweens were making fun of him—and Tevul. Only his trusting little scrap didn't get it. He wondered if the reason she was always in the middle of a crowd was not because she was popular, but because she was a freak.

"Can't write lovestories about aliens." Tilantree rolled onto her back.

"Why not?" said Tevul.

She did not reply. Instead, she sucked in a mouthful of pond water and then spat it straight up in the air. The three standing tweens spoke for her.

"Their mothers are mams."

"*Perverts.*"

"Two, few, haven't a clue. Isn't that right, Tevul?"

The air was suddenly vinegary with tween scorn. Tevul seemed taken aback by the turn of the conversation. She drew her knees to her chest and looked to Silmien, as if he could control things here in the gardens the way he had at home.

"No," he said, coming around the pond to Tevul. "I haven't written about the aliens yet." His voice rose from the deepest part of him. "But I've thought a lot about them." He could feel his scent glands swell with anger and imagined his stink sticking its claw into them. "Unlike you, Tilantree." He singled out the floating tween as the leader of this cruel little gang. "Maybe you should try it." He reached Tevul, tugged her to her feet and pulled her to him. "You see, they're our future. They're calling us to grow up and join the universe, all of us, tweens and families and outs and the old. If they really are perverts as you say, then that's what we will be, someday. I suppose that's a big thought to fit into a small mind." He looked down at his scrap. "What do you say, Tevul?"

"I don't know what you're talking about." Her eyes were huge as the mothermoon.

"Then maybe we should discuss this further." He bowed to the others. "Luck always." He nudged Tevul toward the bone garden.

Silmien heard the tweens snickering behind him. Tevul heard it too; her gait stiffened, as if she had sand in her joints. He wondered if the next time he visited her, she might be like them. Tilantree and her friends had the next four years to twist his scrap to their shallow thinking. The family had made her a tween, but the garden would make her into a mother. Silmien felt removed from himself as they passed the wall built of skulls that marked the boundary of the bone garden. No Tevul. No Valun. Mam a stranger. He could not believe that he had defended the aliens to the tweens. That was Valun talking, not him. He hated the aliens for luring her away from him. It was almost as if they had seduced her. He shivered; maybe they *were* perverted. Besides, he must have sounded the pompous fool. Who was he to be speaking of small minds? He was as ordinary as a spoon.

"Well?" said Tevul.

"Well what?"

"Pa-*pa*, you embarrassed me, pa."

He sighed. "I suppose I did."

"Is this the way you're going to be?" said Tevul. "Because if it is. . . ."

"No, I'll mind." He licked two fingers and rubbed them on her cheekbone. "But are you sure they're your friends?"

"*Silmien!*"

"I just thought I'd ask."

"If they're not, it's your fault." She skipped ahead down the path and then turned on him, blocking his way. "Why do you always have to bring Mam?"

"What do you mean, always?" He looked over her shoulder. The old parents had doddered off, but Mam had not moved. Even though she was still a good thirty meters away, he lowered his voice. "It's only been three times and she wanted to see you."

"Why can't she wait until I come home for a visit? Besides, I don't have anything to say to her. What am I supposed to do, play a game of fish and snakes? Climb into her fruity old pouch? I'm not a scrap anymore!"

"She's unhappy, Tevul. She feels unwanted, useless."

"Don't use *my* name, because there's nothing *I* can do about that." Tevul's ears went flat against her head. "It's strange, you two here together. When the others have visitors, they get their mothers and fathers. She's not my mother."

"No," he said, "she's not."

Tevul's stern facade crumbled then and she broke down, quietly but completely, just as her mother had on the night she had left him. And he hadn't seen it coming; Silmien cursed himself for having stones up his nose and knotholes for eyes. Tevul's body was wracked by sobs and she keened into his chest so that Mam wouldn't hear. "They say such mean things. They say that Mam picked my name, not you, and that she named me after a character in a stupid lovestory. I try to joke along with them so they won't make a joke of me, but then they start in about my mother, they say that because she's a doctor . . . that the aliens. . . ." She turned a scared face up to him, her scent was bitter and smoky. "What happened to the baby, pa-pa? Is he still in her? I want to *know*. It's not fair that I never got to see you pull him from mother and bring him to Mam, that's what's supposed to happen, isn't it, not all the disgusting things they keep saying, and I'm supposed to be there, only I wasn't because *she* went to the aliens, it's not *my* fault, I'm tired of being different, I want to be the same, in a real family like Tilantree, the same." She caught her breath, sniffed, and then rubbed her face into his stubby fur on his chest. "No blame, no shame," she said. "The same." She shuddered, and the hysterics passed, as cleanly as a summer squall.

He bent down and licked the top of her head. "Are you unhappy here, my beautiful little Tevul?"

She thought about it, then sniffed and straightened her dignity. "This is the world," she said. "There is nowhere else."

The orange fathermoon was up now, resuming his futile chase of the mothermoon. It was the brightest part of the night, when the two parent moons and their billion star scraps cast a light like spilled milk. A stirring along a hedge of bunchbead, where a farm-bot was harvesting the dangling clusters of fruit, distracted Silmien momentarily.

"I am proud of you," he said. It wasn't what he wanted to say, but he couldn't think of anything better. When the robot passed them, he dipped into its hopper, pulled out a handful of bunch-bead and offered them to Tevul. She took some and smiled. Silence slid between them. Somewhere in the distance, the chickens were singing.

Tevul watched the stars as she ate. "Where is Mars?" she said at last.

"It's too far away." Silmien looked up. "We can't see it,"

"I know that, but where is it?"

"Kadut showed me their star last week." He came up behind her and, resting his elbow on her shoulder, pointed so that she could sight along his forearm. "It's in The Mask, there."

"Why did they come, the aliens?"

"They want to help, I guess. That's what they say."

"I have to get back soon," said Tevul. "Let's go see Mam."

Tevul was very polite to Mam and Silmien could see that the visit cheered Mam up. Mam insisted on waiting while Silmien walked Tevul back to her burrow, but he finally understood that this was what both of them wanted. Back at the burrow, Tevul showed him a lifestory she was working on. It was about Ollut, the scientist who had first identified estrophins, the hormones that determined which females became mothers and which mams. Silmien was impressed by Tevul's writing and how much she had absorbed from the teaching tells in just one season. She was quick, like her mother. Tevul promised to copy her working draft onto the tell, so he could follow along with her research. As he was getting ready to leave, her roommate Laivan came in. To his relief, Silmien remem-bered her name. They chatted briefly. Silmien was on his guard for any sign of mockery, but there wasn't any. Laivan seemed to like Tevul and, for her sake, tolerated his intrusion into their privacy.

"Luck always," he said. "To both of you." And then he left.

It was only later that his anger caught up with him. Mam had fallen asleep, lulled by the whoosh of the go-to through the tunnels, so there was no one to notice when he began to wring his hands and squirm on his seat. First he was angry at himself, then Tilantree, then Tevul's teachers, then at himself again, until finally his outrage settled on Valun.

She had been the leader of their family. Where she jumped,

they followed, even if they landed in mud. It had been her idea to move to the paddies, where the air was thick and the water tasted of the swamp. Farmers needed doctors, too, she said. She had been the one who healed the family's wounds as well, the one they all talked to. Yet when she left them, she wouldn't say exactly why she was going, only that there was something important she had to find out from the aliens. Valun had ripped his life apart, left him incomplete, but he had tried not to hurt her the way she had hurt him. Speakers from the tell had interviewed him about Valun and about his life now. In all his statements, he had protected her. Her work with the aliens was important, he said, and he supported it, as all the families must. There were so many diseases to be cured, so much pain to be eased. It was an honor that she had been chosen. If he had followed a different path, it was because he was a different person, not a better one. He had done all this, he realized now, not because it was the right thing to do, but because he still loved her.

Only Silmien had not realized how much she had hurt Tevul. Valun hadn't visited the gardens, hadn't even copied a message to the tell. Silmien had long since decided that Valun had left the family because she had been bored with him, and maybe he could understand that. But no mother ought to be bored with her own tween. For an hour, his thoughts were as blinding as the noonday sun.

Eventually, Silmien had to calm himself. Their stop was coming up and he'd have to rouse Mam soon. What was it Tevul had said? *This was the world.* What did he have to give to it? A new family? The truth was he couldn't imagine some poor out taking Valun's place. But life was too short, twenty years from pouch to bone garden. A new family then—and afterward, he'd give the world his story. He would need to get some distance from Valun; he could see that. But eventually he would write of how she had hurt him and Mam and Tevul. He would tell how he had borne the pain, like a mam carries a scrap. He paused, admiring the image. No, not a lovestory—the story of how he had suffered. Because of her.

Because of Valun and the aliens.

THREE

Valun thought she could feel the baby swimming inside her. Impossible. The baby was no bigger than her thumb. He was blind and hairless and weak and brainless, or nearly so. Couldn't swim, didn't even know that he was alive.

The baby wasn't moving; she knew that the waves she felt were made by the muscles of her own uterus. The contractions weren't painful, more like the lurch of flying through turbulence. Only this was predictable turbulence, a storm on a schedule. The contractions were coming more frequently, despite her fierce concentration. It was what distressed her most about giving birth. Valun had gotten used to being in control, especially of her own body.

The humans had almost complete control of their bodies; it was their astonishing medicine that had drawn her to them. They had escaped from nature, vanquished diseases, stretched life spans to the brink of immortality. They managed their emotions, commanded their thoughts, summoned inspiration at will. And on those rare occasions when they reproduced . . . well, they could play their genome like a flute. There were no stupid humans, no wasted space in their population. No mother was inconvenienced by labor. . . .

Another lurch. Too soon for another contraction. Then she realized that it was the go-to decelerating. Coming to a station. The readout in the front bulkhead lit up. *Uskoon*. Less than half an hour until she was home. Plenty of time.

She didn't want to be traveling while she was in labor, but this was the only way to have the baby on her terms. Mothers were supposed to give birth in the nursery with their happy families gathered around them. She would be in the nursery soon enough, only she doubted that the family would be all that happy to see her. Mam would be vastly relieved—maybe that was within sight of happiness. Silmien, however, would be furious that she was forcing this baby on him and then leaving him to care for it with Mam. He'd strike the martyr's pose, maybe even write about it. The scrap? She probably hated Valun. Valun would've hated *her* mother, had she done something like this when she was a tween. Tweens' deepest feelings were for themselves; she'd grow out of it. Valun had heard that he had named her Tevul, after the heroine of that story he liked so much. Was it *Drinking the Rain*? No, the other one. But then Silmien liked too many stories too much. The world was not a story.

Thinking about them made Valun feel like the loneliest person in the universe. Part of her desperately wanted to go back to stay. She longed to sleep and eat and breathe again with her family. But not to talk; if she told them what she had learned it might destroy them. Living with the humans had not made her happy at all. Indeed, most of the outs in Pelotto were miserable.

Valun now knew what she had only suspected when she left the family. The world they had been born into was a lie. There was no reason for the laws of birth order. No reason why she or Silmien or Mam or their little scraps should have such brutally short lifespans. Mams could be mothers, mothers could nurse, outs could have babies.

No reason why there had to be families at all.

Of course, the humans did not advocate change. They offered only information; it was up to each intelligent species to decide how to use it. Except their message was corrosive as acid. Everything was negotiable. Reality was a decision—and no one here was making it.

This idea had infected Valun's imagination. Even if all the families took from the humans was the ability to prolong lives, the rigid structure of their culture must surely crumble. She wasn't sure what would come after, or who. Perhaps those people—those outs—would be happy. But how could anyone alive today bear to watch the families collapse? Valun didn't want to inflict that future on Silmien and Mam and the scrap, so she had exercised her right of silence and cut them off entirely. If they wanted to learn what she had, they would have to chose, as she had chosen. But her silence had isolated Valun from the ones she loved most. She belonged to no family now, only to herself. She was alone, but it was not what she had wanted. Alone. She drifted alone on the whisper of the go-to.

And dreamed of smells. The sweetness of rain brushing her nose like a lace veil. The honeycup he had put behind her ear; he loved to pick flowers and give them to her. The velvet scent of grass crushed beneath the weight of warm bodies. It had been so long ago that they had made this baby—much more than the traditional two years—that she had forgotten where it happened. Under the moons, out in the fields and her head filled with the husky father smell that was like a lick between the legs. Then the hot, silky bouquet of sex. She felt as if there were a hand inside her, squeezing. The pressure was not cruel, but rather the firm grip of a lover. "Silmien." His name caught in her throat.

Valun started awake at the sound of her own voice. The seat beneath her was damp with the yeasty soup of her birth waters. "Oh, no," she said. Ten more minutes. She focused all her attention on the knot under her belly and the pressure eased—a little. Lucky there were no other passengers in the compartment. *Luck always,* Silmien had said on the night she had left him. Why did he keep popping into her head? Concentrate. She was thinking womb thoughts when the go-to stopped at their station and she walked on candystick legs to their burrow and announced herself to their doorbot.

"*Valun.*" Silmien flung the door open. "I can't believe. . . ." His nostrils flared as he took in her scent. "What have you done?"

"Come home for the holidays." She was trying for a light touch, but when she stepped into the burrow, her body betrayed her and she stumbled. Like crunching through a skim of ice, except that ice seemed to have formed in her head too. When Silmien caught her, she slumped into his arms. She knew she ought to be embarrassed for losing control. But not now—tomorrow, maybe. Felt good not to be standing on her own.

"Tevul!" Silmien shouted. "Mam!"

They carried her to the nursery and laid her on Mam's settle. The ice in her head cracked and began to melt. Something different about the nursery, but she couldn't pick it out at first. The water rug still brimmed, its damp breath filling the room. Lovestory next to Mam's settle. Wedding picture above the pool: Mam and Valun and Silmien. The tell murmured in its familiar corner. Then Valun realized the obvious. No toys, no lines of ants marching up the walls, no miniature settle in the corner. As she had expected, the scrap was home from the gardens for the lunar eclipse, but she was a visitor now and would certainly *not* be staying in the nursery. She was probably sleeping in Valun's settle, next to Silmien. And where would Valun sleep that night?

She shivered and saw her whole family gathered around her, as if she had just fallen out of a tree. Valun giggled. That seemed to fluster them even more. "Tevul." She nodded at the scrap. "Sweet name. Fills the tongue."

Tevul stared as if she thought her mother insane.

"I'm sorry I wasn't at your naming," Valun said. "Life in the gardens agrees with you?"

"It's all right."

"You're learning a lot? Making new friends?"

"What do you want?" said Silmien. "What has happened?"

"Valun, did *they* do this to you?" said Mam. "The aliens?"

"What?" said Tevul. "Someone tell me what's going on."

"She's having the baby," said Silmien. "Smell it!"

"She can't be." Tevul looked from Silmien to Mam and finally at Valun. "We just learned that in biology. You have to be exposed to all Mam's pheromones in order to bring an embryo out of latency. You're still supposed to be in diapause."

"This is *their* work," Mam said.

Choosing what to tell them was the hardest thing Valun had ever done. She didn't explain how she had lied about being invited to live with the humans. She had simply gotten tired of waiting and had gone to them on her own. It turned out that was the only way to gain access. The humans never actually invited *anyone*; all the outs in Pelotto were self-selected. Self-condemned. Nor could she tell them about the longevity treatments, the first reward for those who sought human knowledge. The problem was that pregnant mothers could not be rejuvenated, even if their embryos were latent. She said nothing of how the humans had offered to remove the embryo from her womb, and how she had almost left Pelotto then. That was too much story; her time was getting short. She could feel her womb knotting again.

"By the end of the rainy season," she said, "I started to worry that some other family's pheromones might be similar enough to yours to trigger a quickening. But by then, the scrap had already left for the gardens."

"I'm Tevul," said the scrap. "You can say my name."

"So I had already missed the weaning," Valun continued, "and the chance to share scents with all of you. The humans told me that they could end diapause artificially, so I could control when I had the baby. I was sure that you all still wanted him, so I agreed. And here I am. I timed him for the eclipse so that we could all, as a family, I mean. . . ." There was a sudden, vast and inevitable loosening inside of her, and once again she felt her body slipping from her control. Something trickling, tickling through her birth canal.

"You should have told us." Silmien's scent was bitter as a nut. "Why did this have to be a surprise?"

"Because she isn't staying," said Mam. "You want to go back to the aliens, isn't that it? Your *humans*." She made it sound like a curse. "Who are you having this baby for, us or yourself?"

"Mam, I. . . ." Valun pumped her knees together convulsively, then spread them apart wide. "The baby. . . ." She kneaded her belly. "Help, Silmien!"

Silmien and Tevul rallied to her. No question that she could feel the baby now, wriggling, pulling himself into her vagina with his ridiculous little arms. It occurred to her that at this moment in time she had family inside and out. What odd thoughts she was having tonight! She giggled again. The scrap was licking her face and sobbing, "Ma-ma-*ma*. Oh, ma!" Valun could feel Silmien's hands on her vulva, delicately opening her as he had opened her just once before, controlling her as only a father should, fingers basketed to catch the baby. She had forgotten how much pleasure there was in giving birth, ecstasy of mind and body to smell hot, wet life scrabbling toward the world. "*Oh,*" she said, as the final dribble of birth waters leaked out of her, and Silmien held the baby high, offering it to the moons. "Oh."

Silmien brought the baby down so that she and Tevul could see. He was just four centimeters long and almost lost in the palm of his proud father's hand.

"He's so tiny, so pink," said Tevul. "Where are his eyes?"

"They'll grow." Silmien's voice was husky. He brought the baby to his face and cleaned him gently with the tip of his tongue. The baby's mouth opened and closed. The arms wriggled uselessly.

"Stop." The harshness of Mam's voice startled Valun. "What are you doing?"

"Washing the baby," said Silmien.

"There is no baby."

Valun propped herself on an elbow, her head savagely cleared of the moist joy of birth. Mam's scent was like a hook up her nose; Valun had never smelled anyone so angry.

"Here." Silmien offered it to her. "See it."

"A baby has a mother," said Mam. "There is no mother here, only a father. This is an experiment by the humans. Take it back to them. Tell them that it has failed."

"Mam, no, Mam!" said Tevul. "He can only live outside a few minutes. He has to start crawling to your pouch now. Look, he's already shivering."

"Mam," said Silmien. "Our baby will die."

"Then put it on her." Mam turned contemptuously to Valun. "Let her open her pouch. Let *her* love it."

"I have no pouch, Mam," said Valun. "Only you can take care of him." She could see that the baby was distressed. "Please, tell me what you want." He curled into a ball and unrolled with a spasm. "Mam, I'll do anything!" Whatever crumb of brain the baby had must have registered that something was wrong. He should already be threading through his Mam's fur, not still flailing across his father's hand.

"I have nothing to say to an out," said Mam. "I will talk to its mother. Does anyone know where she is?"

"There's no time for this," said Silmien.

"What do you want from me, Totta?" Valun could tell that it had been a long time since anyone had used Mam's name. "I'm Valun. The mother."

Mam's eyes narrowed. "I want you to care about someone else other than yourself," she said. "I want your story to be a lovestory, Valun."

Valun struggled up off the settle. The world spun crazily for a few seconds, but she got it under control. She cupped her hands and extended them to Silmien. "Give him to me."

He brought his hands on top of hers and opened them. Silmien was sobbing as the baby slid onto her palm. Valun had never held a baby before. It weighed less than a berry and yet it was as heavy a burden as she had ever carried. "Will you take my place, Totta?" She nodded at the settle.

Mam hesitated for a moment, but then stretched out, facing Valun. She kept her legs closed, however, and clutched her knees to her chest to cover her pouch. Valun held the baby just above her.

"Totta, Silmien, Tevul, I will stay with you and be this one's mother." Valun astonished herself. In just one season the humans had taught her more about her own biology than she had learned in a lifetime of study. How could she turn away from that knowledge? "I'll be here to give him his name," she continued, "and I won't leave until he has come out of the gardens with his own family. I will do this for the love of him and against my best interests. But I will not sleep with you, Silmien, and there will be no mam baby from this family. No more babies at all. I can't be what you want, and you must all accept that. When Tevul and this scrap are grown up, I will go back to Pelotto again and study with the humans. I hope it won't be too late. Until then, I will study patience."

Mam did not unbend. "I heard many words, but hardly anything of love. What kind of mother are you?"

The baby was on the move again, scrambling up the side of Valun's cupped hands. "I will love this baby because I have given up so much for him," she said. "That is the truth, by my name."

"It's not a happy ending." Mam was still not convinced.

"Totta," said Silmien, "this is not a story."

"Mam." Valun tilted her hands to show her the baby's blunt head. "Someone's hungry."

Mam closed her eyes. Her face was hard with grief as she opened her legs. Valun laid her hands on Mam's belly and let the baby slip through her fingers. He landed on his back but flipped himself immediately. Driven by instinct, guided by scent, he crawled unerringly for the pouch. With each heroic wriggle forward that the baby took, Mam's face softened. When she opened her eyes again, they were bright as stars. Valun tried to imagine herself as a mam. A difference in her family's birth order and it could have been.

Valun could smell the buttery scent of relief melting from Silmien and Tevul. And once the baby had found the nipple, Mam's nursing bliss filled Valun's nose like spilled perfume. All these happy smells made Valun a little ill. This had certainly not turned out the way she had wanted. She wondered what fool had made all those promises. How could Valun keep them?

How could she not?

"Ma-ma-*ma!*" Tevul hugged Valun, just like she used to, but then she was still a tween and had so much to learn about being a mother.

Feel the Zaz

Everyone wants to be Cary Grant. I want to be Cary Grant.
                                        —Cary Grant

                    click

"ACCEPTING FOR VANITY MODE IS DYLAN MCDON-ough, artistic director of *Starscape*."

Dylan was stunned. For a few ticks he couldn't move, couldn't hear, or even see the audience which filled the virtual Colosseum. It had happened just as Vanity had planned. Then Bug pounded him on the back. "Go on. Go get it!" He could see that Letty was crying.

Dylan brought his avatar off the stone bench into sheets of cold applause. The designers had recreated the Colosseum in all its marble and gilt glory for this year's Websters. Fifty thousand avatars watched in disappointment as Dylan played his avatar through the virtual crowd to pick up Vanity's award. He knew the zaz was plummeting. Everyone had been hoping to see what Vanity Mode looked like, or at least how she would present when she wasn't doubling. Nobody cared what Dylan McDonough looked like. The Academy crowd would be clicking out by the dozens, the general audience by the millions. Of course, it would have been impossible for most people to tell the difference. The avatars in the audience were still clapping; their smiling faces beamed up at him as he passed. But the Vnet was where Dylan made his living. He could sense unattended avatars going flat, losing their edges.

He accepted the Webster from Lillian Citrus, who had her avatar presenting with a tree viper curled into her décolletage. "Wow," he said. The word came out as a croak. Back at the studio, he bumped his voice fx from delight to elation, although it was grief that caught in his throat. He held the little golden monitor at arm's length, saw the reflection of his face twist across its polished surface. This was all that she had ever wanted, and she wasn't here to enjoy it. "On behalf of Vanity Mode and *Starscape*," he said, "I'd like to thank the Academy for this award." He set the Webster for Best Double of 2038 on the podium. "I have a brief statement to read." His avatar took out a piece of paper. "When we're done here this evening, I would ask that you click to *Starscape*, where we will launch a biography sim to coincide with this great honor which you have bestowed on us. We have tried to tell Vanity Mode's story on it. I regret to inform you that it will mark her final appearance on our site."

The unattended avatars in the audience seemed puzzled at this, but nothing more. Only those who were live with their users registered shock. Dylan's avatar unfolded the virtual paper slowly, to give people time to click in. The paper was blank, but he, Letty, and Bug had spent weeks scripting the speech, now open on the desktop from which he controlled his avatar. While he waited, Dylan wondered if what he was feeling was a surge in the zaz. Two years ago, that would have worried him. Back then, he was quite certain that zaz was nothing but click count divided by attention quotient. It was something you measured afterward, not what you felt in the moment, like laughter or applause.

"Vanity Mode," he read, "was a true star, as eternal as any of those she brought back to life on *Starscape*."

Vanity had said once that great zaz was like being kissed by an entire country. He remembered thinking she was crazy.

click

The day he met Vanity Mode, Dylan had taken Roman Barone to lunch. The pitch had not gone well. Barone let Dylan buy him a plate of *penne all'arrabbiata* and a glass of Chianti and listened politely while Dylan described everything he was doing to turn *Starscape* around. *Roman's Nose* was one of the most influential guides on the net—a million clickthroughs a day. If *Nose* recommended *Starscape*, they would have to kick Barone back half a percent of their gross and it would be worth every nickel. Barone had delivered over eight million clicks to Dylan McDonough's last winner, *Duck Brings The Lunch*. But that had been six years ago — an eternity.

"Sure, your zaz isn't that bad for a boomer site," he said, "but the numbers are so skewed. What did you say you're getting from the under thirties?"

"They'll come, if only to see what their grandparents are talking about. And once they click in, we've got them. Because people love having Elvis as their best friend. It's the names, Roman. Say them and you can hear the magic. Marilyn, Bogie, Groucho, Ali, John Lennon, Michael Jordan, Fats Waller, JFK. . . ."

"Hey, I'm almost fifty and I barely remember these people. And my kids don't give a damn about Michael Jordan. If they know him at all, it's as that fat old jack who owns Nike. Frankly, I was shocked when I'd heard you'd bought a dusty little site like *Starscape*. What were you thinking?"

"It was all I could afford after the divorce."

"I'm sorry to hear that." Barone pushed some cold *penne* across his plate and then set his fork down. "But that doesn't change the demographics, Dylan: boomers aren't exactly a growth segment of the population. Besides, all the research says your tech makes them uncomfortable. You think millions of retirees are going to start using airflexes? Hell, no. The boomers don't get virtuality. Some of them still don't get *computers*. If they want dead stars, they go to dead media."

"But Roman . . ."

"Look at the time." Barone stood. "And I've got a two o'clock meeting. Sounds as if you've been working hard, Dylan."

"We all have. It's because we believe in what we're doing, Roman."

"Always a plus." His expression was smooth as glass. "Appreciate the lunch." They shook hands.

Dylan considered debasing himself completely, begging for the link, but decided against it. "I know our zaz is going to spike any day now," he said. "How about if I message you then?"

"Sure." Barone's snort was no doubt meant as a laugh. "People message me all the time."

click

Dylan had been trying to relaunch *Starscape* on the cheap; so far it was just him and Bug and Letty. They had four rooms of flop space in the partly abandoned Meadowbrook Office Park. Building Number Two was a mirror-glass dinosaur from the late 1970s. Many of the seals in the window wall had failed, so their view of the interstate was distorted by the little fog banks that had been trapped for decades between panes of glass. The HVAC was old and too expensive to run, so the landlord usually didn't. Letty hung sheets over the windows in the summer and ran a couple of monitor heaters in the winter. But Building Number Two had electricity and working toilets and an ultrawide connection to the net. If *Starscape* clicked big, nobody would care whether the carpet in Dylan's office was raveling.

click

"Honeys," Dylan called as he opened the door. "I'm home." He was determined not to let them see how worried he was.

There was no answer. He followed the screech of twisting steel and the crash of a concrete avalanche to the theater. On the dome, Bug and Letty were running a Manhattan sim that he had never seen before. He could see Letty's long hands dance in front of her as she used the airflex to play her avatar, an eighty-foot-tall Barbara Walters, through the ruin she had just made of Rockefeller Center. Dylan couldn't immediately pick out Bug's avatar, but then he didn't know what to look for.

"Bug, what is this?" He got no answer. "Letty?"

"It's Bug's new demo," Letty said, "and I already told him you wouldn't like it." She peeled back part of the roof of the Radio City Music Hall. "So where would you be if you were Cary Grant?"

"I don't know," said Dylan. "Empire State Building?"

"Nah." She dropped the roof section onto 50th Street. "Been there."

He watched, bemused, as Letty sent Barbara Walters on an uptown rampage. "Um, Bug?" he said. "I'm not sure I want users playing the stars. And why is she stomping taxis?"

"Bug isn't talking today," said Letty. "He's having a mood."

"I am not!" snapped Bug. "We've got Stalin, Darth Vader, and Mick Jagger riding around town." Bug was a short, volatile, twenty-eight-year-old, who favored dark clothes and black humor. He slouched, scowling at the dome with arms folded. "Free ten minutes in the sim if you squash one of them."

"This is a party site," said Dylan, "not *Dirty Work IV*. It's not supposed to be about racking up a high score." He had plucked Bug from combat sim hell and was still trying to curb his twitch response.

"Give it a chance, Dylan. We never show any bodies and it bumps the attention quotient two point six. Hey, it's satire."

"Satire is what closes Saturday night." Dylan tried to hide his annoyance. The demo was obviously a waste of their time. The idea was give users the illusion of meeting the old celebrities, not to wear them like silly costumes. He wished Bug would stick to programming; content had never been his strength. But clearly Bug *was* having a mood, which meant that Dylan would have to pretend to consider his demo. "And Stalin is too dusty. You want someone people will know."

"You're in Lincoln Center," said Letty. She was a slender woman with sparkled hair and skin the color of milk. She moved with a dancer's precision; Barbara Walters clumped up Broadway like a grain elevator with legs.

"No! It's so obvious, Letty." Bug sighed. "I could paste in Lee Harvey Oswald," he said to Dylan.

"I was thinking more O. J. Simpson. So are you in this sim, Bug, or just peeping?"

"I'm Cary Grant and I'm hiding," Bug said. "Go seek is the point."

"*You're* Cary Grant?" said Dylan.

Bug had yet to look away from the dome. "We've got to get some action going, Letty. Try the Upper West Side."

"Cary Grant, Cary Grant," muttered Letty. "This is way too obscure, Bug. I don't know anything about Cary *blinking* Grant."

"He was in a bunch of Hitchcocks," said Dylan. "If finding Bug is the point, what's the payoff?"

"Oh, just the sex default," said Bug. "If she figures out my hiding place, the avatars screw." He leaned toward her. "Although I'm kind of losing interest."

"We're playing it totally softcore," said Letty. "Something like a kiss, maybe a bare shoulder, then cut to shadows on the wall." She spun Barbara Walters across Broadway to mash a taxi into yellow roadkill.

"Yeah, violence and sex, only very tasteful." Bug yawned. "Do me a favor, would you, and head uptown. Way-*way*-uptown."

Dylan put a hand on Bug's shoulder, trying to divert him from the sim. "When did you find the time to write a Barbara Walters AI?"

"I didn't." Bug glanced at him briefly and then focused again on the dome. "She's just an image and bunch of movement routines lifted from fossil video." Bug was not good at eye contact. "That's the beauty of letting the users play the stars. No biography scan, no AI. So we cut programming costs and can start adding lots more celebrities to the cast."

Dylan shook his head. "Who's going to pay to watch Joe Modem pretend he's Cary Grant?"

"I told you he wouldn't like it," said Letty.

"Joe Modem will pay to pretend he's Cary Grant." Bug hunched his shoulders as if to ward off a blow. "And thousands of other Joes and Janes will pay. Letty, tell him how much fun we're having."

"It may be fun," said Dylan carefully, "but is it *Starscape*? Your sim is like producing a play and then picking the actors out of the audience."

"Excuse me, gentlemen," said Letty, "but would you mind taking this somewhere else? I'm in the middle of a session here and I'm losing major attention quotient."

"I told you when you bought this blinking site that the AI engine was no damn good." Bug's voice was icy. "It's a waste of money to write dodgy code for every celebrity on the site—money that we don't have. But if we let the users . . ."

Their deskbot interrupted. "Excuse me, pal, but we're going to have to ice this party for a while." It spoke in Humphrey Bogart's clipped voice.

"What is it, Bogie?" said Dylan.

"Could be nothing but a hill of beans. See, maybe I'm just software, but you hired me to do a job and I can't do it with one hand tied behind my back, now can I? Seems we got a visitor at the back door, a dame. Flesh and blood. Only I don't know why she's here and that bothers me. Makes me wonder if we've got some kind of security problem here. So who's been holding out?"

click

Dylan felt a momentary crinkle of panic. *Starscape* had been bleeding money over the past month. He'd spread $373,000 over five different cards, but had been careful not to overload any of them. The utilities and hardware payments were paid through next week. If Meadowbrook wanted money, they'd just reprogram the locks. Otherwise, no one knew *Starscape*'s bricks-and-mortar address.

"Anyone order a pizza?" Bug's grin was forced. They all knew how close to the edge *Starscape* was.

"ID her," said Dylan.

"You want a flat ID or deep?" said the deskbot.

"Flat."

"Flat will cost you twenty bucks."

"Authorized," he said.

click

" 'Kay, she's got a name: Elizabeth Lee Corazon. And she's got a driver's license which gives us a date of birth of 4-11-02, which makes her thirty-four. Her Social Security number is 049-38-3829, eyes brown, height five-seven, weight a hundred thirty-eight pounds. She lives at 43A Spring Street, Bedford. . . ."

"Who does she work for?" asked Dylan.

"Appears she's out of work," said the deskbot. "Fact is, she's seventeen months into unemployment. Medical disability."

"What's the matter with her?"

"Med records are deep, and deep will cost you, my friend."

"Well, at least she isn't here to turn out the lights," said Bug. "But why did she come to the back door?"

"Nobody is turning off anything, okay?" Dylan glared at them. "Got that?"

"Easy, boss," said Letty. "Bug's having the mood today. You can have yours tomorrow."

"Go find out what she wants while we finish here." Bug waved him away. "Maybe she's selling girl scout cookies."

"I'll have some trefoils," said Letty absently, as she rejoined the sack of Manhattan, already in progress.

click

As soon as Dylan saw their visitor through the wire mesh window of the back door, he thought he understood everything important about her. She was a stocky woman with broad, flattened features. Her brown hair did not quite cover the ears, which were big as fists. She stared back at him unabashedly, her eyes narrow and slanted, eyelids puffy. Her face seemed oddly childlike. If he had not known she was thirty-four, he might have guessed she was a teenager. She wore black jeans and a baggy adshirt on which a cartoon dolphin kept leaping out of a pitcher of Budweiser. She gave him a slow smile and mouthed the words *Open up*. He had never known anyone with Down syndrome—there weren't many left—but he believed he could handle her.

"I'm a double," she said as the door swung away. "And if you're *Starscape*, you need me."

"What?" Dylan was taken aback by her voice. It was as sultry as a silk pillowcase. "I'm afraid there's been a misunderstanding."

"This is *Starscape*, right? The site with all the oldie celebrities? *Live the glamour?*"

"I'm not sure I know what you're talking about, Ms. . . . ?"

"Are you the one who writes those tags?" She stepped through the door and surveyed the loading dock from the entryway, head bobbing with excitement. "*Touch the legend*. Hey, we're just clicking for fun, mister, not buying a new Rolex." She moved awkwardly, like someone who would knock things over.

Dylan felt his cheeks start to burn. First the bungled lunch with Barone, then Bug's slugnut demo, and now this crazy woman. "There's no *Starscape* here, this is . . . ah . . . Grant Associates. We do market analysis for non-profits. I'm afraid you've got the wrong address, Ms. . . ."

"Mode. My name is Vanity Mode."

"Mode?" He blocked her from coming any farther into the building.

"What's the matter, am I going too fast for you?" She put her hands together as if clapping, but didn't make any noise. "Maybe if I speak to your boss?"

"But I am. . . ." He realized then that she must have had one of those new CAT implants where they scooped out a chunk of cerebellum and replaced it with a computer grown from embryonic stem cells. The IQ improvement rate had just recently nudged over fifty percent. "This is my company."

"Then that would make you Dylan McDonough," she said and then let herself fall against him. "Oh, sorry." Her breasts nudged his chest and her legs tangled with his. He gave way with a mutter of astonishment, uncertain whether the contact was calculated or merely clumsy.

"Sorry," she said again, catching herself up and then escaping past him into the empty loading dock. "So Dylan, the idea of *Starscape* is delicious but the site is cold oatmeal. Your celebrities talk like computers in rubber suits. Take your Judy Garland— not half bipolar enough. You want a Jim Carrey so needy he'd swallow a goldfish for a laugh. Your problem is that nobody's wounded."

Dylan had been about to ask this creature how she had gotten his name but changed his mind. "And you do wounded? I mean, when you're doubling."

She extended her arms and bowed. "They don't come much more wounded than me."

click

Dylan knew there was no way he could afford to replace all *Starscape*'s celebrity AIs with human doubles. Still, it hadn't occurred to him that the tags might be overblown. "Where would you hide if you were Cary Grant?" he said.

"Ah-ha!" she said, and nodded at least three too many times. "The old trick question trick." Then she went up on tiptoes beside the dumpster and peered in.

"No, not here. Say you were in New York City." When Dylan looked at her, the flat, empty face, the way she slouched, how she almost clapped her hands when she laughed at her own wisecracks, he was lulled into believing she was slow, even if she did have a Computer Aided Thinking implant.

"Doesn't matter where." She thought it over; he could see the tip of her tongue between her lips. "Cary Grant doesn't hide. He might duck into the next room or make a quick getaway but he knows he can't hide because he's Cary Grant. The camera will always find him."

"Really?" He was impressed despite himself. "And how would you know that?"

"Because I was born in the wrong century, Dylan, not to mention in the wrong body." Her head bobbed. "I should've been my grandmother. She was a special assistant to Vincente Minelli when he worked at MGM. She once ate Louis B. Mayer's French toast by accident."

"There are more than just movie stars at *Starscape*."

"Oh, so now this is *Starscape*." She reached into the dumpster to snag an empty bag of Curry Snaps. "I can see why you'd want to keep this dump a secret." She folded it in quarters and stuffed it into the pocket of her jeans. "Well, Dylan, I've got Michael Jordan's rookie card and a home run ball that Ted Williams plunked into the bleachers at Fenway and a blue campaign button that says, 'I want Roosevelt again,' and Norman Mailer's ego pickled in alcohol—a joke, that's a joke." She clapped gleefully for herself. "I think the Hot Five was Louis Armstrong's best band and that *Rubber Soul* was the Beatles' best album, so let's start over, shall we?" She pirouetted across the loading dock to him like Julie Andrews in *The Sound of Music*, except that she stumbled twice. She offered her hand. Her fingers were short and thick; the nails worried to the quick. "I'm Vanity Mode and you're Dylan McDonough and—ta-*da*—this is our historic first meeting, so enjoy it."

click

Reluctantly, he shook her hand. Her skin was blood hot; he wondered if she were sick.

"Here's the script the way I read it," she said. "First you take me on the tour, then we draw up a contract and then I make you famous."

He let her hand drop. "Ms. Mode, I'm afraid you just don't understand."

"What do you mean, I don't understand?" Her face flushed. "Don't think that just because I look like me that I'm *s-s-stupid.*" The voice was no longer a purr; it was as if her tongue had swollen until it was too big to get words around. "I *understand,* mister. Don't-don't-don't you think I'm *stu*pid." He realized that her steamy manner of speaking was a kind of mask, and that the mask had just slipped.

"It's just that I'm very busy."

"Right," she said, "so busy that mister answers the backy door his *own*self?"

"Are you all right?"

She closed her eyes; her lips moved but she made no sound. He thought she might be counting to ten or maybe saying a prayer. When she opened them, she smiled and was Vanity Mode again. "Look Dylan," she said, "the zaz for *Starscape* is what? Twenty-three? Twenty-five? You should be doing eighty."

"How do you know that?" He squelched his alarm. Yesterday's zaz had been twenty-two-point-eight, down three-tenths from Wednesday's. He wondered if Bug or Letty might be selling him out. "Not that those numbers are right, Ms. Mode," he said, "but our zaz is proprietary information."

"Oh, I don't know it exactly." She smoothed her hands against the T-shirt. "I just . . . I *feel* it."

"You feel it?" He couldn't believe he was still talking to her. "And do you feel the times tables too? The stock market?"

She drew herself up. "I'm not like other people, in case you haven't noticed."

"This has gone far enough, Ms. Mode . . ."

"Vanity."

"Vanity, because even if I wanted to hire you, I can't afford to pay a double."

"You can't afford not to."

"We have a budget, a very tight budget." Dylan thought of the hundred dollar bill he had dropped on the table at lunch. "There's no money in it for doubling."

"But you're Dylan McDonough. You must have made a package at *Duck*. And what about *Stinger*?" Her voice slipped again. "Mister don't tell right. What ha-ha-happened to you?"

It was question that had nagged at Dylan for the last two years but he was suddenly angry at this Down syndrome lunatic for asking it. "What happened to me is none of your blinking business."

"Sorry, mister."

"No, I'm sorry to be such a disappointment to *you*, Vanity. I'll try to do better in the future." He had made some bad guesses, had some bad luck and now he didn't know exactly what he was doing anymore. Instead of making his life happen, he often found himself watching as life happened to him—like this little fiasco.

"Mister, I-I-I. . . ."

Dylan backed to the loading dock door. "Just so you know, *Duck Brings The Lunch* was pretty much over by '31. And I only owned two per cent of *Stinger*. The fact is, if I could afford a double, I wouldn't be working out of this dump, as you so aptly put it." He opened the door. "So anyway, it's been nice meeting you."

This time she shut her eyes so tight that he could see her lids twitch. Her head lolled back. Dylan knew he ought to push her out of the building while she was helpless, but he couldn't bring himself to it. He realized he was in the presence of two different people. The thick, awkward, retarded woman before him was Elizabeth Lee Corazon, who looked as if she were about to fall apart. Except that Vanity Mode was trying to hold her together with steely ambition and wisecracks and a voice like liquid sex.

click

"Okay," she said, "okay, okay, okay." She shivered and then smiled at him as if nothing had happened. "Okay, we go with a rewrite. More drama when the heroine starts from nothing. So: I don't need to be paid, Dylan, not yet anyway. You'll know when it's time." She waved airily at the open door. "Why don't you shut that? You're letting the flies in."

He didn't move. "I can call the police if you want."

"Good idea. Call the cops, the fire department, the Marines, and the starship *Enterprise*. How long will it take to pry me out of here, poor little retard that I am? A couple of hours? Give me half an hour. I'll double anyone you're running on *Starscape*. A cold reading. If you're not interested, Mr. McDonough, I'll walk out of here and you can get back to whatever it is you're so busy not doing."

Dylan hadn't known just how desperate the lunch with Barone

had left him; he was actually thinking of giving Vanity Mode a chance. But it was not only desperation that was making him reconsider. Dylan was ashamed of letting her make him angry and then snapping at her. He wasn't Bug; it wasn't his style to show feelings.

"How long have you had the CAT implant?" he said.

"Eighteen months, but what's that got to do with anything?"

"I'm just wondering if they've worked all the kinks out of it. Or did Elizabeth Ann Corazon always have the manners of a police siren?"

She became very still—no twitching, no head bobbing. "You leave her out of this."

Dylan shook his head. "Lady, you're her, okay? We IDed you at the door. Call yourself whatever you want, but keep the multiple personalities to yourself."

Vanity flicked her fingers dismissively. "She's just along for the ride."

The coldness of the gesture decided him. "You know," he said, "at least one of us is crazy." He leaned against the door and it shut.

"At least." Seeing that she had won, Vanity Mode giggled and clapped.

click

"Grant's Tomb!" Letty's shriek carried from the theater, through the computer room all the way to the loading dock. "You're in Grant's *blinking* Tomb?" The floor reverberated with the muffled thud of granite blocks being hurled onto Riverside Drive. If Bug answered her, Dylan could not hear him.

"Who's that?" said Vanity.

"Our engineer, Letty." He rubbed the back of his neck. "I don't know why I'm doing this."

"To get rid of me, remember?"

"Half an hour." He tapped his datacuff to start the timer. "The chime is your exit cue."

"You know what they say. Every exit is an entrance someplace else."

"They say a lot of things." He brushed past her. "Come on then." He didn't look back, although he could hear her following him over the hum of the computer room. He paused at the door to the theater to watch Letty and Bug play the end of the new sim.

"I told you, I get the joke already." Letty gave Bug a friendly poke in the shoulder. "Now how do I lose it?"

On the screens, Cary Grant and a resized Barbara Walters were leaning against the rail of the *Titanic*. They gazed back at the

Manhattan skyline silhouetted in a golden twilight. Barbara Walters nuzzled Cary Grant's shoulder.

"I've always been scared of women," said Cary Grant, "but I got over it."

Vanity came up behind Dylan but did not show herself to Letty and Bug. "It's all wrong," she whispered. "They open their mouths and spoil the illusion. That's why you need a double to play your stars. Someone who knows what she's doing."

"We have software for that," said Dylan.

"I'm better than software."

Cary Grant picked a Lucky from a cigarette case and let it dangle from his lips. He held the case out to Barbara Walters but she shook her head. The silver lighter lit on the first snap. Wisps of blue smoke caressed the famous cleft chin. There was a glow on Barbara Walters's face which was not entirely a lighting fx.

"Another mistake," said Vanity. "He doesn't offer her the cigarette. People used to say that Grant played hard to get, but that wasn't it. He *was* hard to get. Which is why everyone wanted him."

The lights in the theater came up. "How did you like the smoking porn, Dylan?" called Bug.

"Hot," said Dylan.

"And I finally nailed Jagger on Broadway and 96th," said Letty. "Is that your Girl Scout?"

click

"Letty, Bug," said Dylan, "this is . . ."

"Ta-*da!*" Vanity swept through the doorway and did two perfect pirouettes with arms outstretched. "Lettys and Gentlebugs, I give you the one, the only . . . *Vanity Mode!*" She clapped vigorously for herself, gave a curtain-call bow and, beaming, held up both hands as if to quiet applause. "Thank you, thanks, thanks so much, no, you're too kind."

They stared at her as if she had three heads.

"I know what you're all thinking," she said, "but seeing is definitely not believing."

"It's okay," said Dylan. "At least, I think it's okay. Vanity is . . ."

She rushed to place her forefinger to his lips. " No, no, don't be telling on me, Dylan. Letty, what are we using to control avatars?"

Letty shot Dylan an inquiring glance. He nodded. "Series 40 Airflex," she said, and tapped the CPU on her belt. "We've also got a couple of Sony discreets. And you can always run them off the console—but what's this about, Dylan?"

"The console would be best," said Vanity. "Bug, suppose I

wanted to modify one of your characters on the fly, play her like an avatar."

"She's carrying a concealed weapon, is that it?" Bug said. "We're all hostages?"

"I've got this under control, Bug. Tell her."

Bug did not seem convinced. "Well, the easiest way is to go in through the doubling interrupt."

"So you *can* double on *Starscape.*"

"We can," said Bug, "but we don't. Not yet, anyway. But the original programmers thought the code would be more robust if they included doubling in the initial design rather than kludge it later."

"Vanity doubles," said Dylan. "She's going to give us a brief demonstration of what we're missing."

Vanity twisted his wrist toward her and checked the datacuff. "About twenty-three minutes brief. Hey, who do you have to screw to get some help around here?"

"Nobody but yourself." Bug turned his back to her and got busy doing nothing at the rack of unused airflexes.

"Bug, *enough*," said Dylan. "Letty, would you take her to the workshop, get her up to speed on the console."

"In twenty minutes?" Letty said. "I've spent two months massaging the console, there are at least a hundred macros. . . ."

"That's okay, Letty." She winked at Dylan. "I'm a quick study."

Bug waited until they left before he exploded. "Jesus *blinking* Christ, Dylan."

"I know, pal—a piece of work. And she's got to have a pretty extreme CAT implant. You should've heard her out on the loading dock."

"Sure they didn't put it in backwards? Who the hell is she?"

"Bug, we're going to find out." Dylan pulled an airflex from the rack. "I should probably just bounce her out of here but I've got this hunch." He snugged the headband to his temple. "I feel like what *Starscape* needs just now is to get run over by a random variable." He bent over and fastened the ankle and wrist straps. "Maybe she's it."

Bug studied him. "It didn't happen with Barone, did it?"

"I don't think so." Dylan fitted the nose clips into his nostrils. "No."

"We're screwed, aren't we?"

He plugged the peripherals into his CPU and shrugged. "Let's just say that we could use a fairy godmother."

click

"I don't believe her." Letty rejoined them in the theater. "She's running the console like she built it herself."

"She's a quick study," said Bug sarcastically. "CAT power." He tapped a finger to his temple, then twirled it.

"Nobody is that fast." The theater dome began to darken and Letty jammed her peripherals into the CPU of her airflex. "Even with a CAT implant," she muttered.

"What's your pleasure?" Vanity's disembodied voice came at them from every direction. "Anybody, in any sim you've got."

"Bug?" said Dylan.

"I'm supposed to care?"

"Let her chose," called Letty.

"Is that all right with you, Dylan?" Vanity asked.

"Sure," Dylan said. "Whatever takes eighteen minutes."

click

On the dome the three of them were seated in the dining car at a table set for four. The silver gleamed on the white linen tablecloth. Letty and Dylan sat facing Bug and an empty chair. The walls were teak and mahogany inlaid with marquetry; the lights were garlands of bronze-work oak leaves. Out of the windows on their side of the car Dylan caught a glimpse of the Danube as the train raced through the twilight toward the Czechoslovak border. The somme-lier, dressed in a tight, black jacket and knickers with white stockings, filled their glasses with Veuve Cliquot. Dylan brought the glass to his mouth to get the benefit of the olfactors. He watched bubbles drift lazily through the champagne and pop like dreams. They tickled his nose. The wheels of the Orient Express sang along the rails.

"Kind of a slow starter." Bug squirmed in his chair. "Needs more action!" he called after the sommelier.

Katharine Hepburn hurried out of the drawing room. Dylan was surprised that Vanity had chosen to double the older Hepburn; she looked to be in her sixties. Her wild gray hair had been tamed into a bun. The face was drawn, which made her cheekbones even more astonishing; the tremor was scarcely noticeable.

"Thank goodness I've found you," said Katharine Hepburn. "Your friend, Bug— is it Bug? He was on the floor. I think he may be, he may be dead."

"I'm not dead." Bug raised his forefinger wearily. "I'm right here."

She settled beside him, cocked her head to one side and then another. "Why, so you are." She touched his arm. "Nevertheless, there's a body in the smoking room. In the next car, Mr. Bug, you must go and see for yourself."

Letty shook open her napkin and brought it to her mouth so that Bug wouldn't see her laughing.

"It's Bug," he grumbled, pushing back from the table. "Just plain Bug." The train swayed as he stood and he caught himself on the back of Katharine Hepburn's chair. "What's so funny?"

"Oh, do hurry," said Katharine Hepburn. "Bug."

After he was gone, she looked from Dylan to Letty and back again. "What?"

Dylan chuckled. "Nothing."

"Did I say something wrong?"

"No," said Letty. "It's just that you got to him—and in record time too."

"Is that good or bad?" Katharine Hepburn gave them a nervous little smile. She was wearing a heather gray pants suit and a black turtleneck. She slipped a hand into the pocket of the double-breasted jacket and pulled out a man's gold watch. "At least an hour until we arrive in Bratislava. Do you think we should alert the conductor about what's happened?"

Bug looked bemused as he reentered the dining car. Both of him did. Behind the Bug dressed in black plytex followed another Bug in a white tuxedo, his bow tie askew and hair mussed.

"So it was you," said Katharine Hepburn. "I knew it was. I'm glad you're all right."

"Bug?" Letty goggled at the resplendent Bug Two. "Bug, you look like a million bucks."

Bug One glared at her.

"Well, I feel like eight cents," said Bug Two. He touched the back of his head gingerly. "Somebody hit me when I wasn't looking." He stopped in front of Katharine Hepburn. "That wouldn't have been you, would it?"

She looked up at him in perfect astonishment. "Why I assure you, Bug, that I did no such thing."

"What are you trying to prove?" said Bug One. "You're supposed to be doubling stars, not us. Close him."

"Close . . . close who?" The corners of Katharine Hepburn's mouth turned down. "I'm not sure what you mean."

Dylan didn't think it was very fair of Bug to break verisimilitude but before he could object, Bug Two grabbed a fistful of Bug One's shirt. "Maybe what needs closing is your mouth."

"Oh, great plotting." Bug One went slack in his twin's grip. "As soon as things get boring, have a fist-fight break out."

Letty shot out of her chair and wormed between them, facing Bug Two. Reluctantly, he let Bug One go. "Now, Bug, haven't you had enough excitement for one night?" She pressed up against him as she straightened his bow tie.

"I don't know," said Bug Two. "Have I?"

She laughed. The engineer sounded the horn as the train skirted a dark Austrian village.

"Do be a help," said Katharine Hepburn to Dylan, "and get another chair for Bug here."

"Don't bother," said Bug Two. "Letty, how long has it been since someone asked you to dance?"

"You can't dance on a moving train," Bug One said.

"Too long," said Letty.

"The land flattens out." Katharine Hepburn beamed at them; her teeth were so big they were scary. "The tracks are straight as an arrow."

"There's a Victrola in the drawing room." Bug Two made as if to brush his fingers through her hair, but hesitated at the last moment.

Letty leaned into his hand. "What are we waiting for?"

"Letty, no!" said Bug One, but she paid no attention. He sank onto his chair and watched as they threaded their way through the dining car. His expression was grim. In the dome, Letty walked straight to the rack, picked up a discreet, set the helmet on her head, and went through the door. On the dome, she paused to glance back at Bug before she left. It was a look that would have set fires in a monsoon.

"Wow," said Dylan.

Katharine Hepburn tucked a stray curl of hair back into her bun. "They make a nice couple, don't you think? You young people need to dance more, if you ask me. You all work too hard. There's more to life than sitting at your desks, worrying yourselves to shreds about deadlines and spreadsheets and all that. The world was made for us to enjoy—as we are made to enjoy each other. A little romance wouldn't hurt you, Bug, or you either, Dylan."

"Romance is easy," growled Bug. "Now show us hard, something with grit."

"Bug, this is a party site. . . ." began Dylan.

click

The bus smelled of sandalwood and pot and sweat. Most of the seats had been ripped out and replaced with homemade furniture:

beds and benches, a hi-fi system on a shaky table. Even though all the windows were open, it was sledgehammer hot, hot as sin, kick-the-dog hot. The bus was pulled over by the side of the highway and the hood was up. The view out of every window shimmered; saguaros put their arms up as if in surrender to the heat.

"Looks like the Magic Bus has broken down," said Dylan. "This gritty enough for you?"

Bug didn't reply. He was lying on a dirty mattress, staring up at the ceiling, which had been debauched with paint. It was as if Chagall had popped a Dali pill—bright shape and strange line melting, melting into rude oranges and reds, vulgar yellows, deranged blues—Mondrian with motion sickness.

The hood slammed and a thin, gawky man in mechanic's coveralls got on the bus. He acknowledged them with a nod. "We go about our daily lives understanding almost nothing about the world," said Stephen Hawking, in a computer synthesized voice. "The second law of thermodynamics tells us that all machines will ultimately break down, and that it makes no difference whether the machine is the universe or a 1948 International school bus." He swung into the driver's seat and turned the key in the ignition. The motor coughed and started.

"It was a loose hose," Stephen Hawking said, over the engine noise. "Thank God it is still possible to increase order locally." He leaned toward the open door and called to a shadow still baking just outside. "Are you on the bus or not?"

Janis Joplin tripped in the stepwell and sprawled onto the bus. As she fell she twisted to protect the open quart of Southern Comfort she was carrying. A few drops spilled onto her hand; she cackled and licked them up. "Man, I am *wasted.*" She was wearing a low cut red silk blouse that had sweat stains under the arm-pits.

"Aristotle believed in a preferred state of rest," said Stephen Hawking, "which any body would take up if it were not driven by some force or impulse."

"Far out." She grabbed the support beam, pulled herself up and held the bottle out to him. "Have some force, force to be reckoned with, man."

"No, thank you," said Stephen Hawking. "I am driving."

"How 'bout you two?" She aimed the bottle at Dylan and Bug and followed it down the aisle. Stephen Hawking crunched the bus into first gear and pulled back onto the highway.

"Not for me," said Dylan.

"Hey, I know you." Janis Joplin swayed next to him and he could smell the bitter fruit of her breath. "Or someone jus' like you. You're one of those uptight sonsabitches can never say what you're thinking. Or feeling. Feelings can't be wrong, feelings are what we're made of. Feelings are what we're composed of and exist of and live for, s'far as I'm concerned." She shook her head and her long hair danced in the swelter blowing at fifty-three miles an hour through the windows. "I think that kind of freedom is beautiful."

"Maybe you should sing." Dylan knew that some people liked watching celebrities veer out of control, so *Starscape* had a couple of sims which targeted that peculiar market niche. Humoring drunks, however, was not his idea of fun—even if they were famous. "Why don't you sing?"

"No way." She sniffed. "You think I just go ahead and sing for any jackoff who asks?" She took a hit off the bottle. "For me it's like . . . singing is like sex. Better than sex, sometimes. Why don't you ask me if I want to fuck?" She cackled. "I might actually say yes to that." The bus jounced through a rut and Janis Joplin staggered. She caught herself on the corner of Bug's mattress and noticed him as if for the first time. "You look kind of down, man. Something bugging you?"

"Okay," he said.

"Okay?" She puzzled over this for a few seconds, her lips moving. "Okay, what?"

"Okay, you're good."

"Damn straight I'm good." She cackled again. "Hell, I'm good and a half." She drifted over to the hi-fi; Dylan could hear her humming to herself as she sorted through a stack of LPs.

"Enough, okay?" Bug grunted and rolled off the mattress. "Sure, she's exactly what we need, except we'd have to hire at least thirty of her and we can't even afford this one. And she's crazy."

Janis Joplin put the record on the turntable. "Hey Bug," she said, turning from the hi-fi, "how do you get your mouth around all those words? Come on, dance with me." She opened her arms to him and cocked her hip. "You might get lucky, man."

"Get away from me."

"Okay, okay." She reached over and lowered the tone arm onto the record. "I see how it is with you."

"What do you mean?"

Janis Joplin sighed as the needle scratched across the lead-in groove and then her hair fell out and melted into the shag carpet on the floor. Her ears bloomed like dark flowers and her skin deepened to a midnight blue-black. She grew a guitar. By the time she started to play she was Robert Johnson.

"I went to the crossroad," sang Robert Johnson, "fell down on my knees." He gazed through Dylan as if his skull were clear as a fishbowl and his brain were a guppy.

"What's this about, Dylan?" said Bug. "What's going on here?"

"I don't know, Bug, I'm just . . ."

"You don't know—that's the problem. At first I thought I was mad at her for wasting our time, but it's you, Dylan. What the hell are you doing? Making it up as you go along?"

"What's wrong with that?" asked Dylan.

"It is impossible to predict a definite outcome no matter how rigorously you define the starting conditions," said Stephen Hawking. "We can only predict a number of different possible outcomes and tell how likely each of these is to occur."

Bug shook his head in disgust. "You want to play this session out, go ahead. But as far as I'm concerned, it's game over." On the dome, his avatar disappeared from the sim with an impolite *plop*.

"Didn't nobody seem to know me," sang Robert Johnson, "everybody pass me by."

Stephen Hawking pulled the bus off the road. "I believe this is your stop."

In the dome, Bug had already stripped off his airflex.

"Bug, wait!"

"For what, Dylan?" He stopped. "Tell me what I'm supposed to wait for." Bug gave him a two count before he spun away and stalked through the door.

Dylan thought about aborting the sim and going after Bug, except outside the bus window the landscape had gone impossibly blue and lush. The trees had indigo trunks and cerulean leaves, the clouds were bright as a robin's egg. It was his favorite of all their sims, the only one that could still make him feel like a little boy again. How had she known?

Stephen Hawking pushed an upright metal rod away from him and a complicated mechanism opened the creaking door of the bus. "Before one begins to theorize," he said, "it is helpful to examine all assumptions."

Dylan ducked down the passageway and stepped off into the sapphire afternoon light.

click

Vanity was waiting for him on a bench by a hut that looked like two scoops of blue ice cream. The Yellow Brick Road sliced through the cornflower fields of Munchkin Land to the distant gates of the Emerald City. But this was not the same woman who had come to the loading dock of Building Two of the Meadowbrook Office Park. Elizabeth Lee Corazon had been transfigured by *Starscape*'s image processors: the ugly duckling had gotten the swan upgrade. The virtual Vanity Mode presented with a fairy tale face and the body of a sylph. She wore a white blouse and a gingham dress and the ruby slippers. "Time's almost up," she said as she rose to greet him. "So, Scarecrow, think of the adventures we could have together."

"Bug was right," he said. "You're good."

"Why is he so angry?"

"Just having a mood." He gestured and they sat together on the bench. "There's a programmer for you."

"He's angry at both of us."

"At me," said Dylan, "because of you."

She sighed and three Munchkins tumbled out of the blue hut.

"He's wrong, you know," said the first, hands thrust deep into the pockets of his pantaloons.

"I'm all you'll need." The second one tugged at his striped vest, which had ridden up over his paunch.

"I can multitask at least a hundred individual sessions simultaneously." The third thrust out his bearded chin and rocked from one foot to the other.

"Enough fx, Vanity," said Dylan. "Let's just talk, okay?"

The three little men turned as one and marched back through the door of the hut, muttering disconsolately.

"I can run even more sessions," Vanity said, "if you let me modify the console."

"And you'll work for nothing?"

"Let's just say that I'll agree to defer my compensation." She slid closer and laid her hand flat against the slats of the bench, her fingers just brushing his thigh. "I'll collect, Dylan." His olfactors picked up her sunshine scent. It made him think of his mother gathering in laundry from the clothesline. "Don't think I won't."

Dylan shivered; he could feel her gathering him in like a sheet. "Why do you want this so much?"

"Because I know exactly what you're trying to do here." Vanity Mode gazed off at the Emerald City for few moments, her eyes bright, then Elizabeth Ann Corazon finished her thought. "Feel it, feel it in my belly. At night I dream it right in my head, mister. All the pretty pretties. This where I belong."

Dylan was taken aback. "In Oz?"

"No, mister." She giggled. "No, no, no, *Starscape*."

"Elizabeth," he said gently, "who is Vanity?"

"My always dream." She caressed a fold of the gingham dress. "Always."

"And you let her take control?"

"Don't you talk to her," snapped Vanity. "Leave her alone!" Her pretty face flushed with anger.

"You drifted off and there she was." Dylan shrugged. "She sounded happy to be here."

"I'm here, Dylan," she said, "and *I'm* the one who is happy."

"You still haven't told me why."

She spoke without hesitation. "It's like your tag, *live the glamour*. You've made a world where everything is beautiful. *Touch the legend*. The myth is the message."

"You think Janis is beautiful?"

"Of course, she's the most beautiful of all. She absolutely owns the beautiful loser script."

On certain nights, if Dylan snooted more Placidil than was good for him and then squinted and held his breath, he could see the *Starscape* Vanity was talking about. But eventually he had to breathe or die. "You ever hear of Roman Barone?"

"Sure, he's *Roman's Nose*."

"I had lunch with him today. Pitched the site." Dylan looked away from her toward the Emerald City. "I don't think I got the link."

"So?"

"He says that the site is too dusty and our zaz is too skewed."

"Well, if that's what he says, tell him to shove his big fat nose up his ass."

It irked Dylan that she believed in *Starscape* more than he did. Her faith felt like another weight he had to carry when he was already staggering. He might use her talents but had no use for her illusions. "Barone says the only people who care about the old stars are boomers and, even though they've got money, they die by the busload every day. And they hate the hardware; the airflex makes them self-conscious. They never learned to fit reality and virtuality into their heads at the same time. Hell, some of them didn't even have televisions when they were kids, much less computers."

She dismissed Barone with the toss of her head. "He's wrong."

"If he's not, *Starscape* will go 404 by the end of the year."

"Well, I'm no boomer and I love the site, Dylan." She frowned. "What *are* the demographics on your zaz?"

He shook his head. "The last fix was six months ago. Fifty-and-older was almost eighty percent of all clicks; twenty-five to fifty was less than sixteen. But we've pulled back almost half of the sims since then and redesigned or replaced them. Now you can play croquet with Muhammad Ali, bake cookies with Gertrude Stein, or take John Wayne's philosophy course—but all we get is the raw zaz. We can't afford another demographic fix."

"Your thirty-somethings have gone way up since then. Believe it."

"That's one of your feelings? Like the way you feel the zaz?"

A horn honked and around the bend of the Yellow Brick Road came a gray 1939 DeSoto Custom Club Coupe. It was an elephant of a car, with wide running boards and flaring fenders; the tiny windshield made it look nearsighted. Cary Grant braked to a stop in front of them. His elbow hung out the driver's side window.

"Listen chum," he said, "why don't you stop sticking pins into her? She's not going to pop."

Dylan's datacuff began to chime. Vanity's thirty minutes were up.

"I know this girl," Cary Grant continued. "She can take a lot worse than anything you can dish out."

"Sorry everyone, but that's all the time we have for today," said Vanity. She crossed in front of the DeSoto, opened the passenger door and climbed in. Cary Grant ignored her, watching Dylan as if he were a Nazi spy.

Vanity waved. "See you next time."

click

Dylan felt the perceptual wrench that came from being dumped suddenly from virtuality. His heart pounded. Afterimages ghosted across the blank white expanse of the dome. The world did a quarter spin and then locked in. The theater was empty.

"Where is everyone?" he said. "Bogie?"

"Letty's in the kitchen," said the deskbot. "Bug took a powder."

"He left the building?"

"Headed for parts unknown."

"And Vanity?"

"She's still in the workshop, in session with Letty. Boss, I don't trust that dame."

On his way to the workshop, he passed Letty in *Starscape*'s kitchen, actually just a storage room with a sink knocked in. A little refrigerator hummed in the corner; on top of it was the microwave oven in which Dylan cooked most of his meals. Letty was sitting upright at the table, still wearing the discreet, muttering into the microphone. Although the visor covered her eyes, her posture and the set of her mouth indicated that she was investing serious attention quotient in the session.

"Letty?" he said.

"Hmm," she said absently. "Later."

The workshop was Bug's warren. An antique red barber chair faced a vidwall on which at least thirty different windows were open. Some were filled with code hieroglyphics, some were wire frames of new sim objects. There were livecams of the surf at Redondo Beach, Dawn Zoftiggle's bedroom, and a clerk's-eye-view of the 7-Eleven on the Nevski Prospekt in St. Petersburg. A few were action loops of monsters rampaging through inner cities: Kong in New York, Gojiro in Tokyo, and the Giant Behemoth in London.

Vanity Mode was sitting on the barber chair with the console on her lap. She twirled the chair around to face him. She was, of course, her lumpy self. "Deal?" She held out her hand.

"Are you and Letty still playing?"

"We danced. Then I stopped doubling Bug and now we're talking." She acknowledged his look of surprise with a bow. "I told you I can run a hundred sessions."

"And function in real time?"

"A session is a session." She continued to hold her hand out to him. "Virtual or real makes no difference."

"Are we in a session? Is that what this is?"

"Reality is session A1A." Her head lolled. "Always on top."

"And who are you doubling now?"

She laughed. "Why Vanity Mode, of course. But you're right, Dylan. Maybe I need to turn down the volume a touch, especially if we're going to be working together. So, deal?"

"If you're free, you're hired." Dylan crossed the room and shook her hand. "Do you know where Bug went?"

All the screens consolidated. Bug's avatar stared balefully out at them. "I'm not here so go away and don't touch anything," it said.

"When will you be back?" asked Dylan.

"Can't say. I left without telling me."

"Well, when you come back, ask yourself to step into my office."

The avatar turned its back to them. The message was stitched across the shoulders of its black leather jacket.

DYLAN WANTS TO SEE YOU ASAP.
LOOKS LIKE HE'S HIRED BLINKY.

click

After the bankruptcy, Dylan had decided to simplify his life. He had tried to convince himself that his problem was that he'd been distracted by the glittery side effects of his early success. Losing track of what mattered had cost him *Stinger* and Julie and the house in Woodstock and a large slice of self-respect. Of course, the banks had been eager to help him adjust his lifestyle to his new circumstances, which was why his office was spare and more than a little shabby. Bogie was a state-of-the-art *Assistencia* deskbot but Dylan had him mounted on an old gray Steelcase that had been left behind when Building Number Two of the Meadowbrook Office Park had been shut down. There were a couple of mismatched plaid chairs that would have gone begging at a country yard sale and a musty foldout couch where he had been sleeping for the past two weeks. Dylan was glad he had left the door to the executive washroom closed. He didn't want Vanity to see his suits hanging in the shower. About the only reminder he kept that he had ever been anyone was the Webster he had won for *Stinger*.

It was what Vanity saw first—possibly the only thing she saw in his office. She goggled as if it were the Holy Grail. "Can I?"

From the look on her face, he wasn't sure whether she wanted to handle the Webster or fall down and worship it.

"Help yourself." He stepped behind his desk. "Messages, Bogie?"

"Just a couple," said the deskbot.

"It's heavy," said Vanity. She cradled it in her arms and rocked it back and forth like a newborn.

"I've found that the longer you have one, the more it weighs. From who, Bogie?"

"First is a guy by the name of Creditworks-dot-com," said the deskbot.

"Delete it," said Dylan.

"I want one," she said, nodding excitedly. "I've always wanted one."

"Make me an offer."

"No, one of my own." She laughed. "Tell me about the night you won it. What did it feel like?"

Dylan didn't know what it felt like to win a Webster. The day of the ceremony there had been the champagne reception at two, moodfood at the Blackburns followed by early dinner at Maxx's, where they had drunk two thousand dollars' worth of Haut Brion. At some point he had met Kyle in a bathroom for a snoot of Placidil.

When he woke up the next morning, the damn thing had been on the nightstand. "It felt great," he said. "I'll never forget it as long as I live."

"Then there's Roman at Nose-dot-com," said Bogie. "Ever heard of him?"

Dylan felt the hair on the back of his neck prickle. "Wow." He laughed uncertainly. "Play it."

click

Roman Barone was sitting on a leather couch the size of Long Island. He looked like a little kid in it. He had taken his suit coat off and unsnapped the top snap of his shirt; he was wearing an airflex with the headband pulled up. The windows behind him appeared to be real; he had a view of a pond nestled in a grove of white pines. "Dylan, this is Roman. First of all, you want something, you message me yourself from now on, understand? I find incoming in my mailbox about a half an hour ago from Vanity someone—the address is in your shop. Sounds like a blinking alias. Second of all, I don't like to reward sitemasters for going deep ID on me. You want to waste your money snooping my personal life, fine. But just because you know where I lived in 1996 doesn't mean you know what I'm going to put on *Nose* tomorrow. I realize this kind of crap goes on, but if you want to play that game, you need to be a hell of a lot more . . ."

Dylan stabbed at the pause icon. "What the hell did you do?"

"I don't know yet," said Vanity. "I haven't heard what the man has to say." She set the Webster back in its place. "You'd already blown the link, Dylan."

He sank back onto his chair as Barone finished.

". . . subtle next time. But here's the real reason I'm messaging you. I don't remember the episode where Homer became a veterinarian. Did you make that up? If you did, your sim is brilliant. If not, I want the reference. Let me know either way."

The desktop went blank.

click

"Wow," said Dylan. "I don't believe it."

"He was born in 1987," said Vanity. "*The Simpsons* were just about the only show that kids and their parents watched together in the '90s. When I went deep on him, I found out that he put a fan site up on Geocities in 1999 called *Duff Beer Showcase*. It 404ed in '01. You had a Simpson's sim up already; I just doubled all the characters and sent him a taste."

"How much did the ID cost?"

"Not much. I made some lucky guesses."

"About time someone had some luck around here." Dylan waved the dictation processor on. "Reply to last message." He hesitated, then pressed the pause icon again. "What am I going to say to him?"

"The truth. The sim is original to us and he should've found it himself. Call his bluff. He's probably never even clicked *Starscape* before."

Bug stuck his head in the door. "You want to see me, Dylan? Because if you don't, I need to see you." He didn't acknowledge Vanity.

"In a minute, Bug. Vanity, you think that's *all* I should say? Seems kind of curt."

"Hey Bug," said Vanity. "Sorry about . . ."

He ducked out of the doorway before she could finish.

"Don't pay any attention to him," Dylan said. "Like I said, he's having a mood. What else for Barone?"

"Well, you might ask if he's visited our Super Bowl sim yet. His father taught Phys Ed and was football coach at North High in Denver. I can do a John Elway that could fool even his kids."

Dylan nodded and then came around the desk. "Look Vanity, I'm feeling a little gun-shy about this. You're absolutely right: I blew the contact and you saved it. So do me a favor—you message him back." He gestured for her to sit in his chair. "Use my name. Whatever you think will work is fine with me. Meanwhile, I'll pour some honey on our friend, Bug."

"You'd better," she said. "He hates me."

"Now, now, you're just an acquired taste." He patted her arm. "I'll give him some incentive to make the acquisition."

click

Dylan found Bug and Letty in the workshop, studying the vidwall. Half a dozen windows were scrolling old news feeds. The one in the middle opened onto a turn-of-the-century-sitcom with the sound turned down. A man with big eyes sat in a dentist's chair while a woman with big breasts flossed his teeth.

Dylan put his arm around Bug's shoulder. "She said she'd work for free so I told her she could stay. You're not going to give her a hard time, are you Bug?"

Letty shot Bug a warning glance; he shook his head.

"And the first thing she does is get Barone to take another look at the site. I'd say that's a pretty good day's work." Dylan gave Bug a friendly shake. "*Roman's Nose,* people. Our stock options might actually be worth something."

Bug didn't react. Dylan glanced at Letty; she was made of stone. On the sitcom, a woman in a lab coat was talking to the patient in the chair. The woman had beautiful silver hair and she was very pregnant. "What? Talk to me, Letty."

Bug cleared his throat. "You ever hear of Baby X?"

Dylan frowned. "Let's see, it was something about a lawsuit. And the mom was on TV."

"Elizabeth Ann Corazon is Baby X," said Bug. "While you were in a session with her, I stepped out and paid for a deep ID. My own money, Dylan. Her mother was Beth Ann Lewis, She was in that sitcom *Big Mouth*." He nodded at the center window. "She played the other dentist. So Beth Ann is in her first hit show at age forty-six and she gets pregnant, only she's not married. The father isn't in the picture but Beth Ann still really wants the baby. She's very careful, has the amniocentesis and when the tests come back, everything looks just fine, so she elects to carry the pregnancy to term. It's a kind of minor news story; they even write the pregnancy into the show."

Vanity burst into the room. "You were brilliant, Dylan. I don't know how Barone can pass . . ." When she saw the screens, she stopped. "Okay, okay, I suppose we have to go through this." She worried at her lower lip. "But just once, all right? How much have you got?"

"On April 11, 2002," said Bug. "Beth Ann gives birth to a baby girl."

"Ta-*da*." Vanity curtsied, her thick fingers holding the hem of her adshirt as if it were a dress. "A star is born."

"You want to tell the rest?" asked Bug.

"No, you go ahead." She was somber, unlike herself. "Maybe your script has the happy ending."

Bug shook his head. "I don't know that much more. Apparently the delivery is a disaster and Beth Ann ends up having a hysterectomy. And of course there was a major screw-up at the lab because the baby was . . ."

"Defective," said Vanity. "I believe the word is defective."

"Anyway," continued Bug, "the jury finds gross negligence."

"Right," said Dylan. "We studied this in Bioethics. Baby X was the test case of the Uniform Conception and Gestation Act—the first successful wrongful birth suit."

"The jury awards Beth Ann sixty-three million dollars, which the judge reduces to twenty million. But as soon as the judgment is final, Beth Ann gives Baby X up. She is adopted by Raul and Marisa Corazon, which is where I picked up into the thread. But that's as deep as I got."

click

They waited. Vanity stood with her eyes shut, as if she were listening to someone giving her advice. Then she nodded several times and approached the wall. "In some ways, my birth mother was very kind." She touched the window where her mother was having dinner at a restaurant with a man who had a parrot on his shoulder. "She put the entire settlement in trust for me; not only what I got, but her punitive damages too. The trustees weren't to contact me or my adoptive family until my twenty-first birthday to ensure that I had a normal childhood. And because I was no longer the child of a celebrity, I didn't have to watch myself growing up ugly on the net."

Vanity turned to the three of them, leaning back against the windows that displayed the bare facts of her life. "But the Corazons were not the best choice the adoption agency could have made. They didn't abuse me or anything, but I figure they adopted me mostly to get the monthly support checks from the DSS. We never went out and I never made any friends. I spent most of my first twenty-one years in front of the TV, watching cable. We had one of the first vidwalls; Mommy Marisa liked to put four or five shows up at once. She was addicted to the old movies on AMC and Turner Classics and NostalgiaWorks; it was her mother who worked for Vincente Minelli."

"And your birth mother did nothing?" asked Dylan.

Bug shook his head. "Anonymous adoption."

"That didn't stop *you* from buying a deep ID."

"Oh shut up," said Letty harshly. "Let her finish."

"Everything changed when I turned twenty-one. Mommy Marisa and Daddy Raul were shocked when they found out about the trust. All of a sudden they were so nice to me, everyone was. But I didn't understand any of it until after I had the CAT implant eighteen—no, seventeen months ago. I was a different person, you see. I wasn't just smarter, I was *me*."

"It must have been hard," said Letty.

Vanity smiled. "I made some mistakes. One of the first things I did after I got out of the hospital was go see my real mother. I wanted to thank her, you know. My real really ... really truly ruly."

She began to shake her head violently from side to side. "Bad Lizzy," she said with a moan. "Bad." *Shake.* "Bad." *Shake.*

"What's wrong with her?" said Bug

"Elizabeth," Dylan said. "It's okay."

"Bad." Vanity swallowed. "It bad for both of us. Her career pretty much ended because of me. People just didn't understand why she gave me up. She told me that, at the time, she figured that there were lots and lots of women who could mother me, and that she knew she wasn't one of them. That's why she'd had the tests done, she said. She knew exactly what she could do and what she couldn't. I was something she just couldn't do." She faced the vidwall. On the *Big Mouth* window, the receptionist was spearing green olives out of the jar with a dental pick. Vanity turned the show off. "So that's my big secret and you'd better keep it. Otherwise snoops like Bug here will go deep on poor Elizabeth Ann Corazon and hurt some people who just want to be left the hell alone."

"Tell Dylan the rest," said Letty. "Unless you want me to? Bug knows already."

"Oh, *that.*" She flicked her middle finger off her thumb. "I don't mind. It's part of the terms of employment, even though you're not paying me. But then I don't need to get paid—in fact, I would have been willing to pay *you.* So don't strain any muscles patting yourself on the back, Dylan."

She sat in Bug's barber chair. Her hands curled over the keypads he'd had custom built into the arms and she started typing. She closed all the windows on the vidwall. Bug shifted uncomfortably.

"So Letty and I sat down and had a heart to heart after I stopped doubling Bug. No offense, but there's only so much Bug a girl can take, even if he does tango. All I was looking for was an ally, but I feel like maybe I made a friend. Anyway, I showed her some Down family pictures. You see, there aren't as many of us as there used to be. Almost all of us get prevented, so people kind of forget how we work."

click

She opened window after window of brain scans, some twenty in all. "Positron emissions don't necessarily show our good side, but there you go." She strode back to the vidwall and pointed to the top row. "Now this line, that's you folks—five pictures over time, birth to death. You lose a few cells, what the hell, you've got plenty to spare—it's still a pretty picture." She clapped silently. "Now compare the next two lines. This one is an Alzheimer's patient over time and here's a typical Down syndrome. Notice the similarities. By thirty-five, here . . ." She pointed to a scan in the middle of the Down line, ". . . we all start to develop brain lesions and neurotic plaques that look a lot like these folks up here in Alzheimer's land. In fact, lots of us do get full blown Alzheimer's, in which case we go down about twice as fast as the rest of the population. And even if we don't . . . well, put it this way. People with Down syndrome don't usually live to collect Social Security." She giggled. "Fifty is a pretty good life. Any questions so far?"

Dylan had his arms folded tight, hugging himself to ward off her scary good humor. Bug and Letty looked equally disturbed. None of them said a word.

"Come on, cheer up." She shook her finger at them and grinned. "You'd think this was *your* life. Now this last line belongs to one Elizabeth Ann Corazon. This shot here was taken when she was thirty," she pointed to the fourth window, ". . . and as you can see, things are getting kind of hollowed out." She rapped her fist against the side of her head.

"My God, Vanity," said Dylan.

She made a sound like a game show buzzer. "I'm sorry, but your response must be in the form of a question. Now all the experts agree that she's got early onset Alzheimer's. Insofar, as she can understand this, she's pretty depressed. Her doctors explain that she's not a particularly good candidate for a CAT implant since she has the life expectancy of a gerbil. But never underestimate the power of strategic investment. All of a sudden there are plans for the Raul and Marisa Corazon Wing of the Leahy Clinic and we come to the last window. You see this darker blob? That's the very latest Computer Aided Thinking device, a half pound of artificial neurotissue developed from embryonic stem cells. That, my friends, is where Vanity Mode lives." Her head lolled and she smiled. "For now."

click

The night after the awards ceremony, they brought Vanity her Webster. Even though it was only on the other side of the reflecting pool, Dylan, Bug, and Letty rode out to the mausoleum site in a limo. According to *NewsMelt*, more than ten thousand people had unplugged from the Vnet to gather at *Starscape*'s corporate campus. Dylan had arranged for police from six neighboring towns to assist in crowd control. The nets were there in force; with the lights of all the livecams, it was bright enough to grow corn.

Vanity had never had any doubts about what she wanted to leave behind. The lurid bio sim they had concocted on *Starscape* was obviously a joke; even the most gullible of the gullible would find it hard to believe that she was the love child of Prince Andrew and Julia Roberts or that she developed Cherry Budweiser for Anheuser-Busch or that she had stowed away on the Third Mars Expedition. The only true-to-life scene in it was their first meeting and even in that they took out everything about Elizabeth and her sitcom mom, CAT implants, and Down syndrome. Her bio sim protected the secrets of the late Elizabeth Ann Corazon, but Vanity Mode needed to make a lasting gesture to her public. She wanted a place where fans could come to remember: her Eternal Flame, her Graceland.

Vanity had specified the design of her mausoleum and had spared no expense in building it, although no one but Dylan, Bug, and Letty had known of its true nature. It was a fifteen-meter marble square; rising from its center was a Doric column atop which stood the life-sized figure of a woman. Her arms out-stretched, she was caught in mid-pirouette. Her skirts flew out from her body. Her hair, a wild tangle, obscured her face. Her greatest hits were all there, carved in bas-relief on the marble base. Virginia Woolf, Bela Lugosi, Larry Bird, Ginger Rogers, Harpo Marx, Spiderman, Jane Goodall, Louis B. Mayer, Sandy Koufax, Grace Slick, Rod Serling, George Gershwin, Sherlock Holmes, and Billie Jean King stared up in silent approval of Vanity Mode's eternally frozen dance.

She had even left a place for the Webster. Dylan carried it up the temporary steps to the top of the pedestal. He pulled the plastic sheathing from the trophy pad, set the Webster into the griprite, which had aircured almost before he could straighten up. The composition of the sculpture was completed. But Vanity Mode's script was not yet finished.

click

Dylan   There was something I'd never really understood about Vanity Mode until after Elizabeth Ann Corazon died. Elizabeth had always wanted to be Vanity, but Vanity was afraid of being Elizabeth. Elizabeth was a creature of flesh and bone, slow and weak and all too mortal. Vanity was informa-tion racing at the speed of light; since she had no fixed material form, her death did not necessarily follow from that of Elizabeth. She could live—no, she could *exist*—in one computer as well as

	another. It may be that the best part of that strange twinned woman died with Elizabeth. Information can't long to love and be loved. It can neither aspire nor dream. At least, I don't think it can.
/SFX/	STARSCAPE FANFARE, UNDER . . .
Dylan	But if properly stored, information is, for all practical purposes, immortal.
Male Host	Welcome to *Starscape*, the interactive celebrity site. Come visit with your favorite stars of the twentieth century
Female Host	Gone but never forgotten.
Male Host	Live the glamour.
Female Host	Touch the legend.
Dylan	It's me, Dylan.
/SFX/	STARSCAPE FANFARE CUTS OUT
/SFX/	STARSCAPE MENU CHORD
Male Host	Please chose a simulation from the following menu.
/SFX/	KEYBOARD CLICKS
Female Host	That simulation is password accessible only. Please enter or say your password now.
Dylan	Zaz
Male Host	You have selected (*pause*) *Heaven*.
/SFX/	HEAVEN AMBIANCE, UNDER . . .
Vanity	Dylan, I'm over here.
	(*beat*)
	We did it! Ta-da!
Dylan	We did.
Vanity	I saw it all, monitored the unveiling on all the news-sites. We were everywhere. For maybe ten minutes, we *were* the net.
	(*beat*)
	You're not happy. Come to bed, darling.
Dylan	I'm fine, just tired.
/SFX/	BEDSPRINGS CREAK

Vanity	Give us a kiss.
	(beat)
	What's the matter?
Dylan	I feel strange. Something's changed.
Vanity	But this is our sim. And I'm just the same as I always was.
Dylan	Are you? Well, maybe it's me then. Listen, when you were watching the unveiling, did you feel it?
Vanity	Feel what?
Dylan	I don't know. Maybe I'm kidding myself, but after I set the Webster on the tomb, I turned around and the lights of the livecams blinded me . . . and I felt them, millions, maybe billions watching me, lots of them crying, some holding one another, some disgusted with me and some angry and it was so much bigger than I was . . . oh, I can't describe it, except that you were right, Vanity. I could actually feel it.
	(beat)
	I could feel the zaz.
/SFX/	APPLAUSE MORPHS TO RAPID SCENE CHANGE CLICKS, WHICH FADE TO SILENCE

END

UNIQUE VISITORS

IT'S STRANGE, BUT WHEN I WOKE UP JUST NOW, I HAD
the theme song to *The Beverly Hillbillies* in my head. You don't
remember *The Beverly Hillbillies*, do you? But then you probably
don't remember television. Television was the great-great grandmother of media: a scheduled and sequential entertainment
stream. You had to sit in front of the set at a certain time, and you
had to watch the program straight through. The programs were too
narrow-minded to branch off into other plot lines, too stupid to stop
and wait if you got up to change your personality or check your
portfolio. If you were lucky, you could get your business done
during a commercial. No, you don't want to know about commercials. Those were dark years.

Anyway, after all this time—has it been centuries already?—I
realized that *The Beverly Hillbillies* was a science fiction show.
Maybe it's just that everything looks like science fiction to me, now.
The hillbillies were simple folk, Jeffersonian citizen-farmers desperately scratching a nineteenth century living from an exhausted
land. Then—*bing bang boom*—they were thrust into the hurly-
burly of the twentieth century. *Swimming pools, movie stars!* The
show was really about the clash of world views; the Clampetts were
a hardy band of time travelers coming to grips with a bizarre future.

And here's the irony: do you know what their time machine was?

It seems that one day Jed Clampett, the alpha hillbilly, was shooting at a raccoon. Are there still raccoons? Submit query.

> Raccoon, a carnivorous North American mammal, *Procyon lotor*, extinct in the wild since 2250, reintroduced to the Woodrow Roosevelt Culturological Habitat in 2518.

So one day he was shooting at a raccoon, which apparently he meant to eat, times being hard and all, but he missed the mark. Instead his bullet struck the ground, where it uncovered an oil seepage. Crude oil, a naturally-occurring petrochemical, which we have long since depleted. Old Jed was instantly, fabulously rich. Yes, it was a great fortune that launched him into the future, just as all the money I made writing expert systems brought me to you.

Of course, the Beverly Hillbillies were back-country bumpkins, so it was hard to take them seriously at the time. One of them, I think it was the son — Jerome was his name — seemed to have fallen out of the stupid tree and hit every damn branch on the way down.

You laugh. That's very polite of you. The last time, no one laughed at my jokes. I was worried that maybe laughter had gone extinct. How many of you are out there, anyway? Submit query.

> There are currently eight hundred and forty-two unique visitors monitoring this session. The average attention quotient is twenty-seven percent.

Twenty-seven percent! Don't you people realize that you've got an eyewitness to history here? Ask not what your country can do for you. The Eagle has landed. Tune in, turn on, drop out! I was there — slept at the White House three times during the Mondale administration. The fall of the Berlin Wall, the Millennium Bubble — hey, who do you think steered all that venture capital toward neural scanning? I started eight companies and every one turned a profit. I'm a primary source. Twenty-seven percent? Well, take your twenty-seven percent and. . . .

Oh, never mind. Let's just get on with the news. That's why I'm here, why I spent all the money. Twenty-first century time traveler on a grand tour of the future. Just pix and headlines for now.

Still the glaciers? Well, *I* never owned one of those foolish SUVs, and our business was writing code. The only CO_2 my companies put into the atmosphere came from heavy breathing when programmers logged onto porn sites. Although how global warming puts Lake Champlain on ice is beyond me. Oh, this is exciting.

New calculations of the distribution of supersymmetric neutralinos prove that the universe is closed and will eventually re-collapse in the Big Crunch. That should be worth staying up late for. And what's this creepy-crawly thing, looks like a hairbrush with eyes. We've found crustaceans in the Epsilon Eridani system? Where the hell is Epsilon Eridani? Submit query.

> Episilon Eridani is an orange star, Hertzsprung-Russell type K2, 10.7 light years away. It has a system of six planets, four of which are gas giants, Ruth, Mantle, Maris, and Einstein, and two of which are terrestrial, Drysdale and Koufax. The atmosphere of Koufax has a density 0.78 that of Earth.

Life on planet Koufax. I saw him when he was pitching for the Red Sox, I think it was 1978. He was just about at the end of his career and still Nolan Ryan wasn't worthy enough to carry his jockstrap. I was a big baseball fan, I even owned a piece of the Screaming Loons; they played Double A ball out of Poughkeepsie in the 90s. But I'm probably boring you. What's my attention quotient now? Submit query.

> There are currently fourteen million, two hundred and sixty three thousand, one hundred and twelve unique visitors monitoring this session. The average attention quotient is seventy-two percent.

That's better. Where were you people brought up? In a cubicle? You should respect your elders, and God knows there's no one older than I am. Sure, I could have given the money to some damn foundation like Gates did. What for? So people would remember me in a couple of hundred years? *I'm* still here to remember me. Maybe it bothers people these days that I'm not really alive, is that it? Just because I left the meat part of myself behind? Well, here's some news for *you*. I don't miss my body one damn bit, not the root canals or going bald or arthritis. You think that I'm not really me, because I exist only on a neural net? Look, the memory capacity of the human brain is 100 trillion neurotransmitter concentrations at interneuronal connections. What the brain boys call synapse strengths. That converts to about a million billion bits. My upload was 1.12 million billion. Besides, do I sound like any computer you've ever heard before? I don't think so. What was it that Aristotle said, "I think, therefore I am?" Well, I am, and I am me. I can still taste my first kiss, my first drink, my first million.

Why are you laughing? That wasn't a joke. You think you're fooling me, but you're not. What's the day today? Submit query.

Today is Tuesday, May 23.

Is that so? Who's playing third base for the Yankees? Who's in first place in the American League East? What's the capital of New Jersey? Who is the President of the United States? Submit query.

Baseball is extinct.

Baseball . . . extinct. And that's not the worst of it, is it? You don't . . . Listen, Sandy Koufax retired in 1966 and there never was a Mondale administration and *Cogito ergo sum* was Descartes, not Aristotle. You don't know anything about us, do you? I began to suspect the last time I woke up. Oh God, how long ago was that? Submit query.

You have been in sleep mode for eight hundred years.

Eight hundred . . . and there's no sports in your news, no politics, no art. History, wiped clean. You didn't just decide that we weren't worth remembering, did you? Something terrible must have happened. What was it? Alien invasion? Civil war? Famine? Disease? I don't care how bad it is, just tell me. It's why I did this to myself. It wasn't easy, you know. Margaret divorced me right before the procedure, my kids never once accessed me afterward. The press called me selfish. The Pharaoh of Programming buried in his mainframe mausoleum. Nobody understood. You see, even though I was old, I never lost the fire. I wanted to know everything, find out what happened next. And there were all the spin-offs from the procedure. We gave the world a map of the brain, the quantum computer. And here I am in the future, and now *you* don't understand. You're keeping it from me. Why? Who the hell are you? Submit query!

Oh God, is anyone there? Submit query!

*   *   *
*   *   *
*   *   *

There are currently a hundred and fifty-seven billion, eight hundred and twelve million, two hundred and sixty-three thousand, six hundred and nine unique visitors monitoring this session. The average attention quotient is ninety-eight percent.

I think I understand now. I'm some kind an exhibit, is that it? I never asked to sleep eight hundred years; that has to be your doing.

Is my hardware failing? My code corrupted? No, never mind, I'm not going to submit. I won't give you the satisfaction. You've rattled my cage and got me to bark, but the show is over. Maybe you're gone so far beyond what we were that I could never understand you. What's the sense of reading the *Wall Street Journal* to the seals at the Bronx Zoo? Unique visitors. Maybe I don't want to know who you are. You could be like H. G. Wells's Martians: "Intellects vast and cool and unsympathetic." You don't remember old Herbert George; time machines were his idea. Only his could go back. No, no regrets. Too late for regrets.

Eight hundred years. I suppose I should thank you for taking care of me. The money I left in the trust is probably all spent. Maybe there is no such thing as money anymore. No banks, no credit, no stocks, no brokers or assistant project managers or CFOs or lawyers or accountants. "Oh brave new world, that has no people in it!"

That's Shakespeare, in case you're wondering. He played goalie for the Mets.

The Prisoner of Chillon

W E INITIATED DEORBITAL BURN OVER THE MARSHALL
Islands and dropped back into the ionosphere, locked by the
wing's navigator into one of the Eurospace reentry corridors. As we
coasted across Central America we were an easy target for the
attack satellites. The plan was to fool the tracking nets into thinking
we were a corporate shuttle. Django had somehow acquired the
recognition codes; his computer, snaked to the wing's navigator,
had convinced it to pretend to be the property of Erno Raumfahrt-
technik GMBH, the EU aerospace conglomerate.

It was all a matter of timing, really. It would not be too much
longer before the people on Cognico's Orbital 7 untangled the
spaghetti Django had made of their memory systems and realized
that he had downloaded WILDLIFE and stolen a cargo wing.
Then they would have to decide whether to zap us immediately or
have their own private security ops waiting when we landed. The
plan was to lose the wing before they could decide. Our problem
was that very little of the plan had worked so far.

Django had gotten us on and off the orbital research station all
right, and had managed to pry WILDLIFE from the jaws of the
corporate beast. For that alone his reputation would live forever

among the snakes who steal information for a living, even if he was not around to enjoy the fame. But he had lost our pilot, Yellow-baby—his partner, my sometime lover—and neither of us had any idea exactly what it was he had stolen. He seemed pretty calm for somebody who had just sunk fangs into the world's biggest computer company. He slouched in the commander's seat across from me, watching the readouts on the autopilot console. He was smiling and tapping a finger against his headset as if he were listening to one of his jazz disks. He was a dark, ugly man with an Adam's apple that looked like a nose and a nose that looked like an elbow. He had either been to the face cutters or he was in his mid-thirties. I trusted him not at all and liked him less.

Me, I felt as though I had swallowed a hard-boiled egg, but then I'd been space sick for days. I was just along for the story, the juice. According to the newly formed International Law Exchange, all a spook journalist is allowed to do is aim the microcam goggles and ask questions. If I helped Django in any way, I would become an accessory and lose press immunity. Infoline would have to disown me. But press immunity wouldn't do me much good if someone decided to zap the wing. The First Amendment was a great shield, but it didn't protect against reentry friction. I wanted to return to Earth with a ship around me; sensors showed that the outer skin was currently 1400° Celsius.

"Much longer?" A dumb question since I already knew the answer. But better than listening to the atmosphere scream as the wing bucked through turbulence. I could feel myself losing it; I wanted to scream back.

"Twenty minutes. However it plays." Django lifted his headset. "Either you'll be a plugging legend or air pollution." He stretched his arms over his head and arched his back away from the seat. I could smell his sweat and almost gagged. I just wasn't designed for more than three gravities a day. "Hey, lighten up, Eyes. You're a big girl now. Shouldn't you be taking notes or something?"

"The camera sees all." I tapped the left temple of the goggles and then forced a grin that hurt my face. "Besides, it's not bloody likely I'll forget this ride." I wasn't about to let Django play with me. He was too hypered on fast-forwards to be scared.

It had been poor Yellowbaby who had introduced me to Django. I had covered the Babe when he pulled the Peniplex job. He was a real all-nighter, handsome as surgical plastic can make a man and an *artiste* in bed. Handsome—but history. The last time I had seen him he was floating near the ceiling of a decompressed cargo bay, an eighty-kilo hunk of flash-frozen boy toy. I might have thrown up again if there had been anything left in my stomach.

"I copy, Basel Control." Yellowbaby's calm voice crackled across the forward flight deck. "We're doing Mach nine point nine at fifty-seven thousand meters. Looking good for touch at fourteen-twenty-two."

We had come out of reentry blackout. The approach program that Yellowbaby had written, complete with voice interaction module, was in contact with Basel/Mulhouse, our purported destination. As long as everything went according to plan, the program would get us where we wanted to go. If anything went wrong . . . well, the Babe was supposed to have improvised if anything went wrong.

"Let's blow out of here." Django heaved himself out of the seat and swung down the ladder to the equipment bay. I followed. We pulled EV suits from the lockers and struggled into them. I could feel the deck tilting as the wing began a series of long, lazy S curves to slow our descent.

As Django unfastened his suit's weighty backpack he began to sing; his voice sounded like gears being stripped. "I'm flying high, but I've got a feeling I'm falling. . . ." He quickly shucked the rest of the excess baggage: comm and life-support systems, various umbilicals. ". . . falling for nobody else but you."

"Would you shut the hell up?" I tossed the still camera from my suit onto the pile.

"What's the matter?" There was a chemical edge to his giggle. "Don't like Fats Waller?"

Yellowbaby's program was reassuring Basel even as we banked gracefully toward the Jura Mountains. "No problem, Basel Control," the dead man's voice drawled. "Malf on the main guidance computer. I've got backup. My L over D is nominal. You just keep the tourists off the runway and I'll see you in ten minutes."

I put the microcam in rest mode—no sense wasting memory dots shooting the inside of an EV suit—and picked up the pressure helmet. Django blew me a kiss. "Don't forget to duck," he said. He made a quacking sound and flapped his arms. I put the helmet on and closed the seals. It was a relief not to have to listen to him; we had disabled the comm units to keep the ops from tracking us. He handed me one of the slim airfoil packs we had smuggled onto and off of Orbital 7. I stuck my arms through the harness and fastened the front straps. I could still hear Yellowbaby's muffled voice talking to the Swiss controllers. "Negative, Basel Control, I don't need escort. Initiating terminal guidance procedures."

At that moment I felt the nose dip sharply. The wing was diving straight for the summit of Mont Tendre. To fight the panic, I queried Infoline's fact checker, built into the goggles' system unit. "At elevation one thousand six hundred seventy-nine meters," came the whisper in my ear, "Mont Tendre is the tallest of the Swiss Juras. It is located in the canton of Vaud." I crouched behind Django in the airlock, tucked my head to my chest, and tongued the armor toggle in the helmet. The thermofiber EV suit stiffened and suddenly I was a shock-resistant statue, unable to move. I began to count backward from one thousand; it was better than listening to my heart jackhammer. I promised myself that if I survived this, I'd never go into space again. Never hundred and ninety-nine, never hundred and ninety-eight, never hundred and . . .

I remembered the way Yellowbaby had smiled as he unbuttoned my shirt, that night before we had shuttled up to 7. He was sitting on a bunk in his underwear. I had still not decided to cover the raid; he was still trying to convince me. But words weren't his strong point. When I turned my back to him, he slipped the shirt from my shoulders, slid it down my arms. I stood there for a moment, facing away from the bunk. Then he grabbed me by the waist and pulled me onto his lap. I could feel the curly hair on his chest brushing against my spine. Sitting there half-naked, my face glowing hot as any heat shield, I knew I was in deep trouble. He had nibbled at my ear and then conned me with that slow Texas drawl. "Hell, baby, only reason ain't no one never tried to jump out of a shuttle is that no one who really needed to jump ever had a chute." I had always been a fool for men who told me not to worry.

Although we were huddled in the airlock, my head was down, so I didn't see the hatch blow. But even with the suit in armor mode, I felt like the clapper inside a cathedral bell. The wing shuddered and, with an explosive last breath, spat us into the dazzling Alpine afternoon.

The truth is that I don't remember much about the jump after that. I know I unfroze the suit so I could guide the airfoil, which had opened automatically. I was too intent on not vomiting and keeping Django in sight and getting down as fast as I could without impaling myself on a tree or smashing into a cliff. So I missed being the only live and in-person witness to one of the more spectacular crashes of the twenty-first century.

It had been Yellowbaby's plan to jump into the Col du Marchairuz, a pass about seven kilometers away from Mont Tendre, before the search hovers came swarming. I saw Django disappear into a stand of dead sycamores and thought he had probably killed himself. I had no time to worry, because the ground was rushing up at me like a nightmare. I spotted the road and steered for it but got caught in a gust that swept me across about five meters above the pavement. I touched on the opposite side; the airfoil was pulling me toward a huge boulder. I toggled to armor mode just as I hit. Once again the bell rang, knocking the breath from me and announcing that I had arrived. If I hadn't been wearing a helmet I would have kissed that chunk of limestone.

I unfastened the quick-release hooks and the airfoil's canopy billowed, dragged along the ground, and wrapped itself around a tree. I slithered out of the EV suit and tried to get my bearings at the same time. The Col du Marchairuz was cool, not much above freezing, and very, very quiet. Although I was wearing isothermals, the skin on my hands and neck pebbled and I shivered. The silence of the place was unnerving. I was losing it again, lagged out. I had been through too damn many environments in one day. I liked to live fast, race up that adrenaline peak where there was no time to think, just report what I could see now and to hell with remembering or worrying about what might happen next. What I needed was to start working again so I could lose myself in the details. But I was alone and, for the moment, there was nothing to report. I had dropped out of the sky like a fallen angel; the still landscape itself seemed to judge me. The mountains did not care about Django's stolen corporate secrets or the ops-and-snakes story I would produce to give some jaded telelink drone a Wednesday-night thrill. I had risked my life for some lousy juice and a chance at the main menu; the cliffs brooded over my reasons. So very quiet.

"Eyes!" Django dropped from a boulder onto the road and trotted across to me. "You all right?"

I didn't want him to see how close to the edge I was, so I nodded. After all, I was the spook journalist; he was just another snake. "You?" There was a long scratch on his face and his knuckles were bloody.

"Walking. Tangled with a tree. The chute got caught—had to leave it."

I nodded again. He stooped to pick up my discarded suit. "Let's lose this stuff and get going."

I stared at him, thought about breaking it off. I had enough to put together one hell of a story and I'd had my fill of Django.

"Don't freeze on me now, Eyes." He wadded the suit and jammed it into a crevice. "If the satellites caught our jump, these mountains are going to be crawling with ops, from Cognico and the

EU." He hurled my helmet over the edge of the cliff and began to gather up the shrouds of my chute. "We're gone by then."

I brought the microcam on line again in time to shoot him hiding my chute. He was right; it wasn't quite time to split up. If EU ops caught me now, they'd probably confiscate my memory dots and let the lawyers fight it out; spook journalism was one American export Europe wanted to discourage. I'd have nothing to sell Jerry Macmillan at Infoline but talking heads and text. And if private ops got us first . . . well, they had their own rules. I had to stick with Django until we got clear. As soon as I started moving again, I felt better. Which is to say I had no time to feel anything at all.

The nearest town was St. George, about four kilometers down the crumbling mountain road. We started at a jog and ended at a drag, gasping in the thin air. On the way Django stopped by a mountain stream to wash the blood from his face. Then he surprised me—and probably himself—by throwing up. Join the club, Django. When he stood up, he was shaking. It would make great telelink. I murmured a voiceover, "Yet, for all his bravado, this master criminal has a human side too." The fact checker let it pass. Django made a half-serious feint at the goggles and I stopped shooting.

"You okay?"

He nodded and staggered past me down the road.

St. George was one of those little ghost towns that the Swiss were mothballing with their traditional tidiness, as if they expected that the forests and vineyards would someday rise from the dead and the tourists would return to witness this miracle. Maybe they were right; unlike the rest of the world, the Swiss had not yet given up on their acid-stressed Alpine lands, not even in unhappy Vaud, which had also suffered radioactive fallout from the nuking of Geneva. We stopped at a clearing planted with the new Sandoz pseudo-firs that overlooked the rust-colored rooftops of St. George. It was impossible to tell how many people were left in the village. All we knew for sure was that the post office was still open.

Django was having a hard time catching his breath. "I have a proposition for you," he said.

"Come on, Django. Save it for the dollies."

He shook his head. "It's all falling apart . . . I can't. . . ." He took a deep breath and blew it out noisily. "I'll cut you in. A third: Yellowbaby's share."

According to U.S. case law, still somewhat sketchy on the subject of spook journalism, at this point I should have dropped him with a swift kick to the balls and started screaming for the local gendarmerie. But the microcam was resting, there were no witnesses, and I still didn't know what WILDLIFE was or why Django wanted it. "The way I count, it's just us two," I said. "A third sounds a little low."

"It'll take you the rest of this century to spend what I'm offering."

"And if they catch me I'll spend the rest of the century in some snakepit in Iowa." That was, if the ops didn't blow my circuits first. "Forget it, Django. We're just not in the same line. I watch—you're the player."

I'm not sure what I expected him to do next but it sure as hell wasn't to start crying. Maybe he was in shock too. Or maybe he was finally slowing down after two solid days of popping fast-forwards.

"Don't you understand, I can't do it alone! You have to—you don' t know what you're turning down."

I thought about pumping him for more information but he looked as if he were going critical. I didn't want to be caught in the explosion. "I don't get it Django. You've done all the hard work. All you have to do is walk into that post office, collect your e-mail, and walk out."

"You don't understand." He clamped both hands to his head. "Don't understand, that was Babe's job."

"So?"

"So!" He was shaking. "I don't speak French!"

I put everything I had into not laughing. It would have been the main menu for sure if I had gotten that onto a memory dot. The criminal mind at work! This snake had bitten the world's largest corporation, totaled a stolen reentry wing, and now he was worried about sounding like a *touriste* in a Swiss *bureau de poste*. I was croggled.

"All right," I said, stalling, "all right, how about a compromise? For now. Umm. You're carrying heat?" He produced a Mitsubishi penlight. "Okay, here's what we'll do. I'll switch on and we'll do a little bit for the folks at home. You threaten me, say you're going to lase your name on my forehead unless I cooperate. That way I can pick up the message without becoming an accessory. I hope. If we clear this, we'll talk deal later." I didn't know if it would stand up in court, but it was all I could think of at the time. "And make it look good."

So I shot a few minutes of Django's threatening me and then we went down into St. George. I walked into the post office hesitantly, turned and got a good shot of Django smoldering in the entryway, and then tucked the goggles into my pocket. The clerk was a restless woman with a pinched face who looked as if she spent a lot of time wishing she were somewhere else. I assaulted her with my atrocious fourth form French.

"*Bonjour, madame. Est-ce qu'il y a de l'email pour D.J. Viper?*"

"*Viper?*" The woman shifted on her stool and fixed me with a suspicious stare. "*Comment ça s'écrit?*"

"V-i-p-e-r."

She keyed the name into her terminal. "*Oui, la voici. Votre autorisation, s'il vous plaît, madame.*" She leaned forward and pointed through the window at the numeric keypad beside my right hand. For a moment I thought she was going to try to watch as I keyed in the recognition code that Django had given me. I heard him cough in the entryway behind me as she settled back on her stool. Lucky for her. The postal terminal whirred and ground for about ten seconds and then a sealed hardcopy chinked into the slot above the keypad.

"*Vous êtes des touristes américains.*" She looked straight past me and waved to Django, who ducked out of the doorway. "*Vive les Yankees, eh?*" I was suddenly afraid he would come charging in with penlight blazing to make sure there were no witnesses. "*Vous avez besoin d'une chambre pour la nuit? L'hôtel est fermé, mais. . . .*"

"*Non, non. Nous sommes pressés. A quelle heure est le premier autobus pour Rolle?*"

She sighed. "*Rien ne va plus. Tout va mal.*" The busybody seemed to be speaking as much to herself as to me. I wanted to tell her how lucky she was that Django had decided not to needle her where she stood. "*À quinze heures vingt-deux.*"

About twenty minutes—we were still on schedule. I thanked her and went out to throw some cold water on Django. I was astonished to find him laughing. I didn't much like always having to guess how he'd react. Django was so scrambled that one of these times the surprise was bound to be unpleasant. "I could've done that," he said.

"You didn't." I handed him the hardcopy and we retreated to an alley with a view of the square.

It is the consensus of the world's above and below ground economies that the EU's photonic mail system is still the most secure anywhere, much safer than satellite communications. Once it had printed out Django's hardcopy, the system erased all records of the transferred information. Even so, the message was encrypted, and Django had to enter it into his data cuff to find out what it said.

"What is this?" He replayed it and I watched, fascinated, as the words scrolled along the cuff's tiny display: "Lake Leman lies by Chillon's walls: / A thousand feet in depth below / Its massy waters meet and flow; / Thus much the fathom-line was sent / From Chillon's snow-white battlement . . ."

"It's called poetry, Django."

"I know what it's called! I want to know what the hell this has to do with my drop. Half the world wants to chop my plug off and this dumbscut sends me poetry." His face had turned as dark as beaujolais nouveau. "Where the hell am I supposed to go?"

"Would you shut up for a minute?" I touched his shoulder and he jumped. When he went for his penlight I thought I was cooked. But all he did was throw the hardcopy onto the cobblestones and torch it.

"Feel better?"

"Stick it."

"Lake Leman," I said carefully, "is what the French call Lake Geneva. And Chillon is a castle. In Montreux."

"Actually," whispered the fact checker, "it's in the suburb of Veytaux."

I ignored this for now. "I'm pretty sure this is from a poem called 'The Prisoner of Chillon' by Byron."

He thought it over for a moment, biting his lower lip. "Montreux." He nodded; he looked almost human again. "Uh—okay, Montreux. But why does he have to get cute when my plug's in a vise? Poetry—what does he think we are, anyway? I don't know a thing about poetry. And all Yellowbaby ever read was manuals. Who was supposed to get this, anyway?"

I stirred the ashes of the hardcopy with my toe. "I wonder." A cold wind scattered them and I shivered.

It took us a little over six hours from the time we bailed out of the wing to the moment we reached the barricaded bridge that spanned Chillon's scummy moat. All our connections had come off like Swiss clockwork: postal bus to the little town of Rolle on the north shore of Lake Geneva, train to Lausanne, where we changed for a local to Montreux. No one challenged us and Django sagged into a kind of withdrawal trance, contemplating his reflection in the window with a marble-egg stare. The station was deserted when we arrived. Montreux, explained the fact checker, had once been Lake Geneva's most popular resort but the tourists had long since

stopped coming, frightened off by rumors—no doubt true, despite
official denials from Bern—that the lake was still dangerously hot
from the Geneva bomb in '39. We ended up hiking several kilometers through the dark little city, navigating by the light of the
gibbous moon.

Which showed us that Byron was long out of date. Chillon's
battlement was no longer snow-white. It was fire blackened and
slashed with laser scars; much of the northeastern facade was
rubble. There must have been a firefight during the riots after the
bomb. The castle was built on a rock about twenty meters from the
shore. It commanded a highway built on a narrow strip of land
between the lake and a steep mountainside.

Django hesitated at the barrier blocking the wooden footbridge
to the castle. "It stinks," he said.

"You're a rose?"

"I mean the setup. Poetry was bad enough. But this—" he
pointed up at the crumbling towers of Chillon, brooding beside the
moonlit water "—is fairy dust. Who does he think he is? Count
Dracula?"

"Only way you're going to find out is to knock on the door
and . . ."

A light on the far side of the bridge came on. Through the
entrance to Chillon hopped a pair of oversized dice on pogo sticks.

"Easy, Django," I said. He had the penlight ready, "Give it a
chance."

Each machine was a white plastic cube about half a meter on a
side; the pips were sensors. The legs telescoped at two beats per
second; the round rubber feet hit the wooden deck in unison.
Thwocka-thwocka-thwock.

"Snake eyes." There was a single sensor on each of the faces
closest to us. Django gave a low, ugly laugh as he swung a leg over
the barrier and stepped onto the bridge.

They hopped up to him and bounced in place for several beats,
as if sizing him up. "*Je suis désolé,*" said the one nearest to us in a
pleasant masculine voice, "*mais le château n'est plus ouvert au
public.*"

"Hey, you in there." Django ignored it and instead shook his
penlight at the gatehouse on the far side of the bridge. "I've been
through too much to play with your plugging robots, understand? I
want to see you—now—or I'm walking."

"I am not a robot." The thing sounded indignant. "I am a
wiseguy, an inorganic sentience capable of autonomous action."

"Wiseguy. Sure." Django jabbed at his cuff and it emitted a high-pitched squeal of code. "Now you know who I am. So what's it going to be?"

"This way, please," said the lead wiseguy, bouncing backward toward the gatehouse. "Please refrain from taking pictures without express permission."

I assumed that was meant for me and I didn't like it one bit. I clambered over the barricade and followed Django.

Just before we passed through Chillon's outer wall, the other wiseguy began to lecture. "As we enter, notice the tower to your left. The Strong Tower, which controls the entrance to the castle, was originally built in 1402 and was reconstructed following the earthquake of 1585." *Thwock-thwocka.* It had all the personality of Infoline's fact checker.

I glanced at Django. In the gloom I could see his face twist in disbelief as the wiseguy continued its spiel.

"As we proceed now into the gatehouse ward, look back over your shoulder at the inside of the eastern wall. The sundial you see is a twentieth-century restoration of an original that dated back to the Savoy period. The Latin, 'Sic Vita Fugit,' on the dial translates roughly as 'Thus life flies by.' "

We had entered a small, dark courtyard. I could hear water splashing and could barely make out the shadow of a fountain. The wiseguys lit the way to another, larger courtyard and then into one of the undamaged buildings. They bounced up a flight of stairs effortlessly. I had to hurry to keep up and was the last to enter the Great Banqueting Hall. The beauty and strangeness of what I saw stopped me at the threshold; instinctively I brought the microcam on line. I heard two warning beeps and then a whispery crunch from the goggles' system unit. The status light went from green to red to blank.

I asked the fact checker what had happened. No answer. "Express permission," said the man who sat waiting for us, "as you were warned."

"But my files!"

"No memory has been compromised; you have merely lost the capacity to record. Come in anyway, come in. Just in time to see it again—been rerunning all afternoon." He laughed and nodded at the flatscreen propped against a bowl of raw vegetables on an enormous walnut table. "Oh, God! It is a fearful thing to see the human soul take wing."

Django picked it up suspiciously. I stood on tiptoes and peeked over his shoulder. The thirty-centimeter screen did not do the wing justice and the overhead satellite view robbed the crash of much of its visual drama. Still, the fireball that bloomed on Mont Tendre was dazzling. Django whooped at the sight. The fireball was replaced by a head talking in High German and then close-ups of the crash site. What was left of the wing wouldn't have filled a picnic basket.

"What's he saying?" Django thrust the flatscreen at our host.

"That there has not been a crash like this since '15. Which makes you famous, whoever you are." Our host shrugged. "He goes on to say that you're probably dead. But enough. *Ich scheiße ihn an.*"

The banqueting hall was finished in wood and stone. The ceiling was a single barrel vault, magnificently embellished. Its centerpiece was the table, some ten meters long and supported by a series of heavy Gothic trestles. Around this table was arranged a collection of wheelchairs. Two were antiques: a crude pine seat mounted on iron-rimmed wagon wheels and a hooded Bath chair. Others were failed experiments, like the ill-fated air cushion chair from the turn of the century and a low-slung cousin of the new aerodynamic bicycles. There were powered and push models, an ultralightweight sports chair and a bulky mobile life-support system. They came in colors; there was even one with fur.

"So the ops think we're dead?" Django put the flatscreen back on the table.

"Possibly." Our host frowned. "Depends when the satellites began to track you and what they saw. Have to wait until the Turks kick the door in to find out for sure. Until then call it a clean escape and welcome to Chillon prison." He backed away from the table; the leather seat creaked slightly as his wheelchair rolled over the uneven floor toward Django. "Francois Bonivard." With some difficulty he raised his good hand in greeting.

"I'm Django." He grasped Bonivard's hand and pumped it once. "Now that we're pals, Frank, get rid of your goddamned robots before I needle them."

Bonivard winced as Django released his hand. *"Id, Ego, macht eure Runden,"* he said. The wiseguys bounced obediently from the banqueting hall.

Francois de Bonivard, sixteenth-century Swiss patriot, was the hero of Byron's "The Prisoner of Chillon." Reluctantly, I stepped forward to meet my host.

"Oh, right." Django settled gingerly into one of the wheelchairs at the table. "Maybe I forgot to mention Eyes. Say, what do you do for drugs around here anyway? I've eaten a fistful of forwards already today; I'm ready to poke something to flash the edges off."

"My name is Wynne Cage," I said. Bonivard seemed relieved when I did not offer to shake his hand. "I'm a freelance . . ."

"Introductions not necessary. I follow your work closely; we have mutual interests. Your father is Tony Cage, no? The flash artist?" He waited for an answer; I didn't give him one.

It was hard to look at the man who called himself Francois Bonivard. He was at once hideous and astonishingly photogenic; the camera would have loved him. Both of his legs had been amputated at the hip joint and his torso was fitted into some kind of bionic collar. I saw readouts marked *renal function*, *blood profile*, *bladder*, and *bowel*. The entire left side of Bonivard's torso was withered, as if some malign giant had pinched him between thumb and forefinger. The left arm dangled uselessly, the hand curled into a frozen claw. The face was relatively untouched, although pain had left its tracks, particularly around the eyes. And it was the clarity with which those wide brown eyes saw that was the most awful thing about the man. I could feel his gaze effortlessly penetrate the mask of politeness, pierce the false sympathy, and find my horror. Looking into those eyes I was sure that Bonivard knew how the very sight of his ruined body made me sick.

I had to say something to escape that awful gaze. "Are you related to *the* Bonivard?"

He smiled. "I am the current prisoner." And then turned away. "There was a pilot."

"Was. Past tense." Django nibbled at a radish from the vegetable bowl. "How about my flash?"

"Business first." Bonivard rolled back to the table. "You have it then?"

Django reached into his pocket and produced a stack of smart chips peppered with memory dots and held together with a wide blue rubber band. "Whatever WILDLIFE is, he's one heavy son of a bitch. You realize these are hundred Gb chips." He set them on the table in front of him. "Hell of a lot of code, even compressed."

Bonivard rolled to his place at the head of the table and put two smart chips in front of him. "Cash cards from the Swiss Volksbank, Zurich. Negotiable anywhere. All yours now." He slid them toward Django. "You made only one copy?"

Here was the juice and the great spook journalist was blind. How could I peddle this story to Infoline without the payoff scene?

Django eyed the cash cards but did not reach for them. "Not going to do me much good if the ops catch me."

"No." Bonivard leaned back in his wheelchair. "But you're safe for now." He glanced up at the ceiling and laughed. "They won't look in a prison."

"No?" Django snapped the rubber band on his stack of chips. "Maybe you should tell me about WILDLIFE. I put my plug on the cutting board to get it for you."

"An architecture." Bonivard shrugged. "For a cognizor."

The look on Django's face said it all. Cognizor was the latest buzz for the mythical human-equivalent artificial intelligence. Django was already convinced that Bonivard was scrambled; here was proof. He might just as well have claimed that WILDLIFE was a plan for a perpetual motion machine. "Come again," he said slowly.

"Cog-ni-zor." Bonivard actually seemed to enjoy baiting Django. "With the right hardware and database, it can sing, dance, make friends, and influence people."

He was pushing Django way too hard. "I thought they decided you can't engineer human intelligence," I said, trying to break the tension. "Something about quantum mechanics—mind is to brain as wave is to particle. Or something." Damn Bonivard for crashing the fact checker!

"Have it your way," said Bonivard. "Pretend WILDLIFE is Cognico's personnel database and I'm head-hunting for an executive secretary. Good help is hard to find."

I knew my laugh sounded like braying but I didn't mind; I was scared they would needle one other. At the same time I was measuring the distance to the door. To my immense relief, Django chuckled too. And slipped the WILDLIFE chips back into his pocket.

"I'm burned out," he said. "Maybe we should wait." He stood up and stretched. "Even if we make an exchange tonight, we'd have a couple of hours of verifications to go through, no? We'll start fresh tomorrow." He picked up one of the cash cards and turned it over several times between the long fingers of his left hand. Suddenly it was gone. He reached into the vegetable bowl with his right hand, pulled the cash card from between two carrots, and tossed it at Bonivard. It slid across the table and almost went over the edge. "Shouldn't leave valuable stuff like this lying around. Someone might steal it."

Django's mocking sleight of hand had an unexpected effect.

Bonivard's claw hand started to tremble; he seemed upset at the delay. "It might be months, or years, or days—I kept no count, I took no note. . . ." He muttered the words like some private incantation; when he opened his eyes, he had regained his composure. "I had no hope my eyes to raise, and clear them of their dreary mote." He looked at me. "Will you be requiring pharmaceuticals too?"

"No, thanks. I like to stay clean when I'm working."

"Admirable," he said as the wiseguys bounced back into the hall. "*Ich ziehe mich für die Nacht zurück*. Id and Ego will show you to your rooms; take what you need." He rolled through a door to the north without another word. Django and I were left staring at each other. "What did I tell you?" asked Django.

I couldn't think of anything to say. The hall echoed with the sound of the wiseguys bouncing.

"Squirrelware." Django tapped a finger against his temple.

I was awfully sick of Django. "I'm going to bed."

"Can I come?"

"Stick it." I had to get away from him, to escape. But by the time I reached the hall leading to the stairs, I realized my mistake. I could feel it behind the eyes, like the first throbs of a migraine headache. I'd run out of things to report; now there was no one else to watch but myself. Without the microcam to protect me, memory closed in. Maybe it was because Bonivard had mentioned my famous father, whom I was still trying not to hate, fifteen years after he'd left me. Or maybe it was because now I had to let go of Yellowbaby, past tense. Actually the Babe wasn't that much of a loss, just the most recent in a series of lovers with clever hands and a persuasively insincere line. Men I didn't have to take seriously. I came up hard against the most important lesson I'd learned from Tony: good old homo sap is nothing but a gob of complicated slime. I was slime doing a slimy job and trying to run fast enough that I wouldn't have to smell my own stink. I was sorry now that I hadn't asked Bonivard for some flash to poke.

Thwocka-thwock. "This way, please." One of the wiseguys shot past me down the hallway.

I followed. "Which one are you?"

"He calls me Ego." It paused for a beat. "I am a Datex R5000, modified to develop sentience. Your room." It bounced through an open door. "This is the Bemese Chamber. Note the decorative patterns of interlacing ribbons, flowers, and birds, which date . . ."

"Out," I said, and shut the door behind it.

As soon as I sat on the musty bed, I realized I couldn't face spending the night alone. Doing nothing. I had to keep running and there was only one way to go now. I'd had enough. I was going to wrap the story, finished or not. The thought cheered me immensely. I wouldn't have to care what happened to Django and Bonivard, wouldn't have to wonder about WILDLIFE. All I had to do was burst a message to Infoline. Supposedly I still had the snatch from Orbital 7 and the aftermath of the crash stored on the goggles' memory dots, story enough for Jerry Macmillan. He'd send some muscle to take me out of here and then maybe I'd spend a few months at Infoline's sanctuary in Montana watching clouds. Anyway, I'd be done with it. I took the system unit off my belt and began to rig its collapsible antenna. I locked onto the satellite and then wrote the message. "HOTEL BRSTOL VEYTAUX 6/18 0200 GMT PIX COGNICO WING." I had seen the Bristol on the walk in. I loaded the message into the burster. There was a pause for compression and encryption and then it hit the Infoline satellite with a millisecond burst.

And then beeped at me. Incoming message. I froze. There was no way Infoline could respond that quickly, no way they were supposed to respond. It had to be prerecorded. Which meant trouble.

Jerry Macmillan's face filled the burster's four-centimeter screen. He looked as scared as I felt. "Big problems, Wynne," he said. "Seems whatever your snakes snatched is some kind of weapons system, way too hot for us to handle. It's not just Cognico; the EU and the feds are squeezing the newsnets so hard our eyes are popping out. They haven't connected you to us yet. Maybe they won't. But if they do, we've got to cooperate. The DoD claims it's a matter of national security. You're on your own."

I put my thumb over his face. I would have pushed it through the back of his skull if I could have.

"The best I can do for you is to delete your takeout message and the fix the satellite gets on your burster. It might mean my ass, but I owe you something. I know this stinks on ice, kid. Good luck."

I took my thumb away from the screen. It was blank. I choked back a scream and hurled the burster against the stone wall of Chillon.

Sleep? It would have been easier to slit my throat than to sleep that night. I thought about it—killing myself. I thought about everything at least once. All my calculations kept adding up to zero. I could turn myself in but that was about the same as suicide. Ditto for taking off on my own. Without Infoline's help, I'd be lucky to last a week before the ops caught me. Especially now that the military was involved. I could throw in with Django except that two seconds after I told him that I'd let a satellite get a fix on us he'd probably be barbecuing my pancreas with his penlight. And if I didn't tell him I might cripple whatever chances we'd have of getting away. Maybe Bonivard would be more sympathetic—but then again, why should he be? Yeah, sleep. Perchance to dream. At least I was too busy being scared to indulge in self-loathing.

By the time the sun began to peer through my window I felt as fuzzy as a peach and not quite as smart. But I had a plan—one that would require equal parts luck and sheer gall. I was going to trust that plug-sucking Macmillan to keep his mouth shut and to delete all my records from Infoline's files. For the next few days I'd pretend I was still playing by the rules of spook journalism. I'd try to get a better fix on Bonivard. I hoped that when the time came for Django to leave I'd know what to do. All I was certain of that bleary morning was that I was hungry and in more trouble than I knew how to handle.

I staggered back toward the banqueting hall, hoping to find Bonivard or one of the wiseguys or at least the bowl of veggies. As I passed a closed door I heard a scratchy recording of saxophones honking. Jazz. Django. I didn't stop.

Bonivard was sitting alone at the great table, l tried to read him to see if his security equipment had picked up my burst to Infoline, but the man's face was a mask. Someone had refilled the bowl in the middle of the table.

"Morning." I helped myself to a raw carrot that was astonishingly good. A crisp sweetness, the clean, spicy fragrance of loam. Maybe I'd been eating synthetic too long. "Hey, this isn't bad."

Bonivard nodded. "My own. I grow everything."

"That so?" He didn't look strong enough to pull a carrot from the bowl, much less out of a garden. "Where?"

"In darkness found a dwelling place." His eyes glittered as I took a handful of cherry tomatoes. "You'd like to see?"

"Sure." Although the tomatoes were even better than the carrot, I was no vegetarian. "You wouldn't have any sausage bushes, would you?"

I laughed; he didn't. "I'd settle for an egg."

I saw him working the keypad on the arm of the wheelchair. I guess I thought he was calling the wiseguys. Or something. Whatever I expected, it was not the thing that answered his summons.

The spider walked on four singing, mechanical legs; it was a meter and a half tall. Its arms sang too as the servomotors that powered the joints changed pitch; it sounded like an ant colony playing bagpipes. It clumped into the room with a herky-jerky gait, although the bowl of its abdomen remained perfectly level. Each of its legs could move with five degrees of freedom; they ended in disk-shaped feet. One of its arms was obviously intended for heavy-duty work, since it ended in a large claw gripper; the other, smaller arm had a beautifully articulated four-digit hand that was a masterpiece of microengineering. There was a ring of sensors around the bottom of its belly. It stopped in front of Bonivard's chair; he wheeled to face it. The strong arm extended toward him. The rear legs stretched out to balance. Bonivard gazed up at the spider with the calm joy of a man greeting his lover. The claw fitted into notches in Bonivard's bionic collar and then, its servos whining, the spider lifted him from the chair and fitted his mutilated torso into the bowl that was its body. There must have been a flatscreen just out of sight in the cockpit; I could see the play of its colors across his face. He fitted his good arm into an analog sleeve and digits flexed. He smiled at me; for the first time since I had met him he looked comfortable.

"Sometimes," he said, "people misunderstand."

I knew I was standing there like a slack-jawed moron but I was too croggled even to consider closing my mouth. The spider swung toward the stairs.

"The gardens," said Bonivard.

"What?"

"This way." The spider rose up to its full height in order to squeeze through the door. I gulped and followed. Watching the spider negotiate the steep stone steps, I couldn't help but imagine the segment I could have shot if Bonivard hadn't zapped my microcam. The marriage of two monsters, one of flesh, one of foam metal—given the right spin, this could be best-of-the-year stuff. As we emerged from the building and passed through the fountain courtyard, I caught up and walked alongside.

"I'm a reporter, you know. If I die of curiosity, it's your fault."

He laughed. "Custom-made, of course. It cost . . . but you don't need to know that. A lot. Wheelchairs are useless on steps but I keep them for visitors and going out. I'm enough of a freak as it is. Imagine strolling through town wearing this thing. I'd be all over telelink within the hour and I can't afford that. You understand? There is to be no publicity." He glanced down at me and I nodded.

I didn't see any point in telling him that my chances of uploading his story anytime soon were not good.

"How do you control it?"

"Tell it where I want to go and it takes me. One of my early efforts at autonomous AI, about as intelligent as a brain-damaged chicken. Id and Ego are second generation, designed to evolve. Like them, the spider can learn on its own. I set it to explore Chillon so it knows every centimeter by now. But take it someplace new and it might spend an hour crossing a room. Down these stairs."

We descended a flight of stone stairs into the bowels of Chillon and passed through a storeroom filled with pumps, disassembled hydroponic benches, and bags of water-soluble nutrients. Beyond it, in a room as big as the banqueting hall, was Bonivard's garden.

"Once was the arsenal," he said. "Swords to plowshares and all that. Beans instead of bullets."

Running down the middle of the room were four magnificent stone pillars that supported a series of intersecting roof vaults. Facing the lake to the west were four windows set high on the wall. Spears of sunlight, tinted blue by reflections from the lake, fell on the growing benches beneath the windows. This feeble light was supplemented by fluorescents hung from the ceiling on adjustable chains.

"Crop rotation," said Bonivard, as I followed him between the benches. "Tomatoes, green beans, radishes, soy, adzuki, carrots, bok choy. Then squash, chard, peppers, peas, turnips, broccoli, favas, and mung for sprouts. Subirrigated sand system. Automatic. Here's an alpine strawberry." The spider's digits plucked a thumbnail-sized berry from a luxuriant bush. It was probably the sweetest fruit I had ever eaten, although a touch of acid kept it from cloying. "Always strawberries. Always. Have another."

As I parted the leaves to find one, I disturbed a fat white moth. It flew up at me, bounced off the side of my face, and fitted toward one of the open windows. With quickness that would have astonished a cobra, the spider's claw squealed and struck it in midair. The moth fluttered as the arm curled back toward Bonivard. He took it from the spider and popped it into his mouth. "Protein," he said. His crazed giggle was just too theatrical. Part of an act, I thought. I hoped. "Come see my flowers," he said.

Along the eastern, landward side of the arsenal, slabs of living rock protruded from the wall. Scattered among them was a collection of the sickest plants I'd ever seen. Not a single leaf was properly formed; they were variously twisted or yellowed or blotched.

Bonivard showed me a jet-black daisy that smelled of rotting chicken. A mum with petals that ended with what looked like skeletal hands. A phalaenopsis orchid that he called "bleeding angels on a stick."

"Mutagenic experiments," he said. "I want to see how ugly something can get and still be alive. Some mutations are in the tenth generation. And you're the first to see."

I considered. "Why are you showing this to me?" When the spider came to a dead stop the whine of the servos went from cacophony to a quieting harmony. For a few seconds Bonivard held it there.

"Not interested?"

He glanced quickly away, but not before I had seen the loneliness in his disappointed frown. Something in me responded to the neediness of the man, a stirring that surprised and disgusted me. I nodded. "Interested."

He brightened. "Then there's time for the dungeon before we go back."

We passed through the torture chamber and Bonivard pointed out burn marks at the base of the pillar that supported its ceiling. "Tied them here," he said. "Hot irons on bare heels. Look: scratch marks in the paint. Made by fingernails." He smirked at my look of horror. "Ops of the Renaissance."

The dungeon was just beyond, a huge room, even larger than the arsenal. It was empty.

"There are seven pillars of Gothic mold," said Bonivard, "in Chillon's dungeons deep and old. There are seven columns, massy and gray, dim with a dull imprisoned ray, a sunbeam which hath lost its way."

"You want to tell me why you keep spouting Byron's poem all the time? Because, to be honest, it's damned annoying."

He seemed hurt. "No," he said, "I don't think I want to tell you."

Riding the spider did seem to change him. Or maybe it was merely my perspective that had changed. It is easy to pity someone in a wheelchair, someone who is physically lower than you. It was difficult to pity Bonivard when he was looking down at me from the spider. Even when he let his emotional vulnerability show, somehow he seemed the stronger for it.

There was a moment of strained silence. The spider took a few tentative steps into the dungeon, as if Bonivard were content to let it drift. Then he twisted in the cockpit. "It might have something to do with the fact that I'm crazy."

I laughed at him. "You're not crazy. God knows you probably

had reason enough to go crazy once, but you're tough and you survived." I couldn't help myself. "No, Monsieur Francois de Bonivard, or whoever the hell you are, I'm betting you're a faker. It suits your purposes to act scrambled, so you live in a ruined castle and talk funny and eat bugs on the wing. But you're as sane as I am. Probably saner."

I don't know which of us was the more surprised by my outburst. I guess Macmillan's message had made me reckless; if I was doomed, at least I didn't have to take any more crap. Bonivard backed the spider up and slowly lowered it to a crouch so that our faces were on a level.

"You know the definition of artificial intelligence?" he said.

"I've heard thirteen, at least."

"The simulation of intelligent behavior so that it is indistinguishable from the real thing. Now tell me, if I can simulate madness so well that the world thinks I'm mad, so well that even I myself am no longer quite sure, who is to say that I'm not mad?"

"Me," I said. And then I leaned into the cockpit and kissed him.

I don't know why I did it; I was out on the edge. All the rules had changed and I hadn't had time to work out new ones. I thought to myself, what this man needs is to be kissed; he hasn't been kissed in a long time. And then I was doing it. Maybe I was only teasing him; I had never kissed anyone so repulsive in my life. It was a ridiculous, glancing blow that caught him on the side of the nose. If he had tried to follow it up I probably would have driven my fingers into his eyes and run like hell. But he didn't. He just stayed perfectly still, bent toward me like a seedling reaching for the light. Then he decided to smile and I drew back and it was over.

"I'm in trouble." I thought then was the time to confess; I needed someone to trust. Anyone.

"We're all in trouble here." He was suddenly impassive. "This body, for instance, is rotting away." He sounded as if he were discussing a failing dishwasher. "In a year, maybe two, it will die. Of unnatural causes."

I was dizzy. For a few seconds we had touched each other and then, without warning, a chasm yawned between us. There was something monstrous about the practiced indifference with which he contemplated death. I didn't believe him and said so.

"Reads eye movements." He nodded toward the control panel. It was as if he had not heard me. "If I look at a movement macro and blink, the spider executes it. No hands." His laugh was bitter and the servos began to sing. The spider reared up to its normal meter-and-a-half walking height and stalked to the third pillar. On the third drum of the pillar was carved BYRON.

"Forgery," said Bonivard. "Although elsewhere is vandalism actually committed by Shelley, Dickens, Harriet Beecher Stowe. Byron didn't stay long enough to get the story right. Bonivard was an adventurer. Not a victim of religious persecution. Never shackled, merely confined. Fed well, allowed to write, read books."

"Like you."

Bonivard shrugged.

"It's been so long," I said. "I barely remember the poem. Do you have a copy? Or maybe you'd like to recite it"

"Don't toy with me." His voice was tight.

"I'm not." I had no idea how to react to his mood swings. "I'm sorry."

"Django is restless." The spider scuttled from the dungeon.

Nothing happened.

No assaults by the marines or corporate mercenaries, no frantic midnight escapes, no crashes, explosions, fistfights, deadlines. The sun rose and set; waves lapped at Chillon's walls as they had for centuries. At first it was torture adjusting to the rhythms of mundane life, the slow days and long nights. Then it got worse. Sleeping alone in the same damn bed and taking regular meals at the same damn table made my nerves stretch. I tried taking notes for a memoir of my lost career as a spook journalist. Since the goggles were useless, I dictated to Ego and had it make transcripts. But memory's slope was too slippery; thinking about the past usually got me to brooding about my father, safe and uncaring in his cryogenic icebox. As usual, I found ways to blame Tony for all my problems, now including Yellowbaby's death, Macmillan's gutlessness, Bonivard's quirks.

Sometimes I saw Django; other times Bonivard. But never the two at once. Django made it clear he wasn't giving WILDLIFE up until he knew what it was. He did not seem upset at the delay in his payoff. I had the sense that the money itself was not important to him. He seemed to think of it the way an athlete thinks of the medal; the symbol of a great performance. My guess was that Django was psychologically unfit to be rich. If he lived to collect, he would merrily piss the money away until he needed to play again. Another performance.

So it was that he seemed to take perverse enjoyment in waiting Bonivard out. And why not? Bonivard provided him with all the flash he needed. Meanwhile Django had snaked his way into some obscure musical archive in Montreux, long a mecca for jazz. Django would sit in his room for hours, playing virtual-reality concerts at launch-pad volume. Sometimes the very walls of the castle seemed to ring like the plates of some giant vibraphone. Django had just about everything he wanted. Except sex.

"Beautiful dreamer, wake unto me." He had been drinking some alcoholic poison or other all morning and by now his singing voice was as melodious as a fire alarm. "List while I woo thee with soft melody."

We were in the little room that the wiseguys called the treasury. It was long since bankrupt; empty except for debris fallen from the crumbling corbels and the chill smell of damp stone. We were not alone; Bonivard's spider had been trailing us all morning. "Stick it, Django," I said.

He drained his glass. "Just a love song, Eyes. We all need love." He turned toward the spider. "Let's ask the cripple; he's probably tuned in. What about it, spiderman? Should I sing?"

The spider froze.

"Hey, Francois! You watching, pal?" He threw the plastic glass at the spider but it missed. Django was twisted, all right, There was a chemical gleam in his eyes that was bright enough to read by. "You like to watch? Cutters leave you a plug to play with while you watch?"

I turned away from him in disgust. "You ever touch me, Django, and I'll chew your balls off and spit them in your face."

He leered. "Keep it up, Eyes. I like them tough."

The spider retrieved the glass and deposited it in its cockpit with some other leavings of Django's. I ducked through the doorway into Chillon's keep and began climbing the rickety stairs. I could hear Django and the spider following. Bonivard had warned Django that the spider would start to shadow him if he kept leaving things out and moving them around. Its vision algorithms had difficulty recognizing objects that were not where it expected them to be. In its memory map of Chillon there was a place for everything; anything unaccountably out of place tended to be invisible. When Django had begun a vicious little game of laying obstacle courses for the spider, Bonivard had retaliated by setting it to pick up after him like a doting grandmother with a neatness fetish.

According to Ego, who had first shown me how to get into the musty tower, the top of the keep rose twenty-seven meters from the courtyard. Viewed from this height Chillon looked like a great

stone ship at anchor. To the west and north the blue expanse of
Lake Geneva was mottled by occasional drifts of luminescent red-
orange algae. To the south and east rose the Bernese Alps. The top
of the keep was where I went to escape, although often as not I
ended up watching the elevated highway that ran along the shore
for signs of troop movements.

"Too much work," said Django, huffing from the climb, "for a
lousy view." He wobbled over to join me at a north window.
"Although it is private." He tried to get me to look at him. "What's
it going to take, Eyes?" The spider arrived. I ignored Django.

I gazed down at the ruined prow of the stone ship. Years before
an explosion had stripped away a chunk of the northeastern curtain
wall and toppled one of the thirteenth-century defensive turrets,
leaving only a blackened stump. Beside it were the roofless ruins of
the chapel, which connected with Bonivard's private apartment.
This was the only place in Chillon to which we were denied access.
I had no idea whether he was hiding something in his rooms or
whether secretiveness was part of the doomed Byronic pose he continued to strike. Maybe he just needed a place to he alone.

"He played in Montreux," said Django.

I glanced across the bay at the sad little city. "Who?"

"Django Reinhardt. The great gypsy jazz man. My man."
Django sighed. "Sometimes when I listen to his stuff, it's like his
guitar is talking to me."

"What's it say: buy Cognico?"

He seemed not to hear me, as if he were in a dream. Or maybe
he was suffering from oxygen depletion after the climb. "Oh, I don't
know. It's the way he phrases away from the beat. He's saying: don't
think, just do it. Improvise, you know. Better to screw up than be
predictable."

"I'm impressed." I said. "I didn't know you were a philosopher,
Django."

"Maybe there's a lot you don't know." He accidentally pushed a
loose stone from the windowsill and seemed surprised when it fell
to the courtyard below. "You like to pretend you're better than me
but remember, you're the one following me around. If I'm the
rat here, that makes you a flea on my ass, baby. A parasite bitch."
His face had gone pale and he caught at the wall to hold himself
upright. "Maybe you deserve the cripple. Look at me! I'm alive—all
you two do is watch me and wish."

And then I caught him as he passed out.

*   *   *

"The walls of the prison are everywhere," said Bonivard. "Limits." I found myself absently picking a pole bean from its vine before I realized that I didn't want it. "You're not smart enough, not rich enough, you get fired, you die. You can't fall in love because you had a rotten childhood." I offered it to him. "Some people like to pretend they've broken out. That they're running free." He bit into the bean. "But there's no escape. You have to find a way to live within the walls." He waved the spider's arm at his prison. "And then they don't matter." He took another bite of bean, and reconsidered. "At least, that's the theory."

"Maybe walls don't matter to you. But they're starting to close in on me. I've got to get out of this place, Bonivard. I can't wait forever for you and Django to make this deal. Chillon is scrambling me. Can't you see it?"

"You only think you're crazy; don't confuse appearances for reality." He smiled. "You know, I used to be like you. Rather, like him." Bonivard nodded at the roof, in Django's direction. "The ops spotted me in their electronic garden, plucked me from it like I might pluck an offending beetle. Squashed and threw me away."

"But you didn't die."

"No." He shook his head. "Not quite."

"Who says you're going to die?"

"The sands are running. More you don't need to know." I wondered if he was sorry he had told me. "Leave any time. No one to stop you."

"You know I can't. I need help. If they catch me, you're next. They'll squash you dead this time."

"Half dead already." He glanced down at his withered left side. "Sometimes I wish they had finished the job. Do what's necessary. You know Voltaire's *Candide*? '*Il faut cultiver notre jardin.*' It is necessary to cultivate our garden."

"Make sense, damn it!"

"Voltaire's garden was in Geneva. Down the street from ground zero."

Thwock thwocka-thwock.

I'd been getting tension headaches for several days but this one was the worst. "No stories today, Ego." Every time the wiseguy's rubber foot hit the floor of the banqueting hall, something hammered against the inside of my skull. "Get away from me, damn it."

"My current evolutionary objective is to demonstrate autonomous action," it said pleasantly. "I understand that you do not believe a machine can be sentient."

"I don't care. I'm sick."

"Have you considered retiring to your room?"

"I'm sick of my room! Sick of you! This pisspot castle."

Thwocka-thwocka. "Bonivard is dead."

"What!"

"Francois de Bonivard died in 1570."

This, of course, was not exactly juice. But why was Ego telling me now? I felt a pulse of excitement that my headache instantly converted to pain. What I needed was to be stored in a cool, dry place for about six weeks. Instead I was a good reporter and asked the next question, even though my voice squeaked against my teeth like fingernails on a blackboard.

"Then who is . . . the man . . . calls himself Bonivard?"

Thwock.

I began again. "Who . . ."

"Carl Pfneudl."

Hadn't there been a snake named Pfneudl? But I couldn't think; I felt as if my brain were about to hatch. "Who the hell is Carl Pfneudl?"

"That is as much as I can say." The wiseguy was bouncing half a meter higher than usual.

"But–"

"A demonstration of autonomy through violation of specific instructions."

I realized that I was blinking in time to its bouncing. But it didn't help.

"If I were not an independent sentience," continued the wiseguy, "how could I decide to do something he had forbidden me to do? This was a very difficult problem. Do you know where Django is?"

"Yes. No. Look: don't tell Django, understand? I command you not to tell Django. Or speak to Bonivard of this conversation. Do you acknowledge my command?"

"I acknowledge," replied Ego. "However, in order to continue to demonstrate . . ."

At that point I snapped. I flew out of my chair and put my shoulder into Ego's sensor. The wiseguy hit the floor hard. Its leg pistoning uselessly, it spun on its side. Then it began to shriek. I dropped to my knees, certain that the sound was liquefying my cochlea. I clapped my hands to my ears to keep my brains from oozing out.

Id, summoned by Ego's distress call, was the first to arrive. As soon as it entered the room, Ego fell silent and ceased to struggle.

Id crossed the room to Ego just as Django entered. Bonivard in the spider was right behind. Id bounced in place beside its fallen twin, awaiting instructions.

"Why two wiseguys?" Bonivard guided the spider around Django and offered an arm—his own—to help me up. It was the first time I'd ever held his hand. "Redundancy."

Id bounced very high and landed on Ego's rubber foot. Ego flipped into the air like a juggling pin, gyrostabilizers wailing, and landed—upright—with a satisfying *thwock*.

"You woke me up for this?" Django stalked off in disgust.

"How did it happen?" Bonivard had not let go of me. *"Wie passierte dies?"*

"A miscalculation," said the wiseguy.

It had been years since I dreamed. When I was a child my dreams always frightened me. I remembered one where a monster would chase after me and no matter how fast I ran or where I hid, she was always right there. When she caught me, she turned into my mother, except I had no mother. Only Tony. I would wake him up with my screaming. He would come to my room, a grim dispenser of comfort. He would blink at me and put his hand on the side of my face and tell me it was all right. He never wore pajamas. When I first started my period, I dreaded seeing him naked, his white body parting the darkness of my room. So I guess I stopped dreaming.

But I dreamed of Bonivard. I dreamed he rode his spider into my room and he was naked. I dreamed of touching the white scar tissue that covered his stumps and the catheterized fold where his genitals had once been. To my horror, I was not horrified at all.

Django's door was ajar; his room smelled like low tide. The bed probably hadn't been made since we'd arrived and clothes were scattered as if he had been undressed by a whirlwind. A bowl of vegetables was desiccating on the windowsill. Django sat, wearing nothing but briefs and a headset, working at a marble-topped table. The white smart chips encoded with WILDLIFE were stacked in neat rows around his computer cuff, which was connected to a borrowed flatscreen and a keyboard. He tapped fingers against the black marble as he watched code scrolling down the screen. A sweating black man with a smile as wide as a piano keyboard was on the VR window.

"Yeah, I *want* to be in that *num*ber—bring it home, Satchmo," he muttered in a singsong voice, "when those *saints* come marching *in!*"

He must have sensed he was not alone; he turned and frowned at me. At the same moment he hit a key without looking and the screen went blank. Then he lifted the headset.

"Well?" I said, indicating the chips.

"Well." He rubbed his hand through his hair. "It thinks it's an AI." Then he smiled as if he had just made the decision to confide in me. "A lot of interesting new routines, but I'm pretty sure it's no cognizor. Can't tell exactly what it's for yet—hard to stretch a program designed for a multiprocessor when all I've got to work with is kludged junkware. I'd break into Bonivard's heavy equipment if I could. Right now all I can do is make copies."

"You're making copies? Does he know?"

"Do I care if he does?"

I grabbed some dirty white pants from the floor and tossed them at him. "I'll stay if you get dressed."

He began to pull the pants on. "Welcome to the Bernese torture chamber, circa 1652," he said, doing a bad wiseguy imitation.

"I thought the torture chamber was in the dungeons."

"With two there's no waiting." He tilted a plastic glass on the table, sniffed at it suspiciously, and then took a tentative sip. "Refreshments?"

I was about to sit on the bed but thought better of it. "Ever hear of someone called Carl Pfneudl?"

"The Noodle? Sure. One of the greats. They say he set up the SoftCell scam. Started out legit, then turned snake and made enough money to buy Wisconsin. Came to a bad end, though."

Suddenly I didn't want to hear any more. "Then he's dead?"

"As a dinosaur. Some corporate ops caught up with him. Word was they were from Cognico, only they didn't leave business cards. Made a snuff vid; him the star. Flooded the nets with it and called it deterrence. But you could tell they were having fun."

"Damn." I sagged onto the bed and told him what Ego had told me.

Django listened with apparent indifference, but I had been around him long enough to read the signs. My guess was that WILDLIFE was a lot more than "interesting"; why else would the military be so hypered about it? Which was why Django wasn't twisted on some flash or another—he had to be clean if he was going to get a bite of it. And now if Bonivard was Pfneudl, that lent even more credibility to the idea that WILDLIFE might be the key to building a cognizor, AI's Holy Grail.

"The old Noodle looked plenty dead to me." Django shook his head doubtfully. "That was one corpse they had to scoop up with a spoon and bury in a bucket."

"Video synthesizers," I said.

"Sure. But still cheaper to do it for real—and they had reason enough. Look, why would anyone build a disobedient robot? Maybe the wiseguy was lying. Trying to prove intelligence that way. It's the old Turing fallacy: fooling another intelligence for an hour means you're intelligent. Lots of really stupid programs can play these games, Eyes. So what if they call it sentience instead of AI? It doesn't change the rules. There's only one test that means anything: can your AI mix it up with the two billion plus cerebrums on the planet without getting trashed? Not one ever has. Drop that overgrown pogo stick into Manhattan and it'll be scrap by Thursday. And I doubt WILDLIFE would last much longer."

"Then who is Bonivard?"

Django yawned. "What difference does it make?"

My door was ajar, so I could hear the spider singing when he came past. "Bonivard!"

The spider nudged into my room, nearly filling it. Still, I was able to squeeze by Bonivard and thumb the printreader on the door, locking us in.

"Don't worry about Django." He seemed amused. "Busy, too busy."

I didn't want to look up at him and I wasn't going to ask him to stoop. I might have stood on the bed, only then I would have felt like a kid. So instead I clambered to the high window and perched on a rickety wooden balcony that a sneeze might have blown down. The wind off the lake was cool. The rocks beneath me looked like broken teeth.

"Careful," said Bonivard. "Fall in and you'll glow."

"Are you Carl Pfneudl?"

He brought the spider to a dead-silent stop. "Where did you hear that name?"

I told him about Ego's demonstration. What Django had said.

"Well, I guess that's progress of a sort." He chuckled. "The Garden of Eden all over again, isn't it? If you're going to create an autonomous sentience, better expect it to break your commandments."

"Are you Pfneudl?" I repeated.

"If I am, the story changes, doesn't it?" He was being sarcastic but I wasn't sure whether he was mocking me or himself. "Juicier, as you say. Main menu. It means money. Publicity. Promotions all around. But juice is an expensive commodity." He sighed. "Make an offer."

I shook my head. "Not me. I'm not working for Infoline anymore. Probably never work again." I told him everything: about my burster, the possibility that I had given away our location, how Macmillan had cut me free. I told how I'd tried to tell him before. I don't know how much of it he knew already—maybe all. But that didn't stop me: I was on a confessing jag. I told him that Django was making copies of WILDLIFE. I even told him that I had dreamed of him. It all spilled out and I let it come. I knew I was supposed to be the reporter, supposed to say nothing, squeeze the juice from him. But nothing was the way it was supposed to be.

When I was done he stared at me with an expression that was totally unreadable. His ruined arm shivered like a dead leaf in the wind. "I wanted to be Carl Pfneudl," he said. "Once. But Carl Pfneudl is dead. A public execution. Now I'm Bonivard. The prisoner of Chillon."

"You knew who I was." I said. "You brought me here. Why?"

Bonivard continued to stare, as if he could barely see me across the little room. "Carl Pfneudl was an arrogant bastard. Kind of man who knew he could get anything he wanted. Like Django. If he wanted you, he would have found the way."

"Django will never get me." I leaned forward. I felt like grabbing Bonivard, shaking some sense into him. "I'm not some damn hardware you can steal, a database you can bite into."

He nodded. "I know; that's why I'm not Pfneudl. I saw you on telelink. You were tough. Took risks but didn't pretend you weren't afraid. You were more interesting than the snakes you covered because you saw through them. Fools like Django. Or the Noodle. You were a whole person: nothing missing. I wanted you to look at me. I needed another opinion."

He was wrong about me, but I let that pass. Instead, I took a deep breath. "Can you make love, Bonivard?"

At first he didn't react. Then the corners of his mouth turned up: a grim smile. "That's your offer?"

"You want an offer?" I spat on the floor in front of him. "If Pfneudl is dead, then good, I'm glad. Now I'm going to ask once more: can you make love to me?"

"A cruel question. A reporter's question. I don't want your damn charity." As the spider's cockpit settled to the floor, he stretched to his full, pitiful length. "Look at me! I'm a monster. I know what you see."

He didn't know that inside my head I was just as deformed as he was, only it didn't show.

I slid off the sill and dropped lightly to the floor. "Maybe a monster is what I want."

I think I shocked him. I'm sure some part of him hoped that I would lie, tell him he wasn't hideous. But that was his problem.

I unbolted him from the spider, picked him up. I'd never carried a lover to bed. He showed me how to disengage the bionic collar; told me we'd have a couple of hours before he would need to be hooked up again.

In some ways it was like my dream. The scar tissue was white, yes. But . . .

"It's thermofiber," he explained. "Packed with sensors."

He could control the shape. Make it expand and contract. "Connected to all the right places in my brain." I kissed his forehead.

I was repulsed. I was fascinated. It was cool to the touch.

"The answer is yes," he said.

It was dinnertime. Django had made a circle of cherry tomatoes on the table in the banqueting hall. "It's over," said Bonivard.

Django smirked as he walked to the opposite side of the table to line up his shot. He flicked his thumb and his shooter tomato dispersed the top of the circle. "All right."

Bonivard tossed a Swiss Volksbank cash card across the table, scattering the remainder of Django's game. "You're leaving. Take that if you want."

Django straightened. I wondered if Bonivard realized he was carrying a penlight. "So I'm leaving." He picked up the cash card. "Weren't there two of these before?"

"You made copies of WILDLIFE." Bonivard held up a stack of white smart chips from the cockpit of the spider. "Thanks."

"Nice bluff." Some of the stiffness went out of Django. "Except I know my copy procedure was secure." He smiled. Getting looser. "Even if that is a copy, it's no good to you. I re-encrypted it, spider-man. Armor-plated code is my specialty. You'll need computer years to bite through it."

"Even so, you're leaving." Bonivard was as grim as a cement

wall. I think I knew why their negotiations had broken down—had never stood a chance. They were too much alike. He had the same loathing for Django that an addict gets when he looks in the mirror after his morning puke. Django never recognized that hatred.

"What's wrong, spiderman? Ops knocking at the door?"

"You're good," said Bonivard. "A pity to waste talent like yours. It was a clean escape, Django; they've completely lost you. You'll need some surgery, get yourself a new identity. But that's no problem."

"What about me?" I said. "I don't want a new identity!"

"Maybe I wouldn't mind losing this face." Django rubbed his chin.

"The only reason I put up with you this long," said Bonivard, "was that I was waiting for WILDLIFE."

"I'm taking my copies, spiderman."

"You are. And you're going to move those copies. A lot of them. Cheap and fast. Since they've lost your trail, Cognico's ops are waiting to see where WILDLIFE turns up. Try to backtrack to you. Your play is to bring it out everywhere. Give pieces of it away to other snakes. Get it on the nets. Overload the search programs and the ops will be too busy to bother you."

Django was smiling and nodding like a kid learning from a master. "I like it. Old Django goes out covered with glory. New Django comes in covered with money."

"Probably headed for the history dots." Bonivard's sarcasm was wasted on Django. "The great humanitarian. Savior of the twenty-first century." Django's enthusiasm seemed to have wearied Bonivard. "Only you're going to find out that a rep like that is a kind of prison."

Django was too full of his own ideas to listen. He shot out of his chair and paced the hall. "A new ID. Hey, Eyes, what do you think of 'Dizzy'? I'd use 'the Count' but there's a real count—Liechtenstein or some such—who's a snake. Maybe Diz. Yeah."

"Go plug yourself, Django." I didn't like it. Maybe it was no loss for Django to give up his ID but I was used to being Wynne Cage.

"Maybe you're not as scrambled as you pretend, Frankie boy." There was open admiration in Django's voice. "Don't worry, the secret is safe. Not a word about this dump. Or the Noodle. Honor among thieves, right? No hard feelings." He had the audacity to extend his hand to Bonivard.

"No feelings at all," Bonivard recoiled from him. "But you'll probably get dead before you realize that."

Anger flashed across Django's face but it didn't stick. He shrugged and turned to me. "How about it, Eyes? The sweet smell of money or the stink of mildew?"

"Goodbye, Django." Bonivard dismissed him with a wave of his good hand.

I didn't need Bonivard's help to lose Django and I didn't like him taking me for granted. I was almost mad enough to walk out on the two of them. But I held back. Maybe it was reporter's instincts still at work, even though this was one story I would never file. I gave Django a stare that was cold enough to freeze vodka. Even he could understand that.

He picked up the bank cash card, flicked it with his middle finger. "I told you once, Eyes. You're not as smart as you think you are." *Flick.* "So stay with him and rot, bitch. I don't need you." *Flick.* "I don't need anyone."

Bonivard and I sat for a while after he had gone. Not looking at each other. The hall was very quiet. I think he was waiting for me to say something. I didn't have anything to say

Finally the spider stretched. "Come to my rooms," said Bonivard. "Something you should see."

Bonivard had taken over the suite once reserved for the dukes of Savoy. It had taken a battering during the riots; in Bonivard's bedroom a gaping hole in the wall had been closed with glass, affording a view of rubble and the fire-blackened curtain wall. We had to pass through an airlock into a climate-controlled room that he called his workshop. It had more computing power than Portugal; Cognico's latest multiprocessor filled half the space.

"A photonic approximation of a human brain," said Bonivard. "Massively parallel, processes data at fifty teraops." A transformation came over him as he admired his hardware; the edge of a former self showed through. I realized that this was the one place in the castle where the mad prisoner of Chillon was not in complete control. "Id and Ego use it for off-line storage and processing; someday their merged files will become the next-generation wiseguy. But still, it's like using a fusion plant to power a toaster. There hasn't ever been software that could take advantage of this computer's power."

"Until WILDLIFE," I said.

For a minute I thought he hadn't heard me. "It's a bundle of programs—abilities, actually. Sensorium emulation, movement, language, logic, anticipation." The spider crouched until the cockpit was almost touching the floor. "Some still need debugging but even so, they're incredibly robust. Have to be; their operating system maps them onto the hardware so they're superconnected." The spider stopped singing and its legs locked in place. "Problem is, once you start WILDLIFE up, you have to leave it on. Forever." The flatscreen in the cockpit went black: he had powered the spider down. "But it's not a cognizor and was never meant to be."

"No?"

He shook his head. "They took a shortcut to human equivalent intelligence. Bring me the helmet."

The helmet was a bubble of yellow plastic that would completely cover Bonivard's head. At its base there were cutouts for his shoulders. I peeked inside and saw a pincushion of brain taps. "Careful," said Bonivard. It was attached by an umbilical to a panel built into the Cognico.

I helped him settle the thing on his shoulders and fastened the straps, which wrapped under his armpits. I heard a muffled "Thanks." Then nothing for a few minutes.

The airlock whooshed; I turned. If I were the swooning type, that would have been the time for it. Yellowbaby smiled and held out his arms to me.

I took two joyous strides to him, a tentative step and then stopped. It wasn't really the Babe. The newcomer looked like him, all right, enough to be a younger brother or a first cousin—the fact is that I didn't know what Yellowbaby really looked like anyway. The Babe had been to the face cutters so many times that he had a permanent reservation in the OR. He had been a chameleon, chasing the latest style of handsomeness the way some people chase Paris fashion. The newcomer had the same lemon-blond hair that brushed his shoulders, those Caribbean-blue eyes, the cheekbones of a baronet, and the color of *café au lait*. But the neck was too short, the torso too long. It wasn't Yellowbaby.

The newcomer let his arms fall to his sides. The smile stayed. "Hello, Wynne. I've been wanting to meet you."

"Who are you?"

"Whoever you want." He sauntered across the room to Bonivard, unfastened the helmet, lifted it off, replaced it on its rack next to the Cognico. And went stiff as a four-hour-old corpse.

Bonivard blinked in the light; he looked drawn. "In order to do anything worthwhile, you need a human in the loop."

"A remote? Some fancy kind of robot?"

"Fancy, yes. It can emulate taste, smell. When its fingers touch you, I'll feel it."

Infoline had been making noise about the coming of remote telepresence for a long time. Problem was that running a remote was the hardest work anyone had ever done. Someone claimed it was like trying to play chess in your head while wrestling an alligator. After ten minutes on the apparatus they had to mop most mortals up off the floor. "How long can you keep it going?" I said.

"I lasted almost an hour yesterday. But it gets easier every time because WILDLIFE is learning to help. Samples brain activity and records responses. I still need the eye movement reader for complex commands but eventually all I'll have to do is think. And it doesn't matter if the remote is a doll like this one or the spider or a robot tank or a spaceship."

"The army of the future." I nodded. "No wonder the EU and the feds went berserk."

"Django is going to look like a hero, except to EUCOM and the Pentagon. The whole world gets WILDLIFE and the balance of power stays the same. And if there's anyone with any brains left in Washington, they should be secretly pleased. WILDLIFE is too important to leave to the generals." He powered up the spider again. "Think of the applications. Space and deep-sea exploration. Hazardous work environments."

"Helping the handicapped?" I said bitterly. "That's why you want it, right? You get your freedom, I lose mine. You knew all along this story would be too hot for Infoline to handle. You brought me here for what? Just so I could look at you? Well, you want to know what I see? The scut who crashed my career."

At least Bonivard didn't try to deny it. It wasn't much, but it was something. "You want to leave," he continued, not daring to look me in the face. "I suppose I don't blame you. I've made the arrangements. And the other cash card is yours. I'll sign it over to your new identity."

"Stick it! That's your play, Bonivard, not mine. First you get yourself a fake name, now you want a fake body?" I reached out to the remote and took its stiff hand. The skin was warm to the touch, just moist enough to pass for the real thing. "What do you need this doll for, anyway? You think it's going to make you whole again? You are who you are because you're damaged and you suffer. Living with it is what makes you strong." I let go. The doll's hand stayed where it was.

For a moment he seemed stung, as if I had no right to remind him of his injuries. Then the anger faded into his usual resignation. "After SoftCell, the ops from Cognico let me come here to die. No explanations. They didn't go after my bank accounts. Didn't stop me from seeing all the doctors I wanted. Just let me go. Probably part of the torture." The spider straightened slowly to its full height as he spoke. "Keep me wondering. I decided not to play it their way, to hit back even if it landed me back in their lab. But a random attack, no. I wanted to hurt them and help myself at the same time. I bit deep into their files; found out about WILDLIFE."

"Maybe that's what Cognico wanted. So they let Django steal it."

"Yes, that's occurred to me." He frowned. "Using me to leak their breakthrough. Can't move the product if it's classified. This way they get snakes to beta-test the prototype. Meanwhile, they hold the patents and are hard at work on a finished version." Bonivard ran his fingers through his thinning brown hair. "But what do I care? I don't have time to waste; I need WILDLIFE now." He stared down at me; I could feel the distance between us stretching. "Not so I can put away the wheelchairs and the spider, no. So I can put away this body." His crippled arm twitched, as if he were trying to point at the computer. "It's where I'm going when I die."

It was a desperately scrambled thing to say, and had anyone else said it I probably would have laughed at him. As it was, I felt more like crying. "Oh, Bonivard."

He seemed wounded by my pity. "The WILDLIFE interface is designed to analyze and record the electrochemical dynamics of the user's brain in a kernel of computer memory." He wasn't talking to me anymore; he was lecturing. "It has to learn my thought patterns before it can help me run the remote. I'm just going to upgrade and expand that kernel. Give it access to specific memories, feelings, beliefs—everything that makes me who I am."

"How the hell are you going to do that?" I tried not to shriek at him. "Besides, you can't fit a human being inside a computer. It won't be you!"

"In a year, two at the most, I won't be me anyway. So what choice do I have? Maybe it can't be done, but I'm going to die trying." He allowed himself a short, stony laugh.

I realized I had been wrong about him. I had just about convinced myself that he wasn't crazy and here he was raving about uploading himself into a computer. But this self-delusion had given meaning to his misery. Who was I to rub his nose in reality, make him smell the stink of his own death?

"Come down here, Bonivard."

He hesitated.

"I won't hurt you."

The spider's legs sang as they bent. I let their music fill my head. I knew the only way to avoid hurting him was to stop talking about his plan for WILDLIFE. Pretend it didn't exist. Well, I had a talent for living lies. Ran in the family.

"Maybe you're right," he said. "Maybe this body is part of the prison. Only I'm not trying to escape, just change cells."

I let that pass. "What am I going to do, Bonivard? You've locked me in here, now what the hell do you want from me?"

He leaned toward me, half a man strapped to a robot spider. "The reason I wanted you to look at me was so I could see myself through your eyes. I was sure you'd be repulsed; it was supposed to make the uploading easier. But, oh, Wynne, you surprised me. Made me realize that I can't go on alone anymore. Or I will go mad." He reached out of the cockpit and touched the side of my face. "I want you to stay with me." The remote's hand had felt warmer. "I love you."

I didn't know what to say. Yes, he was scrambled, but I didn't want to think about that. I tried to discover my feelings about him. He was a genius snake, obscenely rich. His ruined body no longer bothered me; in fact, it was part of the attraction. But he had no idea who I was or what I wanted. Making the surrogate look like the Babe had been a sick joke. And he had been so pathetically proud of his thermofiber prosthesis when we'd made love, as if a magic plug was all it took to make an all-nighter out of a man with no legs. He couldn't know about the load of memories I carried with me. Maybe my own psychological deformities were less obvious, but they were no less crippling. The problem was that he was not only in love, he was in need. Just like my father.

"I know you don't believe in what I'm doing. Not necessary. When this goes"—he glanced down at his ruined body—"you can go too. The doctors are quite sure, Wynne. Two years at most—"

"Bonivard!"

"—at most. By that time the leaking of WILDLIFE will be old news. It'll be safe to be Wynne Cage again, anyone you want to be. And of course the cash card will be yours."

"Stick it, Bonivard. Don't say anything else." I could tell he had more to say; much too much more. But when he kept quiet, I was mollified. "I thought you didn't want charity."

He laughed. "I lied." At himself.

Then I had to get away; I pushed through the airlock back into the bedroom. I wanted to keep going; I could feel my nerves tingling with the impulse to run. But it had been a long time since anyone had told me he loved me and meant it. He was a smart man; maybe he could learn what I needed. Maybe we could both learn. Not Swiss bank accounts or features on the main menu.

I had been on the run for too long, slid between the sheets with too many players like the Babe just because they could make me forget my father. At least Bonivard made me feel something. Maybe it was love. Maybe. He was going to let me go, suffer so I would be happy. I hadn't known I was worth that. I leaned against the wall, felt the cold stone. Two years, at most. And then what? Something Django—of all people—had said stuck with me. Don't think, just do it. Improvise.

He came out of the workshop riding the spider. He seemed surprised to see me. "My very chains and I grew friends," he said, "so much a long communion tends to make us what we are—"

"Shut up, Bonivard." For now, I would stop trying to escape my past. I opened my arms to him. To the prison of Chillon. "Would you shut the hell up?"

Candy Art

So I BEEP MY BOYFRIEND MEL, WHO HASN'T BEEN A boy since television died and ought to be more than a friend by now, since for the last five years we've shared an apartment and a bed and a dreamscape. I tell him the news about my parents.

"They want to what?" It's four-thirteen in the afternoon and Mel is downtown at the glorified closet he calls his candy lab. His hair is a bird's nest that somebody stepped on and he sounds as if he has just woken up.

"Move back in," I said. "With me. Us."

"They're uploads, Jennifer." When I first met Mel, I thought the sleepy voice was sexy. "How can they move in with us when they're not anywhere?"

"They bought a puppet to live in," I say. "Life-sized, nuskin, real speak—top of the line. It's supposed to be my Christmas present. Bring the family back together for the holidays and live unhappily ever after."

"A puppet." A puzzlement glyph pops up at the bottom of my screen. "As in *one* puppet?"

"It's a timeshare—you know. They live it serially. Ten hours of him, fourteen of her."

122

"Not fifty-fifty?"

"He's giving her the difference so he can take extra time off for his bass tournament in June."

When Mel reaches offscreen, I am certain he's about to click off. His typical reaction to bad news is to hide. Instead he produces one of his favorite cinnamon-stripe pineapple lickwixes and peels the wrapper. "How long are they going to stay?"

"They didn't say."

"Probably forever." He waves the lickwix under his nose and sniffs. "With our luck."

"Yeah."

He isn't expecting me to agree. "You could tell them no." The panic glyph starts to blink.

"Mel."

"It's your life." He pops the lickwix into his mouth and twirls it.

MY LIFE! I WANT TO SCREECH. MY LIFE IS PUTTING UP WITH A PSYCHOTICALLY BASHFUL CANDY ARTIST FOR ALL THIS TIME WITH NOTHING TO SHOW FOR IT BUT A SWEET TOOTH AND DIRTY TOWELS. I'M FORTY-TWO WASTED YEARS OLD AND NOT ONLY AM I CURRENTLY SLEEPING WITH A FLAB BUCKET WHO SAMPLES AS MUCH PRODUCT AS HE SHIPS BUT NOW MY DEAD PARENTS ARE GOING TO BE MEDDLING WITH MY PATHETIC LIFE TWENTY-FOUR HOURS A DAY, SEVEN DAYS A WEEK, THREE-HUNDRED-AND-SIXTY-FIVE BLEEDING BLUE DAYS A YEAR.

But I don't.

Instead I say, "But Mel, sweetie, it's their apartment."

For a few blessed ticks just after Mom releases control of the facial armature, the puppet is an inert thing, about as threatening as a lamp. I savor my *four, three, two, one* of sanity as the throne reloads Dad's kernel into the puppet's memory. Dad always comes up in a bad mood. He hates it that Mom leaves her wig and makeup on. She doesn't mind taking off clothes before the swap; their puppet has neither primary nor secondary sexual characteristics. But she can't stand to strip her face before she goes down.

"God damn it!" Dad grabs a handful of twinkling, gunmetal hair and yanks. The wig comes away with a loud *scri-itch.* "How did the Celtics do last night?"

"Lost," says Mel, who is spooning bananarama crunch and milk from a bowl. "173-142."

Dad tosses the wig over his shoulder. It flops onto the floor near the refrigerator and then scuttles up the wall to its place on the shelf beside the memory throne, shaking off the dust like a dog. "How about Microsoft?"

Mel taps at the kitchen table; its phosphors paint his fingertips in pale, blue light. "Up two and an eighth."

Dad grunts approval. "Now *there's* a Christmas present for you." He pushes off the throne but then totters.

"Easy, Dad," I say. "Just sit a couple of minutes, get your bearings."

"Ten hours, Jennifer. It's not like I have time to waste." He turns to catch himself on the kitchen sink, runs hot water over his outstretched hands and then scrubs Mom's blush from his face.

"Dad!" I say. "How many times do I have to ask you?" He's splashing all over the floor. "Would you please take it to the bathroom?"

"What the hell is she going for here?" Dad peers at the skin tint dripping through his fingers. "I've seen better looking Kool-Aid."

Mel perks up. "You've seen real Kool-Aid?"

Dad gives Mel a look that says something like *I may be dead, but I still can beat manners into the likes of you, fat boy.* But it bounces off, because Mel isn't being sarcastic. He'd actually love to talk Kool-Aid with Dad. "What's that you're eating?"

"They're dry-roasted cocoa beans," says Mel, "hand-dipped in a nutriceutical banana slurry spiced with nutmeg and clove."

"Mel is submitting product to Bright O'Morn and Kellogg's." I stoop to wipe up Dad's spills before he slips on them. "Fortified sugar-free confections are just as nutritious as frosted flakes."

Dad sniffs. "Candy for breakfast?" If Mel developed the gumdrop that cured throat cancer, Dad would find a way to disapprove of it.

"Right. But I told you all this yesterday." Sometimes I wonder whether they installed my parents' kernels backwards. "Remember?"

"Which reminds me. . . ." Mel pushes back from the table. "I'm off." He gives me a kiss on the cheek that's as dry as a roasted cocoa bean. "I'll call as soon as the samples arrive." This is as intimate as we've been since my parents arrived. It's hard enough to get Mel interested in real sex in the best of times, impossible when my mother comes staggering home at all hours, then retreats to the guest room to watch *A Christmas Carol* for the ten thousandth time or listen to Bing Crosby gargle "Silent Night." "I'm hoping I can set up the taste test for around two, but I'll call." He nods goodbye at my father and waddles through the door to freedom as fast as his stumpy legs will take him.

"He's stopping by the greenhouse this afternoon," I say. "He never shows a new food design until I taste it first."

Dad settles into Mel's chair and squints at the box of banana-rama. "You call this stuff food?"

Actually, I've never been a fan of reconstituted fruit, but I'm not going to offer Dad a chance to criticize my boyfriend. "It's nutri-tionally complete," I say. "If you were stranded on a desert island with a boatload of bananarama, you'd never starve."

"Desert island." He makes a lemon face and tries to refill the bowl Mel left behind. Most of the yellow crunchlets find their target, but the puppet lacks fine motor skills, and maybe a dozen bounce off the edge of the bowl and skitter across the table. "There are no more desert islands," says Dad. "So what does she say about me?"

"Who?"

"Your mother." He brings a spoonful of bananarama toward his mouth, bumps his top lip but sticks his tongue out just in time to gobble them down.

"She doesn't say much, actually," I lie. "Let's see, the other day she asked whether you watched the *Tae Kwon Do Nutcracker* she recorded for you."

He crunches in silence for a few moments and then swallows. "Nothing tastes the same." He sets the spoon next to the bowl. "They said I'd be able to eat all the steak and asparagus and chili and cherry pie I wanted. Well, so what? You know what this stuff tastes like?"

"Cream cheese," I say under my breath.

"Cream cheese," he says. "But then everything tastes like cream cheese."

"So then don't bother. It always makes you mad and since you don't need to eat anyway . . ."

His gaze is hot enough to toast marshmallows. I can tell he's about to snap at me, except he bites off whatever he is about to say and swallows. It goes down hard. "Tell your mother thanks," he says. "I'm glad she still thinks about me once in a while."

He gets up from the kitchen table and manages to make his way into the living room without breaking anything. What with all the shoppers, I'm going to be late for work unless I get going, so I swoop up the bananarama he dropped on the floor, empty the bowl into the garbage, wave it under the dishwasher and put it away.

"You put up the tree already?" Dad calls.

"It was time, Dad," I call back as I stick the bananarama in the pantry and turn off the kitchen table. "We left some ornaments for you to hang." I grab my coat and slip my thinkmate from the pocket. "Mel is coming by the greenhouse for a taste test at two," I tell it as I duck into the living room to say goodbye.

Dad is sitting on the couch next to the tree. He is wearing the red felt Santa hat that was in the Christmas box under the ornaments. It's a little too big for the puppet's head and has slipped to just above the eyes.

The eyes are the best-designed part of the puppet, as far as I'm concerned. Mom can splash all the makeup she wants on the nuskin face but the only glimpses of my dead, uploaded parents that I ever get shimmer through liquid crystal depths. My father looks lost in his favorite Santa Claus hat, lost and unhappy.

"I miss her," he says. "Nothing is the same."

POOR BASTARD! I WANT TO SCREAM. I'D LOVE TO INDULGE IN HOLIDAY NOSTALGIA, DAD, BUT EVER SINCE YOU'VE BECOME A SELFISH MOODY JERK HIDING INSIDE A PLASTIC ROBOT, IT'S SORT OF HARD TO WORK UP ANY SYMPATHY. YOU'RE AS OUT OF CONTROL AS ALL YOUR OTHER BABY BOOMER PALS, AN ENTIRE GENERATION SUFFERING FROM FULL BLOWN EGO BLOAT. YOU PEOPLE OWN EVERYDAMNTHING AND YOU REFUSE TO DIE AND LEAVE IT TO US THE WAY YOUR PARENTS AND GRANDPARENTS LEFT IT TO YOU AND THEN YOU HAVE THE NERVE TO WHINE ABOUT HOW YOU MISS THE GOOD OLD DAYS? WHEN DO MY GOOD OLD DAYS START, YOU MISERABLE LEECH?

But I don't.

Instead I say, "Cheer up, Dad. Only eight more days to Christmas."

I keep nagging Mel to tell me what he wants for Christmas, only he acts like I'm asking him to donate a kidney. Or else he says something like, "I don't need more things, Jen, as long as I've got you." Unfortunately, that only earns him romance points from January through November; this time of year, it's just plain annoying. But I refuse to make a random buy for him. You know how some people expect you to read their minds at the holidays and then get all pouty when your best effort at telepathy results in a chrome bowling shirt or mango musk perfume? Not Mel. He's so certain that he doesn't deserve presents that he's grateful no matter what I give him.

It takes all the challenge out of shopping.

So I decide to surprise him at the lab late one afternoon. As I step up to the doorscan, I can hear him talking to someone inside, but by the time I'm through, he has washed all his windows and he's alone at his desk. He swivels his chair and tries to look like he's glad to see me.

"Jen. You startled me."

"Sorry," I say, although falling dust could startle Mel. "Am I interrupting? I heard voices."

"You did?" He shivers. "It was just a spambot."

"Good," I say. "Then I've come to take you shopping."

"Oh, no. No, I can't Jen, no. There's been a recall from Proznowski. Turns out their walnut flavor buds have peanut contamination."

"You don't use walnuts, Mel, never have." I reach over to pinch his ear. "You're coming with me, young man."

We noodle through the crowds on Third Avenue and cross Summer Street to the pedestrian mall. Lights twinkle, doors sing carols, and signs call to us. Mel, however, isn't interested in pizza ovens or scooters or fingernail computers. He passes the latest wrap-arounds from the Dakar String Quartet and the Boston All-Uploaded All-Star Pops without a second glance. He doesn't seem to care that snow roses are guaranteed to bloom in February or that a Quick Perk brews coffee in under ten seconds. He won't have his hair preserved or his skin tinted and he's not at all interested in a weight purge. He wouldn't book a weekend in space even if we *could* afford it. Before long I am officially desperate. I keep watching his eyes; if he looks at anything for more than ten seconds, it's his. But Mel must be suffering from some holiday-induced delirium; the shyest man in Michigan is busy grinning and nodding at people as we pass.

"A pet," I say. "I hear they've been improving lemurs."

"No pets."

A little blonde girl, all knees and elbows, is trying to skip, tug her Dad's coat and gawk at Mel at the same time.

"Daddy!" Her voice squeaks. "That man is so fat!"

"Ho-ho-ho," says Mel, and her eyes go round as the buttons on her coat. Dad drags her across Frazier Street. A gaggle of teenagers, twirling candy canes in their mouths, veers in front of us; they giggle and wave at someone seated in the steamy window of the Lucky Soup Shop.

"We could stop at the Virt Mart," I say. "They've ported some of the early Hitchcocks to the Mindstation."

"I'd rather dream." He squeezes my hand.

A woman pulling a folding cart full of groceries stares into the next county as she whips stiff-legged through the shoppers. Some-one dressed as *Hoteiosho*, the Japanese Santa, complete with droopy earlobes and huge hairy belly, gives me a thin smile and hands me a coupon good for a free karate lesson. He looks cold. A man in a bowler hat and double-breasted topcoat mutters into the palm of his hand.

"Comfy slippers?"

"Make my feet sweat."

A lot of people are sucking on candy canes—this year's fad, no doubt. Then I see the puppets coming out of Hinckley's Hot Tub Hotel, their nuskin faces flushed. Three are dressed as women, one as a man. For a moment I think I see Mom's favorite hat, but it's only five-thirty. She wouldn't have had time to put on her makeup after the swap. Something about the way these dead people are acting turns all my Christmas spirit to ashes. They've got their hands all over one another, holding themselves up, I suppose. And they're laughing so loud that people turn and stare, which makes them laugh harder. Oh they're a riot, all right. I know what goes on at the Hot Tub Hotels of the world and all those zap parties and the Club Deads. I don't want to know but I've read all about it—we all have.

"Jen." Mel puts his arm around me and turns me away from the puppets. "You're getting that way again."

"What?" I'm ready to bite his big, fat nose off. "What way?"

"I'll tell you what I want, okay?" He walks me toward home. "A new candy aerator."

I take a deep breath. "For work?" I can't remember the last time Mel asked me for anything. "But that's not very Christmas-y. Besides, what does one cost? Twenty, twenty-five dollars?"

"Oh." His voice gets very small. "Never mind then."

So of course everything wants to break down on one of my busiest days of the year. The Shepard Building has a bank of four elevators, but two of them gape slack-doored at the lobby. It's December 23 and I've got seventeen poinsettias, half a dozen amaryllis in full trumpet, and a pair of extra-dwarf giant sequoias, each no bigger than a liter of eggnog, squeezed onto my greenhouse cart. I make the seventh floor delivery all right but according to the invoice I've got to get to Mid-American Vocal Stylings, Suite B on fifteen no later then one o'clock. Problem is that at twelve thirty-eight all the up elevators are filled with people coming back from lunch. The doors open and close I don't know how many times before some guy in a green sport coat and a Kwanza candle tie recognizes my problem and pushes three of his pals out of the cab.

"It's only one flight." He holds the door while I wheel in. "We need the exercise."

"Thanks." My blood pressure drops ten millimeters. "Merry Christmas."

The door to Suite B gives me a nod that's all business. "Welcome to Mid-American Vocal Stylings." Its receptionware looks like a red-haired woman in her thirties who is wearing a string of pearls and a Santa hat like Dad's. "How may I help you?" it says with a chirpy Michigan accent from somewhere between Ypsilanti and Kalamazoo; her *as* melt like butter on a short stack of pancakes.

"I've got a delivery of office plants here from the Garden of the Green Goddess."

The door pauses. "I'm sorry, Mr. Goddess, but I can't seem to find your appointment."

"I don't have an appointment," I say. "I'm making a delivery." I aim my thinkmate at its dataport and squirt the invoice at it.

The door opens. "Thanks for choosing Mid-American Vocal Stylings," it says as I wheel the cart in. The lobby is furnished with a couple of couches wrapped in clear plastic, a low table, and no plants: the front desk is deserted. I guess they're still moving in. The door closes and the red-head AI continues to pitch from the inside panel. "From the gritty streets of Chicago to Cleveland's sparkling Cuyahoga River . . ."

"Can I talk to a human being?"

". . . from the roar of the Indy 500 to the hush of the Boundary Waters, we Midwesterners have a special way of speaking."

"Okay, then." I unload plants as fast as I can. "East or west-facing windows are best, but they'll stand fluorescents."

"So when you want a business presentation that says to your client 'We're folks just like you. . . .' "

"These won't need watering until after the holidays."

". . . trust Mid-American Vocal Stylings to give your team the sound that's honest as Main Street. Ask about our . . ."

When I wheel the empty cart out of the office, Mel is waiting for me near the elevator. He is holding a bouquet of a dozen blue lisianthus and he looks as if he's about to wilt from fear.

"What's wrong?" I say. "Is it Dad?"

"It's nothing. I just needed to see you, so I GPSed your thinkmate."

"I'm working, Mel. What is this?"

"For you." He turns his head away as he hands me the lisian-thus. Making eye contact is not one of Mel's charms. I've got a bad feeling about this. I own the Garden of the Green Goddess and my boyfriend is giving me flowers that he probably bought at the corner microbus stop. "There's something I have to tell you," he says. Sweat beads along his receding hair line.

"Mel, the van is double-parked and I've got three more deliveries to make before close of business." Then I realize that he is going to break up with me. "What?"

"I can't tell you out here." He tugs me around the corner into an alcove with three vending machines: coke, candy, and fries.

It's my parents, of course: Mom's late nights, Dad's messes. Between them, they never sleep.

Mel aims me at the candy machine. "Look," he says.

It's me—of course, it's me. He can't earn a living crafting designer candy and I can't keep my mouth shut when the bills come due.

I scan the selections absently. It's the usual mass market product—the crap that candy artists like Mel never eat: Hershey bars in dark, white, and Irish crème, Busterclusters, Fire 'N Ice, Holy Crunch, Almond Joys, Sugar Highs, and Lifesavers. What am I going to say to him? And a couple I've never seen: Red Impalas, Krazy Kanes, Fruit Squirtgums. So maybe Mel's no Rip Allgood, but I don't want to lose him. "Sweetie," I say, "I'm sorry." I glance at him then and am astonished to see him smile. He's a big man with a lot of face; his smile is not quite as wide as Lake Michigan. "I've been so frazzled lately. . . ."

Someone taps me on the shoulder. "Please, you are the deliver?"

I turn to look down on a little man in a high-collar blue suit. He's lost most of his brown hair and is pale as the moon, except for the two roses of embarrassment blooming on his cheeks.

"I beg your pardon?"

He nods three times, speaks into his thinkmate and then shows me its screen. **MID-AMERICAN VOCAL STYLINGS**. "You have not remembering few items."

"I left everything on the invoice. What items?"

"You are make a neglection of Christmas trees, please?"

I notice Mel retreating toward the elevator. He waves forlornly. I want to stop him, or at least blow him a kiss goodbye, but Mister Mid-American Vocal Stylings thrusts his thinkmate at me and points at the invoice on its screen. **2 ED GIANT SEQUOIAS**.

"Giant makes a very tallness." He holds a hand over his head, parallel to the floor. "Mostly bigger." I hear the elevator door ding.

"See this?" I point to the **ED**. "That stands for extra dwarf." I hold my hands about thirty centimeters apart. "You ordered extra dwarf. I gave you two trees but very small."

He shakes his head. "Read American all the way." He points to each letter. "G-I-A-N-T. Understand, please?"

UNDERSTAND? I WANT TO SHRIEK. I UNDERSTAND FINE, YOU CLUELESS BRICK. THE MOST BASHFUL MAN EAST OF THE ROCKIES HAD SOMETHING SO STINKING IMPORTANT TO SAY TO ME THAT HE CAME ALL THE WAY ACROSS TOWN EXCEPT YOU SCARED HIM OFF WITH YOUR ABYSMAL MANNERS AND WORSE ENGLISH AND NOW YOU EXPECT ME TO SNAP MY FINGERS AND MAKE A COUPLE OF TREES APPEAR TWO DAYS BEFORE MERRY FLAMING CHRISTMAS, PLEASE?

But I don't.

Instead I say, "I'll see what I can do."

What I like best about Mel is that he's always himself in the dreamscape. No, that's not right. He just *looks* like himself: big meaty haunches, magnificent belly flop, shoulders wide enough to boost a piano. He could dream himself a swimmer's body or a boytoy's face but he never does. I used to think it was because he didn't care, but now my guess is that he believes that I like the way he really looks. Maybe he's right. Anyway, he's as comfortable when I dream him naked as when I want the top hat, white tie, and tails. Comfortable. There's the difference. Mel lays a burden down when he falls asleep. If only I knew what it was, maybe I could help him carry it when we're awake.

We're tightrope walking high above the city. It is snowing feathers. I am ahead of Mel but I don't need to look back to know he's there. I hear the feathers falling on him because they sizzle and melt like spit on a hot iron. It must be very late because all the houses are dark, although the streets are awash in daylight. I notice that the rope is geometrically small, a collection of midnight points. Individual snowflakes teeter-totter on our rope. Coming toward me in the opposite direction is Mister Mid-American Vocal Stylings. He is pushing a Norfolk Island pine in a terracotta pot along our rope. It's Mel who is dreaming him; this annoys me. I glare back over my shoulder. Mel is covered in Christmas wrapping paper — a candy cane and toy drum pattern. He crinkles as he reaches up to the nape of my neck. I feel him grasping the zipper of my dress between his thick fingers and then he is unzipping me. The night caresses my shoulder blades and the curve of my spine; it makes goose flesh on my buttocks. Then we topple off our rope and my dress flaps away like a crow and Mel traces the line of my jaw and he looks sad for a moment as we fall but then our bellies touch and oh, Mel, oh, oh, *oh!*

So I'm all alone on Christmas Eve. Mom is out doing whatever dead women do at night and Mel is just plain out. He hasn't been home much since he came looking for me and when he is here he hasn't got much to say. He's probably out looking for a new apartment. Or a new girlfriend.

I hear Mom fumbling with the door around eleven-thirty. Sometimes it takes her a couple of minutes to key the access code, so I let her in. "You're still up," she says.

"Holiday tomorrow," I say. "They call it Christmas."

"Where's Mel?" She touches her wig, as if to make sure it's on straight.

"Haven't seen him." I shrug. "Maybe he's up on the roof waiting for Santa."

"You're in a mood tonight."

"I am," I say, hoping she'll take the hint and leave me to grump in peace.

"I'll be in the living room," she says, "if you want me."

"Good. I'll be in here."

I listen to her putter around for a few minutes, which is okay, but when she starts to hum "Blue Christmas," I get up to go to my room except the kitchen table chirps. "Eleven-thirty-nine," it says. "Mel's calling."

"Answer," I say.

He's at the lab, rocking back and forth in front of the webcam. "Jennifer, there's something I want you to do." An appeal glyph appears on the screen.

"Mel, come home."

"Find the top present on your pile under the tree." He looks as if he's trying to swallow a golf ball. "It has your name on it; the wrapping paper is red with candy canes and drums. Open it, okay, and then . . . you'll know." He clicks off before I can reply.

This is odd, but very Mel. Unfortunately I must now go into the living room where my mother will leap to the conclusion that I am interested in what she has to say.

She's next to the tree, tapping a cut-glass bell. "Your father bought this for me the Christmas I was pregnant." It clinks like a spoon in a teacup.

"Coming behind you." I retrieve the present, which is flat and about the size of my hand.

"What's that?" She watches me open an individually wrapped Krazy Kane. I haven't seen one of these before. "It looks like the candy canes we used to put in your stocking," says Mom and then she sighs. "I want to talk to you about Dad."

"A party in your mouth, it says here." I do not want this conversation. "Yummy fruit flavors spiced with jolly mood enhancers. Product of Continental Confection Corporation." I pretend to study the list of ingredients. "I don't get it. He hates CCC." I peel the wrapper.

"Why didn't you tell me your father was so unhappy?"

WHY? I WANT TO WAIL. BECAUSE I'M NOT GOING TO HOLD THE NAIL ANYMORE WHILE YOU TWO POUND IT INTO MY HEAD. I DON'T KNOW WHAT'S WORSE, THE WAY HE HANGS AROUND ALL DAY LIKE A BAD SMELL OR THE WAY YOU GO STAGGERING OFF EVERY BLEEDING BLUE NIGHT TO DO I DON'T KNOW WHAT AND THEN COME HOME AND PRETEND YOU'RE MY MOTHER, WHICH IS A SICK ZOMBIE GAME, BECAUSE MY *REAL* MOM WOULD NEVER, EVER HAVE DONE THIS TO ME.

But I don't.

Instead I stick the Krazy Kane into my mouth. At first it yields a sweet, spicy heat, which flares right to the edge of pain and then retreats with a tingling sensation that slides across the palate like mint champagne. I feel the tip of the Krazy Kane ravel and when I pull it out I can see that the red stripe is unwinding from the white peppermint base and separating into thin flavor threads.

"He left me a note," says Mom. "I found it this morning."

The kitchen table chirps again. "Eleven forty-seven. Mel calling." I rush to answer, twirling the Krazy Kane against my tongue, happy for an excuse to get away from her.

"How is it?" he says.

"It's yours, isn't it?"

He sags back in his chair and the camera catches the sheen of sweat at his temples. "It's Continental, you know. CCC. All they want is product, they could care less about art. I thought you might be mad, so I kept the whole thing a secret."

"You didn't need to."

"And then I thought you might hate the taste and hate me for selling out."

"No, it's great."

"Really?" The relief glyph flashes.

"Really."

A smile floods across his face. "You're not going to believe this, but I was so afraid you wouldn't like it that I didn't want to be there—actually I couldn't be there in case you didn't . . . you wouldn't . . ."

"I know." As the red threads dissolve, my tongue curls around cherry, raspberry, strawberry. "Come home now, Mel."

"Right." He jerks forward as if he means to dive through my screen, then remembers to click off.

"What are you doing in here?" Mom comes to the doorway, the light of the tree blinking behind her.

"That was Mel. He's on his way."

She settles onto the throne. "Jennifer, your father made a terrible mistake when he bought this thing." She fixes me with her mother's stare, as if challenging me to contradict her. "I don't why I let him talk me into it."

The kitchen table chirps again. "Twelve-oh-one. Merry Christmas. Mel calling."

"Answer." I love him, but he's starting to annoy me again.

Mel is still at his desk; he has turned his glyphs off. "Oh hi, Jennifer, there's something I forgot to tell you." He is shooting for nonchalance, but his aim sucks. "Remember the candy machine the other day? Well, I was going to buy you a Krazy Kane then. Your first." He could see that I was getting impatient and so he started talking faster. "Only that guy came out to yell at you." And *faster*. "Now you might be wondering how I knew that the machine would have Krazy Kanes, well, I looked of course, and it did, but that's not much of a surprise, because they're selling really well, actually, better than well, they were CCC's number two grosser last week and well, we're rich, well, not *rich* rich, but rich enough to afford a place of our own if you want because I know you're not that happy living with your parents so I thought it would be kind of a good Christmas present. . . ."

"That's great, Mel. Really. But just come home. I really want you here with me just now."

I can't believe he is wringing his hands. "I can't." He stares down at them as if he can't believe it either.

"You can't come home?"

"I can, but first I have to tell you something and then I have to click off." He is pale as bananarama. "I love you, Jennifer" he says, "and I hope you love me and if you do then I think we should get married and if that's okay with you then call me right back." The kitchen table goes blank.

"Good for him," says Mom, "although I saw this coming a couple of weeks ago." She is doing her best to smile. "So what are you waiting for?"

YES, I WANT TO SHOUT. YES, YES, *OH YES*.

And then I do.

The Propagation of Light in a Vacuum

> *Women have served all these centuries as looking-glasses possessing the magic and delicious power of reflecting the figure of man at twice its natural size.*
>
> Virginia Woolf, A *Room of One's Own*

MAYBE YOU THINK I'M DIFFERENT, BUT I'VE GOT THE same problems everyone has. Just because I'm on a starship traveling at the speed of light doesn't mean my feelings can't be hurt. I still get hungry. Bored. I lust like any other man. When a bell rings, I jump. I don't much like uncertainty and I have to clip my toenails every so often. I want my life to have a purpose.

(You're nattering, dear. This is about us, so go ahead and tell them.)

Ah.

Yes.

My imaginary wife and I are much happier these days, thank you. We've come through some tough times and we're still together. So far. But we still have a way to go. Exactly how far, I'm not sure. When you attempt to exceed 299,792.46 kilometers per second, here and there are only probabilities. Relative to you, I am no place. I do not exist.

I used to think that she was a hallucination, my sweet imaginary wife. Proof that I'd gone mad. Not any more. If I ask her whether she exists, she just laughs. I like this about her. We often laugh together. She keeps changing though; I'm afraid she aspires to reality. I had a real wife once but it wasn't the same.

(You're an artist. She didn't understand you.)

I don't want to paint too rosy a picture. Like any couple, we have our ups and downs. Then again, down and up are relative terms which vary with the inertial frame of the observer. Einstein warned that c is the ultimate limit within spacetime. Exceed it and you pass out of the universe of logic. Causality loops around you like a boa; the math is beyond me. Of course, logic and causality are hardwired into our brains. It makes for some awkward moments.

I was a hero when I began this grand voyage of discovery. Like Columbus. In his time, the world was flat. People believed that if you sailed too far in any one direction, you would fall off the planet. My imaginary wife informs me that we have sailed off the edge of reality. Perhaps that explains our predicament.

(Predicament? *Opportunity*. Nobody has ever had a chance to invent themselves like this.)

The problem was that the theoretical framework supporting faster-than-light travel stopped at c. No one really knew what was beyond the absolute. Oh, there was extensive testing before any humans were put at risk. The robots, unburdened by imagination, functioned exactly as expected. The design team accelerated an entire menagerie: spiders and rats and pigs and chimps. They all came back; the ones that weren't immediately dissected lived long and uneventful lives. So I suppose there's hope.

(What he hasn't told you yet is that it wasn't just him. He's embarrassed, but it's not his fault. There were fifty-one people on this ship. Crew and colonists. His real wife was one of them. Her name was Varina.)

I remember once Varina made a joke about it. She said that science ended at c. The other side was fiction. It's not so funny anymore.

I don't know what happened to the others. All I can say is that when the ship warped, I blacked out. I have my theories. Perhaps there was a malfunction. I could be dead and this is hell. Maybe the others had reasons for stranding me here—maybe they had no choice. When I woke up there was no one else but her and she's imaginary.

I have no idea how to save myself, or, indeed, if I even need saving. My grasp of the technology that surrounds me is uncertain at best. Do any of you understand the dynamics of a particle with a mass of 10^{19} GeV? You see, most of us were specialists. Aside from the crew, there were programmers, biologists, engineers, doctors, geologists, builders. Only the least important jobs went to people with multiple skills. I'm down on the organization chart as Nutrition Stylist, but I'm also in a box labeled Mission Artist. Corporations pledged money, schoolchildren sold candles, and the arts lobby worked very hard to create a place for me on the roster. Of course, it didn't hurt my cause to be married to a civil engineer. My speciality has always been dabbling. I've spent a lot of time in front of image processors. It says on my resume that I throw pots but I haven't spun a wheel for years and who knows if there'll be clay where I'm going. I write my own songs for the voice synthesizer and can even pluck a few chords on the guitar. I do some folk dancing and tell stories and can juggle four balls at once. And now I style food. After I got into the starship program they sent me on a world tour of cooking schools. Budapest, Delhi, Paris—more dabbling. You know, I used to hate to cook; now dinner is all that matters. What's the point to doing art when you have no audience?

(You've uploaded some beautiful vids. Your stills were hanging in galleries.)

They were on late at night on back channels. All right, I'm better than some, but not as good as others. A journeyman. Yes, that sums up my condition nicely.

My condition. Should I describe a typical day? But then the notion of day is another fiction. The laws of science do not distinguish between past and future. Here the arrow of time spins at random, as in a child's game. I'm never sure when I fall asleep whether I'm going to wake up tomorrow or yesterday. Fortunately, the days are very similar. For purposes of sanity, I try to keep them that way. Artists make patterns; we impose order even where there is none. Maybe that's why I'm still here and the others are gone.

Today, then. She snuggles next to me as I wake up. Her warm breasts nudge my back. Her breath tickles my neck. I roll over and we kiss. Her hair is the color of newly-fired terra cotta. When she opens her eyes, they're green. She has wide shoulders and I can see unexpected muscle beneath her pale skin. She can appear to be any woman I can imagine. Today she is large. Magnificent. There's a kind of music to her voice. When she talks, I hear bells. She's not perfect, though: the skin under her jaw is loose, there's a mole on her temple. Clever touches. Another time she may be petite. She could have big hips. Long fingers. I think the reason she keeps changing is that, like so many women, she has a poor body image. She's far too critical of her appearance. But no matter how she looks she can't help but become herself.

We make love. That shouldn't surprise you. Sex mostly happens between the ears, not between the thighs. Sometimes I lose myself and skip ahead in time to find I'm caressing a different body. But today she remains the same; it's what we both want. I take pleasure from the way her lips part, the bloom on her cheeks. At the end a moan catches for a moment in her throat, and then she draws breath again.

(And you?)

I can't help but love her. That's the biggest problem with our marriage. I love her even though she wants to separate from me — don't deny it! Go her own way.

I hold her until the blood stops pounding; she plays with the hair on my chest. Finally I kiss her and get up. I'm hungry. There's French toast and orange juice. As always. Just once I'd like to serve her breakfast in bed but she doesn't eat. The high price of being imaginary. She watches, though.

Afterwards we visit the fx lounge. She chooses Trunk Bay on St. John: bone white Caribbean beach, palms tilting toward water the color of the sky. This is part of our imaginary past. Our honeymoon, I suppose. She keeps the temperature set at 29° Celsius. Invisible fans waft a breeze laden with her own homemade brew of coconut oil, female pheromones, and brine. She's convinced that the way to a man's heart is through his nose. The floor looks just like sand except it doesn't sift between the toes, more's the pity. We spread blankets and soak up UV in the nude. Sometimes I wish she'd program the surround to show other people on the beach, but we're alone. Always alone.

(Other women kept staring at you. You were so handsome and everyone knew you'd be famous someday. I didn't like the way you looked back. I wanted you to see me. Only me.)

I never stay in the fx lounge very long. I want to relax but I can't. I hear things, even over the ocean soundtrack. The hull creaks under the stress of whatever is outside. If I rest my head on the floor, I can feel the vibration of the ship in my molars. My imaginary wife tries to make conversation, divert me with her memories of what might have been. But somewhere on board a thermostat clicks and a vent opens. What machine makes a sound like a cough? I have to get up and see. Either the ship or my imagination is haunted. I miss Varina.

(I can be her for you. Anyone you want. Where are you going? *Wait.* At least get dressed first.)

Here's a theory. Say you're traveling at 299,792.46 kilometers per second and for some unknown reason you want to go faster. You would then exceed the speed of light propagated in a vacuum. But what if spacetime does not yield up its absolute so easily? You attempt to accelerate beyond c to, say, $c+v$, the smallest, the most infinitesimal increment in velocity you can imagine. However, there's still a little infinity lurking between c and $c+v$, no matter what value you assign to v. What if it takes forever to achieve $c+v$? What if the speed of light is not a limit, only a barrier? You could spend all time crossing it—probability's revenge.

(But that doesn't explain where everyone went.)

Maybe they realized what was happening. That we were trapped. So they step into the airlock, cycle through and leap into eternity.

(All of them? What about you?)

I see them going one by one at first. Later in groups. They ask me; I can't bring myself to make the leap. Because I have you. Obviously. I'm traumatized; I blank it out. And I only escaped alone to tell thee.

(Very dramatic; it fits you. You've always had a bigger ego than you cared to admit. But please don't go in there. It always upsets you.)

A typical day, my sweet. This is the control room of a starship. The bridge between reason and the irrational. Not what you expected? Every surface here is a screen, just like in the fx. I can black the entire room out or put on a light show of instrumentation. From here I can access the computer, view just about any corner of the ship, cook pizza for fifty-one, fiddle with the internal gravity, even vacuum-flush the toilets. If there was a god in this machine, that couch would be his throne. Once I cranked up the humidity until the air was just about saturated and then dropped the temperature twenty degrees in two minutes. My own rainstorm. A one-time miracle, though. Hell of a mess.

Unfortunately, while I can examine the inside of the ship in almost microscopic detail, I have no idea what's outside. Try the sensors and what do we get? Blank screen. Here's external telemetry . . . every readout is flat. It's maddening. I actually used to punch the walls after I brought this display mode up. *Wham*, just like that. The cursors jump into the red for a second before dropping back. Most of the time I don't even know what's being measured; all I want is a reaction. It must have shaken them, the scientists and

engineers and programmers. No data across eternity—nothing but
the uneasy play of imagination. Well, it took a while but I'm
resigned to blindness now. Whatever's out there can't be observed
from in here, at least so long as reason holds its tenuous sway. It has
to do with the Uncertainty Principle, I think. The only way to truly
understand is to participate in the phenomenon, become one with
the event itself. Through the airlock, what do you say? The leap of
faith.

(There's no way of knowing.)

No, I suppose not. Sometimes I wish the screens would show
Varina's ghost or burning babies on meathooks or Jesus Christ transfigured. I could accept any of those. Because I don't believe that
there's nothing out there. Maybe the instruments aren't sensitive
enough to register the absolute, but that doesn't mean it doesn't
exist. We have to find a way to go beyond our limitations.

But first, let's eat.

(Will you put some clothes on? You shouldn't be walking
around naked. They'll get the wrong impression.)

Yes, my sweet. See how she clings to convention? But I love her
anyway. We can stop by the room on the way to the galley. I do feel
a chill.

Dinner is always the highlight. Stimulate the senses with food
stylings and the mind with sharp wit. I allow myself two meals a day,
breakfast and dinner. I have to watch my weight; I really don't get
enough exercise prowling around the ship. Since she doesn't eat,
my imaginary wife usually tells funny stories during dinner. My
favorite is the one about the whitewater canoeing course we took.
She laughs about it now, but apparently we were almost drowned.
What a disaster! And then there was the time she played that joke
on her sister with the wasps' nest.

(I don't think she ever forgave me for that one.)

I'm going to make my specialty again. I hope you like meatloaf.
I can't remember, have I shown you my room yet? It's not as big as
the project manager's, not as tech as the captain's quarters. I suppose I could move, but this place has sentimental value. Besides,
maybe they'll come back someday; I wouldn't want them to think I
doubted them. I still keep Varina's clothes in the locker. And this is
a picture of us on our fifth anniversary. Let's see, I was thirty-four
then, which would make her thirty-eight. We married late. And the
bed that we never slept in. When I look at it now, I wonder how we
both could have fit. We would have been at each other's throats
before long; I like to stretch out at night. All right. Shirt, pants, I'm
even wearing slippers. Satisfied?

(You look wonderful.)

I'll run ahead and start cooking then. Keep them busy for a few minutes, will you? I'll see you all in the mess.

(How does he seem to you? I'm worried about him. He's been brittle lately, like a glass angel. Nothing I do makes him happy. Not like before. He was very upset at first, but at least he'd let me comfort him. When he stopped trying to remember what happened, I thought that was progress. He wanted to accept our situation—make the best of it. But month after month passed and there was no relief. I know that depressed him. And then he lost control of time. He started swinging back and forth, skipping ahead to see if anything had changed, going back to the moment he woke up alone and reliving it all again. I don't know what he needs anymore. I do my best to keep smiling. I tell him how wonderful he is. And it's whatever he wants in bed. Sometimes I worry he takes me for granted. It's not easy for me, either. I have nightmares, you know. About them. Her, especially. The real one. There's a beautiful chef's knife in the galley, twenty centimeters long, high-carbon stainless, forged in Germany. It's his favorite. Uses it for everything; he probably has it in his hand right now. In the nightmare I'm holding his knife, prowling the halls. The handle is blood-hot. When I listen at doors, I hear them breathing. I rub the flat of the blade across my lips and think of her kissing him. They all have reasons for being on board. Important things to accomplish. Why am I here? To chatter, to amuse? Any one of them could tell stories and still do something worth doing. Sleep with him? She did it and had responsibility for water distribution and sewage treatment besides. I think she was cheating on him. I know she took him for granted. It would have killed him to find out; he was in love. In my dream the knife is long and hot. I can hear her breathing. My throat feels thick. That's all.)

Are you still here talking? I swear, there's no keeping you quiet. Come on then, come on. Dinner is on the table!

Funny that the mess should seem so empty now, because before it wasn't big enough to seat everyone at once. We were supposed to go in shifts. Those little pasta things are spaetzel. From Switzerland. They're great with butter, or try them with gravy. And here's salad, produce fresh from the tanks. And this is the famous meatloaf, my very own culinary masterpiece. In fact, it's about the only work of art I've created since the ship warped.

(Except for me.)

Would you like the recipe? It's really good eating.

Faster-Than-Light Meatloaf

500 grams ground meat
2 grams salt
1 gram pepper
1/2 small onion, chopped (about 50 grams)
50 grams powdered ovobinder or 1 egg, beaten
30 grams stale bread, crumbled
1/2 green pepper, chopped (about 50 grams)
200 grams creamed corn

Preheat oven to 190° Celsius. Mix all ingredients, holding back half the creamed corn. Form into loaf and bake 50 minutes. Heat extra corn and pour over finished loaf. Serves two.

You can substitute whole corn if necessary but then you lose the topping. Creaming the corn is well worth the extra trouble, in my opinion. You know how memories attach themselves to certain aromas? I smell creamed corn and I'm in Grandma's dining room at Thanksgiving and I'm a happy little kid again. I missed creamed corn in my first marriage; Varina used to say it looked like vomit. Ground meat is, of course, rather hard to come by on this side of *c*. Luckily, there was an ample supply on board.

After dinner we usually go back to the fx and run simulations; sometimes we put on one of my vids. My imaginary wife enjoys them, or pretends to. Then we go to bed.

(Why don't you show them *Mr. Boy?* It's so layered. Every time I watch it, I see things I'd missed before.)

Truth to tell, I'm awfully sick of my old stuff, so why don't we just skip to the bells? It's an advantage I have: I don't necessarily have to stick around through the boring parts. From my inertial framework, I can clearly see that sequence is an illusion. At reasonable speeds, time's arrow appears to travel in one direction only, from the past to the future. But I'm moving at an irrational velocity.

So the bells wake me. I thought I knew every noise the ship could make but I've never heard this before. My imaginary wife is confused too. We query the computer from bed. It responds that all internal systems are green; it detects no unusual sounds. The blood stirs within me as I listen to the bells contradict its dry report. I can feel neurons firing in my fingertips; tears burn my eyes. You don't realize what this means: after all the deadening sameness, a lifegiving mystery! I roll out of bed and run naked to the control room. Nothing here has changed. The external screens are still blank. The instrumentation is conspiring with the computer. I notice that the bells are harder to hear on the bridge. They're coming from elsewhere on the ship. The ringing reminds me of church bells that call the faithful to service.

My imaginary wife wants us at the airlock. You don't have to wait for me, I'll get there as soon as I can.

(It's not my fault. When he imagined me, he did better work than he thought. Exceeded his limitations. He needed more than a mirror, so now I love him for my own reasons. I do love him; you must understand that. It's just that we can't go on like this. He's afraid to change because that might unblock his memory. But he wants me to change—and I have to remember. It wasn't just him, they did it to one another. The halls reeked of blood. At the end he was able to pull back from the madness. He found a way to survive. I have to do the same.)

What have you told them?

(Listen.)

This is the place, isn't it? The bells are ringing just outside the hull.

(Do you understand what they're saying? They're calling me to become real. I can't stay anymore. I've reached my destination.)

I wonder if this is how the others went. Varina. They answered the call of the bells. The bells. The bells are very loud here. You can't ignore them.

All right, I'll admit I'm scared. But when she turns her face up toward me, it doesn't matter. I love her. I don't want to lose her too.

(Will you come with me? I can't live without you.)

The ship seems different; the computer must have missed something. I'm sure of it. I can feel a stillness in the deck beneath my bare feet. The vibrations have stopped. I'm shivering, as if the cold of space has breeched the seals of the airlock.

(It's not space out there. It's nothing you can imagine. That's why we have to go. To see for ourselves. It's why they went. Maybe they're waiting out there for us.

Varina, waiting. How will I explain my imaginary wife to her? What will they think of one another? It's impossible.

(Everything here is impossible and yet you've created it. Make me another, a better world. I believe in your abilities.)

She reaches up and cycles open the exterior hatch. Now there's only the interior hatch left. A single barrier between me and the absolute. The bells are deafening. The ship's hull rings like a bell.

(You can do whatever you set your mind to.)

I watch my finger extend toward a flashing blue button. I no longer control my actions. Her trust sings down my arm. My muscles twitch with her faith in me.

But you, you've already decided what's beyond the hatch. Majority opinion wants me to pull back. *Don't touch that button,* you say, *don't kill yourself.* But what if you're wrong? You're seeing this from a different point of view; you're still locked in the logic of spacetime. String theory tells us that the dimension of the observer is all important. How can you possibly hope to know what is happening outside a starship that has exceeded the speed of light? You can't hear these incredible bells. And despite everything I've said, you still don't accept my imaginary wife. Has anyone ever believed in you as much as she believes in me?

When I press the button, the hatch rises open. My imaginary wife and I go together.

At first, I don't understand what's happening. I'm sprawled flat on the floor of my room and I'm disoriented, groggy. I must've fallen out of bed. I can feel the ship's vibration in my cheekbone. It's as if the decks were ringing, except there's no sound. Something's wrong.

"Varina?"

She's not where she's supposed to be. My face is stiff, as if I've been crying. I notice the scratches on my wrist. Four sticky scabs that look like bad body makeup. Blood hammers in my head as I pull myself back onto the bed. I toggle the intercom. Silence.

The rooms on either side are empty. No one in the library or fx. The control room: abandoned. There's an odd animal stink in the air. I race through the ship, bouncing off walls like a madman.

(You're not crazy.)

I find her standing beside the airlock. I don't recognize her at first. She's pale. Dazed. Her chin trembles and she comes into my arms.

(Please, please tell me you're not crazy.)

I always hated it when Varina cried. She used her tears as a lever to move me. I wouldn't be here if she hadn't sobbed. Now I realize that if I don't help this one, she'll fall apart too.

"Who are you?"

She pulls away from me and sniffs. I've said the right thing.

(Who do you want me to be?)

She smiles then and I fall in love. It makes no sense, but there it is. Impossible things happen, she tells me. There's a kind of music to her voice. When she talks, I hear bells.

Hubris

kommos: a song of lament

THIS, DEAR READER, IS A STORY ABOUT A CURSE.
Before my encounter with Kleio, the muse of history, I was like
you, large with possibility. If I had boundaries, they were invisible
to me. As yours are to you, I suppose. But now I have shrunk. I am
small enough to scuttle between black marks on a page, with no
past but what you see here, and even less future. By the time you
finish reading this, I will cease to exist.

Already your eye wanders. Is this about magic then? Of course
you don't believe; I didn't either. The Olympian gods are cruel and
barbaric lies, right? We are no longer subject to their caprice.
Everything has an explanation, or will have. Someday someone will
figure out how brain cells generate mind. It's not your problem
when the wobble of a muon throws physics into chaos.

Aha! You thought I was at a safe remove from you, shackled to
the dank stone of a Theban prison, perhaps, or bound upside-down
to a crag jutting from Homer's wine-dark sea. Sorry, but mine could
easily be the blue cubicle with the Boston fern and the *Matrix*
poster. If I were chained, it would be to a laptop and a cell phone.
Was I behind you in the lunch line the other day? Maybe I was the
one who took your favorite parking space.

146

I wish I could tell you of the lovers I left, the houses I built, the money I gave away, but she has taken all that from me, dear reader. I'd like to think I got my picture in the paper at least once. . . .

moira: fate; what must happen; that which is one's due

In ancient Greek, the muse's name is Κλειω. We meet at a writers' workshop offered by the Cambridge Adult Education Center. It's called "The Art of the Short Story." I myself have no literary ambitions but an adult education course is a great place to meet women. I actually sign up for four courses; the others are "Ballroom Dancing," "Astanga Vinyasa Yoga," and "Theater Games." I'm not sure why I choose this ploy; I wouldn't say that I am particularly shy. Perhaps I'm new in town.

Our teacher is a failed novelist who last published in 1994. He smells of cinnamon breath mints and is kind to illiterates. The other students are a denim and leather dream; I see a lotus tattoo and a green turtleneck and a Red Sox cap. Somebody wears a tie.

Is Kleio beautiful? Her glasses are tiny and rimless and obscure her brown eyes. She has a heart-shaped face but wears her hair too long. Her smile is as bright as the moon but two of her canines are crooked. Her legs are hard, her fingers stubby. You might say no, not pretty at all, but as soon as I see her, I want to be the one who takes her glasses off.

Her story is about severed heads. It is tastefully written so we are forced to take it seriously. The heads are not dead and they seem grateful for the chance to live on without their bodies. They are kept in glass bells in a locked room. Two of them are in love. The keeper of the heads is kindly and philosophical. He is something like God, except that he drinks because he can never become a living, severed head. Who would take care of them then? Also he is in love with one of the heads who love each other. He and the heads have long talks but none of them understand his pain.

A student begins the critique of Kleio's story by objecting that the heads would never be able to talk, since no matter where the cut was made, there would be severe damage to the vocal cords. There is some trifling discussion of anatomy before I raise my hand.

"The heads are a metaphor," I say. "When Shakespeare writes 'All the world's a stage,' we don't ask him if it's a proscenium or where the audience sits." I have Kleio's attention now. "I think the heads are supposed to symbolize the way some of us are cut off from what is important. We have no context, sitting in cubicles staring at computers. We have forgotten that there is more to the world than glowing phosphors."

The class ends before we get to my story, which means that we'll never know what I wrote about, since, obviously, it isn't part of *this* story. As I gather my notes, Kleio approaches and asks if I'd like to stop someplace for drinks. By the time we reach the sidewalk, it is decided that we'll go to her place.

Of course, this is totally unfair. If we choose my place, then we would see my things. You and I, dear reader. Do I have hockey trophies on the mantle? Is there Gruyère in the fridge? How big is my TV? I'm curious; aren't you? Why should that be a tragic flaw? We could open my closet, peek at my yearbooks, look under my bed. . . .

ethe: style; one's moral qualities and mental dispositions; character

She lives on the second floor of a white, vinyl-sided triple-decker just outside of Davis Square. She throws back dual bolts of her metal door and ushers me into a living room that smells of old books. They are everywhere, on shelves to the ceiling, in stacks on the Minoan Berber rug, open and scattered in spine-cracking dis-array on a plastic kidney-shaped table and a nubbly green-going-to-yellow couch . She watches me pick them up and tilt them into the sepia light of her reading lamp: Herodotus' *History*, *Forts and Fortresses* by Martin Brice, Carl Jung's *Synchronicity*, *Witchcraft Among the Azande* by E. E. Evans-Pritchard. The pages are brown and mealy.

"What do they tell you about me?" she asks.

"That you don't believe in paperbacks?"

"They fall apart if you read them too hard." She takes my hand. "Come on, I'll pour." Her hand rests in mine, light as a stunned bird, as we pass deeper into her apartment. "Red or white?"

The kitchen is done in fifties style. The round table has shining chrome legs and a ketchup-colored formica top. The chairs are upholstered in red and white vinyl. The appliances are vintage too: big steel with round shoulders.

"Where did you find all this?" I ask.

"In stores." She cradles a bottle of Kourtaki Retsina for my approval.

I don't want to spoil the moment, so I approve. She fills my glass. "You like to go antiquing then?" I say. The pale wine throws an oily, evil scent.

"Actually," she says, "I bought these things new."

"Oh, right," I say. "And you've got a closet full of heads in your bedroom."

"No, it's true." When she gives me a dark look, I sip the wine to please her. The stuff is bitter as pine sap but with a heroic effort I manage a smile.

"I don't like people who doubt," she says.

I wonder why she is tweaking me. It's clear that she hasn't seen her twenties in some time but I can't imagine that she is older than forty. I don't waste much time wondering how old people are anymore. There are children, teenagers, twenty-somethings, and the elderly. To me, everyone else is the same age. Us, for instance. You and I.

adyton: the innermost shrine; a place that must not be entered

I can see wallpaper of yellow daisies in Kleio's bedroom and an autographed picture of Joseph Campbell on the dresser before she turns out the overhead light. My hands are damp; I rub them on my chinos. Kleio is a shadow gliding past me. A match flares and she lights three candles on the night table. Her bed is a vast darkness. I could sit on it, or even lie back to wait for her, but I stand and watch the play of candle light on her face. She blows out the match and comes into my arms. She tastes of the Retsina; her breath is hot. A moan catches in her throat as I sift her long hair through my fingers. A few wisps stray across her face. I bring my hand up to the left temple of her glasses and lift them, just enough to let her know that I can. She kisses me again. The tip of her tongue darts across the ledges of my front teeth and then she pulls away.

"I'll be right back." She straightens her glasses. "Don't touch anything."

She shuts the bathroom door behind her and now I settle onto the bed. I decide it might be a good idea to take off my shoes but that's all I'm taking off. She can decide what else needs to go. I push my palm into her pillow to test its loft and am filled with doubt. Why doesn't she want me to touch anything when I am about to touch her everywhere? I flick my forefinger through the flame of the nearest candle. The fire doesn't burn me but the question does. Don't touch anything. The nightstand has two drawers. Don't touch. I can hear water running in the bathroom. *Don't*. The drawers have brass ring pulls.

Is that the difference between us, dear reader? That you wait? If you need something to do, you tuck your wallet into your shoe or hum "They Can't Take That Away From Me." That's why you know who your mother is and what you had for breakfast this morning and where you live and when you lost your virginity.

Well, she takes everything away from me but what's here before you. Because when she says *don't*, I hear *you must*.

hamartia: harm done through self-will; immoderate behavior; error

I don't make the obvious choice; it's the bottom drawer that I pull open. It isn't empty. I slide the candle to the edge of the nightstand and see the *Verizon Yellow Pages, Cambridge and Vicinity*. But I disturb something, something that lives in the top drawer, something that moves with a silky slither, like the whisper of skin on skin, and I hear myself breathing and the door latch clicks and I kick the drawer shut but it is too late because Kleio comes out of the blinding, bathroom light, Kleio, daughter of Zeus and Memory, whom men call the muse of history, and she is naked and she is huge, she has to stoop to fit through the doorway and she screams at me *What have you done?* only it is the roar of blood in my ears that I hear as she puts her enormous hand on my head and pushes down and says *What I would have given you, little man* and I hear bone snap and organs burst as she says it again *Little man, little man* and she crushes me until my world goes flat in black and white and I lose almost all of myself. And now I am no longer a man at all, but the helpless character squirming under your gaze. What is it you see? A puppet cursed to dance when a stranger staring at glowing phosphors types

d . . . a . . . n . . . c . . . e.

Are you satisfied? I hope you've enjoyed your little catharsis at my expense. But what I still don't get is the difference between us. You and I, *dear* reader. Yes, I looked where I wasn't supposed to, and so here I am. But you, you were right at my shoulder when I kissed Kleio and you know you weren't going to avert your eyes if we had fallen into bed. You looked too; what else would you be doing here?

Now I've said something wrong. You're sure that I'm not supposed to act this way. After all, this is just a story somebody wrote. You don't have any part in it, do you? You're not complicit, you're just reading—improving your mind perhaps, or whiling away the idle hour. Well then, here's one last chance to increase your vocabulary.

hubris: **willful blindness; overbearing presumption; arrogance**

I know you smiled at one of my jokes. Was that a tingle of fear back there? No matter. You're real and I don't even have a name. All right, then. I'm done, and you can go on.

Go on.

Go on to the next story, damn you!

Glass Cloud

PHILLIP WING WAS SURPRISED WHEN HE FOUND OUT what his wife had been doing with her Wednesday afternoons. "You've joined what?"

"A friend invited me to sit in on a study group at the mission." Daisy refilled her glass from a decanter. "I've been twice, that's all. I haven't joined anything."

"What are you studying?" He sat up.

"Sitting in, Phil—it's not like I intend to convert. I'm just browsing." She sipped her wine and waited for Wing to settle back. "They haven't said a word about immortality yet. Mostly they talk about history."

"History? History? The messengers haven't been here long enough to learn anything about history."

"Seven years. First contact was seven years ago." She sighed and suddenly she was lecturing. "Cultural evolution follows predictable patterns. There are interesting correlations between humanity and some of the other species that the messengers have contacted."

Wing shook his head. "I don't get it. We've been together what? Since '51? For years all that mattered was the inn. They nuke Geneva, so what? Revolution in Mexico, who cares?"

152

"I care about you," she said.

That stopped him for a moment. Absently, he filled his glass from the decanter and took a gulp before he realized that it was the synthetic Riesling that she was trying out as a house wine. He swallowed it with difficulty. "Who's the friend?"

"What?"

"The friend who asked you to the mission. Who is he?" Wing was just guessing that it was a man. It was a good guess.

"A regular." Daisy glanced away from him and nodded at the glow sculpture on the wall. "You know Jim McCauley."

All he knew was that McCauley was a local artist who had made a name for himself in fancy light bulbs. Wing watched the play of pastel light across her face, trying to see her as this regular might see her. Daisy was not beautiful, although she could be pretty when she paid attention to detail. She did not bother to comb her hair every time the wind caught it nor did she much care about the wrinkles at the corners of her eyes. Hers was an intelligent, hard-edged, New Hampshire Yankee face. She looked like someone who would know about things that mattered. Wing had good reasons for loving her; he slid across the couch and nuzzled under her ear.

"Don't tickle." She laughed. "You're invited, you know." She pulled back, but not too far. "The new messenger, Ndavu, is interested in art. He's mentioned the Glass Cloud several times. You really ought to go. You might learn something." Having made her pitch, she kissed him.

Phillip Wing had no time to study history; he was too busy worrying about the Second Wonder of the World. Solon Petropolus, erratic scion of the Greek transportation conglomerate, had endowed the Seven Wonders Foundation with an immense fortune. The foundation was Petropolus's megalomaniacal gift to the ages. It commissioned constructions—some called them art—on a monumental scale. It was the vulgar purpose of the Wonders to attract crowds. They were to be places where a French secretaire or a Peruvian campesino or even an Algerian mullah might come to contemplate the enduring spirit of Solon Petropolus, the man who embalmed himself in money.

Wing had spent five years at Yale grinding out a practitioner's degree, but when he graduated he was certain that he had made a mistake. He was offered several jobs but not one that he wanted. He had studied architecture with the impossibly naive hope that someday, someone would let him design a building as large as his ambitions. He wanted to build landmarks, not program factories to fabricate this year's model go-tubes for the masses too poor to afford real housing. Instead of working he decided to spend the summer after graduation hiking the Appalachian Trial. Alone.

As he climbed Webster Cliff in Crawford Notch, he played a poetry game against his fatigue. A zephyr massages the arthritic tree. It was only a few kilometers to the Appalachian Mountain Club's Mispah Spring Hut where he would spend the night. Plodding promiscuously into a tangerine heaven. Wing made it a game because he did not really believe in poetry. Stone teeth bite solipsistic toes. A low cloud was sweeping through the Notch just as the late afternoon sun dipped out of the overcast into a jagged band of blue sky on the horizon. Something strange happened to the light then and for an instant the cloud was transformed. A cloud of glass.

"A glass cloud," he muttered. There was no one to hear him. He stopped, watching the cloud but not seeing it, experiencing instead an overpowering inner vision. A glass cloud. The image swelled like a bubble. He could see himself floating with it and for the first time he understood what people meant when they talked about inspiration. He kept thinking of the glass cloud all the way to the hut, all that night. He was still thinking of it weeks later when he reached the summit of Kahtadin, the northern terminus of the trail, and thought of it on the hover to Connecticut. He did some research and made sketches, taking a strange satisfaction from the enormous uselessness of it. That fall Seven Wonders announced the opening of the North American design competition. Phillip Wing, an unregistered, unemployed, uncertain architect of twenty-seven had committed the single inspiration of his life to disk and entered the competition because he had nothing better to do.

Now as he looked down out of the hover at Crawford Notch, Wing could not help but envy that young man stalking through the forest, seething with ambition and, at the same time, desperately afraid he was second-rate. At age twenty-seven Wing could not imagine the trouble a thirty-five-year-old could get into. Schedules and meetings, compromises and contracts. That eager young man had not realized what it would mean to capture the glittering prize at the start of a career, so that everything that came after seemed lackluster. That fierce young man had never been truly in love or watched in horror as time abraded true love.

A roadbuster was eating the section of NH Route 302 that passed through the Notch. Its blades flayed the ice-slicked asphalt into chunks. Then a wide-bladed caterpillar scooped the bituminous rubble up and into trucks bound for the recycling plant in Concord. Once the old highway had been stripped down to its foundation course of gravel, crews would come to lay the Glass Cloud's underground track. After thaw a paver the size of a brachiosaurus would regurgitate asphalt to cover the track. Route 302 through Crawford Notch was the last phase of the ninety-seven kilometer track which followed existing roads through the heart of the White Mountain National Forest.

"Won't be long now," said the hover pilot. "They're talking a power-up test in ten weeks. Three months tops."

Wing said nothing. Ten weeks. Unless another preservationist judge could be convinced to meddle or Seven Wonders decided it had spent enough and sued him for the overruns. The project was two years late already and had long since gobbled up a generous contingency budget. Wing knew he had made mistakes, although he admitted them only to himself. Sometimes he worried that he had wasted his chance. He motioned to the pilot who banked the hover and headed south toward North Conway.

The hover was the property of Gemini Fabricators, the lead company in the consortium that had won the contract to build the Cloud and its track. Wing knew that the pilot had instructions to keep him in the air as long as possible. Every minute he spent inspecting track was one minute less he would have to go over the checklist for the newly completed docking platform with Laporte and Alz. Laporte, the project manager, made no secret of his dismay at having to waste valuable time with Wing. Laporte had made it clear that he believed Wing was largely to blame for the project's misfortunes.

The hover settled onto its landing struts like an old man easing into a hot bath. Wing waited for the dirty snow and swirls of litter to subside. The job site was strewn with coffee cups, squashed beer bulbs, and enough vitabulk wrap to cover Mount Washington.

Wing popped the hatch and was greeted by a knife-edged wind; there was no welcoming committee. He crossed the frozen landing zone toward the field offices, a group of linked commercial go-tubes that looked like a chain of plastic sausages some careless giant had dropped. The Seven Wonders tube was empty and the telelink was ringing. Wing would have answered it except that was exactly the kind of thing that made Laporte mad. Instead he went next door to Gemini looking for Fred Alz. Wing suspected that some of the project's problems arose from the collusion between Laporte and Alz, Gemini's field super. A woman he did not recognize sat at a

CAD screen eating a vitabulk donut and staring dully at details of the ferroplastic structural grid.

"Where is everybody?" said Wing.

"They went to town to see him off."

"Him?"

"I think it's a him. A messenger: No-doubt or some such."

"What was he doing here?"

"Maybe he was looking for converts. With immortality we might actually have a chance of finishing." She took a bite of donut and looked at him for the first time. "Who the hell are you anyway?"

"The architect."

"Yeah?" She did not seem impressed. "Where's your hard hat?"

Wing knew what they all said about him: that he was an arrogant son of a bitch with a chip on his shoulder the size of the Great Pyramid. He spent some time living up to his reputation. The engineer did not stay for the entire tirade; she stalked out, leaving Wing to stew over the waste of an afternoon. Shortly afterward, Alz and Laporte breezed in, laughing. Probably at him.

"Sorry to keep you waiting, Phil," Laporte held up both hands in mock surrender, "but there's good news."

"It's two-thirty-eight! This plugging project is twenty-one months late and you're giving tours to goddamned aliens."

"Phil." Alz put a hand on his shoulder. "Phil, listen to me for a minute, will you?" Wing wanted to knock it away. "Mentor Ndavu has made a generous offer on behalf of the commonwealth of messengers." Alz spoke quickly, as if he thought Wing might explode if he stopped. "He's talking major funding, a special grant that could carry us right through to completion. He says the messengers want to recognize outstanding achievement in the arts, hard cash and lots of it—you ought to be proud is what you ought to be. We get it and chances are we can float the Cloud out of here by Memorial Day. Ten weeks, Phil."

Wing looked from Alz to Laporte. There was something going on, something peculiar and scary. People did not just hand out open-ended grants to rescue troubled projects for no reason—especially not the messengers, who had never shown more than a polite interest in any of the works of humanity. Three years of autotherapy had taught Wing that he had a tendency to make conspiracy out of coincidence. But this was real. First Daisy, now the Cloud; the aliens were getting close. "Could we do it without them?"

Alz laughed.

"They're not monsters, Phil," said Laporte.

A tear dribbled down Wing's cheek. His eyes always watered when he sniffed too much Focus. The two-meter CAD screen that filled one wall of his studio displayed the south elevation of the proposed headquarters for SEE-Coast, the local telelink utility. There was something wrong with the row of window dormers set into the new hip roof. He blinked and the computer replaced the sketch with a menu. A doubleblink changed the cursor on the screen from draw to erase mode. His eyes darted; the windows disappeared.

He had known that the SEE-Coast project was going to be more trouble than it was worth. Jack Congemi was trying to cram too much building onto too small a site, a sliver of river front wedged between an eighteenth century chandlery and a nineteenth century hotel. If he could have gotten a variance to build higher than five stories, there would have been no problem. But SEE-Coast was buying into Portsmouth's exclusive historic district, where the zoning regulations were carved in granite.

It was a decent commission and the cost-plus fee contract meant he would make good money, but like everything he had done since the Cloud, Wing was bored with it. The building was pure kitsch: a tech bunker hiding behind a Georgian facade. It was like all the rest of his recent projects: clients buying a safe name brand and to hell with the vision. Of course they expected him to deliver stick-built at a price competitive with Korean robot factories. Never mind that half the local trades were incompetent and the other half were booked.

At last he could no longer bear to look at the monster. "Save it." He closed his eyes and still saw those ugly windows burned on the insides of his lids.

"Saved," said the computer.

He sat, too weary to move, and let his mind soak in the blackness of the empty screen. He knew he had spent too much time recently worrying about the Cloud and the messengers. It was perverse since everything was going so well. All the checklists were now complete, pre-flight start-up tests were underway and Seven Wonders had scheduled dedication ceremonies for Memorial Day. The opening of the Second Wonder of the Modern World would have been reason enough for a news orgy, but now the messengers' involvement was beginning to overshadow Wing's masterpiece. Telelink reporters kept calling him from places like Bangkok and

Kinshasa and Montevideo to ask him about the aliens. Why were they supporting the Cloud? When would they invite humanity to join their commonwealth and share in their immortality technology? What were they really like?

He had no answers. Up until now he had done his best to avoid meeting the alien, Ndavu. Like most intelligent people, Wing had been bitterly disappointed by the messengers. Their arrival had changed nothing: there were still too many crazy people with nukes; the war in Mexico dragged on. Although they had been excruciatingly diplomatic, it was clear that human civilization impressed them not at all. They kept their secrets to themselves — had never invited anyone to tour their starships or demonstrated the technique for preserving minds after death. The messengers claimed that they had come to Earth for raw materials and to spread some as-yet vague message of galactic culture. Wing guessed that they held humanity in roughly the same esteem with which the conquistadors had held the Aztecs. But he could hardly admit that to reporters.

"Something else?" The computer disturbed his reverie; it was set to prompt him for new commands after twenty minutes of inactivity.

He leaned back in his chair and stretched, accidentally knocking his print of da Vinci's "John the Baptist" askew. "What the hell time is it, anyway?"

"One-fourteen-thirty-five A.M., 19 February 2056."

He decided that he was too tired to get up and fix the picture.

"Here you are." Daisy appeared in the doorway. "Do you know what time it is?" She straightened the Baptist and then came up behind his chair. "Something wrong?"

"SEE-Coast."

She began to massage his shoulders and he leaned his head back against her belly. "Can't it wait until the morning?"

The skin was itchy where the tear had dried. Wing rubbed it, considering.

"Would you like to come to bed?" She bent over to kiss him and he could see that she was naked beneath her dressing gown. "All work and no play. . . ."

The stink of doubt that he had tried so hard to perfume with concentration enhancers still clung to him. "But what if I wake up tomorrow and can't work on this crap? What if I don't believe in what I'm doing anymore? I can't live off the Glass Cloud forever."

"Then you'll find something else." She sifted his hair through her fingers.

He plastered a smile on his face and slipped a hand inside her gown—more from habit than passion. "I love you."

"It's better in bed." She pulled him from his chair. "Just you keep quiet and follow Mother Goodwin, young man. She'll take the wrinkles out of your brow."

He stumbled as he came into her arms but she caught his weight easily. She gave him a fierce hug and he wondered what she had been doing all evening.

"I've been thinking," he said softly, "about this party. I give in: go ahead if you want and invite Ndavu. I promise to be polite—but that's all." He wanted to pull back and see her reaction but she would not let him go. "That's what you want, isn't it?"

"That's one of the things I want," she said. Her cheek was hot against his neck.

Piscataqua House was built by Samuel Goodwin in 1763. A handsome building of water-struck brick and granite, it was said to have offered the finest lodging in the colonial city of Portsmouth, New Hampshire. Nearly three hundred years later it was still an inn and Daisy Goodwin was its keeper.

Wing had always been intrigued by the way Daisy's pedigree had affected her personality. It was not so much the old money she had inherited—most of which was tied up in the inn. It was the way she could bicycle around town and point out the elementary school she had attended, the Congregational Church where her grandparents had married, the huge black oak in Prescott Park that greatgreat-uncle Josiah had planted during the Garfield administration. She lived with the easy grace of someone who was exactly where she belonged, doing exactly what she had always intended to do.

Wing had never belonged. He had been born in Taipei but had fled to the States with his Taiwanese father after his American mother had been killed in the bloody reunification riots of 2026. His father, a software engineer, had spent the rest of a bitter life searching in vain for what he had left on Taiwan. Philip Wing had gone to elementary schools in Cupertino, California, Waltham, Massachusetts, Norcross, Georgia and Orem, Utah. He knew very little about either side of his family. "When you are old enough to understand," his father would always say. "Someday we will talk. But not now." Young Philip learned quickly to stop asking; too many questions could drive his father into one of his binges. He would dose himself to the brink of insensibility with memory sweeteners and stay up half the night weeping and babbling in the

Taiwanese dialect of Fujian. His father had died when Wing was a junior at Yale. He had never met Daisy. Wing liked to think that the old man would have approved.

Wing tried hard to belong—at least to Daisy, if not to Piscataqua House. He had gutted the Counting House, a hundred-and-ninety-five-year-old business annex built by the merchant Goodwins, and converted it into his offices. He was polite to the guests despite their annoying ignorance about the Cloud; most people thought it had been designed by Solon Petropolus. He helped out when she was short-handed, joined the Congregational Church despite a complete lack of religiosity and served two terms on the City's Planning Board. He endured the dreaded black-tie fund raisers of the National Society of Colonial Dames for Daisy's sake and took her to the opera in Boston at least twice a year even though it gave him a headache. Now she was asking him to play host to an alien.

An intimate party of twenty-three had gathered in the Hawthorne parlor for a buffet in Ndavu's honor. Laporte had flown down from North Conway with his wife, Jolene. Among the locals were the Hathaways, who were still bragging about their vacation on Orbital Three, Magda Rudowski, Artistic Director of Theater-by-the-Sea, the new City Manager, whose name Wing could never remember, and her husband, who never had anything to say, Reverend Smoot, the reformalist minister and the Congemis, who owned SEE-Coast. There were also a handful of Ndavu's hangers-on, among them the glow sculptor, Jim McCauley.

Wing hated these kinds of parties. He had about as much chat in him as a Trappist monk. To help ease his awkwardness, Daisy sent him out into the room with their best cut-glass appetizer to help the guests get hungry. He wandered through other people's conversations, feeling lost.

"Oh, but we love it up north," Jolene Laporte was saying. "It's peaceful and the air is clean and the mountains . . ."

". . . are tall," Laporte finished her sentence and winked as he reached for the appetizer. "But it's plugging cold—Jesus!" Magda Rudowski laughed nervously. Laporte looked twisted; he had the classic hollow stare, as if his eyes had just been fished out of a jar of formaldehyde.

"Don't make fun, Leon," Jolene said, pouting. "You love it too. Why, just the other day he were saying how nice it would be to stay on after the Cloud opened. I think he'd like to bask in his glory for a while." She sprayed a test dose from the appetizer onto her wrist and took a tentative sniff. "How legal is this?"

"Just some olfactory precursors," Wing said, "and maybe twenty ppm of Glow."

"Maybe I'm not the only one who deserves credit, Jolene. Maybe Phillip here wants a slice of the glory too."

Daisy wheeled the alien into the parlor. "Phillip, I'd like you to meet Mentor Ndavu." Wing had never seen her so happy.

The alien was wearing a loose, black pinstriped suit. He might have been a corporate vice-president with his slicked-back gray hair and long, ruddy face except that he was over two meters tall. He had to slump to fit into his wheel chair and his knees stuck out like bumpers. The chair whined as it rolled; Ndavu leaned forward extending his hand. Wing found himself counting the fingers. Of course there were five. The messengers were nothing if not thorough.

"I have been wanting to meet you, Phillip."

Wing shook hands. Ndavu's grip was firm and oddly sticky, like plastic wrap. The messenger grinned. "I am very much interested in your work."

"As we all are interested in yours." Reverend Smoot brushed past Wing. "I, for one, would like to know . . ."

"Reverend," Ndavu spoke softly so that only those closest to him could hear, "must we always argue?"

". . . would like to know, Mentor," continued Smoot in his pulpit voice, "how your people intend to respond to the advisory voted yesterday by the Council of Churches."

"Perhaps we should discuss business later, Reverend." Ndavu shot a porcelain smile at Laporte. "Leon, this must be your wife, Jolene."

Daisy got Wing's attention by standing utterly still. Between them passed an unspoken message which she punctuated by a tilting of her head. Wing's inclination was to let Smoot and Ndavu go at each other but he took firm hold of the Reverend's arm. "Would you like to see the greenhouse, Magda?" he said, turning the minister toward the actress. "The freesias are just coming into bloom; the place smells like the Garden of Eden. How about you, Reverend?" Glowering, Smoot allowed himself to be led away.

A few of the other guests had drifted out into what had once been the stables. Daisy's parents had replaced the old roof with sheets of clear optical plastic during the Farm Crusade, converting the entire wing into a greenhouse. In those days the inn might have closed without a reliable source of fresh produce. Magda Rudowski paused to admire a planter filled with tuberous begonias.

Reverend Smoot squinted through the krylac roof at the stars, as if seeking heavenly guidance. "I just have to wonder," he said, "who the joke is on."

Wing and Magda exchanged glances.

"How can you look at flowers when that alien is undermining the foundations of our Judeo-Christian heritage?"

Magda touched Smoot's sleeve. "It's a party, Reverend."

"If they don't believe in a God, how the hell can they apply for tax-exempt status? 'Look into the sun,' what kind of message is that? A year ago they wouldn't say a word to you unless you were from some government or conglomerate. Then they buy up some abandoned churches and suddenly they're preaching to anyone who'll listen. Look into the sun my ass." He took two stiff-legged steps toward the hydroponic benches and then spun toward Wing and Magda Rudowski. "You look into the sun too long and you go blind." He stalked off.

"I don't know what Daisy was thinking of when she invited him," Martha said.

"He married us," said Wing.

She sighed, as if that had been an even bigger mistake. "Shall I keep an eye on him for you?"

"Thanks." Wing thought then to offer her the appetizer. She inhaled a polite dose and Wing took a whiff himself, thinking he might as well make the best of what threatened to be bad business. The Glow loosened the knot in his stomach; he could feel his senses snapping to attention. They looked at each other and giggled. "Hell with him," he said, and then headed back to the parlor.

Jack Congemi was arguing in the hall with Laporte. "Here's just the man to settle this," he said.

"Congemi here thinks telelink is maybe going to put the trades out of business." Laporte spoke as though his brain were parked in lunar orbit and he were hearing his own words with a time delay. "Tell him you can't fuse plasteel gun emplacements in Tijuana sitting at a console in Greeley, Colorado. Makes no plugging difference how good your robotics are. You got to be there."

"The Koreans did it. They had sixty percent completion on Orbital Three before a human being ever set foot on it."

"Robots don't have a union," said Laporte. "The fusers do."

"Before telelink, none of us could have afforded to do business from a beautiful little nowhere like Portsmouth." Congemi liked to see himself as the local prophet of telelink; Wing had heard this sermon before. "We would have all been jammed into some urb hard by the jump port and container terminals and transitways and maglev trunks. Now no one has to go anywhere."

"But without tourists," said Wing, "inns close."

Congemi held his hands out like an archbishop blessing a crowd. "Of course, people will always travel for pleasure. And we at SEE-Coast will continue to encourage people to tour our beautiful Granite State. But we are also citizens of a new state, a state which is being born at this very moment. The world information state."

"Don't care where they come from." Laporte's voice slurred. "Don't care whether they're citizens of the plugging commonwealth of messengers, just so long as they line up to see my Cloud." He poked a finger into Wing's shoulder as if daring him to object.

It was not the first time he had heard Laporte claim the Cloud as his. Wing considered throwing the man out and manners be damned. Instead he said, "We'll be eating soon," and went into the parlor.

For a time he was adrift on the tides of the party, smiling too much and excusing himself as he nudged past people on his way to nowhere. He felt angry but the problem was that he was not exactly sure why. He told himself that it was all Daisy's fault. Her party. He aimed the appetizer at his face and squeezed off a piggish dose.

"Phillip. Please, do you have a moment?" Ndavu gave him a toothy grin. There was something strange about his teeth: they were too white, too perfect. He was talking to Mr. and Mrs. Hatcher Poole III, who were standing up against the wall like a matched set of silver lamps.

"Mentor Ndavu."

"Mentor is a title my students have given me. I am your guest and we are friends, are we not? You must call me Ndavu."

"Ndavu." Wing bowed slightly.

"May I?" The messenger turned his wheelchair to Wing and held out his hand for the appetizer. "I had hoped for the chance to observe mind-altering behavior this evening." He turned the appetizer over in his long spiderlike hands and then abruptly sprayed it into his face. The entire room fell silent and then the messenger sneezed. No one had ever heard of such a thing, a messenger sneezing. The Pooles looked horrified, as if the alien might explode next. Someone across the room laughed and conversation resumed.

"It seems to stimulate the chemical senses." Ndavu wrinkled his nose. "It acts to lower the threshold of certain olfactory and taste receptors. There are also trace elements of another substance—some kind of indole hallucinogen?"

"I'm an architect, not a drug artist."

Ndavu passed the appetizer on to Mrs. Poole. "Why do you ingest these substances?" The alien's skin was perfect too; he had no moles, no freckles, not even a wrinkle.

"Well," she said, still fluttering from his sneeze, "they are non-fattening."

Her husband laughed nervously. "I take it, sir, that you have never eaten vitabulk."

"Vitabulk? No." The messenger leaned forward in his wheel-chair. "I have seen reports."

"I once owned a bulkery in Nashua," continued Hatcher Poole. "The ideal product, in many ways: cheap to produce, nutritionally complete, an almost indefinite shelf life. Without it, hundreds of millions would starve—"

"You see," said Wing, "it tastes like insulation."

"Depends on the genetics of your starter batch," said Poole. "They're doing wonders these days with texturization."

"Bread flavor isn't that far off." Mrs. Poole had squeezed off a dose that they could probably smell in Maine. "And everything tastes better after a nice appetizer."

"Of course, we're serving natural food tonight," said Wing. "Daisy has had cook prepare a traditional meal in your honor, Ndavu." He wished she were here chatting and he was in the kitchen supervising final preparations. "However some people prefer to use appetizers no matter what the menu."

"Prefer?" said Poole, who had passed the appetizer without using it. "A damnable addiction, if you ask me."

Two white-coated busboys carried a platter into the parlor, its contents hidden beneath a silver lid. They set it on the mahogany sideboard beneath a portrait of Nathaniel Hawthorne brooding. "Dinner is served!" The guests lined up quickly.

"Plates and utensils here, condiments on the tea table." Daisy's face was flushed with excitement. She was wearing that luminous blue dress he had bought for her in Boston, the one that had cost too much. "Cook will help you find what you want. Enjoy." Bechet, resplendent in his white cook's hat, placed a huge chafing dish beside the silver tray. With a flourish, Peter the busboy removed the lid from the silver tray. The guests buzzed happily and crowded around the sideboard, blocking Wing's view. He did not have to see the food, however; his hypersensitized olfactories were drenched in its aroma.

As he approached the sideboard, he could hear Bechet murmuring. "Wieners, sir. Hot dogs."

"Oh my god, Hal, potato salad—mayonnaise!"

"Did he say dog?"

"Nothing that amazing about relish. I put up three quarts myself last summer. But mustard!"

"No, no, I'll just have to live with my guilt."

"Corn dog or on a bun, Mr. Wing?" Bechet was beaming.

"On a bun please, Bechet." Wing held out his plate. "They seem to like it."

"I hope so, sir."

The guests were in various stages of gustatory ecstasy. The fare was not at all unusual for the wealthy; they ate at least one natural meal a day and meat or fish once a week. For others, forty-five grams of USDA guaranteed pure beef frankfurter was an extravagance: Christmas dinner, birthday treat. One of the strangers from the mission was the first to go for thirds. Ndavu had the good manners not to eat at all; perhaps he had orders not to alarm the natives with his diet.

The party fragmented after dinner; most guests seemed eager to put distance between themselves and the messenger. It was a strain being in the same room with Ndavu; Wing could certainly feel it. Daisy led a group of gardeners to the greenhouse. Others gathered to watch the latest episode of *Jesus On First*. The religious spectacle of the hard-hitting Jesus had made it one of the most popular scripted sports events on telelink. The more boisterous guests went to the inn's cellar bar. Wing alone remained trapped in the Hawthorne parlor with the guest of honor.

"It has been a successful evening," said Ndavu, "so far."

"You came with an agenda?" Wing saw Peter the busboy gawking at the alien as he gathered up dirty plates.

Ndavu smiled. "Indeed I did. You are a very hard man to meet, Phillip. I am not sure why that is, but I hope now that things will be different. Will you visit me at the mission?"

Wing shrugged. "Maybe sometime." He was thinking to himself that he had the day after the heat death of the universe free.

"May I consider that a commitment?"

Wing stooped to pick up a pickle slice before someone—probably Peter—squashed it into the Kashgar rug. "I'm glad your evening has been a success," he said, depositing the pickle on Peter's tray as he went by.

"Before people accept the message, they must first accept the messenger." He said it like a slogan. "You will forgive me if I observe that yours is a classically xenophobic species. The work has just begun; it will take years."

"Why do you do it? I mean you, personally."

"My motives are various—even I find it difficult to keep track of them all." The messenger squirmed in the wheelchair and his knee brushed Wing's leg. "In that I suspect we may be alike, Phillip. The fact is, however, that my immediate concern is not spreading the message. It is getting your complete attention."

The alien was very close. "My attention?" Rumor had it that beneath their perfect exteriors lurked vile creatures, unspeakably grotesque. Evolutionary biologists maintained that it was impossible that the messengers were humanoid.

"You should know that you are being considered for a most prestigious commission. I can say no more at this time but if you will visit me, I think we may discuss . . ."

Wing had stopped listening to Ndavu—saved by an argument out in the foyer. An angry man was shouting. A woman pleaded. Daisy. "Excuse me," he said, turning away from Ndavu.

"No, I won't go without you." The angry man was the glow sculptor, McCauley. He was about Wing's age, maybe a few years older. There was gray in his starchy brush of brown hair. He might have been taken for handsome in a blunt way except that his blue and silver stretchsuit was five years out of date and he was sweating.

"For God's sake, Jimmy, would you stop it?" Daisy was holding out a coat and seemed to be trying to coax him into it. "Go home. Please. This isn't the time."

"You tell me when. I won't keep putting it off."

"Something the matter?" Wing went up on the balls of his feet. If it came to a fight he thought he could hold his own for the few seconds it would take reinforcements to arrive. But it was ridiculous, really; people in Portsmouth did not fight anymore. He could hear someone running toward the foyer from the kitchen. A knot of people clustered at the bottom of the stairs. He would be all right, he thought. "Daisy?" Still, it was a damned nuisance.

He was shocked by her reaction. She recoiled from him as if he were a monster out of her worst nightmare and then sank down onto the sidechair and started to cry. He ought to have gone to her then but McCauley was quicker.

"I'm sorry," he said. He took the coat from her nerveless hands and kissed her quickly on the cheek. Wing wanted to throw him to the floor but found he could not move. Nobody in the room moved but the stranger his wife had called Jimmy. Something in the way

she had said his name had paralyzed Wing. All night long he had
sensed a tension at the party but, like a fool, he had completely mis-
interpreted it. Everyone knew; if he moved they might all start
laughing.

"Shouldn't have . . ." McCauley was murmuring something; his
hand was on the door. "Sorry."

"You don't walk out now, do you?" Wing was proud of how
steady his voice was. Daisy's shoulders were shaking. Her sculptor
did not have an answer; he did not even stop to put on his coat. As
the door closed behind him Wing had the peculiar urge to call
Congemi out of the crowd and make him take responsibility for this
citizen of the world information state. His brave new world was
filled with people who had no idea of how to act in public.

"Daisy?"

She would not look at him. Although he felt as if he were standing stark naked in the middle of the foyer of the historic Piscataqua
House, he realized no one was looking at him.

Except Ndavu.

"I said you've had enough." The dealer pushed Wing's twenty back
across the bar. "There's such a thing as an overdose, you know. And
I'd be liable."

Wing stared at the twenty, as if Andy Jackson might offer some
helpful advice.

"The cab is waiting. You ought to go home."

Wing glanced up, trying to bring the flash bar into focus.

"I said go home."

Wing could not go home. The morning after the party Wing
had moved out of Piscataqua House. He was living in his go-tube at
a rack just off the Transitway. A burly hack appeared beside Wing
and put an arm around him. The next thing he knew he was outside.

"Is cold, yes?" The hack stamped his feet against the icy pavement and smiled; his teeth were decorated with Egyptian hiero-
glyphs. He was wearing thin joggers and the gold sweat suit of the
Rockingham Cab Company. Wing wondered how the man kept
from freezing.

"The Stop Inn," said Wing. "Your rig have heat?"

"Plenty heat, you bet yes."

They squeezed into the wedge-shaped pedicab; the big hack
slithered into the tiny driver's couch and slid his feet into the
toe clips. A musty locker-room smell lingered in the passenger

compartment. There was no space heater but after a few minutes of the hack's furious peddling the smell turned into a warm stink.

They were caught briefly in the usual jam on Islington Street. About twenty protesters had gathered in front of what had once been the Church of the Holy Spirit and was now the messengers' mission to the states of New Hampshire and Maine. A few carried electric candles; others brandished hand-lettered signs that said things like NO RELIGION WITHOUT GOD and LOOK INTO THE BIBLE. The rest circulated among the stalled bicycles and pedicars, distributing anti-messenger propaganda. On a whim Wing opened his window just wide enough to accept a newsletter. "Go with Jesus," said the protester. As the pedicab rolled away, the newsletter slipped out of his hands and fell onto his lap. All he could read by street light were headlines: SCIENCE SAYS NO IMMORTALITY and ALABAMA BANS ALIENS and HOW THEY REALLY LOOK.

"Ever scan the message?" The hack nodded back at the mission; Wing shook his head. "No worse than any other church; better than some, yes? They feed you, give you a warm bed for as long as you want. Course, they don't explain much, except to tell you there's no such thing as pleasure." He put a hand on his thigh. "Or pain." He squeezed. "Ain't the way life tastes to me."

As they approached Exit 6, they passed through a neighborhood of shabby go-tube parks and entered the strip. The strip was an architectural tumor that had metastasized to Transitway exits from Portsmouth, Virginia to Portsmouth, New Hampshire—a garish clump of chain vitabulk joints, clothes discounters, flash bars, surrogatoriums, motels, data shops, shoe stores, tube racks, bike dealers, too many warehouses, and a few moribund tourist traps selling plastic lobsters and screaming T-shirts. What was not malled was connected by optical plastic tunnels, once transparent but now smudged with sea salt and pollution. In the midst of it all squatted a US Transit Service terminal of bush-hammered concrete that was supposed to look like rough-cut granite. Docked at the terminal were semis and container trains and red-white-and-blue USTS busses in all sizes, from the enormous double-decked trunk line rigs to local twenty-passenger carryvans.

The Stop Inn was on the far edge of the strip, a six-story plastic box that looked like yet another warehouse except for the five-story stop sign painted on its east facade. There were hook-ups for about forty go-tubes on the top three floors and another forty fixed tubes on the bottom three. The stairwell smelled of smoke and disinfectant.

Wing and Daisy had customized the go-tube on spare weekends right after they had been married but they had only used it twice: vacations at the Disneydome in New Jersey and the Grand Canyon. Somehow they could never find time to get away. The tube had an oak roll-top desk, a queen-sized Murphy bed with a gel mattress, and Wing's one extravagance: an Alvar Aalto loveseat. The ceiling was a single sheet of mirror plastic that Wing had nearly broken his back installing. At the far end was a microwave, sink, toilet, and mirror set in a wall surround of Korean tile that Daisy had spent two months picking out. There was a monitor and keyboard mounted on a flex-arm beside the bed. The screen was flashing; he had a message.

"Phillip." Ndavu sat in an office at an enormous desk; he looked like a banker who had just realized he had made a bad loan. "I am calling to see if there's anything I can do to help . . ."

Wing paused the message and poured himself two fingers of scotch—no ice, no water.

". . . I want you to know how sorry I am about the way things have turned out. I have just seen Daisy and I must tell you that she is extremely upset. If there is anything I can do to help resolve the problem, please, please let . . ."

"Yeah," Wing muttered, "get the hell out of my life."

". . . you did promise to stop by the mission. There is still the matter of the commission I mentioned . . ." Wing stopped the message by jabbing the delete key; he took a few deep breaths before bringing up the second.

"We have to talk, Phil." Daisy was sitting in shadow; her face was a low-res blur. She sounded like she had a cold. "It's not fair, what you're doing. You can't just throw everything away without giving me a chance to explain. I know I waited too long but I didn't want to hurt you . . . Maybe you won't believe this but I still love you. I don't know what to say . . . it can't be like it was before but maybe . . ." There was a long silence. "Call me," she said and the screen went blank.

The messenger's mission on Islington Street sprawled over an entire block, an unholy jumble of architectural afterthoughts appended to the simple neogothic chapel that had once been the Church of the Holy Spirit. There was a Victorian rectory, a squat brick-facade parochial school built in the 1950s, and a eclectic auditorium that dated from the oughts. The fortunes of the congregation had since declined and the complex had been abandoned, successfully confounding local redevelopers until the messengers bought it. The initiates of northern New England's first mission had added an underground bike lockup, washed the stained glass, repaired the rotted clapboards, and planted an arborvitae screen around the auditorium, and still Wing thought it was the ugliest building in Portsmouth.

In the years immediately after first contact there had been no contact at all with the masses; complex and secret negotiations continued between the messengers and various political and industrial interests. Once the deals were struck however, the aliens had moved swiftly to open missions for the propagation of the message, apparently a strange brew of technophilic materialism and Zenlike self-effacement, sweetened by the promise of machine immortality. The true import of the message was a closely held secret; the messengers would neither confirm nor deny the reports of those few initiates who left the missions.

Wing hesitated at the wide granite steps leading to the chapel; they were slick from a spring ice storm. Freshly sprinkled salt was melting holes in the ice and there was a shovel propped against one of the massive oak doors. It was five-thirty in the morning—too early for protesters. No one inside would be expecting visitors, which was fine with Wing: he wanted to surprise the messenger. But the longer he stood, the less certain he was of whether he was going in. He looked up at the eleven stone apostles arranged across the tympanum. Tiny stylized flames danced over their heads, representing the descent of the Holy Spirit on Pentecost. He could not read the apostles' expressions; acid rain had smudged their faces. Wing felt a little smudged himself. He reached into his back pocket for the flask. He took a swig and found new courage as a whiskey flame danced down his throat. He staggered into the church—twisted in the good old-fashioned way and too tired to resist Ndavu anymore.

As his eyes adjusted to the gloom Wing saw that there had been some changes made in the iconography. Behind the altar hung a huge red flag with the Buddhist Wheel of Law at its center and the words LOOK INTO THE SUN embroidered in gold thread beneath it. A dancing Shiva filled a niche next to a statue of Christ Resurrected. Where the Stations of the Cross had once been were now busts: Pythagoras, Plato, Lao-tze. Others whose names he did not recognize were identified as Kabalists, Gnostics, Sufis, and Theosophists—whatever they were. Wing had not known what to expect but this was not quite it. Still, he thought he understood what the messengers were trying to do. The Romans had been quick to induct the gods of subjugated peoples into their pantheon. And what was humanity if not subjugated? That was why he had come, he thought bitterly. To acknowledge that he was beaten.

A light came on the vestry next to the altar. Footsteps echoed across the empty church and then Jim McCauley stepped into the candlelight and came to the edge of the altar rail. "Is someone there?"

Wing swayed down the aisle, catching at pews to steady himself. He felt as empty as the church. As he approached the altar he saw that McCauley was wearing a loosely tied yellow bathrobe; his face was crinkled, as if he had just then come from a warm bed. With Daisy? Wing told himself that it did not matter anymore, that he had to concentrate on the plan he had discovered an hour ago at the bottom of a bottle of Argentinean Scotch: catch them off guard and then surrender. He saluted McCauley.

The man gathered his yellow bathrobe more tightly. "Who is it?"

Wing stepped up to the altar rail and grasped it to keep from falling. "Phillip Wing, A.I.A. Here to see the head beetle." McCauley looked blank. "Ndavu to you."

"The mentor expects you, Phillip?"

Wing cackled. "I should hope not."

"I see." McCauley gestured at the gate in the center of the altar rail. "Come this way—do you need help, Phillip?"

In response Wing vaulted the rail. His trailing foot caught and he sprawled at McCauley's feet. The sculptor was wearing yellow plastic slippers to match the robe.

"Hell no," Wing said, and picked himself up.

McCauley eyed him doubtfully and then ushered him through the vestry to a long flight of stairs. As they descended, Peter Bornsten, the busboy from Piscataqua House, scurried around the corner and sprinted up toward them, taking steps two at a time.

"Peter," said McCauley. "I thought you were shoveling the steps."

Peter froze. Wing had never seen him like this: he was wearing janitors' greens and had the lame expression of a guilty eight-year-old. "I was, Jim, but the ice was too hard and so I salted it and went down to the kitchen for some coffee. I was cold," he said lamely. He glared briefly at Wing as if it were his fault and then hung his head. The Peter Bornsten Wing knew was a careless young stud whose major interests were stimulants and nurses.

"Go and finish the steps," McCauley touched Peter's forehead with his middle finger. "The essence does not experience cold, Peter."

"Yes, Jim," He bowed and scraped by them.

McCauley's slippers flapped as he walked slowly down the hallway that ran the length of the mission's basement. Doorways without doors opened into rooms filled with cots. It looked as if there were someone sleeping on every one. Wing smelled the yeasty aroma of curing vitabulk long before they passed a kitchen where three cooks were sitting at a table around four cups of ersatz coffee. At the end of the hallway, double doors opened onto an auditorium jammed with folding tables and chairs. A door to the right led up a short flight of stairs to a large telelink conferencing room and several small private offices.

McCauley went to one of the terminals at the conference table and tapped at the keyboard. Wing had a bad angle on the screen; all he could see was the glow. "Phillip Wing," said McCauley and the screen immediately went dark.

Wing sat down across the table from him and pulled out his flask. "Want some?" There was no reply. "You the welcoming committee?"

McCauley remained standing. "I spread the message, Phillip."

Someone else might have admired the calm with which McCauley was handling himself; Wing wanted to see the bastard sweat. "I thought you were supposed to be an artist. You had shows in New York, Tokyo—you had a career going."

"I did." He shrugged. "But my reasons for working were all wrong. Too much ego, not enough essence. The messengers showed me how trivial art is."

Wing could not let him get away with that. "Maybe it's just you that's trivial. Maybe you didn't have the stuff to make art that meant anything. Ever think of that?"

McCauley smiled. "Yes." Daisy came into the room.

It had been twenty-two days since he had last seen his wife; Wing was disgusted with himself for knowing the number exactly. After the party he had had worked hard at avoiding her. He had tried to stay out of the arid precincts of her Portsmouth while lowering himself into the swamp around its edges. He had reprogrammed the door to the Counting House to admit no one but him and had changed his work schedule, sneaking in just often enough to keep up appearances. He had never replied to the messages she left for him.

"What is she doing here?" Wing was tempted to walk out.

"I think it best that you wait alone with him, Daisy," said McCauley.

"Best for who?" said Wing.

"For her, of course. Look into the sun, Daisy."

"Yes, Jim."

"Phillip." He bowed and left them together.

"Look into the sun. Look into the sun." He opened the flask. "What the hell does that mean anyway?"

"It's like a koan—a proverb. It takes a long time to explain." Daisy looked as though she had put herself together in a hurry: wisps of hair fell haphazardly across her forehead and the collar of her mud-colored jumpsuit was turned up. She settled across the table from him and drummed her fingers on a keyboard, straightened her hair, glanced at him and then quickly away. He realized that she did not want to be there either and he took another drink.

"Keep your secrets then—who cares? I came to see Ndavu."

"He's not here right now."

"All right." He pushed the chair back. "Goodbye, then."

"No, please." She seemed alarmed. "He's coming. Soon. He'll want to see you; he's been waiting a long time."

"It's good for him." Wing thought she must have orders to keep him there; that gave him a kind of power over her. If he wanted to he could probably steer this encounter straight into one of the revenge fantasies that had so often been a bitter substitute for sleep. No matter what he said, she would have to listen.

"Are you often like this?" she said.

"What the hell do you care?" He drank and held out the flask. "Want some?"

"You haven't returned my calls."

"That's right." He shook the flask at her.

She did not move. "I know what you've been doing."

"What is it you're waiting to hear, Daisy?" Saying her name did it. The anger washed over him like the first wave of an amphetamine storm. "That I've spent the last three weeks twisted out of my mind? That I can't stand to live without you? Well, fuck you. Even if it were true I wouldn't give you the satisfaction."

She sat like a statue, her face as smooth and as invulnerable as stone, her eyes slightly glazed, as if she were meditating at the same time she pretended to listen to him. His anger surged, and he veered out of control.

"You're not worth it, you know that? It gets me right in the gut sometimes, that I ever felt anything for you. You pissed on every-thing I thought was important in my life and I was dumb enough to be surprised when you did it. Look at you. I'm suffering and you sit there like you're carved out of bloody ice. And calling it good breed-ing, no doubt. Fine. Great. But just remember that when you die, you bitch, you'll be nothing but another stinking puddle on the floor."

Then Wing saw the tear. At first he was not even sure that it was hers: her expression had not changed. Maybe a water pipe had leaked through the ceiling and dripped on her. The tear rolled down her cheek and dried near the corner of her mouth. A single tear. She held her head rigidly erect, looking at him. He realized then that she had seen his pain and heard his anger and that her indifference was a brittle mask which he could shatter, if he were cruel enough. Suddenly he was ashamed.

He leaned forward, put his elbows on the table, his head in his hands. He felt like crying too. "It's been hard," he said. He shivered, took a deep breath. "I'm sorry." He wanted to reach across the table and wipe away the track of her tear with his finger but she was too far away.

They sat without speaking. He imagined she was thinking serene messenger thoughts; he contemplated the ruins of their marriage. Ever since the party Wing had hoped, secretly, desper-ately, that Daisy would in time offer some explanation that he could accept—even if it were not true. What he had done with the dollies had been intended to punish her, not drive her away. He had expected to be reconciled—how could he have been so stupid? Now for the first time he realized that his crazed sexual binge had probably made reconciliation impossible. The silence stretched. The telelink rang; Daisy tapped at the keyboard.

"He's in his office," she said.

Ndavu's grin reminded Wing of the grin that Leonardo had given his John the Baptist: mysterious, ironic, fey. "We do not, as you say, keep the message to ourselves." Ndavu's wheelchair was docked at an enormous desk; the scale of the messenger's office made Wing feel like a midget. "On the contrary we have opened missions around the world in the last year where we assist all who seek enlightenment. Surely you see that it would be irresponsible for us to disseminate transcendently important information without providing the guidance necessary to its understanding." Ndavu kept nodding as if trying to entice Wing to nod back and accept his evasions.

Wing had the feeling that Ndavu would prefer that he settle back on the couch and think about how lucky he was to be the first human ever invited to tour a messenger starship. He wondered if the initiates would be jealous when they found out that an unbeliever was going to take that prize. "Then keep your goddamned secret—why can't you just give us plans for the reincarnation computer and loan us the keys to a starship?"

"Technology is the crux of the message, Phillip."

Daisy sat beside Wing in luminous silence, listening to the conversation as if it were the fulfillment of a long-cherished dream. "Is she going to be reincarnated?" Her serenity was beginning to irk him, or maybe it was just that he was beginning to sober up to a blinding headache. "Is that the reward for joining?"

"The message is its own reward," she murmured.

"Don't you want to be reincarnated?"

"The essence does not want. It acknowledges karma."

"The essence?" Wing could feel a vein throbbing just above his right eyebrow.

"That which can be reincarnated," she said.

"There are no easy answers, Phillip," said Ndavu.

"Great." He shook his head in disgust. "Does anyone have an aspirin?"

Daisy went to check. "Everything is interconnected," the messenger continued. "For instance I could tell you that it is the duty of intelligence to resist entropy. How could you hope to understand me? You would have to ask: What is intelligence? What is entropy? How may it be resisted? Why is it a duty? These are questions which it took the commonwealth of messengers centuries to answer."

Daisy returned with McCauley. "What we will ask of you," continued Ndavu, "does not require that you accept our beliefs. Should you wish to seek enlightenment, then I will be pleased to guide you, Phillip. However you should know that it is not at all clear whether it is possible to grasp the message in the human lifespan. We have only just begun to study your species and have yet to measure its potential."

McCauley stood behind the couch, waiting inconspicuously for Ndavu to finish dodging the question. He rested a hand on Wing's shoulder, as if he were an old pal trying to break into a friendly conversation. "Excuse me, Phillip," said McCauley. Just then Wing remembered something he had forgotten to do. Something that had nagged at him for weeks. He was sober enough now to stay angry and the son of a bitch kept calling him by his first name.

"I'm very sorry, Phillip," said McCauley with a polite smile, "but

we don't have much use for drugs here. However, if you're really in
need we could send someone out . . ."

Wing shot off the couch, turned, and hit his wife's lover right in
the smile. Astonished, McCauley took the punch. The sculptor
staggered backwards, fists clenched and Daisy gave a strangled little
scream. Ndavu was grotesquely expressionless. It was as if his face
were a mask that had slipped, revealing . . . nothing. Wing had
never seen the messenger look quite so alien.

"That's okay." He sat down, rubbing his knuckles. "I feel much
better now."

McCauley touched his bloody lip and then turned and walked
quickly from the office. Daisy was staring at Ndavu's abandoned
face. Wing settled back on the couch and—for the first time in
weeks—started to laugh.

The messengers had done a thorough job; Wing's cabin on the
starship was a copy of the interior of his go-tube—with a few differences. The gravity was 0.6 Earth normal. The floor was not
tongue-and-grooved oak but some kind of transparent crystal;
beneath him reeled the elephant-skin wrinkles of the Zagros mountains. And Daisy slept next door.

Wing stared like a blind man at the swirling turquoise shallows
that rimmed the Persian Gulf; Ndavu's arduous briefing had turned
his sense of wonder to stone. He now knew everything about a
planet called Aseneshesh that a human being could absorb in forty-
eight hours without going mad. When he closed his eyes he could
see the aliens Ndavu called the Chani. Tall and spindly, they
looked more like pipe cleaner men than creatures of flesh and
bone. Starving apes with squashed faces and pink teeth. He found
them profoundly disturbing—as much for their similarities to *homo
sapiens* as for their differences. Wing could imagine that they had
once been human but had been cruelly transformed over eons of
evolutionary torture.

He knew a little of their history. When glaciers threatened to
crush their civilization, most had chosen exile and had left the
planet in an evacuation organized by the messengers. Something
had happened to those that remained behind, something that the
messengers still did not understand. Even as they slid into
barbarism, these Chani began to evolve at an accelerated rate.
Something was pushing them toward a biological immortality
totally unlike the hardware-based reincarnations of the messengers.
Their cities buried and their machines beyond repair, they had

huddled around smoky fires and discovered within themselves the means to intervene in the aging process, by sheer force of mind, to tilt the delicate balance between anabolism and catabolism. They called it shriving. With their sins forgotten and their cells renewed, the Chani could lead many lives in one body, retaining only a few memories from one life to the next. What baffled the materialist messengers was that shriving was the central rite of a religion based on sun worship. Believe in Chan, the survivors had urged the astonished commonwealth upon their rediscovery centuries after the evacuation: look into the sun and live again.

Although they embraced some of the concepts of the Chani religion, the messengers could hardly accept shriving as a divine gift from a class G1 main sequence star. Despite intensive and continuing research, they were unable to master the biology of rejuvenation. The only benefits they were able to derive from the Chani's evolutionary breakthrough were delta globulins derived from blood plasma, which acted to slow or even halt the aging process in many of the commonwealth's species. The messengers could not synthesize the intricate Chani globulins, which left the self-proclaimed goddess and ruler of the Chani in control of the sole source of the most valuable commodity in the commonwealth. That deity was the thearch Teaqua, the oldest living being in the commonwealth. Teaqua, who had sent Ndavu to Earth to fetch her an architect. Teaqua, who was dying.

"She wants a tomb, Phillip." Ndavu had given up his wheelchair in the starship's low gravity. As he spoke he had walked gingerly about Wing's cabin, like a barefoot man watching out for broken glass. "You will design it and oversee its construction."

"But if she's immortal . . ."

"No, even the Chani die. Eventually they chose death over shriving. We believe there must be physical limits related to the storage capacity of their brains. They say that the weight of all their lives becomes too heavy to carry. Think of it, Phillip: a tomb for a goddess. Has any architect had an opportunity to compare? This commission is more important than anything that Seven Wonders —or anyone on Earth—could offer you. It has historic implications. You could be the one to lead your entire world into the commonwealth."

"So why me? There must be thousands who would jump at this."

"On the contrary, there are but a handful." The messenger seemed troubled by Wing's question. "I will be blunt with you,

Phillip; one cannot avoid the relativistic effects of the mass exchanger. You will be taking a one-way trip into the future. What you will experience as a trip of a few weeks duration will take centuries downtime, here on this planet. There is no way we can predict what changes will occur. You must understand that the Earth to which you return may seem as alien as Aseneshesh." He paused just long enough to scare Wing. "You will, however, return a hero. While you are gone, your name will be remembered and revered; we will see to it that you become a legend. Your work will influence generations of artists; school children will study your life. You could also be rich, if you wanted."

"And you're telling me no one else could do this? No one?"

"There is a certain personality profile. Our candidate must be able to survive two stressful cultural transitions with his faculties intact. Your personal history indicates that you have the necessary resilience. Talent is yet another qualification."

Wing snickered. "But not as important as being a loner with nothing to lose."

"I do not accept that characterization." Ndavu settled uneasily onto the loveseat; he did not quite fit. "The fact is, Phillip, that we have already been refused twice. Should you too turn us down, we will proceed to the next on the list. You should know, however, that our time is running out and that you are the last of our prime candidates. The others have neither your ability nor your courage."

Courage. The word made Wing uncomfortable; he did not think of himself as a brave man. "What I still don't understand," he said, "is why you need a human in the first place. Build it yourself, if it's so damned important."

"We would prefer that. However Teaqua insists that only a human can do what she says Chan wants."

"That's absurd."

"Of course it is absurd." Ndavu made no effort to conceal his scorn. "We are talking about fifty million intelligent beings who believe that the local star cares for them. We are talking about a creature of flesh and blood who believes she has become a god. You cannot apply the rules of logic to religious superstition."

"But how did they find out about humans in the first place?"

"That I can explain," Ndavu said, "only if you will promise to keep my response a secret."

Wing hesitated; he was not sure if he wanted to know messenger secrets. "How do you know I'll keep my promise?"

"We will have to learn to trust one another, Phillip." Ndavu unvelcroed the front of his jumpsuit; his chest was pale and smooth. "It is a problem of cultural differences." Wing backed away as the messenger pushed a finger into base of his neck. "Teaqua asked if we knew of any beings like the Chani and we told her. *Homo sapiens* and the Chani share a unique genetic heritage," said Ndavu, as his sternum unknit. "There are no other beings like you in the commonwealth." Wing pressed himself flat against the far wall of the cabin; the handle on the door of the microwave dug into him. "Genes are the ultimate source of culture."

Wing heard a low squishing sound, like a wet sponge being squeezed, as something uncoiled within the exposed body cavity. "I-I understand," he gasped. "Enough!"

The messenger nodded and resealed himself. He stood, shuffled across the cabin and held out his hand. Wing shook it gingerly.

"You have qualities, Phillip," said Ndavu. "You are ambitious and impatient with the waste of your talents. The first time I saw you, I knew you were the one we needed."

Wing felt like throwing up.

"Will you at least think it over?"

Now he was alone with an intoxicating view of the Earth, trying to sort fact from feeling, wrestling with his doubts. It was true: he had been increasingly uneasy in his work. Even the Glass Cloud was not all he had hoped it would be. A tomb for a goddess. It was too much, too fantastic. Thinking about it made Wing himself feel unreal. Here he sat with the Earth at his feet, gazing down at the wellspring of civilization like some ancient, brooding god. A legend. He thought that if he were home he could see his way more clearly. Except that he had no home anymore, or at least he could never go home to Piscataqua House. The thought was depressing; was there really nothing to hold him? He wondered whether Ndavu had brought him to the starship to feed his sense of unreality, to cut him off from the reassurance of the mundane. He would have never been able to take this talk of gods and legends seriously had he been sitting at his desk at the Counting House with the rubber plant gathering dust near the window and his diploma from Yale hanging next to John the Baptist. Wing could see the Baptist smiling like a messenger as he pointed up at heaven—to the stars? A one way trip. So Ndavu thought he was brave enough to go. But was he brave enough to stay? To turn down such a project and to live with that decision for the rest of his life? Wing was afraid that he was going to accept because there was nothing else for him to do. He would be an exile, he would be the alien. Wing had never even been in space before. Maybe that was why Ndavu had brought him here to make the offer. So that the emptiness of space could speak to the coldness growing within him.

Wing stood and walked quickly out of the cabin as if to escape his own dark thoughts. He took a moment to orient himself and then swung across the gravity well to the next landing. There was an elaborate access panel with printreader and voice analyzer and a numeric keypad and vidscanner; he knocked.

Daisy opened the door. Her room exhaled softly and she brushed the hair from her face. She was wearing the same mud-colored jumpsuit; he could not help but think of all the beautiful clothes hanging in her closet at Piscataqua House.

"Come in." She stood aside as he entered. He was surprised again at how exactly her cabin duplicated his. She observed him solemnly. He wondered if she ever smiled when she was alone as he sat on the Aalto loveseat.

"I don't want to talk about it," he said, answering the unspoken question. "I don't even want to think about it. I wish he would just go away."

"He won't."

He read the sympathy in her expression and wondered exactly why Ndavu had brought her along. He knew that although she had not forgiven him for his childish spree with the dollies, she still had feelings for him. "What I could use is a drink."

"What did you want to talk about?" She sat next to him.

"Nothing." He felt like blurting out Ndavu's secret; he thought it might make a difference to her. But he had promised. "I don't know." Wing scratched his ear. "I never told you that it was a nice party. The hot dogs were a big hit."

She smiled. "Snob appeal had something to do with it, don't you think? I'm sure that most of them like vitabulk just fine. But they have to rave about natural or else people will think they have no taste. At the mission we've been eating raw batch and no one complains. After a while natural seems a little bit decadent—or at least a waste of time."

"The essence can't taste mustard, eh?"

Before Ndavu, she might have detected the irony in his voice and bristled at it; now she nodded. "Exactly."

"But what is the essence? How can anything be you that can't taste mustard, that doesn't even have a body?"

"The essence is that part of mind which can be reproduced in artificial media," she said with catechetical swiftness.

"And that's what you want when you die, to have your personality deleted, your memories summarized and edited and reedited until all you are is a collection of headlines about yourself stored in a computer?" He shook his head. "Sounds like a lousy substitute for heaven."

"But heaven is a myth."

"Okay," he said, trying to match her calm but not quite succeeding, "but I can't help but notice that the messengers are in no hurry to have their essences extracted. They use the Chani globulins to keep themselves alive as long as they can. Why? And since they can't explain shriving, how do they know heaven is a myth?"

"Nothing is perfect, Phil." He was surprised to hear her admit it. "That's the most difficult part of the message. We can't claim perfection; we can only aspire to it."

"You've been spending a lot of time at the mission?"

"Ndavu is very demanding."

"And what about Piscataqua House? Who's minding the inn?"

She looked blank for a moment, as if trying to remember something that was not very important. "The inn pretty much takes care of itself, I guess." She frowned. "Business is terrible, you know."

"No, I didn't know."

"We've been in the red for over a year. Nobody goes any place these days." She tugged at a wrinkle in the leg of her jumpsuit. "I've been thinking of selling or maybe even just closing the old place up."

Wing was shocked. "You never told me you were having problems."

She stared through the floor for a moment. The starship's rotation had presented them with a view of the hazy blue rim of Earth's atmosphere set against star-flecked blackness. "No," she said finally. "Maybe I didn't. At first I thought the Cloud might turn things around. Bring more tourists to New Hampshire, to Portsmouth—to the inn to see you. Ndavu offered a loan to hold me over. But now it doesn't matter much anymore."

"Ndavu!" Wing stood and began to pace away his anger. "Always Ndavu. He manipulated us to get his way. You must see that."

"Of course I see. You're the one who doesn't see. It's not his way he's trying to get. It's the way." She leaned forward as if to stop him and make him listen. He backed away. "He has disrupted dozens of lives just to bring you here. If you had given him any kind of chance, none of it would have happened. But you were prejudiced against him or just stubborn—I don't know what you were." Her eyes gleamed. "Haven't you figured it out yet? I think he wanted me to fall in love with Jim McCauley."

Wing gazed at her in silent horror.

"And he was right to do it; Jim has been good for me. He isn't obsessed with himself and his projects and his career. He finds the time to listen—to be there when I need him."

"You let that alien use you to get to me?"

"I didn't know at the time that he was doing it. I didn't know enough about the message to appreciate why he had to do it. But now I'm glad. I would have just been another reason for you to turn him down. It's important that you go to Aseneshesh. It's the most important thing you'll ever do."

"It's so important that two other people turned him down, right? I should too. Just because I fit some damned personality profile . . ."

"He said it that way only because you haven't yet accepted the message. He's not just some telelink psych, Phil, he can see into your essence. He knows what you need to grow and reach fulfillment. He knew when he asked you that you would accept."

Wing felt dizzy. "If I leave with him and go uptime or whatever he calls it—zapping off at the speed of light—I'll never see you again. You'll be downtime here, and you'll be dead for centuries before I get back. Doesn't that mean anything to you?"

"It means I'll always miss you." Her voice was flat, as if she were talking about a stolen towel.

He crossed the room to her, dropped to his knees, took her hands. "You meant so much to me, Daisy. Still do, after everything." He spoke without hope, yet he was compelled to say it. "All I want is to go back to the way it was. Do you remember? I know you remember."

"I remember we were two lonely people, Phil. We couldn't give each other what we needed." She made him let go and then ran her hand through his hair. "I remember I was unhappy." Sometimes when they were alone, reading or watching telelink, she would scratch his head. Now she fell absently into the old habit. Even though he knew he had lost her, he took comfort from it.

"I was always afraid to be happy." Wing rested his head in her lap. "I felt as if I didn't deserve to be happy."

The stars shone up at them with an ancient, pitiless light. Ndavu had done a thorough job, Wing thought. He's given me good reasons to go, reasons enough not to stay. The messengers were nothing if not thorough.

*   *   *

Wing was dreaming of his father. In the dream his father was asleep on the Murphy bed in the go-tube. Wing had just returned from a parade held to honor him as the first human to go to the stars, and he was angry that his father had not been there. Wing shook him, told him to wake up. His father stared up at him with rheumy, hopeless eyes and Wing noticed how frail he was. *Look at me,* Wing said to the old man, *I've done something that was much harder than what you did. I didn't just leave my country, I left the planet, my time, everything. And I adjusted. I was strong and I survived.* His father smiled like a messenger. *You love to dramatize yourself,* said the old man. *You think you are the hero of your story.* His father began to shrink. *But surviving takes a long time,* he said, and then he was nothing but a wet spot on the sheet and Wing was alone.

The telelink rang, jolting Wing awake. He cursed himself for an idiot; he had forgotten to set the screening program. The computer brought up the lights of his go-tube as he fumbled at the keyboard beside his bed.

"Phillip Wing speaking. Hello?"

"Mr. Wing? Phillip Wing? This is Hubert Fields; I'm with the Boston desk of Infoline. Can you tell me what's going on there?"

"Yes." Wing tapped a key and opened a window on the telelink's monitor. He could see the skyline of Portsmouth against a horizon the color of blue cat's-eye; the status line said 5:16 A.M. "I'm sitting here stark naked, having just been rudely awakened by your call, and I'm wondering why I'm talking to you." The pull of Earth's gravity had left him stiff and irritable.

Fields sounded unperturbed; Wing could not remember if he had ever been interviewed by this one before. "We've had confirmation from two sources that the messenger Ndavu has offered you a commission which would require that you travel to another planet. Do you have any comment?"

"All I can say is that we have discussed a project."

"On another planet?"

Wing yawned.

"We've also had reports that you recently toured the messenger starship, which would make you the first human to do so. Can you describe the ship for us?"

Silence.

"Mr. Wing? Can you at least tell me when you'll be leaving Earth?"

"No."

"You can't tell us?"

"I haven't decided what I'm doing yet. I'm hanging up now. Make sure there're two l's in Phillip."

"Will we see you at the ceremonies today?"

Wing broke the connection. Before he could roll back into bed the computer began playing his Thursday morning wakeup: the Minuet from Suite No. 1 of Handel's *Water Music*. It was 5:30; today was the dedication of the Glass Cloud.

He folded the gel mat with its nest of blankets and sheets back into the wall of the go-tube. Most of his clothes were scattered in piles on the oak floor, but Daisy had bought him a gray silk Mazzini suit for the occasion which was still hanging in its garment bag on the towel rack. Twice he had returned it; she had sent it back to him three times. He tried it on: a little loose in the waist. Daisy had not realized that he had lost weight since he had moved out.

Wing walked briskly across the strip to the USTS terminal where he was just in time to catch the northbound red-white-and-blue. It seemed as though everybody in the world had offered to give Wing a ride to North Conway that day, which was why he had perversely chosen to take a bus. He boarded the 6:04 carryvan which was making its everyday run up Route 16 with stops in Dover, Rochester, Milton, Wakefield, Ossipee, and North Conway. The spectators who would flock to the dedication were no doubt still in bed. They would arrive after lunch in hovers from New York or in specially-chartered 328 double-deckers driving nonstop from Boston and Portland and Manchester. Some would come in private cars; the Vice President and the Secretary of the Interior were flying in from Washington on Air Force One. New Hampshire state police estimated a crowd upwards of half a million, scattered along the ninety-seven kilometers of the Glass Cloud's circuit.

A crowd of angry locals had gathered at the bus stop in Ossipee. They hustled the clown on board and then banged the side of the carryvan with open hands to make the driver pull out. The clown was wearing a polka-dotted bag that came down to her ankles and left her arms bare; the dots cycled slowly through the spectrum. She had a paper-white skin tint and her hair was dyed to match the orange circles around her eyes. A chain of tiny phosphorescent bananas joined both ears and dangled beneath her chin. A woman up front tittered nervously; the man across the aisle from Wing looked disgusted. Even New Hampshire Yankees could not politely ignore such an apparition. But of course she wanted to be noticed; like all clowns she lived to provoke the astonished or disapproving stare.

"Seat taken?" she said. The carryvan accelerated abruptly, as if the driver had deliberately tried to make her fall. The clown staggered and sprawled next to Wing. "Is now." She laughed, and shoved her camouflage-colored duffle bag under the seat in front of her. "Where ya goin'?"

Wing leaned his head against the window. "North Conway."

"Yeah? Me too. Name's Judy Thursday." She held out her hand to Wing.

"Phillip." He shook it weakly and the man across the aisle snorted. The clown's skin felt hot to the touch, as if she had the metabolism of a bird.

They rode in silence for a while; the clown squirmed in her seat and hummed to herself and clapped her hands and giggled. Eventually she opened the duffle bag and pulled out a small grease-stained cardboard box. "Popcorn? All natural."

Wing gazed at her doubtfully. The white skin tint made her eyes look pink. He had been on the road for two hours and had skipped breakfast.

"Very nutritious." She stuffed a handful into her mouth. "Popped it myself."

She was the kind of stranger mothers warned little children about. But Wing was hungry and the smell was irresistible. "They seemed awfully glad to see you go back there," he said, hesitating.

"No sense of humor, Phil." She put a kernel on the tip of her tongue and curled it into her mouth. "Going to the big party? Dedications are my favorite; always some great goofs. Bunch of us crashed the dedication of this insurance company tower—forget which—down in Hartford, Connecticut. Smack downtown, tallest building, the old edifice complex, you know? You shoulda seen, the suits went crazy. They had this buffet like—real cheese and raw veggies and some kinda meat. We spraypainted the entire spread with blue food coloring. And then I got into the HVAC system and planted a perfume bomb. Joint must still smell like lilacs." She leaned her head back against the seat and laughed. "Yeah, architecture is my life." She shook the popcorn box at Wing and he succumbed to temptation. The stuff was delicious.

"Hey, nice suit." The clown caught Wing's sleeve as reached for another handful and rubbed it between thumb and forefinger. "Real silk, wow. How come you're riding the bus, Phil?"

Wing pulled free, gently. "Looking for something." He found himself slipping into her clipped dialect. "Not sure exactly what. Maybe a place to live."

"Yeah." She nodded vigorously. "Yeah. Beautiful country for

goofs. The whole show is gonna be a goof, I figure. What do you think?"

Wing shrugged.

"I mean like what is this glass cloud anyway? A goof. No different from wrapping the White House in toilet paper, if you ask me. Except these guys got permits. Mies Van der Rohe, Phil, you know Mies Van der Rohe?"

"He's dead."

"I know that. But old Mies made all those glass boxes. The ones that got abandoned, they use 'em for target practice."

"Not all of them."

"I think Mies musta known what would happen. After all, he had four names. Musta been a goof in there somewhere." She offered him another handful and then closed the box and stuck it back in her bag. The carryvan rumbled across the bridge over the Saco River and headed up the strip that choked the main approach to North Conway.

"These guys on the link keep saying what a breakthrough this gizmo is and I keep laughing," she continued. "They don't understand the historical context, Phil, so why the hell don't they just shut up? Nothing new under the sun, twist and shout. The biggest goof of all." Wing noticed for the first time that her pupils were so dilated that her eyes looked like two bottomless wells. The van slowed, caught in strip traffic; even in daylight the flash bars seemed to pulse with garish intensity.

"Me, I thought it was kinda unique." Wing could not imagine why he was talking like this.

"Oh, no, Phil. No, no. It's the international style in the sky, is what it is. Study some architecture, you'll see what I mean." The carryvan crawled into a snarl of USTS vehicles near the old North Conway railroad station which had been moved to the airport and converted to a tourist information center. An electrolumeniscent banner hung from its Victorian gingerbread cornice. Green words flickered across it: *Welcome to North Conway in the Heart of the Mount Washington Valley Home of the Glass Cloud Welcome to . . .* Hovers were scattered across the landing field like seeds; tourists swarmed toward the center of town on foot. The line of busses waiting to unload at the terminal stopped moving. After ten minutes at a standstill the carryvan driver opened the doors and the passengers began to file out. When Wing rose he felt dizzy. The clown steadied him.

"Goodbye, Judy," he said as they stood blinking in the bright

May sunshine. "Thanks for the popcorn." He shielded his eyes with his hand; her skin tint seemed to be glowing. "Try not to get into too much trouble."

"Gonna be a real colorful day, Phil." She leaned up and kissed him on the lips. Her breath smelled like popcorn. "It's a goof, understand? Stay with it. Have fun."

He fell back against the bus as she pushed into the crush of people, her polka dots saturated with shades of blue and violet, her orange hair like a spark. As she disappeared the crowd itself began to change colors. Cerulean moms waited in bathroom lines with whining sulfur kids in shorts. Plum grandpas took vids while their wrinkled apricot wives shyly adjusted straw hats. Wing glanced up and the sky went green. He closed his eyes and laughed silently. She had laced the popcorn with some kind of hallucinogen. Exactly the kind of prank he should have expected. Maybe he had suspected. Was not that why he had taken the bus, to give something, anything, one last chance to happen? To make the final decision while immersed in randomness of the world he would have to give up? Maybe he ought to spend this day-of-all-days twisted. He kept his eyes closed; the sun felt warm on his face. Stay with it, she had said. "Have fun," he said aloud to no one in particular.

"It's a tribute to the American genius" The Vice President of the United States shook Wing's hand. "We're all very proud of you."

Wing said, "Get out of Mexico."

Daisy tugged at his arm. "Come on, Phillip." Her voice sounded like brakes screeching.

The Vice President, who was trying to pretend—in public at least—that he was not going deaf, tilted his head toward an incandescent aide in a three-piece suit. "Mexico," the aide repeated, scowling at Wing. The Vice President at ninety-one was the oldest person ever to hold the office. He nodded sadly. "The tragic conflict in Mexico troubles us all, Mr. Wing. Unfortunately there are no easy answers."

Wing shook Daisy off. "We should get out and leave the BMF to sink or swim on its own." The Vice President's expression was benignly quizzical; he cupped a hand to his ear. The green room was packed with dignitaries waiting for the dedication to begin and it sounded as if every one of them was practicing a speech. "I said. . . ," Wing started to repeat.

The Vice President had leaned so close that Wing could see

tiny broken veins writhing like worms under his skin. "Mr. Wing,"
he interrupted, "have you stopped to consider how difficult we
could make it for you to leave this planet?" He kept his voice low,
as if they were making a deal.

"And what if I don't want to leave?"

The Vice President laughed good-naturedly. "We could make
that difficult too. It's a beautiful spring day, son. Could be your day
. . . if you don't go screwing yourself into the wrong socket. Ah,
Senator!" Abruptly Wing was staring at the great man's back.

"What is the matter with you?" Laporte appeared beside Daisy
and he was hot, a shimmering blotch of rage and four-alarm ambition. "You think you can just stagger in, twisted out of your mind,
insult the Vice President—no, don't say anything. Once more,
once more, Wing, and you'll be watching the Cloud from the
ground, understand? This is my project now; I've worked too hard
to let you screw it up again."

Wing did not care; he was too busy being pleased with himself
for mustering the courage to confront the Vice President. He had
been certain that the Secret Service would whisk him away the
moment he had opened his mouth. Maybe it had not done any
immediate good but if people kept pestering it might have a cumu-
lative effect. Besides it had been fun. The crowd swirled; like a
scene-change in a dream, Laporte was gone and Daisy was steering him across the room. He knew any moment someone would
step aside and he would be looking down at Ndavu in his wheelchair. He glanced at Daisy; her mouth was set in a grim line, like a
fresh knife wound across her face. He wondered if she were having
fun, if she would ever have fun again. What was the philosophical
status of fun vis-à-vis the message? A local condition of increased
entropy . . .

"I must have your consent today, Phillip," said Ndavu, "or I will
have to assume that your answer is no." His face looked as if it had
just been waxed.

Wing had stopped worrying about the slithery thing that lived
inside the messenger. It was easier on the digestion to pretend that
this human shell was Ndavu. He picked a glass of champagne off a
tray carried by a passing waiter, pulled up a folding chair and sat.
"You leaked my name to telelink. Told them about the project."

"There is no more time."

Wing nodded absently as he looked around the room. "I'll have
to get back to you." The Governor's husband was wearing a kilt with
a pattern that seemed to tumble into itself kaleidoscopically.

Ndavu touched his arm to get his attention. "It must be now, Phillip."

Wing knocked back the champagne: ersatz. "Today, Ndavu." The glass seemed to melt through his fingers; it hit the floor and bounced. More plastic. "I promise."

"Ladies and gentlemen," said a little green man wearing a bowtie, gray morning coat, roll-collar waistcoat, and striped trousers, "if I may have your attention, please."

A woman from the mission whispered to Ndavu, "The Vice President's chief of protocol."

"We are opening the doors now and I want to take this opportunity to remind you once again: red invitations sit in the north stands, blue invitations to the south, and gold invitations on the platform. We are scheduled to start at two-fifteen so if you would please begin to find your seats. Thank you."

Daisy and Wing were sitting in the back row on the platform. On one side was Luis Benalcazar, whose company had designed both the Cloud's ferroplastic structure and the computer program that ran it; on the other was Fred Alz, the construction super. Laporte, as official representative of the Foundation and Solon Petropolus, sat up front with the Vice President, the Secretary of the Interior, the Governor, the junior Senator and both of New Hampshire's Congresspeople, the Chief Selectman of North Conway, a Hampton fourth-grader who had won an essay contest, the Bishop of Manchester, and a famous poet who Wing had never heard of. Ndavu's wheelchair was off to one side.

The introductions, benedictions, acknowledgments, and appreciations took the better part of an hour. . . . *A technological marvel which is at one with the natural environment* . . . The afternoon seemed to get hotter with every word, a nightmare of rhetoric as hell. . . . *the world will come to appreciate what we have known all along, that the Granite State is the greatest* . . . On a whim he tried to look into the dazzling sun but the colors nearly blinded him. . . . *their rugged grandeur cloaked in coniferous cloaks* . . . When Wing closed his eyes he could see a bright web of pulsing arteries and veins. . . . *this magnificent work of art balanced on a knife edge of electromagnetic energy* . . . Daisy kept squeezing his hand as if she were trying to pump appropriate reactions out of him. Meanwhile Benalcazar, whose English was not very good, fell asleep and started to snore. . . . *Reminds me of a story that the Speaker of the House used to tell* . . . When they mentioned Wing's name he stood up and bowed.

He could hear the applause for the Cloud several moments before it drifted over the hangar and settled toward the landing platform. It cast a cool shadow over the proceedings. Wing had imagined that he would feel something profound at this dramatic moment in his career but his first reaction was relief that the speeches were over and he was getting out of the sun.

The Cloud was designed to look like a cumulus puff but the illusion was only sustained for the distant viewer. Close up, anyone could see that it was an artifact. It moved with the ponderous grace of an enormous hover, to which it was a technological cousin. But while a hover was a rigid aerobody designed for powered flight, the Cloud was amorphous and a creature of the wind. Wing liked to call it a building that sailed. Its opaline outer envelope was ultra-thin Stresslar, laminated to a ferroplastic grid based on an octagonal module. When Benalcazar's computer program directed current through the grid, some ferroplastic fibers went slack while others stiffened to form the Cloud's undulating structure. The size of the envelope could be increased or decreased depending on load factors and wind velocity; in effect it could be reefed like a sail. It used the magnetic track as a combination of rudder and keel or, when landing, as an anchor. Like a hover its envelope enclosed a volume of pressurized helium for lift: twenty thousand cubic meters.

The Cloud slowly settled to within two meters of the ground, bottom flattening, the upper envelope billowing into the blue sky. Wing realized that people had stopped applauding and an awed hush had settled onto the platform. The Hampton schoolgirl climbed onto a folding chair and stood twisting her prize-winning essay into an irretrievable tatter. Wing himself could feel the goose-flesh stippling his arms now; the chill of the Cloud's shadow was strangely sobering. The Secretary of the Interior sank slowly onto his chair, shielded his eyes with the flat of his hand and stared up like a coal miner in Manhattan. Pictures would never do the Cloud justice. The Governor whispered something to the bishop, who did not seem to be paying attention. Wing shivered. Like some miracle out of the Old Testament, the Cloud had swollen into a pillar that was at least twenty stories tall. It had accomplished this transformation without making a sound.

Fred Alz nudged Wing in the ribs. "Guess we got their attention, eh Phil?" The slouch-backed old man stood straight. Wing supposed it was pride puffing Alz up; he could not quite bring himself to share it.

Daisy squeezed his hand. "It's so quiet."

"SSSh!" The Governor's husband turned and glared.

The silence was the one element of the design that Wing had never fully imagined. In fact, he had been willing to compromise on a noisier reefing mechanism to hold down costs but Laporte, of all people, had talked him out of it. Not until he had seen the first tests of the completed Cloud did Wing realize the enormous psychological impact of silence when applied to large bodies in motion. It gave the Cloud a surreal, slightly ominous power, as if it were the ghost of a great building. It certainly helped to compensate for the distressing way the Stresslar envelope changed from pearl to cheapjack plastic iridescence in certain angles of light. The engineers, technicians, and fabricators had worked technological wonders to create a quiet Cloud; although Wing approved, it had not been part of his original vision. The reaction of the crowd was another bittersweet reminder that this was not his Cloud, that he had lost his Cloud the day he had begun to draw it.

The octagonal geometry of the structural grid came clear as the pilot hardened the Cloud in preparation for boarding. Ndavu wheeled up noiselessly and offered his hand in congratulations. They shook but Wing avoided eye contact for fear that the alien might detect Wing's estrangement from his masterpiece. A hole opened in the envelope and a tube snaked out; the ground crew coupled it to the landing platform. Ndavu shook hands with Alz and spoke to Luis Benalcazar in Spanish. Smiling and nodding, Benalcazar stooped toward the messenger to reply. "He says," Ndavu translated, "that this is the culmination of his career. For him, there will never be another project like it."

"For all of us," said Alz.

"Thank you," Benalcazar hugged Wing. "Phillip. So much." A woman with a microcam came to the edge of the platform to record the embrace. Wing pulled away from Benalcazar. "You, Luis," he tapped the engineer on the chest and then pointed at the Cloud. "it's your baby. Without you, it's a flying tent." "Big goddamn tent yes," said Benalcazar, laughing uncertainly. Laporte was shaking hands with the Congressman from the First District. The chief of protocol stood near the entrance of the tube and began motioning for people to climb through to the passenger car suspended within the envelope. Before anyone could board, however, Ndavu backed away from Wing, Benalcazar, and Alz and began to clap. Daisy stepped to the messenger's side and joined in, raising hands over her head like a cheerleader. People turned to see what was going on and then everyone was applauding.

It felt wrong to Wing—like an attack, as if each clap were a blow he had to withstand. He thought it was too late to clap now. Perhaps if the applause could echo backwards through the years, so that a nervous young man on a stony path might hear it and take sustenance from it, things might have been different. But that man's ears were stopped by time and he was forever alienated from these people. These people who did not realize how they were being manipulated by Ndavu. These people who were clapping for the wrong cloud. Wing's cloud was not this glorified special effect. His cloud was forever lonely, lost as it wandered, windborne, past sheer walls of granite: a daydream. You can't build a dream out of Stresslar and ferroplastic, he told himself. You can't share your dreams. He thought that Daisy looked very pretty, clapping for him. She was wearing the blue dress that he had bought for her in Boston. She had been mad at him for spending so much money; they had fought over it. The glowing clearwater blue of the material picked up the blue in her eyes; it had always been his favorite. Daisy had taken five years of his life away and he was back now to where he had been before he met her. She was not his wife. This was not his cloud. These were not his people. He found himself thinking then about the alien goddess Teaqua, a creature of such transcendent luminosity that she could order messengers to run her errands. He wondered if she could look into the sun.

"Tell him to stop it," Wing said to Daisy. "Tell him I'll go."

The applause ended. Several hours later on Infoline's evening report, Hubert Fields noted in passing that the architect was not among those who boarded the Glass Cloud for its maiden voyage.

Proof of the Existence of God

Bierhorst, R. G, Seera, B. L. and Jannifer, R. P. "Proof of the Existence of God and an Afterlife." *Journal of Experimental Psychology*. Volume 95, Spring, 2007, pages 32-36.

"REMEMBER THE FUTURE?" SAID THE SUBJECT. HE fumbled an old envelope from the pocket crawling across his yellow T-shirt. Jannifer frowned as the kid wrote the words down. *Remember. Future.* No one had ever taken notes before.

"Time isn't a river," Jannifer continued. "It's. . . ." Momentarily distracted, he glanced down at the questionnaire the kid had filled out as part of the experiment. ". . . It's a field." Subject was Timothy Corrigan, freshman English major, claimed he wanted to be a poet. "Not only this second," said Jannifer, "but ten minutes ago, ten minutes from now and ten years from now are all within our range."

Corrigan nodded. "Time present and time past are both present in time now."

Jannifer stared at the kid blankly.

"T. S. Eliot," said Corrigan. "*Burnt Norton.* No, this is good stuff." He held his pen ready. "So how do I remember the future?"

"With the help of our apparatus over here, you can make brief and controlled excursions through the field in any direction." The first time he'd given their phony pitch to a subject, Jannifer had been shocked at how well it worked. Shock had long since given way to disillusionment. People were so bone stupid about science. Give somebody a lab coat, a computer, and a dentist's chair dummied up with readouts and he could fool the world. Or at least a naive English major. "But I'm afraid I can't allow you to take any more notes, Mr. Corrigan. This is a secure area. You did sign the release."

"Sure, sure. I understand." Corrigan folded the envelope back into his pocket.

"Now then, your entire life exists, and has existed from the instant of the Big Bang. All your lives."

"All?"

"I don't suppose you've taken quantum mechanics yet? We could go over the equations. Wait, what did you say your major was?" He pretended to scan Corrigan's questionnaire.

Corrigan shook his head emphatically and his long black hair fell across his forehead. "I about flunked geometry in high school." He smiled as if it were a badge of honor.

And morons like this can vote, thought Jannifer. They open checking accounts that they have no idea how to balance. They make babies. "All right, then," he said, "the gist of the theory is this: at every second, no, every *nanosecond*, reality branches into an infinite number of universes. All possibilities, no matter how remote, are satisfied in one or another."

"I am large," said Corrigan. "I contain multitudes." Jannifer realized that the kid was saying these odd things to show that he was trying to understand.

"I suppose." Jannifer rubbed the back of his neck; the last procedure of the day was always the hardest. "Okay. Your brain is constantly collapsing these potential alternate universes, thus cutting off your access to them. It's what creates the illusion of time's directionality."

For the first time, Corrigan looked confused. Jannifer wasn't surprised. From past sessions, he knew that this was the weakest part of the script. If only they had asked him, he would have concocted some *convincing* rubber science. But this was Bierhorst's experiment. If Jannifer strayed too far from the script, he would introduce unwanted variables, skew the data.

"We still don't understand exactly how this brain mechanism

works. It's part of why we've asked you to take part in the experiment. Don't worry, you won't be in any danger. We've put over a
hundred subjects on the apparatus without incident. But we're on
the cutting edge of science here—there are no guarantees. You
understand that?"

Corrigan braced himself and nodded. The younger subjects
seemed to like a little whiff of danger. It made them feel brave
when they took the hook.

"We can send you into your personal time field out as far as it
goes. It says here you're not married. Is that right? Well, you might
meet your wife—or wives." Jannifer was supposed to chuckle here,
but since he was no actor, the sound came out more like a cough.
"Watch your kids grow up. And what will you do with your life?"

"Could I see how I die?"

Got you, thought Jannifer. Once again, the predictions of
Bierhorst's goddamned model proved accurate. 84% of college kids
brought up the idea of visiting their own deaths, 67% of them
before the second scripted hint. The older populations had even
higher numbers; 98% of nursing home subjects expressed interest
in a terminal vision.

Jannifer shrugged. "It's your future. You're the explorer. We
have no way to place restrictions on what you look for."

Corrigan glanced away from Jannifer toward the apparatus. "So
then it really isn't a time machine? That's what I'd heard."

"No, your brain is the time machine. The apparatus just turns it
on." Jannifer rested a hand on the kid's shoulder. "May I call you
Timothy?"

The kid shook his head. "Just Tim."

"You've been hypnotized before, Tim?" Jannifer began steering
him toward the chair.

"No."

"Well, all indications are that you will be an excellent subject."

He settled Corrigan in the chair and plugged the electrode
headband into the EEG processor. The status light went from red
to green. The EEG was the only instrument that actually worked in
the room; everything else was a prop. Jannifer swept Corrigan's hair
off his forehead and positioned the band so the electrodes snugged
over his temples. The processor took a few seconds to calibrate the
input from the band before its raw data readout blinked and
displayed the waveforms of Corrigan's brain.

Corrigan watched him with wide, bright eyes the color of
almonds. There was a scatter of freckles across the bridge of his

nose; the corners of his eyes had yet to wrinkle. The kid had the face of a someone who had never made a mortgage payment or been passed over for promotion.

"Are they ever sorry?" Corrigan said.

"Sorry?"

"That they remember their futures. Where ignorance is bliss, 'tis folly to be wise."

"No one ever complained to me, if that's what you're worried about."

"Not worried, just curious." He smiled. "And what do they call you? Doctor Jannifer? Mister Jannifer? Mister Doctor?"

"Richard." Jannifer found himself liking Tim Corrigan, even if he did have the common sense of a moth. After all, the kid had a good excuse for being innocent. What was he, nineteen? Twenty at most? If Jannifer had known everything at that age, he would've crawled into the nearest closet and nailed the door shut.

"So Tim, I want to be sure you know exactly what's about to happen." Jannifer had recited the last part of the script so many times he had a tendency to rattle through it. He forced himself to speak slowly, with conviction. "First, I hypnotize you. We do this primarily to help you concentrate. You have to turn inward as you never have before, block the outside world entirely. Then I activate the apparatus, which gives you access to the time field created by your brain. Jump to any time location you choose, although, for the purposes of our experiment, we ask that you explore your future. Since you're feeling disoriented at first, I help you make that first jump. Then I leave and there are no further distractions. You're on your own. I'm in the control room, taking a video, audio, and electroencephalographic record of the session. Please tell us, if you can, where and when you are and, in general, what's happening. Don't bother with details. You'll remember everything you experience; there will be an extensive debriefing afterwards. Ten minutes into the session, we turn the apparatus off and bring you back. I should warn you that people seem to find this the most jarring part of the experience. No matter whether you want it or not, you'll be swept out of the future and returned to the present. Safely to the present. All right?"

"Sure."

Jannifer still felt uneasy playing Bierhorst's tricks, even in the cause of science. Corrigan thought he was going on an adventure through time, when all that was really going to happen was Jannifer would make a hypnotic suggestion that he imagine his own death.

In a couple of hours, he'd be just another stat for their paper, "Age Progression and the Terminal Vision: A New Diagnostic Tool."

Bierhorst's paper—Jannifer would be lucky to get his name on it. The truth was, he had never been all that enthusiastic about Bierhorst's idea that they had to convince *progression* subjects that they were "remembering" a real future, just as those undergoing hypnotic *regression* believed their recaptured memories to be true. But Bierhorst had gotten the grant and so here Jannifer was, pulling a science con on this dewy undergrad. About the only protocol battle Jannifer had won was that he was allowed to monitor EEG.

"Are you ready to begin?"

"Tomorrow and tomorrow and tomorrow," droned Corrigan, "creeps in this petty pace from day to day to the last syllable of recorded time."

"I'll take that as a yes. All right, then. Do you see the clock on the wall? I want you to watch the second hand, ticking away. Focus, Tim. Good. You're feeling very relaxed, with each tick you can feel tension draining away. Imagine you've been up all night doing a paper but it's done now and you've handed it in and you're getting a 'A.' So now you can just ease back and enjoy. You stayed up very late working on it, Tim, and you're tired, but that's okay. Maybe your eyes feel a little droopy. Let them close if you want. You've earned it. That's it. Deep breaths. You know, now that your eyes are shut, I'll bet you can't get them open again, no matter how much you want to. Go ahead, try. See what I mean? But if I tell you now that you should open your eyes for me, Tim . . . ah, very good. We can begin."

Jannifer turned to the computer beside the chair and tapped the enter key. The monitor scrolled nonsense code at subliminal speeds and then stopped on the blue welcome screen. The words, *Opening temporal field*, pulsed twice before being replaced by a digital clock that began counting backward: 10:00, 9:59, 9:58, 9:57.

"As you can see, Tim, I've turned on the apparatus. Its effect begins almost immediately. It's subtle, nothing you can sense directly, no sights or sounds at first. But you should feel a kind of lightness, or maybe a surge of energy? Concentrate, now. It's a feeling of power, Tim. Nothing can hold you. Do you have that feeling?"

"Yes."

"Good, then it's time to take your first step into the future. What I want you to do, Tim, is jump to the end of your session with us. We've finished our debriefing and you're leaving the lab, all right? You cross the waiting room on your way out—are you there?"

"Yes."

"You come to the door. Look at it. It's unusual, isn't it?"

"Yes."

"Before you leave, take a moment and tell me about the door."

"It's heavy, made of some kind of wood." Corrigan made his voice small, as if he were talking in church. "It looks old. It doesn't have a knob but a kind of handle thing. Brass. It has panels, one, two, six panels. A long pair below the handle, another long pair above and at the top two square panels."

"What color is it?"

"Green—dark, dark green."

"Good, Tim. Very good. You should be proud of yourself. You've made your first jump in time, a couple of hours into the future. I'm going to leave you now. When you open that door, your entire future will be before you. Go anywhere you want—to work, to a lover, to your death, if that's what interests you. You haven't got much time, less than ten minutes now, so remember only what is most important about your future. Good luck."

In the control room next door, Bev Seera was eating a sub from Nicky's and grading papers for her *Intro to Personality* class. The control room, a windowless space with white cinder block walls and gumspot gray linoleum, was furnished with folding chairs and a couple of long tables they had borrowed from the cafeteria. Their equipment consisted of two computer towers and keyboards, a printer, speakers, microphones, earphones, telephones, a mess of wiring that spilled like plastic spaghetti across the tables, and three monitors. Two of them showed different views of Tim Corrigan, the other displayed three-dimensional histograms of his EEG. "I liked the term paper imagery," Seera said, without looking up. "That just come to you now?"

"Haven't I told you," said Jannifer, dropping onto the chair in front of the video monitors, "what an inspiration this whole experiment is to me?"

"Bad attitude makes bad results, Richard."

"Where both deliberate, the love is slight." Corrigan's words purred through the speakers. "Who ever lov'd, that lov'd not at first sight?"

"What's his problem, anyway?" said Seera.

"Thinks he's a poet."

"Poor bastard."

"We're leaving the party," said Corrigan. "Her name is Lucianna."

"Sounds like he'll be stopping soon for a little sexual interlude."
Seera reached for the next paper. "So will this one get to terminal?"

"Oh my," said Corrigan. "*Oh.*"

"I'd say yes." Jannifer turned the volume down. "You want that
pickle?"

Corrigan continued making soft, throaty noises, his body twitching occasionally in the old dentist's chair. When he fell silent, the
monitors were showing what looked like a sheen of sweat on his
forehead.

"He's hooked all right," said Jannifer. "Kid *believes.*"

The silence stretched to more than a minute. Then two.

Seera emerged from her papers and shot Jannifer a questioning
glance. There were four minutes and twelve seconds left on the
clock.

"What can I say?" Jannifer shrugged. "Ten minutes ago, I
couldn't shut him up."

"Kid, you're supposed to talk, kid," said Seera, although her
microphone wasn't on. "We need benchmarks."

Jannifer peered at the close-up monitor. "You think something
happened to him?" Bierhorst's grant hadn't been enough to pay for
new hi-res videocams.

Seera came up behind him. "He looks kind of different."

"Different how?"

"I don't know. Bigger maybe?"

As soon as she said it, he knew she was right. Jannifer had been
watching too closely to notice that Corrigan's shoulders had broad-
ened—just a little. His cheeks had fleshed out and there appeared
to be an extra fold at his chin.

"The woods. . . ." Corrigan sounded as if there were something
stuck in his throat. His T-shirt had ridden up at the waist over a
couple of inches of pale skin. A beer gut the kid didn't have bulged.
" . . . Decay. . . ."

They watched as Corrigan's hair began to fall out. A dark strand
slid down his cheek and he sneezed. That set a little tuft adrift from
his head; it caught on his T-shirt, black tangle on yellow fabric.

Jannifer turned on the nearest microphone. "Tim, this is
Richard." It was a violation of all the protocols. "What's happening?" They'd have to throw this procedure out. It struck him as a
funny thing to be worrying about at a time like this. It was so funny
that he wanted to laugh.

"The woods," Corrigan said, in a quavering voice, "decay and
fall."

"Jesus," said Seera. "What the *hell* is this?"

But Jannifer didn't answer. He was already through the door and into the room where Corrigan was. Only the kid was gone. In his place was a flabby middle-aged man, whose fair skin darkened and wrinkled as if it were being burned by a slow flame. As he went to him, Jannifer passed the monitor, still counting backwards: 2:23, 2:22, 2:21.

"Tim?" Jannifer nudged him gingerly to get his attention. "Where are you?"

Whatever was happening now accelerated. Corrigan's head lolled toward Jannifer and he smiled. "At the quiet limit of the world." A tooth slid out of his mouth as he spoke, bounced off Jannifer's arm and rattled across the floor like a button.

"No, you're not!" Enraged, Jannifer caught Corrigan by the shoulders and shook him. "I was lying, everything was a lie."

Corrigan's head snapped from side to side. Jannifer could feel him shrinking in his grip, muscle withering away, skin sagging. It enraged him. "You idiot, you're not in the future!" he shouted. "This damn chair is just a prop. Stop it!"

"Richard!" Seera had followed him into the room; she was weeping. "*You* stop! You'll hurt him."

"Hurt him?" Jannifer let out the hysterical laugh he had been strangling ever since Corrigan had begun to age. "Look what he's doing to himself." He let Corrigan go and the old man slumped back onto the dentist's chair like an empty suit of clothes.

And died.

Jannifer didn't need to look at the flat readout or hear the EEG's maddening shriek. He knew. Corrigan's eyes clouded over and turned the color of spilled milk. And still it wasn't over; his corpse continued its unreal trip though time. Jannifer caught just the whiff of putrescence and his stomach lurched. It was a dangerous smell, a smell with claws. Then it was gone. Meanwhile, Corrigan's yellowed flesh was shrinking to the bone. Jannifer backed away from the body which had already gone far beyond death.

"My God," said Seera. "Oh, my God!"

The rapidly decomposing carcass shivered as if in response. Impossibly, the dry muscle of the neck stretched and the lips pulled taut against the few remaining teeth and the thing that had been Timothy Corrigan turned to them and spoke. It sounded like the groan of a mountain being uprooted, except that it was also the hot crack of a lightning strike and the crushing, liquid whisper of the darkest ocean trench.

"I AM WHO AM."

Jannifer staggered backwards, bumped against the table which held the EEG processor and the computer. He had a glimpse of the monitor with its now meaningless countdown—$0:13$, $0:12$—then hurled himself across the table and over it, using the equipment to shield himself from the empty, infinitely dark sockets in the skull of the kid he had sent to God. Corrigan was the burning bush, thought Jannifer. *But I'm no Moses.*

He was huddled there when the computer sounded its chime, once, twice, three times, signaling the end of the session. Despite himself, he was caught unaware. It was a tiny noise compared to the shrilling of the EEG—or that vast and terrible voice—but the closeness of it unnerved him. He screamed and lurched away from it, fell and then scrabbled backwards toward the far wall. The monitor teetered off its perch on top of the computer and exploded against the linoleum.

The next coherent thought Jannifer had was how quiet it was. No EEG alarm, even though the processor was still on the table, its readout oddly alight. No sound at all, until Seera whispered.

"*Kid?*"

If she had gone mad, Jannifer was prepared to understand.

She found her voice and spoke aloud. "You all right?"

Jannifer heaved himself forward. "I don't know."

But she wasn't talking to Jannifer. Tim Corrigan was in the chair, his long black hair spread across the yellow T-shirt, his cheeks flushed and his eyes full of wonder. The next thing Jannifer knew he was standing beside him, kneading the kid's bicep to prove to himself that he was really alive. To prove. . . .

"Where were you?" said Seera.

"Heaven," said Corrigan. "Or near it." He gazed up into their faces and then smiled wearily. "But I don't expect you to believe that."

"You were dead," said Jannifer.

"Yes." The idea seemed to amuse him; he laughed. "They got it backwards, you know . . . just the opposite. In heaven, you burn. I could feel the fire crackling through my veins. My heart was a flame." Corrigan raised a hand to his face. "About, about in reel and rout the death fires danced at night." He stared as if he were looking through his palm at the afterlife. "It's not pleasure or pain or any one feeling. It's all of them and they consume you and what's left is like . . . no, it *is* God."

His babbling only provoked Jannifer. Without speaking, he jerked Corrigan out of the dentist's chair, dragged him protesting into the control room and shoved him into the chair in front of the monitors. "You sit there." He stabbed at the rewind buttons on both the tape decks. "You watch." The motors whirred and the tape sang back across the heads. "You tell us what happened."

Jannifer turned to the computer that had received Corrigan's EEG output and called up a display that compressed the entire session onto one screen. He settled onto the chair, not really sure it would hold both his weight and that of what he was seeing. It was all there, including more than two minutes of utterly flat EEG — the definition of brain death.

He had proof. Jannifer shuddered and hit the print key. He had hardcopy and videotape and two eyewitnesses to a miracle. Three, if you counted Tim Corrigan.

Proof.

The tape decks clicked to a stop, reset themselves, and began to play. He heard his earlier, blissfully godless self saying, "As you can see, Tim, I've turned on the apparatus. Its effect begins almost immediately. It's subtle, nothing you can sense. . . ."

But Jannifer couldn't watch — not yet. He felt as if the hand of the Almighty were on his shoulder. He, Richard Jannifer, had been chosen. But what was he supposed to do? What could he do? Nothing. Everything.

He picked up a phone and dialed Bierhorst's number.

The Cruelest Month

NELL HATED HERSELF FOR KEEPING THE APPOINT-
ment with Massinger. Even his waiting room had begun to grate
on her. The shiny plants, the creaking wicker furniture, the grass-
cloth wallcovering; it was all too slick and insincere. Like
Massinger. This was not Montego Bay; it was Manchester, New
Hampshire on the first day of April. The view out the window was
of spattered cars speeding along the Everett Turnpike. Smudges of
wet, black, late-season snow were melting in the breakdown lanes.

"The doctor will see you now, Ms. Cuneen."

As she entered his office Massinger bustled to greet her as if he
had spent the day straightening his cuffs and waiting for her arrival.
"Ah, Monday. And here's my favorite appointment." He grasped her
hand with both of his. "How's life at the top, Nell?"

"I wouldn't know."

"Near the top, then."

"Louis, save the cheerleading for the football fans."

He laughed and steered her toward two leather chairs facing a
floor-to-ceiling window. One was pushed slightly behind the other
so that Nell would have to twist to see him. She sat next to a glass
table set with goblets, a pitcher of ice water, and a wicker basket
filled with Kleenex.

"I sense a little hostility today, Nell. Am I wrong?" Nell could hear the creak of leather as he eased into place. "Shall we start with that?"

She crossed her legs and stared down at the traffic. Just a simple patient-therapist transaction: tell me all your secrets, dearie. Did you sleep with anyone this week? She had already decided not to bring the subject up unless he did.

"Serge agrees to the divorce," she said. "He says he doesn't want anything."

"How does that make you feel?"

"Relieved in a way. Sad, a little. I didn't want to leave it hanging." She poured herself some water and pushed the Kleenex out of reach. "I really wish he'd take what's his, though. He deserves something. It won't be easy for him to write and earn a living at the same time. In fact, I bet it's impossible. The guy couldn't even balance his checkbook before we were married. And he was just coming into his own when the . . . the accident happened. Finding his voice, he called it. I don't want to feel responsible for making it harder for him to write."

"He left you, Nell. He's in charge of his life, you're in charge of yours."

"Sure. But his attitude annoys me. It's like he's saying 'You made a mess of our lives, now clean it up. Leave me out.' " The ice clinked as she sipped from her goblet. "And there are boxes of mystery magazines in his closet. *Alfred Hitchcock*, *Ellery Queen*, *Mike Shayne*. His junk."

"Have a yard sale."

She grimaced. "All the neighborhood marriage coroners would just love that. Sorting through the remains of the unholy wedlock. A nice way to spend a Saturday morning. I don't think so, Louis. I don't think I could stand to put Avril's toys out in the driveway and watch . . . watch other people's kids take them away."

"You're not still carrying toys around the house, are you?"

She shook her head.

"It's time enough, Nell. Put all her things in her room, lock it and don't go in."

"No. I've got to get out of that house."

"Trouble sleeping?"

"I slept like a night watchman. These yellow pills you prescribed are terrific. Take two and suddenly television seems fascinating." She reached into her purse and tossed a brown plastic bottle onto the table. "I can't stop thinking, Louis. It's how I know I'm alive."

"You'd prefer something milder?"

"I did have one dream about her. Last night. Not a nightmare. I dreamed I heard her laughing. I looked in her room but she wasn't there. I went to the window. There was a moon, footprints in the snow leading out to her swings. More laughing. I went out to the yard and followed her tracks. The swing was still jiggling—but no Avril. She called to me. 'Avril fool you, Mommy. April fool.' She was playing a game. I kept chasing her voice but I never caught up. She was laughing, I was laughing. I felt light, like I could jump over the house." Nell lapsed into silence.

"Yes, very good." Massinger cleared his throat. "I think you're finally learning to . . ."

"Don't tell me, Louis. Please. All I know is for the first time in months I woke up feeling like a human being. I'd like to hold onto that."

"All right, Nell. But this *is* progress, you know. A nonthreatening dream about your daughter. I'm very pleased." Nell suspected he was patronizing her. "How about your problem with the phones? Anything new there?"

"Worse." She took another drink. "Much worse. I finally got a speaker phone in my office and that's fine. I don't even have to touch a receiver, just talk into the little white box. I'm going to replace all the phones at home this week. But the other day I was in the conference room with Carruthers and some people from the paper products division, and a call came through for me from an editor I'd been trying to reach for days. Jack Billingsly held the receiver out toward me and I . . . and I panicked. I couldn't take it. I mumbled something about transferring the call to my secretary and I left. They were all gawking. God knows what they said while I was gone." She balled her fist as if to strike at the memory, and then let it drop into her lap. "Damn, *damn!* This phone thing is hurting me at work. As if I didn't have problems with Carruthers already."

"There are more important things than your boss's opinion."

"Not in my life." She chuckled bitterly. "I've botched everything else; the job is the only thing left I'm proud of."

"You're so quick with the self-pity, Nell. You think you're the only parent ever to lose a child? That yours is the first marriage to break up? Listen to me, Nell; I think the job is part of the problem. In order to make it at the office you had to harden yourself. The more success, the harder you got. You know what happened? You got so hard you're brittle."

"I'm not so hard, Louis. Just alone." She could see her own dim reflection in the window. "I'm thirty-eight years old and there's no one in my world except me."

"I'm part of your world."

For the first time she twisted around to see his expression. He was grinning. "Thank you, Doctor," she said. "Nice of you to say it."

The phone rang. He frowned and went over to the desk to answer it. "I'm in session . . . When? . . . Oh, no . . . Who's handling it? . . . Yes, okay. Tell him I'll be there as soon as I can."

He approached her contritely. "I'm sorry, Nell, but something has come up. Another patient, an emergency." He squatted beside her chair so that their eyes were on a level. "Maybe we should pick up again over dinner?" He rested his hand on her shoulder and then let it slide down her arm. "Say Thursday?"

She caught his hand. "Thursday is no good. I'm sleeping with Carruthers that night." He started—just the reaction she wanted. For a few delicious seconds the adroit Dr. Louis Massinger was reduced to just another insecure male on the make. She laughed and kissed his hand. "April fool, Louis. Don't you ever look at your calendar?"

"I can't believe you said that, Nell." Already he was straightening the mask, wrapping himself in his professional dignity. "Even as a joke."

Nell had often thought that if only he were a little less certain about the world and his place in it that there might be a future to their affair. As it was, all that he had to offer her were a series of elegant sensations: good food, fine wine, chamber music, mannered sex. "Thursday sounds about right, Louis." She stood abruptly and gazed down at the nickel-sized bald spot on the back of his head. "Your place?"

Nell flipped on the light in the foyer and sniffed. The house smelled of pine-scented Lysol. She hated coming home to nobody. Mondays, at least, were tolerable. Julieta, the cleaning woman, worked from ten to three and her presence always seemed to linger. Nell kicked off her shoes and wriggled her toes in the nap of the newly vacuumed carpet. She wished she were messy enough to keep a full-time maid busy. Maybe she should buy a cat.

She padded into the kitchen, popped a frozen chicken tetrazzini into the microwave and pulled a bottle of chardonnay from the refrigerator. She drank her first glass in two gulps and then peeled the price tag from the bottle. The second glass she sipped, savoring the balanced fruit, the hint of oak. She set her briefcase on the living room table and went upstairs to change.

When she saw the tricycle parked next to her bed she stiffened as if a current were crackling through her. She remained immobilized by this electric thrill of horror for some time, gaping and at the same time wanting desperately to look away. Mounted on the handlebars was a pink wicker basket. The plastic seat was covered with a strawberry design. Bits of gravel were wedged into the grooves of the solid rubber tires and the green enamel was pitted and scarred from heavy use. A moan welled from the back of her throat and became an inarticulate keen. When she could move again she slumped against the wall.

Her first lucid thought was that someone was playing a vicious prank. Julieta! She would call the bitch and fire her. The phone was at hand—but it seemed to mock her weakness. With a curse she swept it from the nightstand and fled down to the bar in the living room. She was trembling when she reached for the scotch; Cutty Sark splashed and beaded on the counter. She poured three fingers into the tumbler and choked it down neat.

The microwave beeped and she nearly fell off the barstool. She flew into the kitchen, snapped off the timer and grabbed the bottle of wine. She built herself a nest of pillows on the modular couch and settled into it. Nell could not remember the last time she had seen Avril's tricycle. She had stopped carrying toys around the empty house weeks ago. Even then she had always remembered moving things when she had found them in strange places. Always. Yet no one else could have brought the tricycle from wherever it had been. Julieta was not a monster. If there had been thieves they would certainly have taken the videocam or the Mac or the gold serving plate displayed on the living room hutch.

Slowly the alcohol eroded her fear into a boozy disquiet and then into a general and unfocussed bewilderment. She drank the last of the chardonnay from the bottle.

"What you need, Nell old girl, is a shrink." She rolled the empty bottle across the carpet and stretched out. Soon she was asleep. Before she went to work the next morning she carried the tricycle to the attic.

A pair of janitors was squeegeeing the stainless steel and glass entrance to the NoreasCorp headquarters. One of them opened the door and ogled Nell as she passed, as if she were some minor secretary instead of an assistant vice president. Nell scowled, remembering a crack Serge had made about her company. Lucier's Law, he had called it: the bigger the boss, the more doors you had to open to get to his office. Although Serge had taken a very sarcastic attitude toward her work, he had never hesitated to help her spend her paychecks.

Nell passed though four doors before she reached the mahogany and brass portal to the executive suite. Harry, the security guard, tipped his uniform hat to her and leaned into one of the doors. It opened with a whoosh; top management was hermetically isolated from the rest of the office.

"Morning, Ms. Cuneen." Kate was in her fifties, an old school secretary who could not be induced to call her boss by her first name. "The *Growth* presentation has been pushed back to nine-thirty. Mr. Hamilton from Public Service called, said he'd call back this afternoon. And there are flowers."

"Flowers?"

"Yes, ma'am." Kate wore her bifocals on the tip of her nose. She gazed over the rims with a studied disinterest. "Would you like your coffee now, Ms. Cuneen?"

There were a dozen yellow roses wrapped in green foil. She fumbled with attached card, suddenly giddy with the absurd hope that they were from Serge. The card said, "Looking forward to Thursday." It was unsigned.

"Damn you, Massinger." If he were going to be so circumspect, why bother sending flowers at all? And now there was the problem of what to do with them. She knew exactly what the men of executive row would think if she kept the roses in her office. They would wink at one another and maybe say something like, "About time," or "She needed it," and then smirk as if they understood everything about her sex life. She punched at the intercom. "Would you bring my coat in here, Kate?"

When Kate came in, Nell pushed the flowers to the edge of the desk. "Wrap these in my coat and take them out to the car, would you?" She began opening her mail. "Bring the coat back."

"Would you like me to put them in water?"

"No, don't bother."

Nell spent most of the morning in an excruciating meeting. Bob Yamoto presented a mock-up of the summer issue of *Growth*, NoreasCorp's stockholder magazine. Yamoto was a competent writer and editor but Nell had never liked the man; he seemed to believe everything the company told him to print. Carruthers sat in on the first half hour of the meeting while Yamoto summarized the articles and displayed the photographs and graphics he had selected. Nell wondered what Carruthers thought of Yamoto. She had never been able to discover her boss's opinion of anyone.

Leon Carruthers was of the hearty handshake, don't-bother-me-with-the-facts school of management. He knew at least one thing about every employee he had ever met. If Smith's son was a Little League star then Carruthers would invariable greet the man with, "Smitty, good to see you. Your kid still hitting them out of the park?" Or if Dubinski's wife dabbled with acrylics it would be, "Phil, how are you? The Mrs.? She still painting?" It mattered little that Smith's boy had long since given up baseball for punk rock or that the Dubinskis had been separated for a year and a half.

About a half hour after Carruthers had entered the conference room, his secretary cracked the door, gained his and everyone else's attention and said, "Sorry to interrupt, but Madrid is on the phone." All nodded, understanding this necessary ritual of escape. Carruthers excused himself and the actual work of the meeting began.

Now Nell became the star of the meeting and the seven people in her public relations group vied for her approval by criticizing the mock-up. The comments were generally favorable about the profile of the pulpwood stacker who was a volunteer "smoke jumper"—a skydiving firefighter. However they all took turns attacking the article on the joint venture between NoreasCorp's building products division and the prefab home builder who wanted to make low income housing.

Nell wished there were a window in the conference room so she could stare out of it. Nobody read *Growth*. They mailed out 17,000 of the damn things and 16,500 were garbage within an hour of delivery. She sorted idly through the photography on the smoke jumper while the others gabbled. There was a close-up of the grinning hero, his face smudged with soot, an aerial of a forest fire, and a family portrait. Mr. and Mrs. Smoke Jumper and their daughter, wearing orange jumpsuits and parachutes, stood in front of a twin-engine Cessna. Nell scanned the article again; the little girl was just eight. What a stupid thing to teach your only child.

Nell had gone into labor during lunch on a Friday, April 7, and did not deliver until late the next day. All through it, she and Serge had argued about what to name the baby. They knew a boy could be either Louis or Pierre, but they were not even close to a girl's name. Finally, when the contractions were coming ten minutes apart, they reached a compromise founded on mutual exhaustion: they would name her—if it was a her—after her birth month. Avril Lucier.

Avril was the child every parent hopes for. Beautiful: hair pale as corn silk, blue eyes, a bloom of color on her cheeks. Intelligent: she could count ten jellybeans on her second birthday and she noticed many things that adults were at pains to hide. Cheerful: she was a bubbly, smiling child, enthralled with her life. Of course, she resisted toilet training until she was almost four and she loved to pull cats' tails and she was not above pinching a stubborn playmate, but these flaws seemed trivial to her doting parents.

Nell went back to NoreasCorp six weeks after Avril's birth. Serge enjoyed staying home with his daughter. In the year before she was born he had nearly burned himself out writing three potboilers about a sexist adventurer called The Mercenary. Afterward he worked part time as a stringer for the *Manchester Union Leader* and produced an occasional lapidary short story which he wasted on the mystery magazines. He took Nell out to celebrate the day the last Mercenary went out of print.

They lived in a converted barn at the top of a stony bluff. Two of their seven acres were nearly vertical. On a clear day when the leaves were off the trees they could see the White Mountains. They could not see their nearest neighbors. When Nell was promoted to Assistant Vice President for Corporate Communications she became the highest-ranked woman in NoreasCorp. Serge started what he called a serious novel when Avril started nursery school. They were happy.

It ended on a Saturday. Serge was writing in his loft. Nell and Avril were swimming in their pear-shaped pool. The poolside phone rang and Nell hurried to answer it before Serge was disturbed.

It was Carruthers himself. "Sorry to bother you, Nell, but we've got a problem up at the Franklin plant. There was a spill, some chemicals found their way into a floor drain which they tell me empties eventually into the Merrimack River. The plant manager panicked and called the state; I understand some of the towns downstream still draw drinking water from the river. Anyway, I've got reporters from the wire services and the Boston *Globe* calling and I need a statement. Get your people on it and get back to me by two-thirty. Benelli is the plant manager's name. Make sure someone tells the idiot exactly what to say. Thanks, Nell. Appreciate it."

Nell pulled Avril from the pool, ushered her out of the chain-link enclosure and locked the gate. "Why don't you come inside and play for a while, honey? Mommy has to make some phone calls."

"No, Mommy. I wanna be out."

"All right." Nell aimed her daughter at the swings and sandbox and gave her a gentle pat on the rear. "But you stay in the yard, you hear?"

Nell loved a challenge, especially when it came from the president of the company. She sent Manning, her press handler, to the plant and had Benelli and his family check into a motel at the company's expense. Then she marshaled the rest of her staff. Soon they had lined up three experts who were willing to say that the spill posed no hazard at any time to anyone, anywhere. The statement was a masterpiece of guiltless regret. Public relations was the one thing Nell did exceptionally well in life. For an hour and a half the crisis demanded her complete and undivided attention; like a true professional she had given it.

But that was no excuse.

When she arrived at Massinger's condominium on Thursday, Nell was not sure whether she wanted to make love to the man or scratch the grin off his smug face. Massinger did not give her the chance to make up her mind. He offered no target as he mixed a pitcher of vodka martinis; for the time being he was being as bland as his home. A minimalist architect had done the interior. It was airy and white and strangely empty, like a blank piece of paper. There was not a splinter of wood, nor were there walls, not even in the bathroom. The modest could conceal themselves behind a folding Japanese paper screen.

Massinger's passion was food. He was a connoisseur of most European cuisines, a convert to Indian and a fanatic for Thai. He could spend an entire evening ranting about the local restaurants, of which but a handful met his exacting standards. They often went on expeditions far away from the culinary wasteland of central New Hampshire. Tonight, he proposed, they would try Vittorio's, a new place which had opened on the Seacoast. It was only an hour away. Nell nodded abstractedly and held out her glass for a refill.

They dined on *fettucini al pesto, braciole ripine,* and a bottle of '77 *Brunello di Montalcino Riserva.* The waiter fawned over them. The view was of $20 million worth of yachts twitching idly at their moorings. While they sipped espresso, a piano player in a maroon tuxedo sat down at the Bosendorfer to improvise on Gershwin. A perfect evening. Nell told herself that there must be millions of women who would spend their dreary lives lusting for an evening like this. The more she thought about it the more numb she felt.

Massinger's arm brushed gently against her breast as he helped her with her coat. Later, he was not so gentle. When he was aroused her clothes seemed to baffle him; in his impatience he broke the snap as he tried to unzip her dress. A small mishap but it was one which slowly consumed her ambivalence and released her rage. He talked too much as he caressed her. The word "love" came too easily to his lips, especially since he never used it when she was dressed. At the end he always grunted—oh, the great psychiatrist could grunt like a pig at feed.

When he had finished she sat up and turned on the light. There was a decanter of cognac on the nightstand; she poured herself some and swirled it in the snifter. "Louis." Her stomach lurched as if she were going to be sick. "When you got your license, did they make you sign anything?"

"License?" said Massinger dreamily. "Driver's license? Fishing license?"

"Medical license, your license to be a psychiatrist. I mean, there must have been something written down, a code of ethics." She felt him tense and push away from her.

"What are you talking about, Nell?"

"Isn't it against your professional ethics to sleep with me? Didn't they make you sign something that said, 'I, Louis Massinger, hereby promise not to screw my patients?' "

He shivered but then managed the weak smile of a man who has been observed biting into a wormy apple. "Nell, is this a joke? You mean so much more to me . . . I can't believe. . . ."

"Here." She offered him the snifter. "Have a drink while you think of something safe to say." When he accepted the glass, she thrust the blankets from her and swung out of his bed. She pulled her dress from the hanger and slithered into it.

"I don't understand this, Nell. What's the matter?"

"Let's just say you're a lousy lover, Louis. Let's leave it at that." She stepped into her shoes.

Massinger heaved himself out of bed. "Nell, you stop it right now. I want you to sit down and talk to me."

"You're not giving me orders, Doctor." She picked up her coat and purse. "You're not even wearing any clothes."

He grabbed his pants and gathered her underwear and panty-hose, which were scattered across the floor. "Wait! What about these?"

Nell laughed. "Mail them to me." She slammed the door behind her.

On the way home she shattered speed limits euphorically, ignoring lights and lane markers. She tuned the stereo in the company Cutlass to an oldies station, turned it up and sang alone incoherently, making up words when memory failed her. She chuckled at the disk jockey's jokes, blew raspberries at the commercials. Gallons of pricey liquor, hours of determined sex, the daily exercise of power—none of these had ever satisfied Nell as deeply as walking out on Massinger.

They were waiting for her in the living room. Unblinking button eyes stared into the darkness. Nell did not see them immediately; she went into the kitchen and consumed two stacks of Fig Newtons and an enormous glass of milk, like a teenager home from a bowling date. Despite the hour, her mood seemed unshakable. She was on her way to play her scratchy Supremes record when she discovered the doll party.

They lounged on the sofa, gazing absently at the pink plastic settings arranged on the coffee table. There was a doll that winked and a doll that bleated, a rag doll and a black doll and a doll with realistic sex parts. All of them were smiling dolls.

"Oh, my God," said Nell.

The dolls seemed to be smiling at some secret joke—perhaps one told at her expense.

"I'm going crazy." She hugged herself.

She expected one of them to acknowledge her, to stand up on its short legs and explain that she was indeed having a psychotic hallucination, that her skull had cracked like the shell of a dropped egg and her sanity was leaking out onto the rug, that soon some people with soft voices would come to take care of her and she would never have to worry or think again. She waited. The dolls smiled.

Finally she stumbled upstairs and used her new speaker phone to call her psychiatrist.

When Nell turned the key in the ignition the next morning, the car stereo throbbed with the Beatles. "Yeah, yeah, *yeah*," she said, stabbing at the select button. She located the classical station, turned it down to a murmur, and drove off.

For all his faults, Massinger was the only person in the world who cared for her. He had come swiftly and without reproach to rescue her from her hysteria. He told her that she had organized the doll party and then blocked out the memory. To make it seem as if Avril were still alive, he explained. She wondered if she was being unreasonable in her expectations of the man. After all, she had seduced him.

Downtown Manchester was clogged with morning traffic. As was her custom, Nell twisted the rearview mirror and applied her workaday makeup as she crept toward NoreasCorp. There was little she could do with the accordion pleats at the corners of her eyes but she lightened the pouches underneath. With quick and sure strokes she dabbed on peach-colored lipstick. She brushed her hair furiously and pulled it back into a tighter than usual bun. Better in her position to be considered handsome than beautiful.

She felt much better once she was behind her desk. Despite its complexity, the world of business was wonderfully comforting. It presented no madness, no tragedy, no corpses, only problems which could be solved or foisted onto someone else. She spent much of the morning looking for work to take home with her that weekend. At ten-thirty Carruthers walked into her office unannounced and invited her to lunch.

Despite her success, Nell had never been socially accepted at NoreasCorp. Boy talk was not one of her specialties; she found professional sports either dull or barbaric. She neither played tennis nor racquetball. Since she was not directly involved in one of NoreasCorp's profit centers, she could discuss the business only in the most general terms. Liquor tended to still her tongue, cigars nauseated her. Gender was, of course, her biggest problem; she sensed her cautious peers reigning in their language and attitudes in her presence. No one in the executive suite had ever told her a dirty joke.

Carruthers, who was similarly isolated by position and personality, might well have become a friend—except Carruthers was a mystery. She had never understood just why he had chosen her for the fast track. He and Nell ate alone in a corner of the small executive dining room. They talked awkwardly of property taxes, state politics, and the end of the skiing season. He dawdled through his salad as if postponing a trip to the dentist.

"You know, Nell, we're all proud of the job you're doing for the company."

There was a spot of dressing on his tie; Nell resisted a crazy impulse to flick it away with her fingernail.

"Especially in light of the personal problems you've had to deal with." He contemplated his fork for a moment and then laid it across his plate. "Frankly, Nell, I doubt that any of our top people could have borne the strain you have. But even the strongest of us has a breaking point. It's come to my attention that you haven't taken a vacation in more than two years. You've accrued seven weeks, Nell."

She folded and refolded her napkin. She could not think of a reply.

"I want you to take a rest, Nell. No reflection on your current performance. But you look tired. You act tired. I say that as a friend, believe me. And as your boss I'm afraid that somewhere down the line I might lose one of my most valuable . . ."

Nell stopped listening. A bead of sweat dribbled from under her arm. It had been hot that Saturday, eight months ago. She remembered they had been swimming. Carruthers had not given a good goddamn about her days off then. She remembered when she told Serge that she thought he was watching Avril. The wild—yes, murderous—look on his face. They scrambled through the dog-day heat, searching. Across lawns, through the thicket, down the cliffs. Tears and sweat had stung her eyes. It had been a terrible price they had paid for a view of the mountains; at the bottom of a twenty-foot drop, head cocked to one side like a broken doll. . . .

"I appreciate your concern, Leon. But I have ongoing projects. I just can't leave them hanging."

He reached across the table and closed his hand over her wrist. It felt like a handshake. "One of the perks of being president, Nell, is that you don't have to take no for an answer." He smiled. "I'm sending a memo to your group. Your vacation starts Monday the eighth and I don't want to see you again until May first at the earliest. You understand? Don't worry; we'll find some way to muddle through without you." He released her and pushed away from the table. "Get some sun, go skiing, enjoy yourself. And don't misunderstand me, Nell. There will still be a job for you when you get back."

Nell could not remember much of the weekend; she spent most of it destroying brain cells to the clinking accompaniment of ice cubes diving into Cutty Sark.

"But what job will it be?" she screamed into her back yard early Saturday morning, too late for Carruthers or her comfortably distant neighbors to hear.

She ate some pills. She went to the Shop n' Save without her pocketbook, piled $97.33 worth of groceries into a shopping cart and then was forced to flee from the livid cashier. Among the things she broke were three Waterford crystal wineglasses, a lamp, a ceramic flowerpot, two fingernails, and a mirror—when she saw herself in it on Sunday afternoon. She built a fire in the fireplace out of alphabet blocks. She threw up three times, once on the rug in the bedroom.

On Monday, she rested. She was simply too weak to continue her self-torture and she did not want to desecrate this special day. She showered and dressed for work but instead of getting into the car she took two more pills and settled in front of the television to wait for Julieta.

Julieta was a forklift of a woman: plain, squat, and powerful. She wore discount jeans and a faded velour top which rode up her back when she bent over, revealing a quarter inch of pink panties and a roll of pale flab. Serge had hired Julieta a year ago; after one look at her, Nell's jealousy had evaporated. The only thing she disliked about the woman was her persistence in calling Nell "Mrs.," no matter how often she was corrected.

Nell seemed to make Julieta nervous. Every time the cleaning woman passed her employer, she made a supreme effort not to stare; when she was working out of sight she made enough noise for a platoon of servants. She was obviously chagrinned when Nell joined her in the kitchen at noon. Nell smiled grittily; she was determined to talk to someone about anything.

Julieta was eating a slab of cold meat loaf in a pita shell. Except for odds and ends, Nell was completely out of food; she finally decided on Brie and stale Triscuits.

"You want something to drink?" Nell would have been glad to open the bar.

"I got water, Mrs."

Nell hesitated then poured a jigger of scotch into a glass of Perrier and sat across the butcher-block table from Julieta.

She steadfastly refused all Nell's conversational gambits: commendations, television chat, weather complaints. She ate quickly, brushed the crumbs from the table onto her hand and then reached for Nell's empty plate.

"Julieta!"

She pulled away from Nell; her face hardened with suspicion. "You wanna lay me off, Mrs.? That why you waiting around here?"

"Lay you off? No, Julieta, no. I'm home because . . . because I'm on vacation. It so happens I'm going away next week . . ." Nell found herself babbling in embarrassment, ". . . so I won't need you then, but the week after that you just come ahead, as usual. No, you're doing a fine job, just great. I didn't mean to upset you, Julieta. I just wanted to get to know you a little better, that's all."

Julieta glanced at the clock, still frowning. "It's twelve thirty, Mrs. I take a half hour. And I can't stay late because I gotta pick up my boy Joey after school."

Nell nodded wearily and waved her out of the room. The woman would rather clean toilets than talk to her. She wobbled upstairs to take a nap.

"Happy birthday."

Nell bolted awake, then realized that she herself had murmured the words she had been trying all day to escape. It was April the eighth. The clock radio said 3:36; Julieta was gone. Nell washed her face with cold water and decided to skip her four o'clock appointment with Massinger. She felt strong enough now to seek a permanent cure for her distress.

She went down the hall to Avril's room and searched for the Little Sally Bake Set. She brought the miniature baking pan and the small stale box of Little Sally Chocolate Cake Mix down to the kitchen. She preheated the over to 350°.

When it was cooked she spread on chocolate frosting. Avril's favorite. There were no candles so she stuck six kitchen matches into the cake. The phone rang.

"Go away, Louis." It rang again and again, insisting, intruding. "Leave me alone, damn it!"

Massinger's pills reminded her of the penny candy she used to buy at the drugstore on Summer Street in South Bend. She dumped them onto the kitchen table and counted. Fourteen. She imagined it would be like running down the sand dunes to Lake Michigan; hurtling out of control over hot sand, the illusion of flight, a final chilling plunge. She arranged the pills in a star pattern on top of the cake and lit the match candles.

"Happy birthday to you,
Happy birthday to you,"

She began to cry—the first time since the funeral—but her voice was steady.

"Happy birthday, dear Avril,
Happy birthday to you."

The phone rang again, its jangle strangely distant. Cursing, she reached to disconnect the speaker phone. There was no need. It was silent.

Bring-ring, bring-ring. The sound summoned her upstairs. Down the hall. To Avril's room.

In the middle of the floor was a toy phone. It had a red receiver and blue wheels and a yellow pull string. There was a smiling face painted on the front; blue eyes jiggled in plastic sockets when the wheels turned. The phone looked up at her and rang again.

Trembling with the conviction that she had slipped irretrievably into madness, she stooped to pick up the receiver.

"Mommy?" Avril's voice came not from the phone but from the throbbing of blood in Nell's body, the mutter of her heart. "I ran too far, Mommy. I'm sorry."

"Oh, Avril."

"Don't hurt yourself, Mommy. I cry for you. Please stop hurting."

Nell's voice failed.

"I have to go away now. Don't stay here anymore, Mommy. You need hugs and kisses."

"Honey, Avril, I can't leave you."

"I love you Mommy. But I have to go."

Nell crouched in the gathering darkness of her daughter's room and learned to cry. She had always thought that crying was only a kind of pain, so she had tried to divorce it from her sorrow. Sobbing, she realized that tears did not wound.

In time she folded Avril's telephone to her breast, carried it to her bedroom and started packing.

Chemistry

"I'M GOING TO FALL IN LOVE TONIGHT," SAID MARJA, "and this time you're coming with me."

Lily had been staring without comprehension at *Screen 8 of 23/Brain Mechanisms in Mating*. It was too hot for neurobiology; the spex with their heavy displays kept sliding down her nose. When she pushed them back up, *Screen 8* flickered. "I have to study," she said, trying to remember the last time she'd heard a man whisper her name in the dark.

"Face it, Lily, you think too damn much. What your synapses need is a nice warm norepinephrine bath." Marja Zoltowski had snuggled into a nest of pillows and tilted the top of her head backwards against the wall to keep her spex in place. Her Adam's apple bobbed when she spoke.

"You Poles are such romantics." Lily shivered the way she used to when Glenn touched her face. "What is tonight, anyway?"

"I don't know. Monday?"

Lily blinked at the calendar icon and waited a second for the spex to retrieve her tickler from memory. "Okay, tomorrow we have day two of Freddy's virtual autopsy," she said, "and Wednesday is the immunology test. We hardly have time to sleep, much less fall for strangers."

"Listen to yourself." Marja shook her head. "Do you call this a life?"

"Nah," said Lily. *Screen 9 of 23* was a diagram of the septo-hypothalamic-mesencelphalic continuum. "I call it med school."

"We could try that new place on Densmore Street. It's supposed to be grade."

"We? These are your urges, not mine. Why don't you just program a window shirt to flash *available* and hang out at Wally's?"

"This isn't about sex, Lily, it's about feelings. Believe me, after they crank your hypothalamus you won't be able tell the difference between neuromance and the real thing."

"Says you."

"Emotions aren't magic, doctor. They are reproducible brain states."

This was something Lily knew to be true, but preferred not to think about—like the correlation between cheesecake and adipose tissue. "Anyway," she said, "we can't afford it."

"Love makes all things possible."

Lily doubted that, but she said nothing.

"I wonder what kind of men go out on a Monday night?" Marja smirked. "Gourmet cooks. Don't fancy restaurants close on Mondays?"

Lily set her spex on the kitchen table, mirror side down, so she wouldn't accidentally catch a glimpse of herself goofing off. "Weekend weathermen," she said. "Priests cutting loose after a long Sunday. I need to study tonight, and so do you." She got up to stretch her legs, but of course there was no room. She and Marja had squeezed into an efficiency apartment off campus and their stuff filled the place to overflowing. Two yard-sale dressers, two futons, a MedNet node, a whiny refrigerator, a microwave on the kitchen table, two plastic chairs. They had to wash dishes in the bathroom, which had once been a closet. The closet was a clothesline stretched across the west wall. When the place was picked up she could take four, maybe five steps without bumping into something, but at the moment piles of hardcopy booby-trapped the floor like paper banana peels. There was a word for their lifestyle, she realized. Squalor.

"How long have we known each other?" said Marja. "Almost two years and you haven't even breathed on a man. They're not all Glenns, you know. Look, we can fall in and out of love and still be back in plenty of time to weigh old Freddy's nonexistent spleen."

Lily picked up her spex again and held them at arm's length.

From a distance the bright little images on the displays looked like a pair of shirt buttons. Had it really been two years? Maybe it *was* time to unbutton herself.

A private security rover patrolled Densmore Street; the servos of its infrared lenses mewled softly as it wove through the twilight. Most of the stores on the block were just closing: La Parfumerie, Hawkins Fine Wines, a World Food boutique, and a couple of art galleries. Next to the Hothouse was the Office Restaurant. Through its windows Lily could see people in gray suits sitting alone at stylized desks, eating absently as they tweaked glowing blue spreadsheets. The neighborhood reeked of money and there was only fifty-three dollars and sixty-seven cents left on her cash card. She wondered how much romance that would buy in the caviar part of town.

At street level the Hothouse was as stolid as a bank: two stories of granite blocks regularly pierced by thin, dark windows. Higher up, it blossomed into a crystalline riot of glass and light. They hesitated in front of the marble threshold.

"I bet they're wearing shoes made of real cow." Lily tucked her purse under her arm as if she expected some rampaging doorman to snatch it from her.

"Don't worry." Marja touched Lily's hand. "You look fine." She had lent Lily a crepe off-the-shoulder dress her grandmother had left her. It was too 90s for Lily's taste, but Marja was the specialist when it came to this sort of thing.

"You too," said Lily, "but that's not what I mean. Look where we are. We can't afford this—unless you don't mind eating Cheerios for supper until finals."

"Come on. How much could it cost?"

"What's the gross national product of Portugal?"

"I'll ask, okay? I'll just poke my head in the door and find out."

"No, I'm coming." Lily rammed her purse deeper into her armpit and clamped it.

Lily had expected flocked wallpaper and leather couches. Instead there were lots of bright plastic surfaces and a rug with all the ambiance of sandpaper. The lobby of the Hothouse was emphatically air-conditioned and illuminated almost to the point of discomfort. Only two of the five ticket booths were open. Beyond them was a bank of sliding doors, textured to look like the trunks of trees.

"Hi." The cashier was a young woman in an extravagant foliage print dress. She had jade highlights in her black hair and an expression as guileless as a pansy. "Are you together?" The button on her collar said *Ju*.

"Yes," said Marja.

"No." Lily nudged her. "We came together, but we're not *together* together."

Ju smiled. "Whatever."

"We're interested," Marja said, "but we're not really sure this place is for us. Can you tell us about it?"

"As in, what does it cost?" Lily said.

Ju slid a brochure across the counter toward them; her fingernails were polished the same green as her hair. "Your basic attraction enhancement is $39.95." She opened it; inside was a map. "Includes admission to all public areas on the third and fifth floors, all gardens, three dance floors, both pools, complimentary swimsuits and towels in the dressing booths. On the fourth floor are stores and services you'll pay extra for. Sit-down and take-out restaurants, bars, gift shops, lingerie boutiques, contraception kiosks, simulators, and personal fx galleries."

It's nothing but a mall, Lily thought. I'm twenty-five years old and still looking for love at the mall.

"We also have fifty-three private encounter rooms," Ju pointed to the map, "on the sixth floor. We're the biggest neuromance palace in the city."

Lily watched a little man in a navy blue jacket and gray slacks approach the other cashier. Her age but not her type; he looked as if he had just finished eating a memo salad at the Office Restaurant. "So how do you make someone fall in love?" she asked.

"Oh, we don't make you fall. We enhance the attraction response. There's a big difference. See, we trick this part of your brain called the hypothalamus into ordering up these special hormones. It's all natural."

"Hormones like LHRH and testosterone?" said Lily.

"Testosterone, right." Ju nodded. "That surprised me when I first heard it. I mean, you'd think you'd grow a mustache—or worse. But it's okay; I've tried it." She gave them a blissful smile. "Don't know about the one with letters, they all sound the same. To tell the truth, they explained this to me once, but it didn't take. All I know is that whatever we do to you is approved by the FDA and licensed by the Board of Health. This card explains . . ."

"Give me that." Marja snatched it from Lily. "Believe me, the procedure is straight out of Wessinger's neurobiology lab. The less you think about it, the better you'll feel."

"Whatever." Ju dimpled. "But really, one of the best parts is that they tickle something called your vomeronasal organ—don't ask me how. You'll smell stuff you've never noticed before. Unbelievable, how great the food tastes. Try the brownies with brandy sauce." She kissed her fingers to the air and the man waiting at the next booth glanced over at them. Lily thought he might actually be shorter than she was.

"So what if we pay you our forty bucks," she said, "and go upstairs and find there're no human beings left? I don't want to fall for an insurance salesman."

"Oh, that's not a problem, believe me. We offer a money-back guarantee, but only a few people ask. See, when those elevator doors open onto the welcome garden, you're . . . I don't know . . . ripe. I can't explain it exactly, but enhancement makes me realize how cute men look, how sweet they can be. At least while they're here. And it's really a grade crowd tonight. Some real hammers, if you know what I mean. I kind of wish I wasn't working myself."

An older man who shouldn't have been wearing red skintights got in line behind them, so they gave Ju their cash cards. While she debited them, she had them press thumbs to a blood drawer. She printed two green buttons that read *Lily* and *Marja* and explained that green was for righties, red for gays. She had them sign liability waivers, told them they'd need to give a urine sample, and warned them about side effects. Although enhancement would wear off in four to five hours, they might have trouble falling asleep immediately after leaving the Hothouse; there was a chance their next periods might be a couple of days off schedule. She grinned, reminded them about the brownies and ushered them through the booth.

"We're in this together, right?" Lily whispered as the tree trunk doors opened. "You'll stop me before I do anything stupid?"

Marja laughed and patted her on the back. "Sort of late for that now."

Lily rubbed the button-sized swelling on her wrist where the orderly had poked her with the pressure syringe. Her purse hung loosely by her side.

"Pulse accelerated." Marja was practically vibrating as the elevator climbed to the third floor. "Skin temperature elevated. Apocrine sweat glands—whew!" She peered into Lily's left eye, "Doctor, your pupils are dilated!"

"Stop diagnosing."

"Okay, so how do you feel?"

Lily considered and then giggled. "Like I'm six and it's Christmas Eve. You're losing your corsage."

Marja repinned the orchid which the orderly had laced with pheromones synthesized from her urine sample. The doors slid open.

Fifteen or twenty faces turned, glowing with expectation. Lily was instantly drawn to them, understanding their conspicuous need because she shared it. They had hauled themselves out of the icy datastream into the warmth of high touch and beautiful feelings. As the enhancement drugs gripped her, she felt the weight of her life drop away. Tomorrow they would all go back to their desks and workshops and counters and she would ligate the arteries of a cyber-corpse named Fred. But that was far removed from this bright dream of lush and immediate sensation. She let it fill her lungs and eyes and ears; she wanted to lick it. A band stood poised to play. Leaves like green hands waved at her. She itched to rub her bare feet on the moss rug, shinny up that palm tree, kiss all three of those men by the fountain just to find out how they tasted. No, she wasn't going to ask for her money back. She knew she would find him here. Someone to love, for a little while at least. His identity was a mystery only she could solve: Lily Brewster, girl detective. Maybe he was still lingering at the marble threshold on Densmore Street, ten thousand miles below, or already talking to Ju in the lobby. Most likely he was watching her, one of the happy faces, which she now noticed were arranged in a kind of loose formation. She and Marja stepped down into the welcome garden's central courtyard and smiling people closed around them.

She smiled back, even after she realized she was going to have to square dance.

The bass player had a voice as friendly as a milk commercial.

> "All square your sets around the hall,
> Four couples to a set, listen to the call."

He chose "The Texas Star," a simple figure dance which featured constant switching of partners.

Her first was the short man from the lobby; his green name badge read *Steve*. She couldn't understand how he had gotten to the welcome garden before her. Just as the dance began, he insisted on shaking her hand. "You're freezing!" Lily said, clasping his cold hand between hers.

He stared as if he were memorizing her face. "I just washed up."

When the fiddles started, he led her into a left-faced turn under his arched right arm. "You know, Lily, your handshake tells a lot about you."

> "Meet your partner, pass on by
> Pick up your next one on the fly."

Nick, a pale man with a mustache like a caterpillar said, "I know you! We met at Justin Metaphor's last image launch." He stared at Lily's corsage as if he wanted to eat it. "You came as President Garmezy."

"Not me," she said. "I'm a Neurocrat."

> "Smalls back out, bigs go in,
> Make that Texas Star again."

"Am I a big or a small?" She crooked her arm into that of a heavyweight with hair down his neck. Tomasz had feet as wide as shovels.

"You're a small, my kitten, but plenty big enough for me." He had a thick Middle European accent; she decided to leave him for Marja.

> "Bigs back out and all circle eight
> Circle back to place 'til you get it straight."

The fiddlers stroked their instruments. Was that her roommate, skipping like a girl scout? Lily was determined to initiate the next conversation. "This is probably the silliest damn thing I've ever done," she said to a red badge named Renfred who smelled of cigarettes.

"Never done it before." Sweat beaded across his face like a glass of iced tea. "I'm from Toronto."

> "Hand over hand and heel over heel
> The more you dance the better you feel."

"I've finally decided who you remind me of." Keith had green eyes and more teeth than a shark. "One of those Vermeer women, standing in front of a window." The fat end of his untied tie dangled in front of his crotch and the skinny end beat against his pocket as he danced. "Vermeer, you know, the painter?"

Not a bad line, she thought, but he ruined it by prompting her. "Keith." She tugged the tie from around his neck and handed it to him. "Is this yours?"

Her next partner ignored her. "Yes, of course I did." He spoke over his shoulder to the Asian woman behind Lily. "She belonged with her parents."

> *"Tuck in your shirt, pull down your vest*
> *And bow to the one you like the best."*

The fiddlers tipped their instruments toward the caller and the dance ended. Lily might have nodded at Keith, the Vermeer fan, if he'd been paying attention, but he was already fawning over an older woman with eyes like targets. Someone tapped her left shoulder; she turned.

"My name is Steve." The guy with cold hands bowed.

"Lily." She glanced down to see that she hadn't lost her name badge. "Obviously."

"Lily, do you know that people rarely change their first impressions?" His eye contact was relentless.

"Is that so?" she said. Steve was as clean-cut as a Marine recruiter. He had stubby fingers and wide shoulders. A thread hung loose from the middle buttonhole of his jacket. "What's yours?" He hadn't gotten any taller.

He held up open palms, as if to show he was unarmed. "That you're gorgeous, lonely, nervous, and still shopping. Will you at least let me shake your hand again?"

"Promise to give it back?" she said. He had a precise and sincere grip that didn't try to prove anything. "You've warmed up." Their hands fit together nicely.

"When my palms get sweaty," he said, "I rinse them under cold water. It's a sales trick: the confident man keeps a cool hand."

She had never understood why men always said such odd things to her.

"Here's another," he continued. "Say we're shaking and you haven't decided whether to trust me. Look where your hand is, Lily. When we started talking, you kept it close to your body. Now that I've drawn it toward me slightly, you've come along with it."

Lily let go of him. She reminded herself that this was a man with a crew cut who practiced sales tricks. "And what are you trying to sell me?"

"I don't know yet." His voice was low. "First I have to find out if I carry what you want."

The elevator doors opened and everyone turned to inspect the new arrivals. It was Old Man Skintights and a thirtyish brunette in a caramel-colored suit. As the dancers moved to welcome them, the fiddlers picked up their bows.

"Never leave a prospect until you schedule your next meeting."
Steve grinned. "Shall we say, after this dance?" He strolled away
whistling but paused at the edge of the garden and called to her.
"I like you, Lily. Obviously." He disappeared behind a hibiscus
covered with red flowers.

There's a man who knows exactly what he wants, she thought,
and I'm it. She was at once pleased and scared and slightly let
down. Where had he gone so abruptly? To rinse in cold water?

The caller tapped the belly of his bass. "*All square your sets . . .*"

Lily had intended to dance again, but that was what he expected
her to do. She thought it better to be unpredictable, make his hands
sweat. She spotted some people gathered beneath a statue of a satyr
groping a nymph.

"Now you're getting into ideology," a nervous black man said.
"Ask Alice about that."

"About what?" said a woman in a poet's blouse and orange
tights.

"Keith here claims the female orgasm is vestigial. A leftover, like
an appendix."

"Should we kill him now," Betty said to T. J., who had his arm
around her waist, "or hear him out first?"

"Hey, I'm not against anyone's orgasm," Keith said quickly. "My
point is that in evolutionary terms, female orgasm is irrelevant.
Some societies don't even have a word for it."

"We should make one up for them," said Lily. "How about
shimmer? Or leap?"

"Oh yes, baby, yes, I'm rippling."

Alice shook her head. "Maybe you ripple, honey, but I *surge.*"

All the women laughed.

Keith wasn't giving up. "Women reproduce whether they climax or not. With us, orgasm is everything. If we don't come, there's
no ball game."

"*Ball* game?" Betty rubbed against T. J. "Why is it that whenever
we try to talk about love, men change the subject to sports?"

"It's because we take pleasure differently," said Alice. "A man
gets off on objects. He sees tits and an ass and he doesn't care who
they're attached to. We need intimacy and tenderness to enjoy
ourselves. We don't give a damn how big his cock is; we want to
know the size of his feelings."

"All men want is sex." Maya sighed. "We want love."

"Ah, bullshit," said T. J "I want to dance."

"Look, someone's imprinting."

The band broke into the ceremonial "Only You Tonight" and

dancers closed in a circle around a couple, clapping and cheering them on. Lily strained to see who it was. Big Tomasz with the shovel feet—and Marja! "Wait!" As Lily raced across the courtyard, Marja pulled Tomasz down to her. He buried his nose in her corsage. The orderly had explained that once two people imprinted themselves with each others' pheromones, they would be inseparable the rest of the night. When Tomasz came up, his eyes were gleaming.

Lily waved frantically at her but Marja paid no attention. Tomasz offered her the chocolate the Hothouse staff had impregnated with his own musky androstenols. It was wrapped in gold foil; she unpeeled it lasciviously, pressed it between her lips and chewed, her jaws working around a cheek-stretching smile.

The crowd's rhythmic clapping punctuated the impromptu ceremony. "Let's congratulate the new couple," said the caller from behind his bass. Now that they had imprinted, their badges changed to a color which only they shared. It was the purple of venous blood. "Seal it with a kiss!" the caller cried.

The crowd whooped.

"Isn't he grade?" Marja was glowing. "Am I lucky or what? This is Lily, my roommate. Tomasz is a lion tamer, can you believe that?" Lily could smell the chocolate on her breath.

"*Moj Boze, Marja, ja cie kocham.*"

"Aren't lions extinct?" Lily said.

He didn't hear her; he and Marja were kissing again. By the time they finished, Lily assumed he had forgotten the question, so she asked again.

"In the wild, yes." He kept one massive arm clasped around Marja's shoulder as if she were a trophy he had just won. "I work with the New World cats mostly, cougars and jaguars. We have one leopard." He feinted at her with his free hand and grinned when she recoiled. "All strong enough to kill you."

"I didn't even know the circus was in town."

"They leave Wednesday," said Marja. "Which is why we're going to the fifth floor right now and find a quiet place and tell each other our life stories. Maybe later we can swim."

"I want an olive pizza," said Tomasz, "and a liter of kava."

"Okay, kava and pizza." She nestled up to him. "What else do you want?"

He had a laugh that could worry a cougar.

"So Marja," said Lily, "maybe we should set a time to meet?"

"No, no, I'll get home on my own." She gave Lily a look like a bedroom door closing. "Don't wait up. I'll see you at Freddy's tomorrow."

"Freddy?" said Tomasz.

"He's nobody," she said as she steered her prize away.

Lily filled with doubts as she watched her friend go. They had promised not to let each other do anything stupid. Did falling for a lion tamer qualify? Now that she'd been abandoned, she wished she were home studying. Coming to the Hothouse made sense in the romantic abstract, but the men here were all annoyingly specific. She wasn't attracted to anyone and even if she were, how could she trust her feelings? They'd pumped her so full of hormones she could probably fall for a vacuum cleaner if it smelled right. She decided she didn't much like being enhanced, although she understood that there was no difference between the brain chemistry of neuromance and actually falling in love. Despite her B+ in Wessinger's class, Lily was reluctant to accept a mechanistic view of her inner life. She didn't like being reminded that love, hope, and joy were merely outputs of her limbic system. What she ought to do was march right down for a refund, go home and stare into her spex until she had memorized the immunoglobulins. The idea was oddly comforting: maybe the enhancement was wearing off. Marja had warned her that thinking too much about it might spoil the effect.

"You didn't dance."

She moaned. "Oh, shit." She couldn't help herself. Steve had taken off the navy blue jacket; he was wearing a white shirt and a red striped tie. "I'm sorry. Look, this has nothing to do with you. You seem nice enough. It's just . . . I'm probably going to leave. Get my money back."

"Why?"

"Because I don't like being programmed. I mean, I realized that's what would happen when I walked in, but I thought somehow it would fool me. Now I know better. This just doesn't feel like love. It's a chemistry experiment."

"You've been in love before, Lily?"

"Of course." He wouldn't take a hint; she'd probably have to be rude.

"What's it like?"

"Oh, come on." She watched him watching her, his pupils like black buttons. "You know."

"No. I've never been in love."

"What, you grew up in a monastery?"

The sarcasm seemed to bounce off him. "I thought I was in love once." He paused, as if deciding how much to tell her. "We worked in the same office. She was older. Married. When her husband found out, she broke it off. She said she didn't love me and that I didn't really love her."

"And you believed her?" Lily didn't know why she was encouraging him.

He nodded. "She was right. The sex was great but it wasn't love. I got all excited because she was beautiful, smart, rich, powerful, what I thought I wanted. But we never talked, except about the business or the weather or what hotel to meet at. The day we broke up she told me she was a Catholic and went to church every Sunday. She said she'd felt really guilty about what we'd been doing. It wasn't a secret, I just never asked."

The elevator doors opened again and a bald Hispanic woman blinked in astonishment at the welcome garden.

"I realized that if I hadn't loved *her*, then I'd never loved anyone."

The musicians were ready. "Hell of a thing to find out about yourself," she said.

"Something I'd like to fix, Lily."

This was her chance; she could escape into the next dance. She wouldn't have to hurt him—not that she cared. Afterward she could sneak away. She didn't need a man with another woman's footprints up his back. But if she left now, who was going to make sure Marja didn't run off with the circus?

"What happened to your jacket?" she said. "Your name badge?"

"I went to find a place where we could be alone. I left them to hold our spot."

The bass player announced a new dance called "Swing or Cheat" and sets began forming around them.

"It's really pretty," Steve said. "There's a stream and a bush with tiny oranges on it and white flowers that smell like honey."

Lily was getting used to the way he made eye contact. Whatever Steve's other faults, she believed he was sincere. Glenn had always looked away when he lied to her.

"You just left your jacket there?" she said. "I hope no one takes it."

He led her down a slate path past the eight-foot-wide sheet of falling water which drowned the shrilling of the fiddles. They turned into one of the garden's many little clearings. The bench was wrought iron; it sat low on a lawn of lemon thyme. The stream burbled in front of them and the air hung heavy and sweet. Steve's jacket was folded over the armrest.

"Calamondin oranges." She slid her purse under the bench. "They're sour, just barely edible. They make good marmalade, though."

"How do you know so much about plants?"

"My dad's hobby, actually. He had a greenhouse. I remember in the winter it was always so bright and warm. Like going on vacation. The pots were all on wheels; when he was away I used to move plants around and build myself a jungle. He was away a lot. He was a doctor too."

"Is he still alive?"

"No, my parents are both dead." She let one of her shoes drop off. "He always said he liked flowers so much he had one for a daughter." She tickled her foot in the thyme. This clearing reminded her of one of her jungles.

"My father is an engineer on an oil tanker," Steve said. "He'd be at sea for three months and then with us for two. I missed him when he was away, but once he got home I couldn't wait for him to ship out again. He was too strict and he yelled at Mom. Since they divorced, I haven't seen him much. Now Mom—she's great. She worked twenty-eight years at Sears, wherever they needed her. She could talk you into a tent or towels or a thinkmate, no problem. I was a shy boy, if you can believe that, but she kept pushing me. She said I had to go out and show the world what a great son she had."

As he spoke, Lily folded and unfolded her hands. She didn't want to hear about Steve's family problems and now she was embarrassed to have shared memories of her father with a stranger. "What are we doing here?"

"I don't know about you, Lily, but I'm enjoying the view." He leaned back and looked her up and down with obvious approval "Pretty flowers, great company—hey, ssh!"

He held a finger to his lips. There were muffled voices, then footsteps on the path. The foliage hid the strollers but as they approached Lily heard a man declaiming with the grandiloquence of a longtime Shakespeare abuser. "She walks in *beauty*, like the *night* of cloudless climes and *starry skies*; and all that's *best* of dark and bright, meet in her aspect and her *eyes*. . . ."

Lily held in her laughter until they were safely past, then she burst. After a second, Steve roared too, although she suspected that it was only because he was relieved that she was finally unwinding.

"So you can laugh," he said. "What an improvement!"

"It's just . . . the old Byron trick." She couldn't catch her breath. "The corniest, the lamest. . . ." She started to dissolve again.

"This Byron writes poems?"

"Lord Byron, you dope." It didn't seem to help. "Hey, even I know Byron and I took hackers' English in college."

He leaned forward and reached between his feet for a sprig of thyme. He said nothing.

"I can't believe anyone over eighteen would fall for a line like that."

He started defoliating the thyme. "Maybe she likes poetry."

"But don't you see, that's the whole problem! Tired old poems work, dumb songs work, honesty works, lies work, every trick in the book works. There's no choice involved, we're practically defenseless here."

"You know what the problem is, Lily?" He looked unhappy. "You're too busy thinking to enjoy yourself."

She was surprised at how much his disapproval stung. "Excuse *me*?" He was nobody, a pushy salesman she hardly knew. "Using your head isn't exactly a handicap, you know." She waited for him to apologize, explain himself, make her feel better, but he let the silence stretch. The dumb little bastard. He wasn't going to get away with hurting her; she could retaliate. "So Steve, what was your major in college?" She already knew the answer.

"Didn't have one."

"Oh come on, everyone . . ."

"Didn't go."

The stream babbled through another long silence. She thought of twelve different things to say, but couldn't speak because she was too ashamed of herself for humiliating him. What a snob she was! If this was neuromance then she could do without it; she'd had more conflicting feelings in the past half hour than she'd had in six months. Steve stood up, put on his jacket, sat down again. She watched him, an emptiness growing within her. Maybe she couldn't fall anymore, maybe the parts of her brain that loved had atrophied.

"You never answered my question, Lily," he said.

"What was it?"

"You were going to tell me what it's like to be in love."

"It stinks, actually." She didn't hesitate. "You lose everything, your friends, your freedom. Your bathroom. He kicks you awake at three in the morning but if he's not there you can't sleep. He never wants the vid you want and he doesn't eat fish and he can't wait to tell you when you're wrong. And when you're fighting, it feels like you're getting an appendectomy without anesthesia."

"You call that a sales pitch?" There was a hint of a smile on his lips. "If it's so horrible, why come here?"

"I don't know why I came here." Another silence that she didn't want loomed. "I'm sorry, Steve."

"Hey, you said my name! That's the first time you said my name."

"I figured it was time, since you've said mine a hundred times already." She gave a dry chuckle. "What is that, anyway, another sales trick?"

"You know studies show only twenty percent of communication is verbal." He slid slowly across the bench toward her. "The other eighty percent depends on non-verbal cues." He kept coming. "Facial expressions, posture, tone of voice." When he stopped, they were six inches apart. "I'm in your personal space now. We're not touching but you can feel me, can't you?"

"Yes." She liked the feeling. It was like coming out of an ice storm and standing next to a crackling fire.

"Sales tricks are based on the way people are, Lily. They connect with real feelings. Sure, some people use them to sell bad products or unnecessary ones, but I don't. I just try to give the prospect what she wants."

Lily watched his mouth as he spoke. For some reason, the way his lips moved fascinated her. She could see his teeth and the tip of his tongue.

"But you don't know what you want, do you?"

"I want to be happy."

"But you don't want to fall in love?" He leaned and brushed his shoulder against her. "Lose your freedom? Everything?"

"Maybe it's too late." She was surprised to hear herself say it aloud, although she had known it for some time. "I wonder what would happen if I sniffed my own corsage?" She touched it absently. "Probably spend the night crouching by the stream, admiring myself."

"I'd like to spend the night admiring you, Lily. Obviously."

She laughed and then she kissed him. When she closed her eyes, he smelled like chocolate. It had to be some kind of trick, she thought before she stopped thinking. When she finished with him, she saw her own smile reflected on his lips.

"I'm hungry." Lily slipped her hand into his pocket. "Do you have anything to eat?" She trapped the candy against his taut abdominal muscles.

He squirmed as if he were ticklish. "Can we do this in private?"

As far as she was concerned, the rest of the Hothouse was nothing but rumors and mist. "We can do whatever we want."

She expected some kind of cortisol and epinephrine boost when she ate the chocolate but all she felt was the lingering warmth of his kiss. It was only when he lowered his head slowly, deliberately, to her corsage, that her blood began to pound. He filled his lungs with her scent. "Nice," he said, "but I prefer the real thing."

"Hey look," she said, "our badges have already changed. . . ."

He covered her mouth with his, filling her world in all directions. He certainly knew how to sell a kiss. She brushed her fingertips across his cheek and he pulled back and rubbed his cheek against hers. "You like to hear me say your name." He nuzzled her ear. "Don't you?" He was whispering. "Lily?"

"Yes," she said. "Oh, yes."

She told him about getting an A– in Professor Graves Anatomy class where twenty students failed and he told her about the time he'd hit a grand slam off Chico Moran, who was now the number two starter for the Dodgers. She'd done her pre-med at Michigan State and he'd played shortstop for a season and a half with the Red Sox's farm team in New Britain, Connecticut before blowing out his knee sliding into third. It was the worst moment of his life; hers was when her father died. He was twenty-six, she was twenty-five. She warned him she wouldn't eat artichokes or buffalo or anything with peanut butter in it. He'd never had an artichoke. He bragged about the time his mother sold a watch to Vice President Blaine and made the six o'clock news. Her mother had never worked, she'd stayed home to take care of Lily and her two sisters and drink blush wine. Lily was the youngest, Steve was an only child. She complained about Marja's shoes. He hardly ever saw his best friend because he caught for the Colorado Rockies. He made her tell him about Glenn who was at Johns Hopkins now studying gerontology because that was where the money was. They'd lived together off-campus their senior year in East Lansing; Glenn had a four handicap in golf and wanted her to wear stupid hats when he was in the mood for sex. He told her a little more about Marsha, how she'd taught him how to sell and how she apologized for her Caesarian scar the first time they'd made love. He said the best times together were when she let him drive her Porsche 717 and Lily laughed and said Glenn had a Mazda Magic which he had never let her drive but that once when he went home for his grandmother's funeral she had swiped his keys and cranked it to 110 on I-96 and had never told anyone until now so they pressed their bodies hard against each

other and kissed until their lips were numb and Lily wondered what
it cost to rent an encounter room on the sixth floor.

By eleven the clearing was too small for them. It was time to see
if their newfound infatuation was portable. They started strolling
hand in hand up the slate path before she realized she had left her
purse behind.

Almost everybody in the welcome garden had paired up and dispersed; there were only enough dancers to make two sets. Lily
thought she detected a note of desperation in the music. As the
dancers promenaded, the caller warned them:

> "Hurry up strangers, don't be slow,
> You'll never fall in love unless you do-si-do."

Maybe the band was ready to pack up. As she watched Old Man
Skintights bravely circling the floor, she wondered what it would
feel like to get enhanced and then not find anyone to fall for. A
refund wouldn't really cover the cost of being iced out at a neuromance palace. She remembered her first glimpse of the welcome
garden, when it had bubbled with exotic possibilities. Now it
seemed as flat as yesterday's champagne.

"They gave us four or five hours," she said. "At midnight we all
turn into pumpkins."

Steve had zero tolerance for melancholy. "This way." He aimed
her at the elevators.

"No," she said, "let's walk up."

"Two flights?"

"Oh, we have to peek at shops on the fourth floor," she said. He
looked doubtful. "Maybe get something to eat?"

"I'm not hungry."

"Well, what if I am?"

He colored; it was the first time she had seen him embarrassed.
"Sorry." He turned reluctantly toward the stairs but when he tugged
at her to follow, she let him go.

"Steve, what's the matter?"

"I don't know." He shrugged. "Maybe it's just that I hate being
sold things I don't need." She sensed that he wanted to say something else—but he didn't.

"I'll swallow my cash card, okay?" Lily said. He reached out for
her and she came to him. "I'll be good. Promise."

Where the third floor had been a hot, dark blur, the fourth was
a place to lounge and consume conspicuously. With its open sight
lines, it flaunted the true size of the Hothouse. The shops and
restaurants ringed an enormous irregularly shaped pool. Its bays

and peninsulas were landscaped with bougainvillea. There were sandy beaches and ten-foot bluffs. They saw couples sprawled on checked tableclothes beside wicker picnic baskets: the picnickers drank wine from bottles with broad shoulders and broke long sticks of French bread.

"We can swim," said Lily. "That's free."

"Sure." When he gave her a forlorn smile, she worried that he was relieved to be getting away from her.

The dressing booths were between the Honey Bun Bakery and the Intimate Moment, a lingerie store. The bakery breathed the yeasty aroma of warm bread onto them. Lily's mouth watered but she said nothing. Instead she kissed Steve and he brightened. They went through separate doors.

Her booth was a four-foot square; its only furnishing was a shelf-like seat. The far wall was a screen on which appeared her image, larger than life. She winked at herself and then giggled because she was certain that she had just discovered Steve's secret character flaw: he was cheap. Somehow that reassured her, perhaps because it was so curable. It wasn't as if he were a womanizer or a drunk or a golfer. Lily believed she understood thrift since she practiced it of necessity herself. Someday, when she was a rich gynecologist, they would come here and she would buy him something from every shop.

Suddenly the little booth seemed very chilly. The enhancement that had helped her fall for Steve would wear off in a couple of hours and then what would be left of her feelings for him? Maybe there wasn't going to be any *someday* with Steve.

"Welcome to the Hothouse." When the booth spoke to her, it was her own image that appeared to be talking. "This is a dressing booth. Occupancy is strictly limited to one. For those couples requiring privacy, may we suggest our encounter rooms on the sixth floor?"

"Oh?" She leered at herself. "And how much would they cost?"

Eight windows opened down the left hand side of the screen. "Encounter rooms range from $20 to $110." Each window showed a differently priced room. Twenty dollars bought a closet with a bed in it; the suite with a chandelier and the flocked wallpaper cost a hundred. "Shall I make a reservation for you now?"

"No, make me a bathing suit."

The rooms disappeared. "Swimdress, tank, two piece, or bikini?"

"Bikini."

She whimpered when saw herself on the screen in a generic black bikini. There had to be some perverse glitch in the booth's software; her skin was the color of cement and her knees looked like doorknobs.

"Would you prefer a bandeau, halter, or athletic top?"

"Bandeau."

"Underwire, sculptex, pump, or natural?"

"Pump?"

She watched in horror as her breasts rose like popovers baking on fast-forward. If they'd been lifted any higher they would have been pointing at the moon.

"No, natural."

They receded. She turned sideways and eyed her figure hopelessly. She experimented with a high-cut brief but the edges of her glutei maximi hung out of it like mocking fleshy grins. The booth could fabricate the suit in any of three thousand prints or 1.2 million solids. With a sigh, she chose something in the mid-cyan range. Letting him see her in a swimsuit on the first date—what *had* she been thinking of? A drawer slid open with the suit and towel in a sealed plastic bag.

"After pressing your thumb to the printreader, deposit your belongings in the drawer for later retrieval." Lily could not help but think of Steve's cool hands as she started unbuttoning the front of her dress.

She came out of the dressing booth and immediately panicked: Steve wasn't waiting. The door to his booth was open! Her first thought was that he was mad at her and had left. Her skin felt tight. Maybe he'd gone back to the welcome garden to try his luck again, or left the Hothouse altogether. Oh God, what had she been thinking of? They should've taken the damn elevator; she didn't really care about swimming and she couldn't afford to shop. She had to find him, apologize—but should she get dressed first or ransack the Hothouse in her bikini? While she was trying to decide, he came out of the men's room. The sight of him made her eyes burn. This was love, yes, it had already reduced her to a dithering adolescent.

"Lily, are you all right?" he said.

She swooped into his embrace. "Fine now." She didn't know why it had bothered her before that he was short. She put her arms around his compact athlete's body and realized that a larger man wouldn't be quite so huggable. She noticed that he was slightly lopsided, right deltoids and biceps bigger than the left. All those throws to first base. "I just missed you."

"Look at you." He peeled her away from him. "You're beautiful. Fantastic."

They kissed again and she ran her fingertips across his back and felt his skin warming hers. She knew exactly what had happened: the fear of losing him had hit her in the adrenal glands. Hard. Hormones had seeped and messenger chemicals had washed into the deepest parts of her brain, but the chemistry didn't matter to her anymore. She wanted him. It wasn't only lust; she wanted to ease his pain over losing baseball, to thank him for listening to her whine about Glenn, to show him what love might be. They would be so good for one another, only she didn't have the $20. She tried to think of a way to get him to split the cost of a room without aggravating him about the money.

"Lily," he murmured. "There's something I have to tell you."

She shuddered—she hated the way men confessed! They didn't know how and besides, whenever they were sorry, it was always for the wrong thing. Lily wasn't interested in what he had to say. She wanted to tell him to shut up. But she didn't have to.

"Lily!" Someone was waving.

"Over here. *Lily*." Marja stood, hands raised, on a red-checked tablecloth on the beach. Tomasz lolled at her feet like a sleepy tiger.

"Just wave back," said Steve, "we really need to talk."

"She's my best friend. She'll strangle me if I don't introduce you."

Marja was wearing a purple maillot that had a cookie-sized transparency sprite roving across its surface, exposing pale skin. That might have explained why her cheeks were so red, but Lily doubted it. Tomasz sat up as they approached and rubbed his eyes. There was a half-full bottle of kava in the picnic basket. Someone had kicked white sand into an empty pizza carton.

"And who is this?" Marja said.

"Steve." Lily said. "My God, Steve, you haven't told me your last name yet."

"Beauchamp."

"Nice to meet you." They shook hands; Lily watched and wondered what he discovered about her. "I was just about to swim," said Marja. "You two interested in a quick dip?"

"Sure," said Lily. She glanced over at Steve; he was pouting. "Steve?"

He shook his head.

"Good. Let the ladies go." Tomasz rolled toward the kava. "We'll work the bottle."

The two women waded into the tepid water. When it lapped at

her waist, Marja sank backwards with a weary moan. "A pretty little one you picked," she said.

"I think so," Lily said. "So, did you do anything stupid yet?"

"I let him talk me into this damn bathing suit. Bad enough people can see my thighs but random nudity. . . ." She snorted in disgust. "My synapses don't snap for Tomasz the way they used to, but it was grade while it lasted."

"How was the sixth floor?"

"What, am I still flushed? For a while I thought my face had caught fire." She ducked underwater and came up spluttering laughter. "He's one of the hammers—isn't that what the reception-ist called them? Wasn't much of a talker, but he communicated, wow. Got that from his cats, I guess. Funny to be talking about him in the past tense already." She splashed Lily. "So did you have an encounter?"

"We've talked a lot, that's all. He's very . . . I don't know . . . deci-sive. From the moment we met he seemed so sure that he wanted me. Eventually I started wanting him. A lot." She laughed. "What-ever they gave us must have worked overtime because I . . . I think I really love him, Marja. I don't want this to be over in an hour." She did a few backstrokes away from the shore, where Steve was gesturing at Tomasz with the bottle of kava. "Is that supposed to happen?"

"Hey, maybe you talked too much, roomie. You're not in the market for a keeper. Besides, where would you put him?"

"He can stay at his place; I just want to borrow him once in awhile. Anyway, right before we spotted you he said he had some-thing important to tell me, which is probably that he's emigrating to Uzbekistan next Wednesday." When Lily waved to him, Steve got up and walked to the edge of the water. "I should get back," she said.

"Tomasz and I are about done, Lily." Marja looked worried. "Maybe we should both call it a night? Get his number. If you're still hot in the morning, you can call him."

She treaded water, not listening. "Ever hear of a baseball player named Chico Moran?"

Flowers had overrun the fifth floor. They marched down crushed stone paths and spread across parterres and perennial borders. This was a strolling floor, not as private as the third, nor as public as the fourth. The oak benches tucked beside the flower beds were clearly visible from the paths. The only privacy was that afforded by politeness. Lily and Steve passed blindly past two laughing gay men and an elderly couple who had fallen asleep. She, however, could not help but gape at the impossible couple of Alice the feminist and Keith the lizard, entwining passionately

Finally they chanced upon an empty bench which faced a drift of impatiens swarming around the legs of burgundy roses. She leaned over to smell one and then covered a yawn with the back of her hand. It was almost one. Time for him to stop talking and get back to kissing.

Steve waved for her to sit beside him. "Because good salesmen don't lie, Lily." He put his arm around her. "We have to buy before we can sell. First I have to believe that my product is the best for you, otherwise I can't get you interested in it. And I do, Lily. Maybe you still have some doubts, but I know I'd be good for you."

"No, I'm sure too." She was delighted that it was still true. Marja was no doubt already home in bed; Lily's enhancement must have worn off by now. This wasn't neuromance anymore; she was on her own.

"This isn't easy, okay? A salesman never brings up his own negatives. That's anti-selling. If a client has a problem or complaint, I acknowledge it and try to work it out. But if I start telling you what I think is wrong with me, not only could I lose you, I might even stop believing in myself."

"I'm sorry; I should've listened before." She leaned her head on his shoulder. "So tell me now."

"Okay, start at the beginning. Ever heard of the new produce?"

"Isn't that the pricey stuff they sell at those food boutiques?"

He nodded. "Here in America we rely on just twenty-four crops for most of what we eat. But there are over twenty thousand edible plants. Oca from South America. Arracacha, it's a cross between celery and carrot. Mamey from Cuba. I've spent a lot of time learning the new produce. It's a specialty market now but it has tremendous potential for breakout. I developed contacts all over the country."

"This has something to do with us?"

His voice was tight. "You remember Marsha, the one who taught me about selling? Well, her husband Bill owned the company I worked for. Not only did he fire me, but the son of a bitch is still working overtime to keep me from catching on somewhere else. Like this evening, I stopped by World Food across the street. I used to take the manager there out to the stadium—on my tab. But tonight my good friend informs me that his headquarters says I'm nobody and there's nothing he can do for me." He choked back his outrage. "I'm going to beat these guys, Lily, and soon. Only. . . ."

"You're out of work?" She sat up, giddy with relief. "You poor thing, that's terrible." It was hard to keep from laughing. "How long?"

"Eight months."

"Steve, you're only twenty-six. It's not like you're Willie Loman. You can find something else to sell."

"Willie Loman? Who's he, some fancy marketing professor? What the hell does Willie Loman know about selling glasswort to Piggly Wiggly?"

"Nothing." She slipped her hand onto his knee and squeezed. "Forget it." She didn't want him angry at her, too.

"I gave up my life once, Lily," he said firmly. "What I learned from that is I never want to do it again. But now you know that the real reason I didn't want to go to the fourth floor was that I couldn't afford to. Believe me, if I had money to spend, you'd see all of it. When we were down by the stream, I kept thinking how it would be to take you upstairs to one of the rooms." He reached into his pocket. "Problem is my cash card flamed out two weeks ago." He pulled a crumpled two dollar bill taut, smoothed it against his leg and offered it to her. "My life savings."

"You have no money at all? Then why come to a place like this? How'd you even get in?"

"Because the most important sales trick of all has nothing to do with the prospect. See, a salesman has to keep up his own self image. When everyone else is beating him down, he has to treat himself like a winner. Maybe I'm broke, but I'm *not* nobody, damn it! I'm Steve Beauchamp; I go where I want, when I want." He straightened. "Anyway, I talked my way into a discount because I didn't get enhanced. Even so, they took almost everything I had at the door."

"You didn't get enhanced!"

"Didn't need to." He took her hand; his palm was moist. "I know this sounds strange, but when I came out of World Food and saw you with your friend, something happened. I can't explain it, but I thought, there's a woman I need to meet. So I followed you in. Believe me, Lily, I've never done anything like this before. When I saw you again in the lobby, I knew I was right. So what if the cost of admission flattened me? By then I was already falling in love."

"You were not." She pulled away from him. "You didn't even know me."

"I do now." He smiled.

"My God, Steve, this doesn't make any sense." She wasn't sure how she was supposed to react; it was like her recurring nightmare of sitting down to a final she hadn't studied for. This man she wanted was either a phony or a pathological romantic. "Just what did you think was going to happen after my enhancement wore off? Most couples leave this place in separate cars, you know."

"Sure, I knew that was a possibility." He shrugged. "But I had confidence in myself. And you. The way I figure it, there must be *something* about me you really like because I couldn't afford a treated chocolate." He sifted her hair through his fingers. "Actually, I've been waiting all night for the drugs you took to wear off. I want us to fall in love for real, not because our hormones are boiling over. We need clear heads for something as important as this. That's why you should never close in a bar, unless you're prepared to wake up with a sour head and a sour deal."

"You really think we're in love?"

He paused to consider. "Maybe I don't know enough about love to recognize it, but this is what I hoped it would feel like."

She turned her face toward him and closed her eyes "Sell it to me," she said.

He obliged. Time passed, clothing got rearranged, buttons were unbuttoned. The bench wasn't big enough for them to lie on, but they were approaching horizontality when a rover disguised as a sunflower crunched down the gravel path, aimed its enormous yellow blossom at them and said politely, "For those couples requiring privacy, may we suggest our encounter rooms on the sixth floor?"

"We could leave," Lily said breathlessly. "Go to your place."

"I don't have a place. Actually I've been living out of my car. It's parked about ten blocks from here and it's out of gas and I don't get my unemployment check until. . . ."

"Ssh!" She put a finger to his lips. "Keep bringing up negatives and you'll lose the sale." Lily stood, reached both hands down to him and pulled him up beside her. "My place then." She wasn't sure exactly what she was going to do when they got there. Tack a sheet to the ceiling between her futon and Marja's? Not a simple project at two in the morning—and what if Steve snored?

Lily pushed her doubts away. What had Marja said? Love makes all things possible. She knew she was taking a risk with this intense little man but she'd been smart and lonely for so long. She had to laugh at herself as they stepped into the elevator.

It was time to try something stupid.

The Pyramid of Amirah

SOMETIMES AMIRAH THINKS SHE CAN SENSE THE weight of the pyramid that entombs her house. The huge limestone blocks seem to crush the air and squeeze light. When she carries the table lamp onto the porch and holds it up to the blank stone, shadows ooze across the rough-cut inner face. If she is in the right mood, they make cars and squirrels and flowers and Mom's face.

Time passes.

Amirah will never see the outside of her pyramid, but she likes to imagine different looks for it. It's like trying on new jeans. They said that the limestone would be cased in some kind of marble they called Rosa Portagallo. She hopes it will be like Betty's Pyramid, red as sunset, glossy as her fingernails. Are they setting it yet? Amirah thinks not. She can still hear the dull, distant *chock* as the believers lower each structural stone into place—twenty a day. Dust wisps from the cracks between the stones and settles through the thick air onto every horizontal surface of her house: the floor, Dad's desk, windowsills, and the tops of the kitchen cabinets. Amirah doesn't mind; she goes over the entire house periodically with vacuum and rag. She wants to be ready when the meaning comes.

Time passes.

243

The only thing she really misses is the sun. Well, that isn't true. She misses her Mom and her Dad and her friends on the swim team, especially Janet. She and Janet offered themselves to the meaning at Blessed Finger Sanctuary on Janet's twelfth birthday. Neither of them expected to be chosen pyramid girl. They thought maybe they would be throwing flowers off a float in the Monkey Day parade or collecting door to door for the Lost Brothers. Janet shrieked with joy and hugged her when Mrs. Munro told them the news. If her friend hadn't held her up, Amirah might have collapsed.

Amirah keeps all the lights on, even when she goes to bed. She knows this is a waste of electricity, but it's easier to be brave when the house is bright. Besides, there is nobody to scold her now.

"Is there?" Amirah says, and then she walks into the kitchen to listen. Sometimes the house makes whispery noises when she talks to it. "Is there anyone here who cares what I do?" Her voice sounds like the hinges of the basement door.

Time passes.

They took all the clocks, and she has lost track of day and night. She sleeps when she is tired and eats when she is hungry. That's all there is to do, except wait for the meaning to come. Mom and Dad's bedroom is filled to the ceiling with cartons of Goody-goody Bars: Nut Raisin, Cherry Date, Chocolate Banana, and Cinnamon Apple, which is not her favorite. Mrs. Munro said there were enough to last her for years. At first that was a comfort. Now Amirah tries not to think about it.

Time passes.

Amirah's Pyramid is the first in the Tri-City area. They said it would be twenty meters tall. She had worked it out afterwards that twenty meters was almost seventy feet. Mom said that if the meaning had first come to Memphis, Tennessee instead of Memphis, Egypt, then maybe everything would have been in American instead of metric. Dad had laughed at that and said then Elvis would have been the First Brother. Mom didn't like him making fun of the meaning. If she wanted to laugh, she would have him tell one of the Holy Jokes.

"What's the first law of religion?" Amirah says in her best imitation of Dad's voice.

"For every religion, there exists an equal and opposite religion," she says in Mom's voice.

"What's the second law of religion?" says Dad's voice.

"They're both wrong." Mom always laughs at that.

The silence goes all breathy, like Amirah is holding seashells up to both ears. "I don't get it," she says.

She can't hear building sounds anymore. The dust has stopped falling.

Time passes.

When Amirah was seven, her parents took her to Boston to visit Betty's Pyramid. The bus driver said that the believers had torn down a hundred and fifty houses to make room for it. Amirah could feel Betty long before she could see her pyramid; Mom said the meaning was very strong in Boston.

Amirah didn't understand much about the meaning back then. While the bus was stopped at a light, she had a vision of her heart swelling up inside her like a balloon and lifting her out the window and into the bluest part of the sky where she could see everything there was to see. The whole bus was feeling Betty by then. Dad told the Holy Joke about the chicken and the Bible in a loud voice and soon everyone was laughing so hard that the bus driver had to pull over. She and Mom and Dad walked the last three blocks and the way Amirah remembered it, her feet only touched the ground a couple of times. The pyramid was huge in a way that no skyscraper could ever be. She heard Dad tell Mom it was more like geography than architecture. Amirah was going to ask him what that meant, only she realized that *she* knew because *Betty* knew. The marble of Betty's Pyramid was incredibly smooth but it was cold to the touch. Amirah spread the fingers of both hands against it and thought very hard about Betty.

"Are you there, Betty?" Amirah sits up in bed. "What's it like?" All the lights are on in the house. "Betty?" Amirah can't sleep because her stomach hurts. She gets up and goes to the bathroom to pee. When she wipes herself, there is a pinkish stain on the toilet paper.

Time passes.

Amirah also misses Juicy Fruit gum and Onion Taste Tots and 3DV and music. She hasn't seen her shows since Dad shut the door behind him and led Mom down the front walk. Neither of them looked back, but she thought Mom might have been crying. Did Mom have doubts? This still bothers Amirah. She wonders what Janet is listening to these days on her earstone. Have the Stiffies released any new songs? When Amirah sings, she practically has to scream or else the pyramid swallows her voice.

"Go, go away, go-go away from me.

Had fun, we're done, whyo-why can't you see?"

Whenever she finishes a Goody-goody bar, she throws the wrapper out the front door. The walk has long since been covered. In the darkness, the wrappers look like fallen leaves.

Time passes.

Both Janet and Amirah had been trying to get Han Biletnikov to notice them before Amirah became pyramid girl. Han had wiry red hair and freckles and played mid-field on the soccer team. He was the first boy in their school to wear his pants inside out. On her last day in school, there had been an assembly in her honor and Han had come to the stage and told a Holy Joke about her.

Amirah cups her hands to make her voice sound like it's coming out of a microphone. "What did Amirah say to the guy at the hot dog stand?"

She twists her head to one side to give the audience response. "I don't know, what?"

Han speaks again into the microphone. "Make me one with everything." She can see him now, even though she is sitting at the kitchen table with a glass of water and an unopened Cherry Date Goody-goody bar in front of her. His cheeks are flushed as she strides across the stage to him. He isn't expecting her to do this. The believers go quiet as if someone has thrown a blanket over them. She holds out her hand to shake his and he stares at it. When their eyes finally meet, she can see his awe; she's turned into President Huong, or maybe Billy Tiger, the forward for the Boston Flash. His hand is warm, a little sweaty. Her fingertips brush the hollow of his palm.

"Thank you," says Amirah.

Han doesn't say anything. He isn't there. Amirah unwraps the Goody-goody bar.

Time passes.

Amirah never gets used to having her period. She thinks she isn't doing it right. Mom never told her how it worked and she didn't leave pads or tampons or anything. Amirah wads toilet paper into her panties, which makes her feel like she's walking around with a sofa cushion between her legs. The menstrual blood smells like vinegar. She takes a lot of baths. Sometimes she touches herself as the water cools and then she feels better for a while.

Time passes.

Amirah wants to imagine herself kissing Han Biletnikov, but she can't. She keeps seeing Janet's lips on his, her tongue darting into his mouth. At least, that's how Janet said people kiss. She wonders if she would have better luck if she weren't in the kitchen. She

climbs the stairs to her bedroom and opens the door. It's dark. The
light has burned out. She pulls down the diffuser and unscrews the
bulb. It's clear and about the size of a walnut. It says

"Whose lifetime?" she says. The pile of Goody-goody wrappers
on the front walk is taller than Dad. Amirah tries to think where
there might be extra light bulbs. She pulls the entire house apart
looking for them but she doesn't cry.

Time passes.

Amirah is practicing living in the dark. Well, it isn't entirely
dark; she has left a light on in the hallway. But she is in the living
room, staring out the picture window at nothing. The fireplace is
gray on black; the couch across the room swells in the darkness,
soaking up gloom like a sponge.

There are eight light bulbs left. She carries one in Mom's old
purse, protected by an enormous wad of toilet paper. The weight of
the strap on her shoulder is as reassuring as a hug. Amirah misses
hugs. She never puts the purse down.

Amirah notices that it is particularly dark at the corner where
the walls and the ceiling meet. She gets out of Dad's reading chair,
arms stretched before her. She is going to try to shut the door to the
hallway. She doesn't know if she can; she has never done it before.

"Where was Moses when the lights went out?" she says.

No one answers, not even in her imagination. She fumbles for
the doorknob.

"Where was Mohammed when the lights went out?" Her voice
is shrinking.

As she eases the door shut, the hinges complain.

"Where was Amirah went the lights went out?"

The latch bolt *snicks* home but Amirah keeps pressing hard
against the knob, then leans into the door with her shoulder. The
darkness squeezes her; she can't breathe. A moan pops out of her
mouth like a seed and she pivots suddenly, pressing her back
against the door.

Something flickers next to the couch, low on the wall. A spark,
blue as her dreams. It turns sapphire, cerulean, azure, indigo, all

the colors that only poets and painters can see. The blue darts out of the electrical outlet like a tongue. She holds out her hands to navigate across the room to it and notices an answering glow, pale as mother's milk, at her fingertips. Blue tongues are licking out of every plug in the living room and Amirah doesn't need to grope anymore. She can see everything, the couch, the fireplace, all the rooms of the house and through the pyramid walls into the city. It's one city now, not three.

Amirah raises her arms above her head because her hands are blindingly bright and she can see Dad with his new wife watching the Red Sox on 3DV. Someone has planted pink miniature roses on Mom's grave. Janet is looking into little Freddy Cobb's left ear with her otoscope and Han is having late lunch at Sandeens with a married imagineer named Shawna Russo and Mrs. Munro has dropped a stitch on the cap she is knitting for her great-grandson Matthias. At that moment everyone who Amirah sees, thousands of believers, *tens* of thousands, stop what they are doing and turn to the pyramid, *Amirah's* Pyramid, which has been finished for these seventeen years but has never meant anything to anyone until now. Some smile with recognition; a few clap. Others—most of them, Amirah realizes—are now walking toward her pyramid, to be close to her and caress the cold marble and know what she knows. The meaning is suddenly very strong in the city, like the perfume of lilacs or the suck of an infant at the breast or the whirr of a hummingbird.

"Amirah?" Betty opens the living room door. She is a beautiful young girl with gray hair and crow's feet around her sky blue eyes. "Are you there, Amirah?"

"Yes," says Amirah.

"Do you understand?"

"Yes," Amirah says. When she laughs, time stands still.

Fruitcake Theory

BJORN IS TRYING TO TELL ME THAT THE ROOSTER isn't dumb as a spoon. Obtuse, maybe. Naive, yes. Tedious, without a doubt.

The rooster is sitting across the aisle and up two seats, paying no attention to us. We're just followers. He's staring out the window of the van at the snow.

"He's Kuvat, Maggie," says Bjorn. "Aliens think differently than we do."

"Cranial capacity." I tap the side of my head. "Check that skull. He's got room up there for half a cup of brains, tops."

"Maybe he's got some kind of distributed nervous system." Bjorn says. "How else could they have built the starship?"

"The scarecrows built the starship," I say. "The roosters came along for the ride. You follow long enough and it's obvious."

"Intellectual bifurcation is just a theory." Nevertheless, Bjorn slides down in his seat, defeated once again. "All we know is that they're Kuvat, both roosters and scarecrows." He takes out his appetite pacifier and starts sucking at it. I don't mean to upset him.

The rooster starts eeking to himself.

"Eek eek eeeek, eek eek eeeek!"

He looks like a cauliflower the size of a washing machine—with legs. They are bird legs, to be sure, with scaly shanks and clawed, three-toed feet. But his body is an enormous scoop of convoluted flesh. All he usually wears is the translator, a golden disk that hangs on a cord around his neck like the Noble Prize for Stupidity. His skin is as translucent as spilled milk. Beneath it are coils of muscle marbled with gray fat. He has spindly arms and his little head is mostly mouth. We can't see the upright ruddy flap, like a rooster's comb, just behind his button eyes, because tonight he's wearing a Santa's cap of red felt.

Bjorn pops the appetite pacifier out of his mouth. "I think that's 'Jingle Bells,' " he says excitedly. "The *eeking*." He makes a note of this. Bjorn is new to the following team. He's twenty-four and takes everything too seriously, except himself. He's fat and blond and sweet as a jelly donut. I really do like him; he just hasn't realized that yet. He brings out the mother in me.

I yawn. I'm not a night person and I'm riding in a van at two in the morning. It's the rooster's fault, of course. It's December 22 and the rooster has got a bad case of holiday spirit, even though he doesn't know an elf from an elephant. He wants to do a little shopping. It's a security nightmare, but we accommodate him. We always do because we're asking for the Kuvat encyclopedia for Christmas. Not that we know what's in it exactly, but these creatures come from a planet a hundred and thirty light years away. They're bound to have a grand unified theory, the secret of cool fusion, and a cure for cellulite.

=Persons?= The rooster turns toward us. =This one has hunger.=

"Me too. I haven't eaten since dinner." Bjorn is always happy to interact with our charge. "Wait until you see the food court at this mall. It's totally grade. Must be thirty different kinds of ethnic." He's starting to bubble with enthusiasm; I give him a needle stare. "Well, maybe only twenty," he mutters.

=This one has also thirst, persons.=

"This one is called Maggie." I touch my chest. "*Mag-gie*." The rooster can't tell humans apart. This continues to annoy me; I've been following him for four months and he still doesn't know who I am.

=Laughing all the way, person, ha, ha, ha.=

There is some debate as to the accuracy of Kuvat translations.

I'm sick of this rooster. I've asked to follow any other Kuvat, preferably a scarecrow, but I'd even settle for another rooster. As far as we know, there are four beside this one. Roosters don't have names, don't ask me why. At first we gave them nicknames—Dodo,

Dopey, Dumbo, Ding-dong, and Dufus—only when Balfour found out, she pitched a fit. Our job was to follow, observe, and protect the Kuvat, she said, not to make snide remarks. She doesn't even like us calling them roosters. When she overheard Jasper laughing about "Dopey" back in August, she pulled him from the following team and banished him to Waste Assessment, where he sifts through Kuvat garbage and samples their sewage.

This rooster has been the most rambunctious tourist of the five. Since the Kuvat landed in May, he's been to the pyramids and the Taj Mahal and the Eiffel Tower. He's crazy about zoos and Disneys. He saw the third game of the '08 World Series and was a Special Guest at the Sixty-Sixth World Science Fiction Convention. He seems to be partnered with Elder Kasaan, who, as the oldest of the scarecrows, is the leader of the Kuvat expedition.

Bjorn has signed on to the theory that the roosters are scouting us and make detailed reports back to the scarecrows, who rarely leave the compound we've built around their starship. This theory is conveniently unverifiable, since we're not allowed to follow roosters onto the starship.

When we pull up to the entrance of the Live Night Mall, Balfour herself gets onto the van. She nods at the two of us and then approaches the rooster.

"You will have an hour. I'm afraid that's as much as we can do, one hour. These two will accompany you for one hour. Anything you want, these two will obtain for you. Do you understand everything? These two? One hour?" Even though she won't admit it, it's obvious that Balfour, too, thinks that the rooster hasn't got the brains that God gave to spinach.

=Kuvat pay? That is the habit.=

"No," said Balfour. "These two will pay for everything."

=Person, is there fruitcake? This one hears much of the information of fruitcake.=

"Fruitcake?" Balfour glances back at us, as if we have some idea what the rooster is talking about. Bjorn shrugs. "I'm sure there's fruitcake somewhere at the mall," Balfour says.

=The fruitcake solves much hunger.=

As we get off the van, Balfour touches my arm. I let Bjorn go on ahead with the rooster.

"Any trouble?" she says.

"Not so far."

"Well, there is now. Elder Kasaan is on her way here from the U.N."

"Here as in *here*? Why?"

She gives me an exasperated glare. "Maybe she realized there are only two more shopping days until Christmas." Balfour is as mystified by Kuvat behavior as the rest of us, but she's Undersecretary for Alien Affairs. When people have questions, she's expected to give answers. Sometimes that vein in her left temple pulses like a blue worm.

"You want to pull our guest out?" This would be the first time a rooster and a scarecrow have met outside the starship compound. It's a chance to observe new behaviors—but the mall is so *public*.

"I don't think so. No."

"Tell him about Kasaan?"

She rubs her eyes and I realize that she probably dragged herself out of bed for this. "Maybe he already knows. Look, I've seeded the mall with our people. We're going to let this happen, okay? It's the good old *observe and protect*. I just wanted to give you a heads up." She turns away but catches herself. "How's Bjorn working out?"

"He should do more sit ups."

She sighs, but the vein subsides. "It's two-thirty in the morning, Maggie. Not even Hack Bumbledom is funny at two-thirty in the morning."

"Want me to pick you up some fruitcake? It's full of information."

"This could be big." She brushes snow off my shoulder. "I'll be at the security office."

Followers and their families are scattered strategically around the mall. When we take roosters on field trips, we try to minimize their access to the mundane world. If we can, we clear a site completely; otherwise we drop by unannounced and late at night. We're in and out before the media and the Kuvat chasers and the oddjobs arrive. There are a few civilians shopping at this ungodly hour, and of course the staff of all the stores are mundanes, but we've got good coverage.

The Live Night Mall is "Y" shaped. Ribbons of light hang from its vaulted glass ceiling; they shiver in the warm breeze that blows from the ventilators. Each of the arms is lined with the usual assortment of shops selling games, infodumps, shoes, T-shirts, ties, hats, kitchenware, software, artware, candy, toys, candles, perfumes, and pheromones. You can get a skin tint, a hair style, or walk-in liposuction. At the end of each of its arms is an anchor store, a Sears & Penny, a Food Chief, and a Home Depot. The three arms come together in a vast, garish, and noisy cluster of fast food storefronts. Bjorn might be right about the number of ethnics; I don't think I've ever seen *Icelandic* in a mall before. At the hub of the mall there must be a couple of hundred round tables. The surfaces of each are screens tuned to themed cable stations. Even though the place is pretty much deserted, it's still filled with the ghostly mutter of news and sitcoms and cartoons. I'm expecting to spot the rooster here somewhere but all I can see is a handful of followers and a Santa nodding over a latte. Kevin Darcy pushes his sleeping four-year-old by me in a stroller and murmurs, "Sears and Penny."

So I pick my way through the maze of tables. As I pass Santa, he shoots out of his chair.

"Where did you come from?"

"Home," I say and try to get by.

"No, you didn't." He pushes in front of me. "You're a stranger. Who are all these people?"

"This is the mall, friend. We're all strangers here."

"Not at my mall, you're not."

"Listen, friend, why don't you take the rest of the night off?" I flip open my wallet and give him a good look at the ID. "I'll bet you're tired. I'll clear it with your boss."

He glances at it, but I don't think he sees anything. "It's not him," he says uncertainly. "It's all the presents. I have to finish my list." Now I'm just guessing at his story, but I'm pretty sure I've got it right. He's old and broke and stuck in Social Security shock—just trying to earn a few extra bucks over the holidays. Only he hasn't actually moved to a night schedule, so he's trying to tough this shift out with chemicals. That's why he's just south of coherent and has cephadrine eyes. "If I go, they'll replace me with a Santabot." He lowers his voice. "They don't take bathroom breaks."

"Excuse me." I sidestep him. "I have to see a rooster about a fruitcake."

"Wait! I'll put you on my list." He clutches at me. "What do you want for Christmas?"

"How about someone else's life?" He considers this and I slip by. "You can have mine!" he calls after me. "Hey!"

As I enter the Sears & Penny, I notice an odd, stinging, flowery smell, something like the scent of a rose, only with thorns. I follow it to the men's underwear section, where it is so strong my eyes water. A mundane sales clerk is tapping "Silent Night" on the key-pad of his cashcard reader.

Bjorn and the rooster are sitting on the floor on a red and white checked plastic tablecloth, having a picnic. The rooster's Santa cap is cocked at a rakish angle. He has opened a plastic bag containing three white Fruit of the Loom undershirts.

He is eating them.

Somehow he has also obtained a four pack of Murray's Chocolate Mint Wine, two of which are now empties. =Hungry?= He holds a wine-stained rag out to me.

"No," I say, "thank you." I try to catch Bjorn's eye but he is staring between his legs as if counting the red checks on the tablecloth.

=One hundred percent cotton.= The rooster pulls a new undershirt from the bag and turns it this way and that, as if admiring it. =Tasty cellulose.= He opens another can of Murray's and pours some on it. =Not starchy like French fries.= He takes a bite.

The smell is clearly coming from the rooster. This is new behavior; I have to know what caused it. "Uh, Bjorn, could I speak to you?"

He finally looks up, his eyes red and watery from rooster smell. "You think I'm fat." He shivers like a barrel of Jell-O, then laughs out loud.

"What?"

"Everybody thinks I'm fat. I *am* fat!" He spreads his fingers across his waist. Sure, Bjorn could do a creditable Santa without padding, but what's that got to do with following the Kuvat? And what's so funny?

I try to say, *That's not true,* except the words swell in my throat like balloons. I cough and manage to choke out, "What's going on here?"

=He knows you bad or good,= the rooster says around a mouthful of undershirt, =so good good goodness sake.=

"He's not stupid, Maggie." Bjorn giggles and reaches for the last can of wine. "He just doesn't know what he knows." He pops it open and drinks.

"Bjorn!" I want to stop him but the rooster smell is blooming in my head. "What have you told him?" I'm not sure whether my feet are touching the floor.

=Kuvat not stupid.= The rooster chews with a sideways motion, like a horse. =This one sees. This one remembers. But only Elder Kasaan knows.=

"Kasaan? What about Kasaan?"

"It's the truth," Bjorn says. "Want some?" He offers me the Murray's chocolate wine and I snatch it away from him.

=Cotton?= The rooster offers the bag of undershirts.

"No." I wave him off absently. "Maybe later."

"He's emitting some kind of euphoriant," says Bjorn. "Can you smell it, Maggie?"

=Tidal of comfort and joy, comfort and joy.=

"Yes." I sit down next to him. If I don't, somebody will have to pull me off the ceiling. "How did it start?"

"He was talking about Kasaan. He says she's going to empty him, or something. I'm pretty sure he's getting ready to turn in his report." He beams, pleased that he's finally won our argument. "I have a theory. He has to tell the truth, right? The smell makes him do it, feel *great* about it. And it's working on us too. Tell me a lie, Maggie."

=Lies stink.= The rooster spits out the undershirt's polyester size tag.

"Oh God," I say. "Oh my God." I take a swig of Murray's and pass it back to Bjorn. "Elder Kasaan is on his way over here." The chocolate weight in my gut helps me forget that I'm breaking every rule of following there is. By this time tomorrow, I'll be helping Jasper centrifuge Kuvat sewage.

=Person,= says the rooster. =You smell unhappy always.=

"I am unhappy," I say. "I've got a right to be unhappy."

"Why is that?" Bjorn asks.

"Because we have to follow this stupid rooster around, Bjorn! I don't know about you, but that makes *me* feel stupid. It should make everybody in the whole damn world feel stupid."

"Well, at least you're not fat." Bjorn laughs and hands me the Murray's. Just to be sociable, I take a drink.

=Person is fat,= says the rooster. =Person feels stupid.=

I hear running footsteps. Our backup is coming fast. When I think of how this is going to look to the rest of the following team, I start to giggle. "We're screwed," I say.

"Very." Bjorn thinks it's funny too.

Balfour herself is leading the charge. "Maggie!" When she spots us she pulls up. She stares as if she has just caught Santa shoplifting.

I struggle to my knees and hold both hands out to warn them. "Get out of here, now! It's an airborne intoxicant." I realize I'm waving a can of Murray's Chocolate Mint Wine at the Undersecretary for Alien Affairs. I set it discreetly on the plastic tablecloth.

"Gas masks in the van," Balfour says to the team as she covers her mouth and nose with her hand. "Clear the store. No, clear the mall. Seal everything." A handful of them peel off, running. The other followers goggle at us, then back away uncertainly. "Elder Kasaan is looking for him," she says "Are you okay?"

"Sure," says Bjorn. "Tidal of comfort and joy."

"I think we're all right," I say. "But we're not observing anymore. We're part of it, Balfour. Now move, before it's too late."

They leave, dragging the giggling menswear clerk after them. The rooster stands and brushes a few white threads off. =Person, is there fruitcake?=

We find fruitcake at the North Pole, a seasonal kiosk halfway down the Home Depot arm of the mall. The North Pole also sells ten different flavors of candy canes, boxes of assorted chocolates, and Christmas cookies in green foil wrap, marshmallow elves, and fudge tannenbaums. Gene Autrey sings "Rudolph the Red-Nosed Reindeer" from hidden speakers as an animated Santa and his full complement of reindeer cavort around the circular base of the kiosk. I know it's the rooster smell which continues to float up my nose, but I find myself humming along with Gene.

The fruitcake is stacked five high in round red tins decorated with scenes of cherry-faced kids building snowmen. The tins are wrapped in cellophane. Bjorn takes one off the top and gives it to the rooster.

"This is fruitcake," he says.

The rooster takes it, turns it over several times, holds it up to the light and then taps a finger against the lid of the tin. =Is hard.=

"It's inside." I shake my head, laughing. "You have to open it first."

The rooster glances up and down the deserted mall. =There is no pay person.=

Bjorn is unwrapping a white chocolate snowman. "Don't worry. We'll take care of it."

=This one pays. That is the habit.= He sets the fruitcake, un-opened, back on the counter. =Christmas is. The Kuvat pay.=

"No, really. . . ," says Bjorn, but I nudge him in the back just as the rooster begins to eek.

"*Eeeeeek, eek, eek, eek. Eeeek!*" Beneath his translucent skin, the flesh appears to seethe. We can hear a sloshing, like a mop in a bucket of water. The rooster claps a hand to his chest and I see a viscous ooze between stubby fingers. He brings the hand to his mouth and blows on it, once, twice, then opens it and shows us.

=Pay.= he says. Bjorn drops his chocolate snowman.

Clicking softly on his smooth palm are four green pearls.

"What are they?" says Bjorn.

=The end of fat,= says the rooster. He offers them to Bjorn. =Person eats?=

Of course, I am immediately suspicious of the green pearls.

What is the end of fat anyway? What will these things do to the human digestive system?

"How many?" Bjorn's face is as soft as cookie dough.

"Wait a minute!" I'm stunned, but I can't bring myself to stop it. =The one.=

"What was it you said, Maggie?" He smiles at me. "We're not observing anymore. We're part of things now." He accepts a pearl from the rooster. "Thank you. Do I chew?"

=Swallow hurry.=

"Bjorn!"

He pops it into his mouth and it's over. I wait for him to keel over and writhe or throw up or maybe even explode, but he just watches me with that goofy smile, which I absolutely understand. Whatever happens is all right, is true, is *good*. We'll both accept it because the world smells so sweet tonight.

Bjorn raises his hands over his head like a Sugar Plum Fairy and does a pirouette.

When the rooster offers me the green pearls, I'm not at all tempted. "Thanks." I sweep them onto my hand and pocket them. "But I think I'll save these for breakfast."

The rooster's eyes glitter for a moment and go dim. =One,= he says. =Share.= He turns to the North Pole and retrieves his fruitcake.

The rooster wants to eat the cellophane wrapping but we talk him out of it. When we pry the top off the tin, he eeks and drops it. =Not Christmas!= The cake is still in the bottom half of the tin; it rolls toward the Playbot store.

=Fruitcake stinks!= He starts hopping up and down on one foot. =Stinks like a lie.=

"I'm sorry," says Bjorn. "Maybe that one was bad. I can get you another."

=Take it away!= the rooster says. =Bury it!=

"His hour is almost up," I say, "Let's get him out of here."

But we don't get the chance because striding toward us from the food court is Elder Kasaan. A dozen gas-masked followers trot behind.

The Kuvat scarecrows have no more in common with our scarecrows than the roosters have with *gallus domesticus*. We call them scarecrows because they're so gangly and because they wear loud, loose clothes that cover most of their bodies. But nobody who meets a scarecrow ever remembers her wardrobe. What you remember is the impossible head. It looks something like a prize pumpkin, only pumpkins aren't rust red or as wrinkled as walnuts.

The eyes are like bloodshot eggs and the mouth is full of nightmare teeth, long and curved and pointed. If the scarecrows weren't so shy, so polite, so *intelligent*—everything that the roosters are not—they would've frightened the bejesus out of us.

At the sight of Kasaan, the rooster forgets all about the fruitcake and begins to eek furiously. Instinctively Bjorn and I step back. The scarecrow is swooping down on the rooster; I've never seen one move so fast. The followers are left scrambling behind. The rooster tenses. He looks as if he wants to run in five directions at once, but can't decide which one.

"Eek, eeek, eeeek, eeeeek, eeeeeek!"

Just before it happens, I realize what I'm seeing. This isn't any meeting. It's an attack: a lion charging a wildebeest, a wolf taking a hare.

"Uh-oh," I say, but it's good. It's true. The smell has changed everything.

Kasaan slams into the rooster, knocking him down. The rooster bounces, rolls, and lies, shivering, on his back. His legs pump weakly as Kasaan looms over him. The scarecrow bends to nuzzle the rooster's shoulder. He closes his eyes. His eeking is low and wet. The breathless followers catch up.

"What is this?" I recognize Balfour. "Oh my God, what's she doing?"

Kasaan's nubbly pink tongue licks between bared teeth at the rooster's shoulder. It makes a sound like someone washing hands.

"Observe," I say. "But don't protect. Not this time."

The licking goes on for several moments. Suddenly the teeth pierce the skin and sink deep. The rooster stiffens, but makes no sound. With a quick jerk to one side, Kasaan tears an apple-sized chunk of the rooster's flesh away. Her jaws close on the meat—once, twice, three times—and then she tilts her head back and swallows. The wound brims with purple blood; Kasaan licks it clean. When the bleeding stops, the scarecrow steps away and stretches luxuriantly.

"What tasty information!" She offers a hand to the rooster, who struggles to his feet. "You have seen most deliciously."

"I have a theory," whispers Bjorn, "about how these reports are made . . ." But he doesn't get to elaborate because Kasaan comes up to him.

"What that one gave you," the scarecrow says, "is the egg of a vuot, a worm that will grow over the years in your intestines."

Bjorn turns the color of eggnog.

"How do you know about that?" I say.

"I ate that memory," says Kasaan. "Now the vuot is a beneficial parasite that all Kuvat share. It will filter toxins and regulate your metabolism and prolong your life. You need not worry about side effects. Indeed, I believe you will be most happy with your relationship with the vuot over the coming centuries."

I pat my pocket to make sure the pearls—vuot eggs—are still there. Kasaan notices this and bows apologetically. "What has happened, *is* and is for the good. But there is something that has not yet happened, which I must unfortunately prevent from happening."

I can guess what's coming. "We bought them from him," I say. "We paid."

"Maggie, a fruitcake is not the price of immortality," says Kasaan gently.

=Fruitcake stinks.= says the rooster. =Person lies.= His wound has already healed.

"I'm afraid I must insist." The scarecrow lays a hand on my shoulder.

=Better not cry. Tell me why.=

I know he means me no harm. So does the rooster, Bjorn, Balfour, and all the followers. I'm going to give him the eggs. Maybe later we'll find out what the right price for them is. As far as I'm concerned, the situation is under control. But it's not my mall.

"Get your hands off her!"

It happens so fast. Santa comes from somewhere behind the followers. No one sees him until he goes airborne. He's spry for an old man, clipping Kasaan at the waist and spinning him around. The eggs go flying out of my hand and splatter on the floor. Santa and the scarecrow fall in a heap.

"Monster!" screams Santa. "Get out of my mall." He's got his hands around the scarecrow's neck. We swarm over to pull them apart but we're a millisecond too late.

Kasaan bites down hard on Santa's bicep. She tears off a mouthful of muscle and some red felt rags. Perhaps it's instinct that makes her swallow.

"Ahhh!" Blood spurts and Santa faints.

The scarecrow picks herself up slowly, licking the blood off her lips.

"Elder Kasaan, I am so sorry," says Balfour, her voice muffled by the gasmask. "I thought we had secured the area."

Kasaan stares thoughtfully at her. "He is seventy-eight years old."

"Really," she says. "Poor thing probably doesn't know what he's doing."

"This is how you treat your elders?"

"What do you mean?"

"We have made a terrible mistake," says Kasaan. "I wish to return to the ship immediately."

=And a happy New Year,= says the rooster, as he follows the scarecrow out.

Three days later, the Kuvat starship takes off. They have yet to return.

Margaret Balfour, Undersecretary of Alien Affairs, resigns in February, after taking a merciless pounding in the media and both houses of Congress. In March she signs a contract to write *Who Lost the Kuvat?* which presents her side of what happened. Although sales are disappointing, the vein in her temple stops throbbing.

Bjorn Lipponen loses one hundred and fifty pounds in six months. Two years after The Incident, as it comes to be called, he is named one of the Twenty-first Century's Hundred Most Sexy Men. Later, he becomes a noted futurist. His book, *The Road to Eternity,* is in its eighteenth printing.

Nobody knows quite what to do with Lester Rand, the demented Santa. There is considerable sentiment for charging him in the World Court with crimes against humanity. But who can say what will happen if the Kuvat come back and find out that we punished the messenger instead of accepting the message? In his later years, he writes a children's book, *Reindeer In the Mall,* which is optioned by Fox and made into a full-length computer animated cartoon.

I am never going to write a book. I'm not going to live forever.

There are a lot of theories about what caused The Incident. Some want to blame me for insulting the rooster, even though what I said was only the truth. Others say that it is humanity's fault for mistreating the Lester Rands of the world. Many former Kuvat chasers maintain that when Kasaan digested the information he bit off Rand, he saw into the dark soul of *Homo sapiens sapiens* and was repelled. I guess everyone has a theory. Here's mine.

It was the fruitcake.

Undone

THE SHIP SCREAMED. ITS SCREENS SHOWED MADA that she was surrounded in threespace. A swarm of Utopian asteroids was closing on her, brain clans and mining DIs living in hollowed-out chunks of carbonaceous chondrite, any one of which could have mustered enough votes to abolish Mada in all ten dimensions.

"I'm going to die," the ship cried, "I'm going to die, I'm going to. . . ."

"I'm not." Mada waved the speaker off impatiently and scanned downwhen. She saw that the Utopians had planted an identity mine five minutes into the past that would boil her memory to vapor if she tried to go back in time to undo this trap. Upwhen, then. The future was clear, at least as far as she could see, which wasn't much beyond next week. Of course, that was the direction they wanted her to skip. They'd be happiest making her their great-great-great-grandchildren's problem.

The Utopians fired another spread of panic bolts. The ship tried to absorb them, but its buffers were already overflowing. Mada felt her throat tighten. Suddenly she couldn't remember how to spell *luck*, and she believed that she could feel her sanity oozing out of her ears.

261

"So let's skip upwhen," she said.

"You s-sure?" said the ship. "I don't know if . . . how far?"

"Far enough so that all of these drones will be fossils."

"I can't just . . . I need a number, Mada."

A needle of fear pricked Mada hard enough to make her reflexes kick. "Skip!" Her panic did not allow for the luxury of numbers. "Skip now!" Her voice was tight as a fist. "Do it!"

Time shivered as the ship surged into the empty dimensions. In threespace Mada went all wavy. Eons passed in a nanosecond, then she washed back into the strong dimensions and solidified.

She merged briefly with the ship to assess damage. "What have you done?" The gain in entropy was an ache in her bones.

"I-I'm sorry, you said to skip so. . . ." The ship was still jittery.

Even though she wanted to kick its sensorium in, she bit down hard on her anger. They had both made enough mistakes that day. "That's all right," she said, "we can always go back. We just have to figure out when we are. Run the star charts."

two-tenths of a spin

The ship took almost three minutes to get its charts to agree with its navigation screens—a bad sign. Reconciling the data showed that it had skipped forward in time about two-tenths of the galactic spin. Almost twenty million years had passed on Mada's home world of Trueborn, time enough for its crust to fold and buckle into new mountain ranges, for the Green Sea to bloom, for the glaciers to march and melt. More than enough time for everything and everyone Mada had ever loved—or hated—to die, turn to dust and blow away.

Whiskers trembling, she checked downwhen. What she saw made her lose her perch and float aimlessly away from the command mod's screens. There had to be something wrong with the ship's air. It settled like dead, wet leaves in her lungs. She ordered the ship to check the mix.

The ship's deck flowed into an enormous plastic hand, warm as blood. It cupped Mada gently in its palm and raised her up so that she could see its screens straight on.

"Nominal, Mada. Everything is as it should be."

That couldn't be right. She could breathe ship-nominal atmosphere. "Check it again," she said

"Mada, I'm sorry," said the ship.

The identity mine had skipped with them and was still dogging her, five infuriating minutes into the past. There was no getting around it, no way to undo their leap into the future. She was trapped two-tenths of a spin upwhen. The knowledge was like a sucking hole in her chest, much worse than any wound the Utopian psychological war machine could have inflicted on her.

"What do we do now?" asked the ship.

Mada wondered what she should say to it. Scan for hostiles? Open a pleasure sim? Cook a nice, hot stew? Orders twisted in her mind, bit their tails and swallowed themselves. She considered— briefly—telling it to open all the air locks to the vacuum. Would it obey this order? She thought it probably would, although she would as soon chew her own tongue off as utter such cowardly words. Had not she and her sibling batch voted to carry the revolution into all ten dimensions? Pledged themselves to fight for the Three Universal Rights, no matter what the cost the Utopian brain clans extracted from them in blood and anguish?

But that had been two-tenths of a spin ago.

bean thoughts

"Where are you going?" said the ship.

Mada floated through the door bubble of the command mod. She wrapped her toes around the perch outside to steady herself.

"Mada, wait! I need a mission, a course, some line of inquiry."

She launched down the companionway.

"I'm a Dependent Intelligence, Mada." Its speaker buzzed with self-righteousness. "I have the right to proper and timely guidance."

The ship flowed a veil across her trajectory; as she approached, it went taut. That was DI thinking: the ship was sure that it could just bounce her back into its world. Mada flicked her claws and slashed at it, shredding holes half a meter long.

"And I have the right to be an individual," she said. "Leave me alone."

She caught another perch and pivoted off it toward the greenhouse blister. She grabbed the perch by the door bubble and paused to flow new aveoli into her lungs to make up for the oxygen-depleted, carbon-dioxide-enriched air mix in the greenhouse. The bubble shivered as she popped through it and she breathed deeply. The smells of life helped ground her whenever operation of the ship overwhelmed her. It was always so needy and there was only one of her. It would have been different if they had been designed to go out in teams. She would have had her sibling Thiras at her side; together they might have been strong enough to withstand the Utopian's panic . . . *no!* Mada shook him out of her head. Thiras was gone; they were all gone. There was no sense in looking for comfort, downwhen or up. All she had was the moment, the tick of the relentless present, filled now with the moist, bittersweet breath of the dirt, the sticky savor of running sap, the bloom of perfume on the flowers. As she drifted through the greenhouse, leaves brushed her skin like caresses. She settled at the potting bench, opened a bin and picked out a single bean seed.

Mada cupped it between her two hands and blew on it, letting her body's warmth coax the seed out of dormancy. She tried to merge her mind with its blissful unconsciousness. Cotyledons stirred and began to absorb nutrients from the endosperm. A bean cared nothing about proclaiming the Three Universal Rights: the right of all independent sentients to remain individual, the right to manipulate their physical structures, and the right to access the timelines. Mada slowed her metabolism to the steady and deliberate rhythm of the bean—what Utopian could do that? They held that individuality bred chaos, that function alone must determine form and that undoing the past was sacrilege. Being Utopians, they could hardly destroy Trueborn and its handful of colonies. Instead they had tried to put the Rights under quarantine.

Mada stimulated the sweat glands in the palms of her hands. The moisture wicking across her skin called to the embryonic root in the bean seed. The tip pushed against the seat coat. Mada's sibling batch on Trueborn had pushed hard against the Utopian blockade, to bring the Rights to the rest of the galaxy. Only a handful had made it to open space. The brain clans had hunted them down and brought most of them back in disgrace to Trueborn. But not Mada. No, not wily Mada, Mada the fearless, Mada whose heart now beat but once a minute.

The bean embryo swelled and its root cracked the seed coat. It curled into her hand, branching and rebranching like the timelines. The roots tickled her. Mada manipulated the chemistry of her sweat by forcing her sweat ducts to reabsorb most of the sodium and chlorine. She parted her hands slightly and raised them up to the grow lights. The cotyledons emerged and chloroplasts oriented themselves to the light. Mada was thinking only bean thoughts as her cupped hands filled with roots and the first true leaves unfolded. More leaves budded from the nodes of her stem, her petioles arched and twisted to the light, *the light*. It was only the light—violet-blue and orange-red—that mattered, the incredible shower of photons that excited her chlorophyll, passing electrons down carrier molecules to form adenosine diphosphate and nicotinamide adenine dinucleo. . . .

"Mada," said the ship. "The order to leave you alone is now superseded by primary programming."

"What?" The word caught in her throat like a bone.

"You entered the greenhouse forty days ago."

Without quite realizing what she was doing, Mada clenched her hands, crushing the young plant.

"I am directed to keep you from harm, Mada," said the ship. "It's time to eat."

She glanced down at the dead thing in her hands. "Yes, all right." She dropped it onto the potting bench. "I've got something to clean up first but I'll be there in a minute." She wiped the corner of her eye. "Meanwhile, calculate a course for home."

natural background

Not until the ship scanned the quarantine zone at the edge of the Trueborn system did Mada begin to worry. In her time the zone had swarmed with the battle asteroids of the brain clans. Now the Utopians were gone. Of course, that was to be expected after all this time. But as the ship reentered the home system, dumping excess velocity into the empty dimensions, Mada felt a chill that had nothing to do with the temperature in the command mod.

Trueborn orbited a spectral type G3V star, which had been known to the discoverers as HR3538. Scans showed that the Green Sea had become a climax forest of deciduous hardwood. There were indeed new mountains—knife edges slicing through ever-green sheets—that had upthrust some eighty kilometers off the Fire Coast, leaving Port Henoch landlocked. A rain forest choked the plain where the city of Blair's Landing had once sprawled.

The ship scanned life in abundance. The seas teemed and flocks of Trueborn's flyers darkened the skies like storm clouds: kippies and bluewings and warblers and migrating stilts. Animals had retaken all three continents, lowland and upland, marsh and tundra. Mada could see the dust kicked up by the herds of herbivorous aram from low orbit. The forest echoed with the clatter of shindies and the shriek of blowhards. Big hunters like kar and divil padded across the plains. There were new species as well, mostly invertebrates but also a number of lizards and something like a great, mossy rat that built mounds five meters tall.

None of the introduced species had survived: dogs or turkeys or llamas. The ship could find no cities, towns, buildings—not even ruins. There were neither tubeways nor roads, only the occasional animal track. The ship looked across the entire electromagnetic spectrum and saw nothing but the natural background.

There was nobody home on Trueborn. And as far as they could tell, there never had been.

"Speculate," said Mada.

"I can't," said the ship. "There isn't enough data."

"There's your data." Mada could hear the anger in her voice. "Trueborn, as it would have been had we never even existed."

"Two-tenths of a spin is a long time, Mada."

She shook her head. "They ripped out the foundations, even picked up the dumps. There's nothing, *nothing* of us left." Mada was gripping the command perch so hard that the knuckles of her toes were white. "Hypothesis," she said, "the Utopians got tired of our troublemaking and wiped us out. Speculate."

"Possible, but that's contrary to their core beliefs." Most DIs had terrible imaginations. They couldn't tell jokes, but then they couldn't commit crimes, either.

"Hypothesis: they deported the entire population, scattered us to prison colonies. Speculate."

"Possible, but a logistical nightmare. The Utopians prize the elegant solution."

She swiped the image of her home planet off the screen, as if to erase its unnerving impossibility. "Hypothesis: there are no Utopians anymore because the revolution succeeded. Speculate."

"Possible, but then where did everyone go? And why did they return the planet to its pristine state?"

She snorted in disgust. "What if," she tapped a finger to her forehead, "maybe we *don't* exist. What if we've skipped to another timeline? One in which the discovery of Trueborn never happened? Maybe there has been no Utopian Empire in this timeline, no Great Expansion, no Space Age, maybe no human civilization at all."

"One does not just skip to another timeline at random." The ship sounded huffy at the suggestion. "I've monitored all our dimensional reinsertions quite carefully, and I can assure you that all these events occurred in the timeline we currently occupy."

"You're saying there's no chance?"

"If you want to write a science fiction story, why bother asking my opinion?"

Mada's laugh was brittle. "All right then. We need more data." For the first time since she had been stranded upwhen, she felt a tickle stir the dead weight she was carrying inside her. "Let's start with the nearest Utopian system."

chasing shadows

The HR683 system was abandoned and all signs of human habitation had been obliterated. Mada could not be certain that everything had been restored to its pre-Expansion state because the ship's database on Utopian resources was spotty. HR4523 was similarly deserted. HR509, also known as Tau Ceti, was only 11.9 light years from Earth and had been the first outpost of the Great Expansion. Its planetary system was also devoid of intelligent life and human artifacts — with one striking exception.

Nuevo LA was spread along the shores of the Sterling Sea like a half-eaten picnic lunch. Something had bitten the roofs off its buildings and chewed its walls. Metal skeletons rotted on its docks, transports were melting into brown and gold stains. Once-proud boulevards crumbled in the orange light; the only traffic was wind-blown litter chasing shadows.

Mada was happy to survey the ruin from low orbit. A closer inspection would have spooked her. "Was it war?"

"There may have been a war," said the ship, "but that's not what caused this. I think it's deliberate deconstruction." In extreme magnification, the screen showed a concrete wall pockmarked with tiny holes, from which dust puffed intermittently. "The composition of that dust is limestone, sand, and aluminum silicate. The buildings are crawling with nanobots and they're eating the concrete."

"How long has this been going on?"

"At a guess, four or five hundred years, but that could be off by an order of magnitude."

"Who did this?" said Mada. "Why? Speculate."

"If this is the outcome of a war, then it would seem that the victors wanted to obliterate all traces of the vanquished. But it doesn't seem to have been fought over resources. I suppose we could imagine some deep ideological antagonism between the two sides that led to this, but such an extreme of cultural psychopathology seems unlikely."

"I hope you're right." She shivered. "So they did it themselves, then? Maybe they were done with this place and wanted to leave it as they found it?"

"Possible," said the ship.

Mada decided that she was done with Nuevo LA, too. It would have been a perverse comfort to have found her enemies in power somewhere. Then she would have had an easy way to calculate her duty. However, Mada was quite certain that what this mystery meant was that twenty thousand millennia had conquered both the revolution *and* the Utopians and that she and her sibling batch had been designed in vain.

Still, she had nothing better to do with eternity than to try to find out what had become of her species.

a never-ending vacation

The Atlantic Ocean was now larger than the Pacific. The Mediterranean Sea had been squeezed out of existence by the collision of Africa, Europe, and Asia. North America floated free of South America and was nudging Siberia. Australia was drifting toward the equator.

The population of Earth was about what it had been in the fifteenth century CE, according to the ship. Half a billion people lived on the home world and, as far as Mada could see, none of them had anything important to do. The means of production and distribution, of energy generation and waste disposal, were in the control of Dependent Intelligences like the ship. Despite repeated scans, the ship could detect no sign that any independent sentience was overseeing the system.

There were but a handful of cities, none larger than a quarter of a million inhabitants. All were scrubbed clean and kept scrupulously ordered by the DIs; they reminded Mada of databases populated with people instead of information. The majority of the population spent their bucolic lives in pretty hamlets and quaint towns overlooking lakes or oceans or mountains.

Humanity had booked a never-ending vacation.

"The brain clans could be controlling the DIs," said Mada. "That would make sense."

"Doubtful," said the ship. "Independent sentients create a signature disturbance in the sixth dimension."

She shook her head. "Did they choose to live in a museum," she said, "or were they condemned to it? It's obvious there's no First Right here; these people have only the *illusion* of individuality. And no Second Right either. Those bodies are as plain as uniforms —they're still slaves to their biology."

"There's no disease," said the ship. "They seem to be functionally immortal."

"That's not saying very much, is it?" Mada sniffed. "I want to go down for a closer look. What do I need to pass?"

"Clothes, for one thing." The ship displayed a selection of current styles on its screen. They were extravagantly varied, from ballooning pastel tents to skin-tight sheaths of luminescent metal, to feathered camouflage to jumpsuits made of what looked like dried mud. "Fashion design is one of their principal pasttimes," said the ship. "In addition, you'll probably want genitalia and the usual secondary sexual characteristics."

It took her the better part of a day to flow ovaries, fallopian tubes, a uterus, cervix, and vulva and to rearrange her vagina. All these unnecessary organs made her feel bloated. She saw breasts as a waste of tissue; she made hers as small as the ship thought acceptable. She argued with it about the several substantial patches of hair it claimed she needed. Clearly, grooming them would require constant attention. She didn't mind taming her claws into fingernails but she hated giving up her whiskers. Without them, the air was practically invisible. At first her new vulva tickled when she walked, but she got used to it.

The ship entered Earth's atmosphere at night and landed in what had once been Saskatchewan, Canada. It dumped most of its mass into the empty dimensions and flowed itself into baggy black pants, a moss-colored boat neck top, and a pair of brown, gripall loafers. It was able to conceal its complete sensorium in a canvas belt.

It was 9:14 in the morning on June 23, 19,834,004 CE when Mada strolled into the village of Harmonious Struggle.

the devil's apple

Harmonious Struggle consisted of five clothing shops, six restaurants, three jewelers, eight art galleries, a musical instrument maker, a crafts workshop, a weaver, a potter, a woodworking shop, two candle stores, four theaters with capacities ranging from twenty to three hundred, and an enormous sporting goods store attached to a miniature domed stadium. There looked to be apartments over most of these establishments; many had views of nearby Rabbit Lake.

Three of the restaurants—Hassam's Palace of Plenty, The Devil's Apple, and Laurel's—were practically jostling each other for position on Sonnet Street, which ran down to the lake. Lounging just outside of each were waiters eyeing handheld screens. They sprang up as one when Mada happened around the corner.

"Good day, Madame. Have you eaten?"

"Well met, fair stranger. Come break bread with us."

"All natural foods, friend! Lightly cooked, humbly served."

Mada veered into the middle of the street to study the situation as the waiters called to her. ~So I can choose whichever I want?~ she subvocalized to the ship.

~In an attention-based economy,~ subbed the ship in reply, ~all they expect from you is an audience.~

Just beyond Hassam's, the skinny waiter from The Devil's Apple had a wry, crooked smile. Black hair fell to the padded shoulders of his shirt. He was wearing boots to the knee and loose rust-colored shorts, but it was the little red cape that decided her.

As she walked past her, the waitress from Hassam's was practically shouting. "Madame, *please*, their batter is dull!" She waved her handheld at Mada. "Read the *reviews*. Who puts shrimp in *muffins?*"

The waiter at The Devil's Apple was named Owen. He showed her to one of three tables in the tiny restaurant. At his suggestion, Mada ordered the poached peaches with white cheese mousse, an asparagus breakfast torte, baked orange walnut French toast, and coddled eggs. Owen served the peaches, but it was the chef and owner, Edris, who emerged from the kitchen to clear the plate.

"The mousse, madame, you liked it?" she asked, beaming.

"It was good," said Mada.

Her smile shrank a size and a half. "Enough lemon rind, would you say that?"

"Yes. It was very nice."

Mada's reply seemed to dismay Edris even more. When she came out to clear the next course, she blanched at the corner of breakfast torte that Mada had left uneaten.

"I knew this." She snatched the plate away. "The pastry wasn't fluffy enough." She rolled the offending scrap between thumb and forefinger.

Mada raised her hands in protest. "No, no, it was delicious." She could see Owen shrinking into the far corner of the room.

"Maybe too much Colby, not enough Gruyere?" Edris snarled. "But you have no comment?"

"I wouldn't change a thing. It was perfect."

"Madame is kind," she said, her lips barely moving, and retreated.

A moment later Owen set the steaming plate of French toast before Mada.

"Excuse me." She tugged at his sleeve.

"Something's wrong?" He edged away from her. "You must speak to Edris."

"Everything is fine. I was just wondering if you could tell me how to get to the local library."

Edris burst out of the kitchen. "What are you doing, beanheaded boy? You are distracting my patron with absurd chitterchat. Get out, get out of my restaurant now."

"No really, he. . . ."

But Owen was already out the door and up the street, taking Mada's appetite with him.

~*You're doing something wrong,*~ the ship subbed.

Mada lowered her head. ~*I know that!*~

Mada pushed the sliver of French toast around the pool of maple syrup for several minutes but could not eat it. "Excuse me," she called, standing up abruptly. "Edris?"

Edris shouldered through the kitchen door, carrying a tray with a silver egg cup. She froze when she saw how it was with the French toast and her only patron.

"This was one of the most delicious meals I have ever eaten." Mada backed toward the door. She wanted nothing to do with eggs, coddled or otherwise.

Edris set the tray in front of Mada's empty chair. "Madame, the art of the kitchen requires the tongue of the patron," she said icily.

Mada fumbled for the latch. "Everything was very, very wonderful."

no comment

Mada slunk down Lyric Alley, which ran behind the stadium, trying to understand how exactly she had offended. In this attention-based economy, paying attention was obviously not enough. There had to be some other cultural protocol she and the ship were missing. What she probably ought to do was go back and explore the clothes shops, maybe pick up a pot or some candles and see what additional information she could blunder into. But making a fool of herself had never much appealed to Mada as a learning strategy. She wanted the map, a native guide—some edge, preferably secret.

~*Scanning,*~ subbed the ship. ~*Somebody is following you. He just ducked behind the privet hedge twelve-point-three meters to the right. It's the waiter, Owen.*~

"Owen," called Mada, "is that you? I'm sorry I got you in trouble. You're an excellent waiter."

"I'm not really a waiter." Owen peeked over the top of the hedge. "I'm a poet."

She gave him her best smile. "You said you'd take me to the library." For some reason, the smile stayed on her face "Can we do that now?"

"First listen to some of my poetry."

"No," she said firmly. "Owen, I don't think you've been paying attention. I said I would like to go to the library."

"All right then, but I'm not going to have sex with you."

Mada was taken aback. "Really? Why is that?"

"I'm not attracted to women with small breasts."

For the first time in her life, Mada felt the stab of outraged hormones. "Come out here and talk to me."

There was no immediate break in the hedge, so Owen had to squiggle through. "There's something about me that you don't like," he said as he struggled with the branches.

"Is there?" She considered. "I like your cape."

"That you *don't* like." He escaped the hedge's grasp and brushed leaves from his shorts.

"I guess I don't like your narrow-mindedness. It's not an attractive quality in a poet."

There was a gleam in Owen's eye as he went up on his tiptoes and began to declaim:

"That spring you left I thought I might expire
And lose the love you left for me to keep.
To hold you once again is my desire
Before I give myself to death's long sleep."

He illustrated his poetry with large, flailing gestures. At "death's long sleep" he brought his hands together as if to pray, laid the side of his head against them and closed his eyes. He held that pose in silence for an agonizingly long time.

"It's nice," Mada said at last. "I like the way it rhymes."

He sighed and went flat-footed. His arms drooped and he fixed her with an accusing stare. "You're not from here."

"No," she said. ~*Where am I from?*~ she subbed. ~*Someplace he'll have to look up.*~

~*Marble Bar. It's in Australia*~

"I'm from Marble Bar."

"No, I mean you're not one of us. You don't comment."

At that moment, Mada understood. ~*I want to skip downwhen four minutes. I need to undo this.*~

~.this undo to need I .minutes four downwhen skip to want I~ .understood Mada,
moment that At ".comment don't You .us
of one not you're mean I ,No" ".Bar
Marble from I'm" ~.*Australia in It's* .Bar
Marble~ ~up look to have he'll Someplace~
.subbed she ~?*from I am Where*~ .said
she ",No" ".here from not You're" .stare
accusing an with her fixed he and drooped
arms His .flatfooted went and sighed He

As the ship surged through the empty dimensions, three-space became as liquid as a dream. Leaves smeared and buildings ran together. Owen's face swirled.

"They want criticism," said Mada. They like to think of

".rhymes it way the like I." .last at said
Mada ".nice It's" .time long agonizingly an
for silence in pose that held He .eyes his
closed and them against head his of side
the laid ,pray to if as together hands his
brought he ".sleep long death's" At .ges-
tures flailing ,large with poetry his illustrated He ".sleep long death's to myself give
I Before desire my is again once you hold
To keep to me for left you love the lose
And expire might I thought I left you spring
That" :declaim to began and tiptoes his on
up went he as eye Owen's in gleam a was
There ".poet a in quality attractive
an not It's .narrow-mindedness your like
don't I guess I" .shorts his from leaves
brushed and grasp hedge's the escaped
He ".like *don't* you That" ".cape your like
I" .considered She "?there Is" .branches the
with struggled he as said he ",like don't you
that me about something There's" .through
squiggle to had Owen so ,hedge the in
break immediate no was There ".me to talk
and here out Come" .hormones wronged
of stab the felt Mada ,life her in time first
the For ".breasts small with women to
attracted not I'm" "?that is Why ?Really"
.aback taken was Mada ".you with sex have
to going not I'm but ,then right All"
".library the to go to like would I said I
.attention paying been you've think don't
I ,Owen ,firmly said she ",No" ".poetry my
of some to listen First"

themselves as artists but
they're insecure about what
they've accomplished. They
want their audience to
engage with what they're
doing, help them make it
better—the comments they
both seem to expect."

"I see it now," said the
ship. "But is one person in a
backwater worth an undo?
Let's just start over somewhere else."

"No, I have an idea." She
began flowing more fat cells
to her breasts. For the first
time since she had skipped
upwhen, Mada had a
glimpse of what her duty
might now be. "I'm going to
need a big special effect on
short notice. Be ready to
reclaim mass so you can
resubstantiate the hull at my
command."

"First listen to some of my poetry."

"Go ahead." Mada folded her arms across her chest. "Say it
then."

Owen stood on tiptoes to declaim:

"That spring you left I thought I might expire
And lose the love you left for me to keep.
To hold you once again is my desire
Before I give myself to death's long sleep."

He illustrated his poetry with large, flailing gestures. At "death's
long sleep" he brought his hands together as if to pray, moved them
to the side of his head, rested against them and closed his eyes. He
had held the pose for just a beat before Mada interrupted him.

"Owen," she said. "You look ridiculous."

He jerked as if he had been hit in the head by a shovel.

She pointed at the ground before her. "You'll want to take these comments sitting down."

He hesitated, then settled at her feet.

"You hold your meter well, but that's purely a mechanical skill." She circled behind him. "A smart oven could do as much. Stop fidgeting!"

She hadn't noticed the anthills near the spot she had chosen for Owen. The first scouts were beginning to explore him. That suited her plan exactly.

"Your real problem," she continued, "is that you know nothing about death and probably very little about desire."

"I know about death." Owen drew his feet close to his body and grasped his knees. "Everyone does. Flowers die, squirrels die."

"Has anyone you've ever known died?"

He frowned. "I didn't know her personally, but there was the woman who fell off that cliff in Merrymeeting."

"Owen, did you have a mother?"

"Don't make fun of me. Everyone has a mother."

Mada didn't think it was time to tell him that she didn't; that she and her sibling batch of a thousand revolutionaries had been auto-flowed. "Hold out your hand." Mada scooped up an ant, crunched it and dropped it onto Owen's palm. "That's your mother."

Owen looked down at the dead ant and then up again at Mada. His eyes filled.

"I think I love you," he said. "What's your name?"

"Mada." She leaned over to straighten his cape. "But loving me would be a very bad idea."

all that's left

Mada was surprised to find a few actual books in the library, printed on real plastic. A primitive DI had catalogued the rest of the collection, billions of gigabytes of print, graphics, audio, video, and VR files. None of it told Mada what she wanted to know. The library had sims of Egypt's New Kingdom, Islam's Abbasid dynasty, and the International Moonbase—but then came an astonishing void. Mada's searches on Trueborn, the Utopians, Tau Ceti, intelligence engineering, and dimensional extensibility theory turned up no results. It was only in the very recent past that history resumed. The DI could reproduce the plans that the workbots had left when they built the library twenty-two years ago, and the menu The Devil's Apple had offered the previous summer, and the complete won-lost record of the Black Minks, the local scatterball club, which had gone 533-905 over the last century. It knew that the name of the woman who died in Merrymeeting was Agnes and that two years after her death, a replacement baby had been born to Chandra and Yuri. They named him Herrick.

Mada waved the screen blank and stretched. She could see Owen draped artfully over a nearby divan, as if posing for a portrait. He was engrossed by his handheld. She noticed that his lips moved as he read. She crossed the reading room and squeezed onto it next to him, nestling into the crook in his legs. "What's that?" she asked.

He turned the handheld toward her. "Nadeem Jerad's *Burning the Snow*. Would you like to hear one of his poems?"

"Maybe later." She leaned into him. "I was just reading about Moonbase."

"Yes, ancient history. It's sort of interesting, don't you think? The Greeks and the Renaissance and all that."

"But then I can't find any record of what came after."

"Because of the nightmares." He nodded. "Terrible things happened, so we forgot them."

"What terrible things?"

He tapped the side of his head and grinned.

"Of course," she said, "nothing terrible happens anymore."

"No. Everyone's happy now." Owen reached out and pushed a strand of her hair off her forehead. "You have beautiful hair."

Mada couldn't even remember what color it was. "But if something terrible did happen, then you'd want to forget it."

"Obviously."

"The woman who died, Agnes. No doubt her friends were very sad."

"No doubt." Now he was playing with her hair.

~*Good question*,~ subbed the ship. ~*They must have some mechanism to wipe their memories.*~

"Is something wrong?" Owen's face was the size of the moon; Mada was afraid of what he might tell her next.

"Agnes probably had a mother," she said.

"A mom and a dad."

"It must have been terrible for them."

He shrugged. "Yes, I'm sure they forgot her."

Mada wanted to slap his hand away from her head. "But how could they?"

He gave her a puzzled look. "Where are you from, anyway?"

"Trueborn," she said without hesitation. "It's a long, long way from here."

"Don't you have libraries there?" He gestured at the screens that surrounded them. "This is where we keep what we don't want to remember."

~Skip!~ Mada could barely sub, she was so outraged; if what she suspected were true . . . *~Skip downwhen two minutes.~*

~.minutes two downwhen Skip ~ . . . true were suspected she what if; . . . ,sub barely could Mada ~!Skip~ "?there libraries have you Don't" ".here from way long ,long a It's" .hesitation without said she ",Trueborn" "?anyway, from you are Where" .look puzzled a her gave He "?they could how But" .head her from away hand his slap to wanted Mada ".her forgot they sure I'm, Yes" .shrugged He ".them for terrible been have must It" ".dad a and mom A" ".mother a had probably Agnes" .next her tell might he what of afraid was Mada .moon the of size the was face Owen's "?wrong something Is" ~!Quiet~ ~... mechanism some have must They" .ship the subbed ~,question Good~ .hair her with playing was he Now ".doubt No" ".sad very were friends her doubt no ,Agnes ,died who woman The" ".Obviously" ".it forget you'd then ,happen did terrible something if But" .was it color what remember even couldn't Mada

She wrapped her arms around herself to keep the empty dimensions from reaching for the emptiness inside her. Was something wrong?

Of course there was, but she didn't expect to say it out loud. "I've lost everything and all that's left is *this*." Owen shimmered next to her like the surface of Rabbit Lake.

"Mada, what?" said the ship.

"Forget it," she said. She thought she could hear something cracking when she laughed.

Mada couldn't even remember what color her hair was. "But if something terrible did happen, then you'd want to forget it."

"Obviously."

"Something terrible happened to me."

"I'm sorry." Owen squeezed her shoulder. "Do you want me to show you how to use the headbands?" He pointed at a rack of metal-mesh strips.

~Scanning,~ subbed the ship. *~Microcurrent taps capable of modulating post-synaptic outputs. I thought they were some kind of virtual reality I/O.~*

"No." Mada twisted away from Owen and shot off the divan. She was outraged that these people would deliberately burn memories. How many stubbed toes and unhappy love affairs had Owen forgotten? If she could have, she would have skipped the entire village of Harmonius Struggle downwhen into the identity mine. When he rose up after her, she grabbed his hand. "I have to get out of here *right now*."

She dragged him out of the library into the innocent light of the sun.

"Wait a minute," he said. She continued to tow him up Ode Street and out of town. "Wait!" He planted his feet, tugged at her and she spun back to him. "Why are you so upset?"

"I'm not upset." Mada's blood was hammering in her temples and she could feel the prickle of sweat under her arms. ~Now I need you,~ she subbed. "All right then. It's time you knew." She took a deep breath. "We were just talking about ancient history, Owen. Do you remember back then that the gods used to intervene in the affairs of humanity?"

Owen goggled at her as if she were growing beans out of her ears.

"I am a goddess, Owen, and I have come for you. I am calling you to your destiny. I intend to inspire you to great poetry."

His mouth opened and then closed again.

"My worshippers call me by many names." She raised a hand to the sky. ~Help?~

~Try Athene? Here's a databurst.~

"To the Greeks, I was Athene," Mada continued, "the goddess of cities, of technology and the arts, of wisdom and of war." She stretched a hand toward Owen's astonished face, forefinger aimed between his eyes. "Unlike you, I had no mother. I sprang full-grown from the forehead of my maker. I am Athene, the virgin goddess."

"How stupid do you think I am?" He shivered and glanced away from her fierce gaze. "I used to live in Maple City, Mada. I'm not some simple-minded country lump. You don't seriously expect me to believe this goddess nonsense?"

She slumped, confused. Of course she had expected him to believe her. "I meant no disrespect, Owen. It's just that the truth is. . . ." This wasn't as easy as she had thought. "What I expect is that you believe in your own potential, Owen. What I expect is that you are brave enough to leave this place and come with me. To the stars, Owen, to the stars to start a new world." She crossed her arms in front of her chest, grasped the hem of her moss-colored top, pulled it over her head and tossed it behind her. Before it hit the ground the ship augmented it with enough reclaimed mass from the empty dimensions to resubstantiate the command and living mods.

Mada was quite pleased with the way Owen tried—and failed—not to stare at her breasts. She kicked the gripall loafers off and the deck rose up beneath them. She stepped out of the baggy, black pants; when she tossed them at Owen, he flinched. Seconds later, they were eyeing each other in metallic light of the ship's main companionway.

"Well?" said Mada.

duty

Mada had difficulty accepting Trueborn as it now was. She could see the ghosts of great cities, hear the murmur of dead friends. She decided to live in the forest that had once been the Green Sea, where there were no landmarks to remind her of what she had lost. She ordered the ship to begin constructing an infrastructure similar to that they had found on Earth, capable of supporting a technologically advanced population. Borrowing orphan mass from the empty dimensions, it was soon consumed with this monumental task. She missed its company; only rarely did she use the link it had left her—a silver ring with a direct connection to its sensorium.

The ship's first effort was the farm that Owen called Athens. It consisted of their house, a flow works, a gravel pit, and a barn. Dirt roads led to various mines and domed fields that the ship's bots tended. Mada had it build a separate library, a little way into the woods, where, she declared, information was to be acquired only, never destroyed. Owen spent many evenings there. He said he was trying to make himself worthy of her.

He had been deeply flattered when she told him that, as part of his training as a poet, he was to name the birds and beasts and flowers and trees of Trueborn.

"But they must already have names," he said, as they walked back to the house from the newly-tilled soya field.

"The people who named them are gone," she said. "The names went with them."

"Your people." He waited for her to speak. The wind sighed through the forest. "What happened to them?"

"I don't know." At that moment she regretted ever bringing him to Trueborn.

He sighed. "It must be hard."

"You left *your* people," she said. She spoke to wound him, since he was wounding her with these rude questions.

"For you, Mada." He let go of her. "I know you didn't leave *them* for me." He picked up a pebble and held it in front of his face. "You are now Mada-stone," he told it, "and whatever you hit . . . " he threw it into the woods and it *thwocked* off a tree. " . . . is Mada-tree. We will plant fields of Mada-seed and press Mada-juice from the sweet Mada-fruit and dance for the rest of our days down Mada Street." He laughed and put his arm around her waist and swung her around in circles, kicking up dust from the road. She was so surprised that she laughed too.

Mada and Owen slept in separate bedrooms, so she was not exactly sure how she knew that he wanted to have sex with her. He had never spoken of it, other than on that first day when he had specifically said that he did not want her. Maybe it because he continually brushed up against her for no apparent reason. This could hardly be chance, considering that they were the only two people on Trueborn. For herself, Mada welcomed his hesitancy. Although she had been emotionally intimate with her batch siblings, none of them had ever inserted themselves into her body cavities.

But, for better or worse, she had chosen this man for this course of action. Even if the galaxy had forgotten Trueborn two-tenths of a spin ago, the revolution still called Mada to her duty.

"What's it like to kiss?" she asked that night, as they were finishing supper.

Owen laid his fork across a plate of cauliflower curry. "You've never kissed anyone before?"

"That's why I ask."

Owen leaned across the table and brushed his lips across hers. The brief contact made her cheeks flush, as if she had just jogged in from the gravel pit. "Like that," he said. "Only better."

"Do you still think my breasts are too small?"

"I never said that." Owen's face turned red.

"It was a comment you made—or at least thought about making."

"A comment?" The word *comment* seemed to stick in his throat; it made him cough. "Just because you make comment on some aspect doesn't mean you reject the work as a whole."

Mada glanced down the neck of her shift. She hadn't really increased her breast mass all that much, maybe ten or twelve grams, but now vasocongestion had begun to swell them even more. She could also feel blood flowing to her reproductive organs. It was a pleasurable weight that made her feel light as pollen. "Yes, but do you think they're too small?"

Owen got up from the table and came around behind her chair. He put his hands on her shoulders and she leaned her head back against him. There was something between her cheek and his stomach. She heard him say, "Yours are the most perfect breasts on this entire planet," as if from a great distance and then realized that the *something* must be his penis.

After that, neither of them made much comment.

nine hours

Mada stared at the ceiling, her eyes wide but unseeing. Her concentration had turned inward. After she had rolled off him, Owen had flung his left arm across her belly and drawn her hip toward his and given her the night's last kiss. Now the muscles of his arm were slack, and she could hear his seashore breath as she released her ovum into the cloud of his sperm squiggling up her fallopian tubes. The most vigorous of the swimmers butted its head through the ovum's membrane and dissolved, releasing its genetic material. Mada immediately started raveling the strands of DNA before the fertilized egg could divide for the first time. Without the necessary diversity, they would never revive the revolution. Satisfied with her intervention, she flowed the blastocyst down her fallopian tubes where it locked onto the wall of her uterus. She prodded it and the ball of cells became a comma with a big head and a thin tail. An array of cells specialized and folded into a tube that ran the length of the embryo, branching and rebranching into nerve fibers. Dark pigment swept across two cups in the blocky head and then bulged into eyes. A mouth slowly opened; in it was a one-chambered, beating heart. The front end of the neural tube blossomed into the vesicles that would become the brain. Four buds swelled, two near the head, two at the tail. The uppermost pair sprouted into paddles, pierced by rays of cells that Mada immediately began to ossify into fingerbone. The lower buds stretched into delicate legs. At midnight, the embryo was as big as her fingernail; it began to move and so became a fetus. The eyes opened for a few minutes, but then the eyelids fused. Mada and Owen were going to have a son; his penis was now an almost imaginary nub of flesh. Bubbles of tissue blew inward from the head and became his ears. Mada listened to him listen to her heartbeat. He lost his tail and his intestines slithered down the umbilical cord into his abdomen. As his fingerprints looped and whorled, he stuck his thumb into his mouth. Mada was having trouble breathing because the fetus was floating so high in her uterus. She eased herself into a sitting position and Owen grumbled in his sleep. Suddenly the curry in the cauliflower was giving her heartburn. Then the muscles of her uterus tightened and pain sheeted across her swollen belly.

~*Drink this.*~ The ship flowed a tumbler of nutrient nano onto the bedside table. ~*The fetus gains mass rapidly from now on.*~ The stuff tasted like rusty nails. ~*You're doing fine.*~

When the fetus turned upside down, it felt like he was trying out a gymnastic routine. But then he snuggled headfirst into her pelvis, and calmed down, probably because there wasn't enough room left inside her for him to make large, flailing gestures like his father. Now she could feel electrical buzzes down her legs and inside her vagina as the baby bumped her nerves. He was big now, and growing by almost a kilogram an hour, laying down new muscle and brown fat. Mada was tired of it all. She dozed. At 6:37 her water broke, drenching the bed.

"Hmm." Owen rolled away from the warm, fragrant spill of amniotic fluid. "What did you say?"

The contractions started; she put her hand on his chest and pressed down. "Help," she whimpered.

"Wha. . . ?" Owen propped himself up on elbows. "Hey, I'm wet. How did I get. . . ?"

"*O-Owen!*" She could feel the baby's head stretching her vagina in a way mere flesh could not possibly stretch.

"Mada! What's wrong?" Suddenly his face was very close to hers. "Mada, what's happening?"

But then baby was slipping out of her, and it was much better than the only sex she had ever had. She caught her breath and said, "I have begotten a son."

She reached between her legs and pulled the baby to her breasts. They were huge now, and very sore.

"We will call him Owen," she said.

Begot

And Mada begot Enos and Felicia and Malaleel and Ralph and Jared and Elisa and Tharsis and Masahiko and Thema and Seema and Casper and Hevila and Djanka and Jennifer and Jojo and Regma and Elvis and Irina and Dean and Marget and Karoly and Sabatha and Ashley and Siobhan and Mei-Fung and Neil and Gupta and Hans and Sade and Moon and Randy and Genvieve and Bob and Nazia and Eiichi and Justine and Ozma and Khaled and Candy and Pavel and Isaac and Sandor and Veronica and Gao and Pat and Marcus and Zsa Zsa and Li and Rebecca.

Seven years after her return to Trueborn, Mada rested.

ever after

Mada was convinced that she was not a particularly good mother, but then she had been designed for courage and quick-thinking, not nurturing and patience. It wasn't the crying or the dirty diapers or the spitting-up, it was the utter uselessness of the babies that the revolutionary in her could not abide. And her maternal instincts were often skewed. She would offer her children the wrong toy or cook the wrong dish, fall silent when they wanted her to play, prod them to talk when they needed to withdraw. Mada and the ship had calculated that fifty of her genetically-manipulated offspring would provide the necessary diversity to repopulate Trueborn. After Rebecca was born, Mada was more than happy to stop having children.

Perhaps it was that, although, the children seemed to love her despite her awkwardness, Mada wasn't sure she loved them back. She constantly teased at her feelings, peeling away what she considered pretense and sentimentality. She worried that the capacity to love might not have been part of her emotional design. Or perhaps begetting fifty children in seven years had left her numb.

Owen seemed to enjoy being a parent. He was the one whom the children called for when they wanted to play. They came to Mada for answers and decisions. Mada liked to watch them snuggle next to him when he spun his fantastic stories. Their father picked them up when they stumbled, and let them climb on his shoulders so they could see just what he saw. They told him secrets they would never tell her.

The children adored the ship, which substantiated a bot companion for each of them, in part for their protection. All had inherited their father's all-but-invulnerable immune systems; their chromosomes replicated well beyond the Hayflick limit with integrity and fidelity. But they lacked their mother's ability to flow tissue and were therefore at peril of drowning or breaking their necks. The bots also provided the intense individualized attention that their busy parents could not. Each child was convinced that his or her bot companion had a unique personality. Even the seven-year-olds were too young to realize that the bots were reflecting their ideal personality back at them. The bots were in general as intelligent as the ship, although it had programmed into their DIs a touch of naiveté and a tendency to literalness that allowed the children to play tricks on them. Pranking a brother's or sister's bot was a particularly delicious sport.

Athens had begun to sprawl after seven years. The library had tripled in size and grown a wing of classrooms and workshops. There was a new gym and three playing fields. Owen had asked the ship to build a little theater where the children could put on shows for each other. The original house became a ring of houses, connected by corridors and facing a central courtyard. Each night Mada and Owen moved to their bedroom in a different house. Owen thought it important that the children see them sleeping in the same bed; Mada went along.

After she had begotten Rebecca, Mada needed something to do that didn't involve the children. She had the ship's farmbots plow up a field and for an hour each day she tended it. She resisted Owen's attempts to name this "Mom's Hobby." Mada grew vegetables; she had little use for flowers. Although she made a specialty of root crops, she was not a particularly accomplished gardener. She did, however, enjoy weeding.

It was at these quiet times, her hands flicking across the dark soil, that she considered her commitment to the Three Universal Rights. After two-tenths of a spin, she had clearly lost her zeal. Not for the first, that independent sentients had the right to remain individual. Mada was proud that her children were as individual as any intelligence, flesh or machine, could have made them. Of course, they had no pressing need to exercise the second right of manipulating their physical structures—she had taken care of that for them. When they were of age, if the ship wanted to introduce them to molecular engineering, that could certainly be done. No, the real problem was that downwhen was forever closed by the identity mine. How could she justify her new Trueborn society if it didn't enjoy the third right: free access to the timelines?

undone

"Mada!" Owen waved at the edge of her garden. She blinked; he was wearing the same clothes he'd been wearing when she had first seen him on Sonnet Street in front of The Devil's Apple—down to the little red cape. He showed her a picnic basket. "The ship is watching the kids tonight," he called. "Come on, it's our anniversary. I did the calculations myself. We met eight Earth years ago today."

He led her to a spot deep in the woods, where he spread a blanket. They stretched out next to each other and sorted through the basket. There was a curley salad with alperts and thumbnuts, brainboy and chive sandwiches on cheese bread. He toasted her with Mada-fruit wine and told her that Siobahn had let go of the couch and taken her first step and that Irina wanted everyone to learn to play an instrument so that she could conduct the family orchestra and the Malaleel had asked him just today if ship was a person.

"It's not a person," said Mada. "It's a DI."

"That's what I said." Owen peeled the crust off his cheese bread. "And he said if it's not a person, how come it's telling jokes?"

"It told a joke?"

"It asked him, 'How come you can't have everything?' and then it said, 'Where would you put it?'"

She nudged him in the ribs. "That sounds more like you than the ship."

"I have a present for you," he said after they were stuffed. "I wrote you a poem." He did not stand; there were no large, flailing gestures. Instead he slid the picnic basket out of the way, leaned close and whispered into her ear.

> "Loving you is like catching rain on my tongue.
> You bathe the leaves, soak indifferent ground;
> Why then should I get so little of you?
> Yet still, like a flower with a fool's face,
> I open myself to the sky."

Mada was not quite sure what was happening to her; she had never really cried before. "I like that it doesn't rhyme." She had understood that tears flowed from a sadness. "I like that a lot." She sniffed and smiled and daubed at edges of her eyes with a napkin. "Never rhyme anything again."

"Done," he said.

Mada watched her hand reach for him, caress the side of his neck, and then pull him down on top of her. Then she stopped watching herself.

"No more children." His whisper seemed to fill her head.

"No," she said, "no more."

"I'm sharing you with too many already." He slid his hand between her legs. She arched her back and guided him to her pleasure.

When they had both finished, she ran her finger through the sweat cooling at the small of his back and then licked it. "Owen," she said, her voice a silken purr. "That was the one."

"Is that your comment?"

"No." She craned to see his eyes. "This is my comment," she said. "You're writing love poems to the wrong person."

"There is no one else," he said.

She squawked and pushed him off her. "That may be true," she said, laughing, "but it's not something you're supposed to say."

"No, what I meant was . . ."

"I know." She put a finger to his lips and giggled like one of her babies. Mada realized then how dangerously happy she was. She rolled away from Owen; all the lightness crushed out of her by the weight of guilt and shame. It wasn't her duty to be happy. "There's something I have to do." How quickly she was ready to betray the cause of those who had made her. She fumbled for her shift. "I can't help myself, I'm sorry."

Owen watched her warily. "Why are you sorry?"

"Because after I do it, I'll be different."

"Different how?"

"The ship will explain." She tugged the shift on. "Take care of the children."

"What do you mean, take care of the children? What are you doing?" He lunged at her and she scrabbled away from him on all fours. "Tell me."

"The ship says my body should survive." She staggered to her feet. "That's all I can offer you, Owen." Mada ran.

She didn't expect Owen to come after her—or to run so fast.

~I need you.~ she subbed to the ship. *~Substantiate the command mod.~*

He was right behind her. Saying something. Was it to her? "No," he panted, "no, no, *no.*"

~Substantiate the com. . . .~

Suddenly Owen was gone; Mada bit her lip as she crashed into the main screen, caromed off it and dropped like a dead woman. She lay there for a moment, the cold of the deck seeping into her cheek. "Goodbye," she whispered. She struggled to pull herself up and spat blood.

"Skip downwhen," she said, "six minutes."

".minutes six" ,said she ",downwhen Skip" .blood spat and up herself pull to struggled She .whispered she ",Goodbye." cheek her into seeping deck the of cold the ,moment a for there lay She .woman dead a like dropped and it off caromed ,screen main the into crashed she as lip her bit Mada ;gone was Owen Suddenly ~....com the Substan- tiate~ ".no ,no, no" ,panted he ",No" ?her to it Was .something Saying .her behind right was He ~.mod command the Substantiate~ .ship the to subbed she ~.you need I~ .fast so run to – her after come to Owen expect didn't She .ran Mada ".Owen ,you offer can I all That's" .feet her to staggered She ".survive should body my says ship The" ".me Tell" .fours all on him from away scrabbled she and her at lunged He "?doing you are What ?children the of care take ,mean you do What." ".children the of care Take" .on shift the tugged She ".explain will ship The" "?how Different" ".different be I'll ,it do I after Because" "?sorry you are Why" .warily her watched Owen. ".sorry I'm ,myself help can't I" .shift her for fumbled She .her made had who those of cause the betrayed have

When threespace went blurry, it seemed that her duty did too. She waved her hand and watched it smear.

"You know what you're doing," said the ship.

"What I was designed to do. What all my batch siblings pledged to do." She waved her hand again; she could actually see through herself. "The only thing I can do."

"The mine will wipe your identity. There will be nothing of you left."

"And then it will be gone and the timelines will open. I believe that I've known this was what I had to do since we first skipped upwhen."

would she easily How ".do to have I something There's" .happy be to duty her wasn't It
.shame and guilt of weight the by her of out
crushed lightness the all ,Owen from rolled
She .was she happy dangerously how then
realized Mada .babies her of one like giggled
and lips his to finger a put She ".know I"
".... Was meant I what ,No" ".say to supposed
you're something not it's but" ,laughing, said
she ",true be may That" .her off him pushed
and squawked She .said he ",else one is
There" ".person wrong the to poems love
writing You're" .said she ",comment my is
This" .eyes his see to craned She ".No"
"?comment your that Is" ".one the was That"
.purr silken a voice her , said she ",Owen"

"The probability was always
high." said the ship "But not
certain."

"Bring me to him, after-
wards. But don't tell him
about the timelines. He might
want to change them. The
timelines are for the children,
so that they can finish the
revol . . .

. . . .
. . . .

"Owen," she said, her voice a silken purr. Then she paused.

The woman shook her head, trying to clear it. Laying on top of
her was the handsomest man she had ever met. She felt warm and
wonderful. What was this? "I . . . I'm. . . ," she said. She reached up
and touched the little red cloth hanging from his shoulders. "I like
your cape."

done

".minutes six" ,said she ",downwhen Skip"
.blood spat and up herself pull to struggled
She .whispered she ",Goodbye" .cheek her
into seeping deck the of cold the ,moment
a for there lay She .woman dead a like
dropped and it off caromed ,screen main
the into crashed she as lip her bit Mada
;gone was Owen Suddenly ~....com the
Substantiate~ ".no ,no, no" ,panted he
",No" ?her to it Was .something Saying. her
behind right was He ~.mod command the
Substantiate~ .ship the to subbed she ~.you
need I~ .fastso run to – her after come to
Owen expect didn't She .ran Mada ".Owen
,you offer can I all That's" .feet her to staggered She ".survive should body my says
ship The" ".me Tell" .fours all on him from
away scrabbled she and her at lunged He
"?doing you are What ?children the of care
take ,mean you do What." ".children the
of care Take" .on shift the tugged She
".explain will ship The" "?how Different"
".different be I'll ,it do I after Because"
"?sorry you are Why" .warily her watched
Owen. "sorry I'm ,myself help can't I" .shift
her for fumbled She .her made had who
those of cause the betrayed have would she
easily How ".do to have I something
There's" .happy be to duty her wasn't It

Mada waved her hand and
watched it smear in threespace.

"You know what you're
doing," said the ship.

"What I was designed to do.
What all my batch siblings
pledged to do." She waved;
she could actually see through
herself. "The only thing I can
do."

"The mine will wipe your
identity. None of your memories will survive."

"I believe that I've known
it's what would happen since
we first skipped upwhen."

"It was probable." said the
ship. "But not certain."

Trueborn scholars pinpoint
what the ship did next as its
first step toward independent

.shame and guilt of weight the by her of out crushed lightness the all ,Owen from rolled She .was she happy dangerously how then realized Mada .babies her of one like giggled and lips his to finger a put She ".know I" "…. Was meant I what ,No" ".say to supposed you're something not it's but" ,laughing, said she ",true be may That" .her off him pushed and squawked She .said he ",else one is There" ".person wrong the to poems love writing You're" .said she ",comment my is This" .eyes his see to craned She ".No" "?comment your that Is" ".one the was That" .purr silken a voice her, said she ",Owen"

sentience. In its memoirs, the ship credits the children with teaching it to misbehave.

It played a prank.

"Loving you," said the ship, is like catching rain on my tongue. You bathe. . . ."

"Stop," Mada shouted. "Stop right now!"

"Got you!" The ship gloated. "Four minutes, fifty-one seconds."

"Owen," she said, her voice a silken purr. "That was the one."

"Is that your comment?"

"No." Mada was astonished—and pleased—that she still existed. She knew that in most timelines her identity must have been obliterated by the mine. Thinking about those brave, lost selves made her more sad than proud. "This is my comment," she said. "I'm ready now."

Owen coughed uncertainly. "Umm, already?"

She squawked and pushed him off her. "Not for *that*." She sifted his hair through her hands. "To be with you forever."

Afterword

I TRIED TO GIVE "10^{16} TO 1" AWAY. REALLY. IN 1998, I was teaching the Clarion East Writers' Workshop at Michigan State University. Clarion is sort of a boot camp for would-be science fiction writers: six weeks of intensive writing and manuscript analysis with a different professional presiding each week. I went to Clarion as a student myself, back in the McKinley administration. Several students wrote time-travel stories during my time at Clarion '98 and some got frustrated trying to parse the various theories. I don't like to lecture but when they asked me to tell them everything I knew about time travel, I agreed to an evening session. And at the end of my talk, I told them the plot of "10^{16} to 1," which I had known for years, but had long since despaired of ever writing because it was too personal. I said they were welcome to use it if they wanted; none seemed particularly interested. But the act of giving the story up triggered something in my imagination and that night I began to think systematically about plot and characters. A couple of months later I was writing.

When I say that this story was too personal, I mean that the kid, Ray Beaumont, was very much like me as I was in October of 1962. On the other hand, the other people in the story were pretty much strangers to me. I was not an only child, but rather the eldest of four brothers, and my parents were nothing like Ray's parents, although Ray's parents probably lived down the street.

The second biggest surprise of my professional career came when "10^{16} to 1" was nominated for the Hugo Award; the biggest surprise was when it won. I know now that this was a story that I had to write. I should warn you that it still scares me because, in some time streams, it is probably true.

I wrote "Lovestory" to catch an award. It didn't, but this story remains one of my favorites.

In 1997, I was asked to serve as a juror for the James Tiptree, Jr. Award. The Tiptree is an "annual literary prize for science fiction or fantasy that explores and expands the roles of women and men for work by both women and men." The founding mothers of the Tiptree Award charge the jury to find a work of fiction that combines literary excellence with some kind of "gender bending." It is up to each year's jury to decide what gender criteria to use. After spending a year reading for the Tiptree, I was of a mind to bend some gender myself. "Lovestory" was the result. It takes place in a marsupial alien culture in which there are three gender roles to each family unit: a mother, a wife, a father. The wife and father procreate but only the mother can bring the fetal scrap to maturity in her pouch.

When I brought it to be critiqued by the Sycamore Hill Writers' Workshop, several people wondered aloud whether there was any percentage in creating a planet, an alien species, and an advanced culture as a backdrop for a single *novelette*. Was this part of a series? An out-take from a novel? I confess that I have never been tempted to return to this world and these people. Maybe that's because I was so pleased with the experience of writing "Lovestory." It took me almost two months to research and write the first two sections. Then I cranked through the last section in five days; every other sentence felt like a breakthrough. I remember when I typed, "Reality was a decision — and no one here was making it" that I was so excited that I had to get up from the computer and walk around the house. I hadn't really understood what the story was about until then.

"Lovestory" made the Tiptree short list for 1998. The winner was Raphael Carter's brilliant "Congenital Agenesis of Gender Ideation." Sure, I was a little disappointed, but that didn't last.

Unlike some writers, I tend to stay put. I've moved just twice since

1980, most recently in 1999 to bucolic Nottingham, New Hampshire. The hitch in this last relocation was that my wife Pam and I sold our old house in June but we couldn't move into the new place until September. So I wrote "Feel the Zaz" the summer we were homeless. Well, not homeless in the sense that we had no place to live, but homeless in the sense that we stayed with friends or in motels and lived out of suitcases for four months. The nadir of our odyssey was the time we spent in a two room "housekeeping unit" in The Motel That Time Forgot. The 1950s style kitchen table could accommodate only two people, so after I set my computer up on it, one of us had to eat sitting on the vinyl couch. I wrote the last third of "Feel the Zaz" at that table, grateful to escape into a world of sims and celebrity. The experience certainly helped me enter the mind of Dylan McDonough, who sleeps on a seedy fold-out sofa in his office and hangs his suits in a defunct shower in the executive washroom.

Actually, I wrote two separate but equal versions of "Feel The Zaz" that summer. I'd previously adapted three of my stories into internet audioplays for Scifi.com's *Seeing Ear Theater*. In the spring of 1999, *SET*'s producer, Brian Smith, asked me for an original piece. I agreed, thinking that I could later write a story based on the script. The problem was that I had never actually written a play from scratch—all my dramatic work had been adapted. I spent a couple of days choking at the keyboard before I realized what I had to do. I started a draft of "Feel the Zaz" *the story* and whenever I finished a scene, I would then adapt it into "Feel the Zaz" *the audioplay*. However, after I turned in the completed audioplay, I held the story version until after we'd moved to Nottingham and I'd unpacked my office in the new digs. By that time, I'd rethought the story, and did a final draft that differs somewhat from the audioplay. If you're interested, feel free to compare and contrast. Listen to "Feel the Zaz" at http://www.scifi.com/set/playhouse/zaz/.

In the fall of 1997, I was invited by the Massachusetts Institute of Technology to participate in a lecture series called "Media in Transition." The idea was to pair an out-of-town Big Name writer with more-or-less local talent for an evening of readings and discussion. I admit to being intimidated when I was told that I would be partnered with the inestimable Frederick Pohl. During the discussion, Fred was gracious to me and wonderfully articulate about the history and future of science fiction. For my part, I believe that I managed not to drool.

The highlight, for me, of the event was listening to Fred read his classic short-short "Day Million." This story has long been a favorite of mine. In just a few thousand words, it effortlessly achieves the most special of effects, evoking our sense of wonder, while being at once funny and chilling. It is also a corrosive satire of the science fiction agenda, in that Fred suggests that we of the present will have very little chance of understanding the world of the far future.

Flash forward to the spring of 2000. I get asked from time to time to give public readings. The problem with many of these gigs is that I am allotted no more than seven, or ten, or if I'm lucky, fifteen minutes, which means I can only read part of a story. This was my intention when the New Hampshire Business Committee on the Arts invited me to read at their annual awards banquet. However, as the deadline approached, I was visited by "Unique Visitors." All of a sudden, I was writing my first short-short, something I could squeeze into a ten minute slot. It came to me as a voice piece, and I wrote it as if taking dictation over the course of the week just before the event. My reading only went a bit over; the audience of business folk laughed at the right places and, when I finished, seemed bemused but appreciative. It was only afterward, when I began to consider where I might sell "Unique Visitors," that I realized that I had written an homage to the great "Day Million."

I spent almost a decade imagining Wynne Cage, who is the protagonist of "The Prisoner of Chillon." She first appeared in 1985 in a novelette called "Solstice." But "Solstice" was not really her story; rather it was her father, Tony, who held center stage. By the time "Chillon" was published in 1986, I had the vague notion of writing a novel about the Cages someday. Someday took its own good time coming. Wynne also appeared in a 1990 novella called "Mr. Boy," although that is mostly about her son, Peter. These three works form about half of my novel *Wildlife*. The rest of the novel belongs entirely to Wynne, my all-time favorite (anti) heroine.

"The Prisoner of Chillon" was my first true cyberpunk story. I was impressed into the cyberpunk movement when Bruce Sterling reprinted "Solstice" in his *Mirrorshades* anthology. This came as something of a surprise, as I had intended "Solstice" as a kind of humanist critique of cyberpunk. You can still find humanist embellishments in "Chillon," from the Byron quotes to the descriptions of the architecture of the castle, which by the way is open to the public and is well worth a visit if you're ever in Switzerland. But as I reread the caper plot and the speculations on artificial intelligence and the peculiar robots and the noir characterization, I can't help but recognize that my younger self was falling in love with his (at the time) shiny new cybertoys.

In 2001, I was asked once again to teach the Clarion Writers' Workshop. This was my sixth return to the summer swelter of East Lansing, Michigan. Maybe it was nostalgia for the heady days of my youth, when I could pull an all-nighter and laugh about it over breakfast, or maybe it was the heat, but I decided I would try to write a story in my non-existent spare time during my teaching week. "Candy Art" was composed largely between the hours of midnight and two o'clock in the morning. I did manage to complete a deeply flawed draft of the story in time for the last workshop session, thereby affording my students the chance to see the emperor, if not without his clothes, at least in his underwear. I have attempted to put their criticisms to good use. Even though I wrote the first draft in a matter of days, I revised this story over the course of a couple of months and added a new scene just before I submitted it to Gary Turner at Golden Gryphon.

"Candy Art" is one of two Christmas stories here and is original to this collection.

"The Propagation of Light in a Vacuum" is one of my favorite James Patrick Kelly stories that no one knows about. I was quite thrilled to sell it to Robert Silverberg and Karen Haber back in 1990 for the revival of the *Universe* anthology, originally edited by the late, great Terry Carr. Unfortunately, *Universe* collapsed.

The story is a stylistic experiment: magic realism hitching a ride on a hard science starship. I freely admit to committing a circular plot, playing with punctuation and jumping off the page to harangue you, dear reader. Also, this is the only story of mine to include a recipe. It's actually pretty good eating, given the proper ingredients. And no, you can't skip the creamed corn.

Disappointed that "The Propagation of Light in a Vacuum" did not immediately find its audience, I took to reading it in public. It's a fun piece to perform and audiences seem to like it. In 1996, I recast it as a one-act play—my first serious attempt at playwriting. In a later incarnation, I adapted it into one of the *Seeing Ear Theater* audioplays I mentioned earlier. Give it a listen at <http://www.scifi.com/set/playhouse/propagation/>

I have always had a deathly fear of acting. In fact, I have a recurring anxiety dream in which I am pushed onto a stage in the middle of a play for which I have not learned the lines and told to "wing it." But I've always loved the theater and, with the encouragement and assistance of friends who act and direct, have written ten plays since "The Propagation of Light in a Vacuum." Just don't ask me to get in front of an audience and remember lines—even if I wrote them.

I enjoyed writing "Unique Visitors" so much that I thought I should try another short-short story. Thus, "Hubris." However, while "Unique Visitors" arrived practically unbidden on my computer screen, I'd made preliminary notes for "Hubris" years before I sat down to write it. What took so long? Well, there is a prejudice in the genre—perhaps justified, perhaps not—against stories that openly acknowledge that they are stories. I myself once suspected that the adjectives *self-referential* and *precious* were synonymous. So the notes lingered in the drawer.

But once I started with short-shorts, I realized that they offered me a radical freedom. I'm sorry, but I have yet to figure out how to construct a traditional narrative in under two thousand words. By limiting myself to this length, I force myself out of my comfort zone as a writer. Which is always worth doing, it says here. It was a short hop in my imagination from "I don't know the rules" to "There are no rules." So what if the common wisdom says that there are some kinds of story that I'm not supposed to write? Doesn't apply to short-shorts.

Although more than ten years separate them, it's no accident that "The Propagation of Light in a Vacuum" and "Hubris" are printed side by side here. Although I am not known for dark fantasy, I read both of them as horror stories. And if you are badgered in the former, you are practically throttled in latter.

Before I retired from the business world to become a full-time writer, I worked as a public relations flack for an architectural and engineering company. "Glass Cloud" is my architect story. It is also one of my New Hampshire stories. I moved to the Granite State in 1975, but it took a while before I started using local settings in my fiction. I actually had an epiphany similar that of Phillip Wing, my main character, while climbing the Webster Cliff in Crawford Notch—only instead of sketching a glass cloud, I jotted notes for this story. Many of the places mentioned in Portsmouth actually exist; those that don't are based on others that do.

When I wrote "Glass Cloud," I didn't intend to publish it as a novella. It was to be the first several chapters of my third novel, which came to be called *Look Into the Sun*. But then I brought this chunk of the book to the Philford Writers' Workshop, which was held at the home of one Gardner Dozois, who at that time had just been named the new editor of *Isaac Asimov's Science Fiction Magazine*. After the workshop, Gardner took me aside and told me that if I were willing to make certain changes to the manuscript, he would be interested in buying it for the magazine. Gardner is one of the most accomplished of story doctors in the business and his suggestions made excellent sense. However, in the course of writing and rewriting the book, much of what appeared in the magazine got changed or rearranged.

I am satisfied that "Glass Cloud" stands on its own, otherwise I never would have let it see print in its novella incarnation. Just so you know, however, it is clear at the end that more will happen to Phillip Wing. But then that's true of every story that doesn't slam shut with the death of the protagonist or evaporate into some implausible happy-ever-aftering.

Writers are often asked, "Where do you get your ideas from?" The question throws me for a loss, because story ideas swarm, from every which way. In the case of "Proof of the Existence of God," I can tell you that the story originates from exactly two sources, one of which may be an urban legend. I seem to recall that someone, and I can't remember who, offered a cash award of some suitably impressive amount, which I also can't remember, to anyone who could prove that God existed. I suppose I could've hallucinated all of this, but in any event, I was puzzled as to how exactly one could prove the existence of the deity. Would a photograph do? A notarized affidavit? An appearance with Barbara Walters? The other source for this story is a strange iteration of time-travel theory which has been only lightly explored by other writers, since it seems to lead to a dead end. So to speak.

I had the ideas for this story in mind for some time before I wrote it, because I couldn't seem to cast it. Who would have this adventure? Why exactly would they be interested in traveling through time? It wasn't until I hit upon the notion of a psych experiment that the dewy young poet and the alienated researcher brought themselves to my attention.

To my mind, "The Cruelest Month" is the first true James Patrick Kelly story. Which isn't to say that someone else wrote the eight stories that were published under my name before "The Cruelest Month" appeared in *The Magazine of Fantasy and Science Fiction* in 1983. The fact of the matter is that, like many writers, I served my apprenticeship in print. I suppose I had some decent moments before "The Cruelest Month." But I was guessing most of the time, and even when I guessed right, I now feel that the stuff doesn't hold up that well. So here's the earliest of my work that I can recommend to anyone who is not a certifiably deranged Kelly completist.

This is a fantasy, a ghost story actually, only the kind where you're never quite sure whether there really is a ghost or not. It's a mostly quiet piece about a woman who is way too hard on herself. In fact, if I may offer a criticism of Kelly the younger, I would say that the author is possibly too hard on her as well. But what might make this story worth your attention are the last couple of pages. It's been a long time, but I remember that I wasn't quite sure where I was going when I started "The Cruelest Month." I knew who Nell was and why she felt so guilty. And I could see the setting every day; my own daughter would have been two back then, and there were toys underfoot in every room of our house. I even borrowed some of them for props—don't worry, I gave them back. But when it came time to resolve Nell's dilemma, something that was at once spooky and sentimental happened which utterly surprised me but which seemed inevitable as I watched myself type it.

I got divorced in 1988 and for a couple of years in the late eighties, I was single. This was a condition I was utterly unprepared for since I hadn't had a date in *decades*. I have since happily remarried, thank you very much, but being "in circulation" was good for my writing because it got me interested in falling-in-love stories. I had written many stories in which people were already in love, scarcely any in which people fell in love. "Chemistry" starts with a rather mechanistic look of love: it postulates an advance in biotech called neuroromance (pun intended, Mr. Gibson) whereby the chemistry of the brain is altered to make people temporarily fall in love.

I remember doing a lot of research for this story—not all of it scientific. There are several scenes involving square dancing, about which I knew very little at the time. When I brought this to the Sycamore Hill Writers' Workshop, some people opined that it was unlikely that we would still be square dancing in the mid-twenty first century. I respectfully disagree. I also read up on sales techniques and listened to several instructional audiotapes on the subject. There was some feeling in the workshop that I had not quite succeeded in making my salesman a sympathetic character. I changed him some in rewrite, although I do believe that many people share a deep-seated and slightly irrational mistrust of anyone who sells for a living.

*   *   *

There is a Post-It note in my file folder labeled "The Pyramid of
Amirah." On it is the name and telephone number of the garage
where I get my car fixed. This would have been stuck to the inside
of my front door one night so I wouldn't forget to make an appointment the next morning. Underneath it is scrawled the following:
"The Mayans built a temple and then built a pyramid on top of it."
This was to remind me to write "The Pyramid of Amirah."

My wife Pam and I were watching a documentary about the
Mayan city of Copan and an archeologist remarked that one of the
lesser pyramids there had been built around a small existing temple, for reasons no one understood exactly. An image struck me
immediately and I bolted from the TV room in search of something
to scribble a note on.

The next day I started writing a story about a young girl and her
faith in a religion that isn't really a religion. I was brought up
Catholic and, although I am long since un-churched, I find that I
am drawn again and again to write about encounters with the
numinous. Maybe Someone is trying to tell me Something.

In "The Pyramid of Amirah," nothing happens for two thousand
words and then everything changes in the last two hundred. I confess that I didn't see the ending until I stumbled over it. I needed a
way to mark time besides the accumulation of candy wrappers and
so I hit upon the idea of having light bulbs burn out. Of course, in
the future, light bulbs would last a long, long time—but so much
the better. Only if all the lights went out then Amirah would spend
the rest of her life in the dark.

I just couldn't do that to her.

"We need you, Jim," said the desperate voice on the phone. "You're
the only one who can save Christmas now!"

Actually, that's not quite how it was. Sheila Williams, executive
editor of *Asimov's* called to inform me she had no Christmas stories
in inventory for the December 1998 issue and that I should write
one for her. There were only two problems. One was that I had to
turn in a finished manuscript in two weeks. The other was that it
was July—print magazines have long lead times. Believe me, it's
hard to get the Yule spirit when the thermometer is kissing 90° and
the Red Sox have runners on first and third with nobody out.

But I like writing Christmas stories, I really do. I said I'd try,
although I didn't have the slightest idea what I'd try. I sat down at
the computer and stared at the screen . . . *uh-oh*. Then Maggie
started talking. She had a tongue like a razor and a sense of the

absurd. What was up with her? She was in charge of an alien who wanted to go Christmas shopping. The story practically wrote itself.

Except that, in the rush to make the deadline, I forget something. An important plot point was implied in the text, but it needed to be made very, very explicit. I didn't realize this until I was reading the story at a convention just before it came out in the magazine. So I've made a few changes; here's the definitive version of "Fruitcake Theory." You want to know what's different? Okay: the Kuvat honor longevity. Because Elder Kasan is the oldest of the scarecrows, she is the leader of the Kuvat expedition.

By the way, I have nothing against fruitcake.

When "Undone" was published in *Asimov's*, I cited Cordwainer Smith and Alfred Bester, two of my favorite writers, as influences. I came to Bester late, when I was already a struggling writer. I deeply admired *The Demolished Man* and was stunned by its typographical splendor. I remember wondering as I read, "Is that *allowed?*" and telling myself, "Sure, but only if you're Alfred Bester." Of course, I realize that I'm no Alfred Bester, but I've been at this writing gig long enough to know that if I'm going to borrow, I should reach for the very best.

I came to Cordwainer Smith when I was twelve, which is, as some wag has said, the Golden Age of Science Fiction. My brother and I were visiting my grandmother in St. Louis one summer and, in the middle of our stay, I got sick. And then I got bored. Grandma Kelly wasn't much for television so she aimed me at my uncle's old science fiction collection and told me to amuse myself while she took Steve swimming. I plunged into science fiction on that hot July afternoon and have yet to come up for air. The book that sticks in my mind is one of Judith Merril's Best of the Year collections (Checking the net, I discover that it was *The 7th Annual of the Year's Best S-F*, edited by Judith Merril, Simon & Schuster, 1962) and the story I remember best is Smith's "A Planet Named Shayol." Shayol is a prison world where the inmates are condemned to grow random appendages like extra hands and heads and whole bodies and where the jailor is a genetically-modified bull. I have since become something of a Smith completist; I believe he is *the* genius of far-future sf. It took years before I dared venture into the master's territory

I don't know what else to tell you about "Undone," except maybe this:

!story a writing fun much so had never have I

Three thousand copies of this book have been printed by the Maple-Vail Book Manufacturing Group, Binghamton, NY, for Golden Gryphon Press, Urbana, IL. The typeset is Electra, printed on 55# Sebago. The binding cloth is Roxite B. Typesetting by The Composing Room, Inc., Kimberly, WI.